PRAISE FOR *THE POISONER*

"Equal parts dark, sumptuous, and spine-chilling, *The Poisoner* is a gothic romance that bites hard with tantalizing fangs and refuses to let go."

—Logan Karlie, author of *Dream by the Shadows*

"Deliciously dark and utterly addictive. With a touch of horror, a delightfully dreary atmosphere, and a romance as venomous as it is swoon-worthy, *The Poisoner* is a must-read for lovers of gothic romance."

—Sophia Slade, author of *Nightstrider*

"Everything my dark little heart desired. Beautifully written with alluring characters."

—Marija Unkind, Goodreads user

"As a gal who is obsessed with *Crimson Peak* & *Penny Dreadful*, I can say for sure—I.V. Ophelia absolutely delivered! From the jaw-dropping aesthetics, the snarky dialogue (accompanied by equally vicious characters), and the unique take on vampires, the storyline grabbed me by the throat and refused to let go."

—Rosie, Goodreads user

"I love the prose in this book, and I love that it's a full sensory experience. Everything is tactile, it has a scent, it has an atmosphere."

—Sarah Keller, Goodreads user

"This book surprised me on almost every level. I was expecting a typical vampire story, but this was so much more and it was deliciously addicting. Dark Gothic vibes, morally gray characters, games of cat and mouse, and some of the sneakiest humor made this hard to put down. It's hard to say I loved these characters, because I'm not sure they deserve it, but I can't help it."

—Kourtney Delair, Goodreads user

"Gross and violent and sexy and totally fucked up. I loved it lol!"

—Melinda, Goodreads user

FRUIT OF THE FLESH
BY I. V. OPHELIA

FRUIT *of the* FLESH

OTHER TITLES BY I.V. OPHELIA

The Poisoner

The Poisoner

The Arachnid

FRUIT *of the* FLESH

I.V. OPHELIA

This is a work of fiction. Names, characters, organizations, places, events, and incidents are either products of the author's imagination or are used fictitiously. Otherwise, any resemblance to actual persons, living or dead, is purely coincidental.

Published by Montlake, Seattle

www.apub.com

EU product safety contact:
Amazon Media EU S. à r.l.
38, avenue John F. Kennedy, L-1855 Luxembourg
amazonpublishing-gpsr@amazon.com

ISBN-13: 9781662534607 (paperback)
ISBN-13: 9781662534591 (digital)

Cover design by Faceout Studio, Molly von Borstel
Cover image: © Alexey Khromushin, © Nadine.de.trevile, © COLOA Studio, © Anastasiia Ageeva, © CreativeStory, © Voin_Sveta, © Soho A Studio / Shutterstock

Additional interior illustration © Sayu / Descendinight

Printed in the United States of America

For those who long to be seen, to be heard, and crave love that consumes—may you eat your fill.

CONTENT WARNING

Fruit of the Flesh is a deliciously dark gothic romance that may contain content that is disturbing for some readers. *Shibari*, specifically *hojo-jutsu*, should not be practiced without an experienced professional. Clay is not body safe, and neither is any porous material. It is not recommended to swim in any fresh body of water in New York City, with or without clothing. Embalming should be done by a licensed mortician up to current, modern standards. This book contains proper BDSM practices including safe words, negotiations, and aftercare. Nothing in this book shall serve as a tutorial.

PROLOGUE

The Artisan

Datura was an unconventional choice of flower, notably in the bouquet of your bride.

Though, I may be just as odd as my intended. Any person in their right mind may think me mad, seeing my earnestness to marry a stranger. But as I assured others, as well as myself, I was completely lucid.

The ceremony was held in the home of her father. Mr. De Villier was a frequent patron of mine, as he was in need of finer finishing pieces for his newly built home—his own art, in a sense. Call me narcissistic, but there is something poetic about getting married under the same roof as some of my most expensive pieces.

The walls were tall and proud like priests, and decorated in a similar manner. Ornate molding and floors made of the rarest wood elevated the domicile into something more than just collections of four walls. Each detail made it known that, even while inanimate, it would always be worth more than you. The glass of the windows alone would strip me of my salary if I happened to break one.

Despite the ostentatious abode, the family received only an intimate gathering for our union.

We stood before the mantel in one of the reception rooms, neatly rearranged to hold the immediate family of the bride.

Her sisters stood staunchly behind her, only one of whom looked enthusiastic about being there. The younger of the two had such a radiant smile, the corners of her lips would touch her ears if it got any wider. She was practically vibrating with excitement for her youngest sister.

The eldest reminded me of one of my statues, but her stare was undoubtedly colder than anything I could carve from dead stone.

Lastly, my dearest bride.

Admittedly, I was hesitant to look down at her. I understood that what may be my most joyous day could be one she had been lamenting. I was reassured that she knew the union would be mostly one of convenience, given both of our needs.

She's the one who chose you, her mother mentioned sourly when I was propositioned.

It dawned on me only then that I had never paid much attention in the time I'd spent working on their home. To have caught the eye of one of the daughters, enough for her to request me personally, was like a bolt out of the blue. I'm sure she had prospects grander than myself, painstakingly curated by the governing power that was her mother.

The afternoon light crept through the windows and cut through the haze of the parlor, daring to illuminate the revenant before me, outlining the silhouette of her face under the veil that shrouded her from view. The only thing that could convince me she was not a vision was the smell of wild blossoms in her bouquet.

Even through the veil, I could see the dress she wore was narrowly ill fitted, a hand-me-down perhaps; I was no stranger to those. But why would she settle for anything other than new? A detail such as this made me wonder about the strange personalities who'd adopted me into their family.

As I lifted the airy fabric, I could have been convinced that God had revealed an angel to me, crowned in a coronet of trumpet flowers among tight orange blossom buds. She gave me a look I recognized, one of cornered fawns or hungry animals. For what, I couldn't know.

The distress was apparent, but something within me suggested it wasn't caused by my presence; it had been fermenting long before.

Her eyes were a deep sepia, and her skin competed in fairness with her gown, two elegant beauty marks to the left of her lips. Even the blond of her hair held a mousy pallidity that made the overall air about her feel frail.

I picked up her hands, running my thumbs over her slight fingers. They were cold, like she had been outside only a moment before. Her knuckles and joints were a gentle rosy color.

"I, Arkady Kamenev," I recited, and her eyes finally met mine, as if I'd startled her from her thoughts, "take thee, Petronille De Villier, to be my wife." I slipped the ruby heirloom onto her finger, letting my touch linger in the moment. "To have and to hold from this day forward, for better or for worse, for richer, for poorer, in sickness and in health, to love and to cherish, and I promise to be faithful to you until death parts us."

"I, Petronille De Villier"—her voice was elegant like a stalk of wild bluebells, each word dangling like a bell in front of me—"take thee, Arkady Kamenev, to be my husband." Her eyes fell to our hands as she slipped the band onto my fourth finger. She was trembling like a leaf in the wind. I clasped my hands over hers in hopes of steadying her. "To have and to hold from this day forward, for better or for worse, for richer, for poorer, in sickness and in health, until death parts us."

"Having witnessed your marriage vows in the eyes of God and before all who are assembled here," the minister droned, looking to the guests, then down to us, "I pronounce you husband and wife. You may now kiss the bride."

As I cupped her face in my hands, hers placed atop mine as if not wanting to part with the security of touch, her eyes were glassy. I kissed her then, her lips trembling as they locked with mine.

Not many people know that tears of various emotions taste different. Tears of joy would typically taste sweet; my bride's tears were acidic as they reached our lips.

CHAPTER ONE

The Performer

For my husband's sake, I believed, in all kindness, he would be better off dead.

There was no trust among the De Villier family, only trust that it would go their way or not at all. I believed as a child that my father was the devil; as an adult, I understood that he was worse.

I knew this to be true. My mother knew it too. My sisters understood this most of all.

Félice squeezed my hand with a firm grip. When I pulled my gaze from her hand, she tilted her head toward the other end of the dining table.

Father was poised there, a foxy glare settled on his face all too naturally. He raised his knife to the corner of his lips, flicking it upward with a mocking smile before it fell again.

I inhaled and put on my best theatrical beam, hoping my eyes would not give way to tears. How well I could hide my dismay depended on the severity of the ache lodged in my throat or how quickly the air could dry my eyes.

The only light left in the room was from the candles, as my mother did not want to insult the guests or myself with unflattering gaslight.

Close family had nearly forgotten my previous occupation; they did not need the association of streetlamps to remind them.

My mother had also made sure the silk stockings fit to a custom length to hide the bruising before she thought it necessary to tailor my sister's old wedding dress to me. More attention was paid to my undergarments than the dress that concealed them.

It was unfair of them to judge me for enjoying the ballet when my parents were the ones who put me and my sisters there. The worst part was, they would never know how alienating it was to be made to quit something that you'd known your whole life. I had no friends of my own, and very little family whom I trusted. My sisters left happily upon being offered an alternative, but I couldn't say I felt the same.

An empty expression peered back at me in the wineglass. The wine itself only disturbed when a bloom of datura wilted from my coronet and landed inside the glass.

A sign? I hoped.

I lifted the cup, but my lips met the back of a hand over the top of the glass.

"That wouldn't be wise," the stranger, my husband, said from beside me, his hand still cupped over my glass, "unless your intent is to become ill."

"How silly of me," I whispered as he took the glass from my hands. My opportunity swept away in an instant.

"Not much of an appetite?" Mr. Kamenev tried to make conversation, gesturing to my untouched plate.

When I'd witnessed him occasionally working in my parents' home, he'd seemed ordinary. But even in the low light, the man had a certain warmth to him. His skin was a soft tan, his hair only a few shades darker. His eyes were prettier up close, an endless green with a deep blue woven through like hand-dyed cloth. We were close enough that I could see the dark freckle on his cheekbone. I feared for the unassuming man and whatever he may have agreed to.

"I guess the excitement stole my appetite." My words came out as a faint hum.

"The excitement stole it? Or was it overstimulation?"

I shrugged and pushed the meat around on my plate with my fork. "Would it be terrible to say it is because of the people?"

"Not at all." A dimple appeared as he seemed amused at my answer. "I am not a fan of crowds either. I am thankful your parents didn't invite more—I can't imagine how I'd fare with such a house at full capacity."

His playful smile was visible for a mere moment before I stared down at my hands. "Trust me, it is as overwhelming as you can imagine."

"Well, we can throw our own *lavish* parties at home instead from now on," he teased. "A quiet night enjoyed with fresh fruit, a good book, burning hickory."

I raised a brow and smiled up at him. "Hopefully you wouldn't mind a guest at one of these humble shut-in parties?"

"I would say yes, but I would have to ask my wife." He grinned, his fingers brushing against mine under the table.

The heat rose to my cheeks faster than if I were hung upside down. He wasn't anything like I thought he would be; I half expected a union more callous, but the curious man seemed to have an interest in me. Perhaps this marriage would not be as arduous as I had initially anticipated.

"I'm surprised," I admitted. "I thought artisans were more social."

"Let's just say there is a reason I prefer the company of my sculptures to actual people." He leaned down by my ear, close enough that I could smell hints of fig and smoky white cedar. "Though, I suppose I wouldn't mind your company, if you allow it?"

"If you won't mind it, neither will I," I whispered.

"Then all we must do is survive the pleasantries, then head home." He ran his thumb over my fingers. I wasn't sure if it was to soothe me or himself. At least we were relatively in agreement.

The sharp chime of cutlery pinging a glass resonated, pulling the attention of anyone who could hear to the end of the table.

Father stood, a champagne flute in his proudly poised hand. "I just wanted to say a few words for the happy couple before we inevitably scatter toward the end of this beautiful feast." His expression gave every indication of happiness, but the sharpness in my father's eyes would never be as warm as his facade.

I glanced at Mr. Kamenev. There was no stiffness in his posture as he devoted his attention. I wondered what it would be like to look at Father and not be riddled with trepidation.

"A toast." Father's voice cut through the air, fluid and eloquent. "May you live as long as you like, and have all you like for as long as you live."

The guests raised their glasses and drank, though Father never took his eyes off me as he peered over the rim of his flute, a subtle smirk playing at the corners of his lips.

As I turned to my new husband, my stomach flipped.

That was when an uncanny twinge in my gut bloomed. Looking into this man's eyes—in that single moment he thought I didn't witness—I saw something lurking beneath the surface, yet to breach.

His cold expression wasn't set on me.

No, he was looking at my father.

Something in his regard made the skin of his face as animated as any porcelain mask. Beautiful and cold. He looked to be made more of stone than he was flesh, a desolate warmth.

When those sharp eyes caught mine, the mask melted. If I were as naive as I was five minutes before, I may have taken it as sincere.

Now I suspected there was something transactional about the kindness, like a buzzard deciding to spend a few innocent moments with a dying woman out of the kindness of its heart.

Mr. Kamenev and my arms looped together with champagne flutes in hand, the crystal glass teasing a cool sensation on my lips.

His gaze lifted from the cup to my eyes, the look almost as chilled as the champagne.

CHAPTER TWO

The Performer

Awkwardness is to be expected on your wedding night, my mother would say. Though I never imagined how truly gauche it would be to bring a stranger into my home.

"It is . . . nice." Mr. Kamenev slid his finger over the surface of a table in the hall, dust pushing into a small pile.

"Let us not begin our union with lies. You can say it."

"Do you not have staff?" He pretended to admire some of the art on the wall.

"No."

"Why is it that you live so differently from your family?"

"Blood will not determine how I live. I am comfortable."

"I see . . ." His voice trailed off.

My fingers hovered over the hallway table for a candle, brushing against the blade of the letter opener and some loose change before grasping the box of matches. My fingers shook as if my bones would rattle and fall apart if I pushed them to be occupied any longer. The match struck once, twice, too many shaky times, with no light in sight.

As I went to strike it again, his hand stopped mine, his arms reaching around me from behind.

His fingers trailed down the back of my hand and pinched the match from me, plucking the box soon after. The match lit with ease. The glow of his hand appeared in the darkness, and he carefully lit my candle.

I gripped the side of the table, unsure if I was embarrassed or bashful. Hosting had never been my strong suit.

"Take a seat, get comfortable." I gestured loosely toward the living room, slipping from him as I cupped the candle. There were no gas lamps in the home; it was too old for that. I never liked the harshness anyway.

He sat down at the small table by the window, placing a bottle of wine from the reception in the middle.

I gathered some glasses from the kitchen and sat across from him, sliding one over along with a corkscrew.

"At least it is quiet," he muttered as he began to drive the screw into the seal.

"Good riddance. I don't think I could have taken any more shrills from my mother." I placed my cheek in my palm as I watched him pour the wine.

"An occasional occurrence, hopefully." There was humor in his tone as he picked up his glass and held it to his nose.

The night was quiet in the street, only the sound of summer insects and the occasional bark of a faraway dog. The cobblestones and footpaths glistened with the memory of rain that had passed not an hour ago.

"Mr. Kamenev, I have a question."

"Arkady," he corrected. "I would say 'Mr. Kamenev' is my father, but I don't even know if that is true," he joked.

"Arkady." I squinted at him, taking a moment to think. "What kind of man are you?"

"Well, what did your father tell you?"

"Nothing. Absolutely nothing." I took a long sip of wine, letting it tickle my sinuses and dry my throat with a single swallow. "I saw your back more often than your face as you worked on their home. You were there almost as often as I was. I didn't know your name until this morning, your face until the evening."

"You were fine with that?" he prodded. "Marrying a man you don't know?"

"I could ask the same of you?"

"A fair question. Though I suppose the next question would be *why*?"

"Because, *why not*?" I shrugged. "You should spend less time asking *why* and more time telling me I won't regret it."

"Wouldn't it be more fun to see for yourself?" He raised a brow over the rim of his glass.

"No, I prefer a more direct approach," I declared, finishing my wine and pushing the cup back to the middle of the table. "What kind of man marries a stranger?"

"Well, then, I can start with an introduction." He filled my glass once again. "I am organized, messy when I need to be, I don't like fish, and I hate the smell of burnt cinnamon."

"Any habits I should be aware of?"

"An introvert, frugal, and a terrible, awful crook." He smirked, pushing the glass my way. "All these questions are about me. What about you? The princess who married the pauper?"

"I'm greedy, selfish, possibly a glutton. Best to be careful, or I may eat you for dinner." I raised my glass, my best attempt at sincerity.

"Now *you* are the one being dishonest." He leaned back in his chair. "Your mother said something during our arrangement."

"She never stops talking. You'll have to be more specific."

"She said you handpicked me." He laughed, shaking his head. "Did I really not need to have a single conversation in order to entice you?"

"I saw you working on the house."

"It's an odd choice, you have to admit."

I twisted the wineglass stem, leaning back in my chair in thought. "You were the first person I thought of when they said they didn't care who it was as long as I got married. So why not the faceless man always in the background?"

He was silent. I glanced up. His face held a look of understanding and patience, but the way he was gripping his glass gave away his distaste.

"I wanted to spite them. The choice of man who would hurt them the most is—"

"A poor man."

"A nobody," I finished. "I needed them to lose."

He nodded in understanding. I'm sure it stung more than he let on.

"What did they lose, aside from a daughter?"

"Opportunity," I said plainly, snatching the bottle and pouring more for myself. "A marriage they can't leverage."

"Were your prospects *that* good?" he teased.

"Only on paper," I mumbled into the glass, drinking down the rest of the wine.

We shared a brief moment of amusement, the tension and awkwardness evaporating the more we drank.

He finished his glass, and the bottle was empty now.

I rose from my seat and reached for his glass, but his hand met mine, and I flinched away.

His eyes flicked from the glass to me, a slow grin playing on his lips at my reaction.

"Are you scared of me?"

"No."

He grabbed my wrist. "You're trembling."

"Iron deficiency."

"Is that so?" Arkady stood suddenly, pulling me close. He leaned down to speak into my ear. "You are like a bird, ready to fly as soon as the cage is open."

"Should I consider fleeing, Mr. Kamenev?" I looked up; he was closer than I thought. His tall, lean body was pressed against mine, leaving barely room enough to turn around. He loomed, like he was waiting for something. Expecting.

"I guess it makes sense for such a frail thing." He didn't answer my question. "Maybe you will wither away before you are able to fly."

"Already comfortable enough for insults, are we?" I swayed, and his grip on my wrist tightened.

"Oh, no, I promise I say it endearingly." He rolled his eyes.

"What are *you* running from, stranger?" I asked, playing with the collar of his shirt. "Debt? Bad habits? Escaping your first family? Murder—"

The pads of his fingers cut me off when they dug into the sides of my neck. My throat bobbed against his palm, my eyes only able to focus on him. My wineglass tipped, shattering under my palm, the shards hot as they threatened to pierce the skin.

If my eyes opened any wider, they might fall from my skull. The grip on my neck was firm, steady, completely secure. His eyes were cold, fixated.

This was when I realized my previous inclinations were correct. I suppose I should have known better. The most dangerous man is an unassuming one.

He smirked, leaning in so that his face hovered over mine. The flickering of the candle dancing around his features.

"No, keep going, I want to hear it," he whispered.

"I knew you would be no different," I spat.

"Different than whom?" He cocked his head, his eyes dark, but I could still see them wander to my lips. "You've got a sharp tongue for a failed *dollar princess*."

"And you are the fool who fell for it," I scoffed. "Did you really think a family like mine would welcome someone like you without strings attached? You are simply the first needy fool they stumbled upon. Just another man."

"Someone like you," he repeated, a cruel smirk pulling at the corners of his lips, his free hand moving a stray piece of hair from my face. The gentle touch was more jarring than the slight grip on my throat. He leaned in to kiss my cheek delicately. "My dear, you are going to learn

very quickly that I am most certainly worse than any man you know. Take comfort that you have such a force on your side."

"For your sake, I hope that is true," I whispered, my head feeling a bit light. "I was wondering when you'd take off the mask."

"I didn't think your father would appreciate such a personality." He sighed, his heavy hand on my hip, fingertips pressing into the skirts. "Rest assured, I'm good at keeping up appearances—as will you be, if you know what's good for you."

A laugh burst from my throat, almost joyous at his proclamation. "Aren't I the one who's better for you? Given that you have no wealth of your own?"

"Will it matter at the end of the day?" He dragged his thumb over my lip, smearing it past the corner, glaring as if to dare me to do something.

"It will." I picked up one leg, trailing my heel up the back of his thigh. "Because if I'm stuck with you"—I hooked my leg behind his, jolting him toward me—"you have to remember that you're also stuck with *me*."

His grip on my neck softened, letting me lean into him, but the closer I got, the more he leaned away. Such a gesture brought me joy, to scare even the most callous of men. How foolish of him to think he could just walk in here and claim what he wanted.

"Aren't you going to do it? To force me? Make my poor little frail body submit to whatever power you feel entitled to?" I mocked. "You were so eager to get your hands on me. Why stop?"

He simply stared, his hand slipping from my throat to my collar, then down to my chest, before falling at my waist. His eyes trailed the path his hand blazed, but he wasn't fully there. He was physically with me, but his mind was somewhere else.

"Make no mistake, Mr. Kamenev"—I sighed—"I do not care about your hunger for money."

"Why doesn't it bother you?" His question seemed genuine, and his brow twitched, the tension in his shoulders looking more uncomfortable by the minute. His gaze didn't even return to me.

"You are doing me a favor as a placeholder"—I played with a piece of his hair—"as I am sure that's all I am to you, anyway."

"So we have an understanding, it seems."

"For now." I smirked and lifted a shoulder. "I would like to be left to my own devices. As long as you can play the fool, I will play the virgin. Do not make demands of me, and I won't make any of you."

He shoved my leg abruptly, my body jolting forward.

All too casually, like we didn't just have that exchange, he retreated. He even took his time digging for the matches as he sat down on the sofa. Even knowing I was right there, he didn't speak a word, he didn't look at me, he didn't acknowledge anything. He simply tucked a cigarette between his lips and nursed the flame from his match.

"Nothing?"

He shook his head, reclining against the sofa as he blew out smoke from his nose.

Leaving me alone, as I wished.

I see your wit, Mr. Kamenev.

I stepped back, unsure of how to feel about my fulfilled wish, and retired to my room in silence. I got my deal, that's all that mattered, but I was left wondering if it was wise to antagonize the snake in my nest.

CHAPTER THREE

The Artisan

It wasn't a chore settling into my wife's townhome. While we did not honeymoon anywhere secretive, it was probably best for her to be somewhere familiar and comfortable.

Besides, moving into my studio would not be the best choice—even *I* would prefer the townhome. It mattered little that it was my wife's.

I lay there on the sofa, the morning light showing the truly distressed state of her home. I couldn't tell if the haze in the air was dust or the steam from my morning brew.

While the domain was expensive, it was ill maintained. Aside from the runner on the stairs and select pieces of furniture, most of it looked like it only existed to hold collections of things like books and trinkets, rather than to serve its intended purpose. It was as though her parents had gifted it to her, but she had no interest in keeping up with it.

Her shelves had run out of space for books a good while ago, stacks forming on the floor. The tables were cluttered, yet each pile seemed to be a specific category, and only she would know the full extent of methodology. The fireplace hadn't held a fire in a long time, or she was very good at maintaining the cleaning, which I highly doubted. The only other signs of life seemed to be the occasional flutter of a moth.

Though I shouldn't complain. Sleeping on the cushions of her sofa was more comfortable than anything in my studio.

I checked my timepiece—not even seven in the morning, yet I couldn't bring myself to sleep in. I supposed that was typical when settling into unfamiliar dwellings.

Up the walls, there were many pieces of art, though not many photographs of the family aside from one ovoid frame of, presumably, a younger vision of Petronille and her sisters.

She had a captivating collection of pinned butterflies, moths, and some other rare insects arranged lavishly in boxes memorializing their deaths.

In front of the window was a small table with two chairs, where we'd sat last night.

Atop a spare chair was what looked like her current project. A set of pointe shoes, the arch of one shoe snapped in half and preworn. The ribbon half sewn on, and the shoe itself serving as a pincushion for her threaded needle.

Draped on the back of the chair was a sort of costume bedazzled with small glass beads and tulle. On another chair in the corner of the room was a pile of flowers well past their freshness beside a collection of letters with unbroken wax seals. I suppose she had many admirers. A shame she didn't bother reading them.

The flowers were not unlike the others that attempted to decorate the home. On the mantel was a small bouquet, withered and dried from the air of time, only a spider finding them pleasing enough to make a home of them. At least the spider earned her keep, trapping a single moth out of however many infested the place.

Peering into the gaunt hallway, I spied a runner ending at a sullen basement door. The padlock dangling on the door a passing temptation to investigate scurrying and scraping from within my mind. As I looked closer, I noticed the runner was more worn than any of the other carpets. I did not know my reasoning for passing as carefully as I did, but the door was beckoning me forward, teasing as to what could be so important that it had to be fashioned with such security.

Despite the teasing questions, I ignored them for a more tempting mystery.

"Hello?" I called up the stairs.

No answer.

"Petronille?" I called again, her name awkward and new in my mouth.

The stairs rasped one by one until I reached the second floor and was presented with an open door to her room.

Within the area, a pale and peaceful pile of blond hair and blankets against a dark and dreary room.

She's much different when she is asleep. Less argumentative. More agreeable.

I watched her from the doorway, the air so thick that I feared she would wake if I disturbed it. The dust fluttered past the windows, a band of glowing nymphs as the sun began to rise above the skyline.

Delicate streaks of light striped across her face, her rising and falling chest, making the silk of the bed and her nightgown glow under its touch.

A moment won't hurt.

As I approached the bed, the floorboards whined in response to my steps.

I would say she reminded me of Sleeping Beauty, but based on her furrowed brow, she may have been more like the title character of "The Princess and the Pea."

Her jaw ticked, her eyes rolling behind her delicate lids, her lashes fluttering occasionally. I was close enough to see the dewy sheen gathering on her skin.

Out of the shadows fluttered a moth. The clumsy flight path of the critter landed him on her pillow. The graceless form crawled closer, climbing through her hair.

What a curious creature.

As I leaned closer, the moth happily rested on her brow, then flicked his wings as he lapped the dewiness forming under her eye. *A tear?*

The powdery wings unfolded as my shadow crept over her face. They were a dusty white with the exception of a red splotch at the widest part of each wing.

Suddenly, I was hit with a wild vision, a strike of inspiration.

While she may be brash and unpleasant past her soft exterior, I could not deny that Petronille was visually pleasing.

The ideas puttered around in the back of my mind . . . I had to go to the studio as soon as I finished my day's arrangements.

As much as I would like to continue watching her sleep, the moths, I am sure, would be better company.

MAN AND WIFE MISSING THREE WEEKS.

"I'm so exhausted, I can't even remember where I put the body!"

> Please alert the metropolitan police if you identify these individuals.

"I tag them all, the logs are accurate, but I cannot for the life of me remember doing it. I'm just thankful that even when running on fumes, I can still do my job—like muscle memory!"

> It is unclear at this time if this missing couple is connected to the Bardugo and Smith disappearances.

"Mm-hmm." I underlined the heading of the paper with my pen, absently staring at the block of text, only able to return to the headline.

"*Arkasha*, did you hear me?" Konstantin stared expectantly.

"What is it, Kostya?" I spoke back.

"You haven't said a word since we got here."

"Not in a talkative mood."

"Is everything all right?"

"Everything is perfect, actually." I folded over my paper. "How's the baby? The wife?"

"Always crying," Kostya groaned, taking an exasperated gulp from his morning beer. "*Both* of them."

"Ah . . ." I sipped my coffee. "So, nothing new?"

"I suppose." Kostya sighed, leaning in his seat and anxiously tipping back the chair. "I'm awful, aren't I?"

"Why would you say that?" I raised a brow, setting my paper down. It seemed the complaint was his way of opening a conversation.

We sat at the café's outdoor tables, early enough that we had our choice of seating and Konstantin could make it to work on time. He tells his wife that his shift starts two hours earlier than it actually does so he can find some peace and quiet.

"I love my wife, and my daughter, they are the most precious things in my life," he started.

"But?"

"*But* I am exhausted. I am awake all through the night helping Emily, I pull longer shifts for peace and quiet—dead men don't cry! Thank Christ!" He pinched the bridge of his nose, taking a breath to calm himself. "I feel like I am constantly awake, riddled with anxiety in my waking hours as well as my sleeping ones, if you can call that sleep."

"You'll be fine, infants grow fast. How is Emily?"

"She is phenomenal with the baby, I don't know how she does it."

"I meant recovery."

"Oh? Yes, she is fine. A bit weak, but that's expected."

I nodded, hoping it would be the last of his complaints. Kostya hadn't been the same since the birth of his daughter. It could be sleep deprivation. It could also be the nature of his work.

Kostya worked as a deputy coroner. He saw many terrible things, and those sights tended to project when you cared about others who would one day, eventually, be on the table as well.

"You aren't too far behind, you know." He gave a light chuckle, smoothing down his neatly groomed mustache. "How are you and the new Mrs. Kameneva?" He put extra emphasis on the feminine-ending vowel.

"She's fine." I forced a smile. "Her couch is more comfortable than the mattress on my studio floor."

He stared blankly at me, frowning when he realized I wasn't attempting to be funny. "A couch, Arkasha? What in the world did you do to her to be cast out to the couch so quickly?"

"I didn't have to do anything—we just talked."

He dragged his palm over his eyes, then the rest of the way over his face with a groan. "You wouldn't know how to swing a cat, dear friend. You are lucky to be born with looks, at least."

"I make my own luck."

"Ah yes, can't forget about that stubborn ego." He clicked his tongue.

I rolled my eyes and finished my drink, then set the cup down. I picked up my paper again but found myself only able to stare at the underlined ink at the top of the page.

An entire section in the newspaper for people who may not even be missing. I wondered how long it would take for the search to end and police to announce they're gone, suspected dead—or worse, used as scapegoats for miscellaneous cold pursuits so authorities can say they've saved the day.

Would someone look for me if I disappeared? No.

If my wife disappeared? Without a doubt in my mind.

Something about it tickled the back of my head. My thoughts have gathered a new pace lately, between my environment and my new union, new home. They've opened my eyes to some things, to alternate lives and social classes that I thought I understood. My new muse may end up teaching me things I never thought to learn.

There are muses for all who dare to feel.

CHAPTER FOUR

The Performer

My mother was right: I was hideous.

The reflection that peered back at me was less than deserving of existing within such an ornate mirror.

Delicate lacings, custom hand stitching, and fine silk clung to my body, but I did not feel as if it fit. Some days I thought my proportions were too long, too stalky and thin.

She was right about another thing—the bruises were unsightly.

I pulled on a long silken robe to cover myself, as if there were anyone else in the room to judge me other than myself.

Despite my less-than-glowing review of my appearance, I tried my best to be presentable. I let my hair down, still curled from its styling the previous night.

Last night . . .

Suddenly my situation settled on me like a new roof on an old brick house.

Arkady hadn't even stepped foot into my room.

A stab of cynicism pierced my gut and squeezed my fluttering heart. It wasn't much of a surprise that he hadn't joined me, more so that there was not even a shallow attempt to engage further. Which, admittedly, is to the credit of my drunken temper.

When you are young, they make it seem like marriage is something to look forward to. The dress out of a princess story modeled after a long line of gowns worn by royalty. The feast as an excuse to splurge, a milestone to be celebrated with traditions kept alive in time.

I knew it would be exciting in some sense, but I couldn't have imagined this. Marriage seemed so much more magical when I was young. Now, it is a convenient piece of paper.

With an exasperated huff, I left my room and peered into the hallway.

Empty.

Every step down the stairs creaked in a different pitch.

There was a haze left by the afternoon light penetrating the living room. The tea table was cluttered with books stacked dowdily upon each other, and the love seat was unkempt from a guest using it to slumber. The candle on the table was burnt to the end of its wick, cool wax pooled in the holder.

Placed upon the table was a business card, writing scrawled across it.

My contact number, call for emergencies only, the "only" underlined several times. Printed on the card was a phone number and the address of a studio. There was no business or studio name aside from his own. *Arkady Kamenev. Artisan.*

His penmanship was terrible, chicken scratch at best. The business card was handmade, as indicated by the basic typeset and a small smudge on his name.

Aside from the measly card, there were no signs of the stray I'd married.

"Look at that one, I don't think I've seen a green that bright before." Lorelei gestured slightly to a woman passing us.

"I thought greens were outdated?"

"I think people say that because they are secretly jealous that they can't afford it. It's even more expensive since the shade was discontinued." She lowered her voice as if sharing some daring secret.

The two of us sat for a leisurely amount of time on the same bench we always frequented at the park. Most days we watched the promenade and took the time to soak in whatever fresh air we could before we spent our days in the musty theater for rehearsal.

"You weren't at the audition yesterday." Lorelei stared doe-eyed at me, endless brown eyes reflecting my pale image. "Your absence threw me enough where I think it was my worst audition yet!"

"I was married," I mumbled.

"Married?" Her mouth hung open in disbelief before smiling wide. "I see, you are joking, that's what you're doing. You've always been so funny!"

"No, I am sincere." I sloped my head to the side to peer at her, holding up my left hand.

The ring was my mother's, refit for a bloodred cabochon-cut ruby just for the occasion. Even when the correct size, the prongs cut between my fingers if placed unfavorably, rejecting the fit. But that part didn't matter. *As long as it's impressive looking, it doesn't matter how it feels,* I'm sure my mother thought.

"Mon Dieu," Lorelei muttered, grasping my hand and holding it close as if she couldn't believe her eyes. "To whom?"

"One of my father's artisans."

"I missed your wedding!" she exclaimed, dropping my hand as her thoughts registered.

"It was uneventful."

"What is he like? What does he look like? How much older is he?"

"I am older than *him*, by three years."

"He is twenty-one?" Lorelei looked horrified. "I don't understand the pairing."

"Ah yes, I'm withering away at twenty-four." I rolled my eyes. "An unorthodox match for an unorthodox family."

"No! I mean, I half expected someone much older," she explained. "Well . . . that should be good for you, no?"

I lifted a shoulder before it slumped again.

"Is he handsome?" Lorelei grinned.

"Very."

"What is his name?"

"Arkady."

Lorelei raised a brow. "And his specialty?"

I plastered a smile across my face. "He works with clay and stone, sculptures mostly," I commented through a taut jaw.

"Lucky for you, I suppose. Well, with all they say about *those* types . . ."

"What is it they say, pray tell?" I rolled my eyes again.

"How do you not know?"

"I loathe gossip, you know this. I haven't read a tabloid in years."

"Painfully boring."

"Guilty."

"Well, that is why you have me to keep you in the know." She glanced over her shoulder before leaning in. "Who else would be able to tell you that sculpting certainly isn't the only thing his hands will be good for—"

"Enough." I pushed her shoulder away.

"What? Am I bringing back wedding-night memories?" she teased.

My face became hot; if I steeped any longer, I would steam.

"Cher seigneur." She grasped my knee. "Did you not?"

I shook my head, focusing only straight in front of me, counting the people who passed.

Shame was the only discernible feeling deep within my chest. It was such a silly thing to be bothered over. It was no one's business other than my own, yet it felt like an objective judgment of my worth. Maybe it was my own insecurities, conveniently read aloud in my head in the voice of my mother.

"Enough about me, how are your endeavors?"

A grin crept across Lorelei's face, further defining her lush cheeks. "I have set my sights on someone new."

I had always been jealous of Lorelei's energy. She was young, sprite-like. I couldn't imagine having that lively energy at all times. I supposed that was a given since she was barely nineteen, hardly a woman.

"Oh?" I turned to her in my seat. "Someone mentioned previously or brand-new altogether?"

"The new ballet master." She shrugged her shoulders in excitement as she clasped her hands.

"I thought you were not going to pursue patrons."

"I pondered on it, but I am young, and it would be a shame to go to waste. Besides, he isn't just *any* patron. I'll never be in the corps de ballet again, I will be a star."

"Lorelei," I warned, "I told you what happens when you go too deep. You won't be able to get out."

"There's too much interest to ignore!"

"Ignore it anyway!"

"When did you become so stuffy?" she grumbled. "You got to have your fun. Maybe you are jealous that I get to have mine?"

My mouth opened to speak, but none of the words I wanted to use would be kind, so I shut it again.

"That's what I thought." She crossed her arms.

That is when I spotted a familiar figure.

In my line of sight, just over Lorelei's shoulder, was a man. A tall and lanky silhouette that resembled his profession entirely.

The coroner stood at the entrance of the park, framed by the iron gates, just waiting.

I supposed the news of my marriage would make its rounds, but I didn't think my patrons would hear so soon. I assumed they would at least know when I wasn't in the next show. I thought I had more time to come up with an explanation.

"I have to get going." I checked my timepiece. Our debates would have to wait for another day.

Lorelei refused to look at me and remained seated.

My shoulders slouched as I dwelled on saying anything more, but I decided against it, departing silently.

I worried for that girl, more than she would care to hear. I remember being foolish once, though I cannot help but wonder why she would choose a life like that. I certainly didn't. It was clear that, even when leaving it all behind, the shadows of my past were not done with me yet.

I don't know why I went. Whether it was morbid curiosity or escaping the stalking of someone worse, I did not know. But I was here now, surrounded by the smell of low-settling smog and fish.

Arkady's studio was by the shipyard, where soot slept and sunshine went to drown. The building was an imposing brick warehouse with a circular window poised below the gable. A narrow smokestack stood erect at the back of the building, erosion stains discoloring the brick on one side. I half expected bodies to wash up beside me on the dock with how bleak the scenery appeared.

I had to push into the sliding door twice, throwing more weight each time, before the rusted metal finally unstuck. It opened up to statues crowded along the edges of the walls, some with sheets over them and others bare. The second circular window at the back of the warehouse was enough to light the floor.

In the middle of the room was one unfinished statue, and Arkady devoting such focus that he did not hear me come in.

The smell of petrichor tickled my nose upon entry. Did it give him performance anxiety, having an army of stone people watching? I could imagine why he'd become such a shut-in. At least the statues couldn't heckle.

Even as he swung the mallet into his chisel, it seemed so effortless, so fluid. Every ripple of his forearm as he tapped along the form, little chips of stone clattering into the floor. The particles shimmered as it puffed into the air. His normally tanned arms now covered in white smears of old clay and dust.

"Is this where you work?" I spoke out. "Quite the audience."

For a moment, his expression was stern when he looked, only for it to become acerbic when he saw it was me. "Mrs. Kameneva."

I wanted to say something back, but the way he addressed me caught me off guard.

"I would have dusted off an extra chair for such an esteemed visit." He leaned back on his stool.

"You can learn a lot by someone's work." I stood straight, looking up at the grand window that made a spotlight on the floor. "I wanted to see the art behind the man."

"Weren't you the one who said something about being left alone?" He raised a brow. "Hypocrite."

I scoffed, glancing back at him.

He squinted with one eye closed, holding a small carving tool in his line of sight toward me.

"What are you doing?"

"Measuring."

"Measuring?"

"Yes." He lowered his hand. "I am working out the proportions." He tapped the stone figure next to him with his tool.

The stone had no face, no hands, just a vague blocky form, but there was something about it that made it human in stature.

"Come closer." He beckoned me. "At least let me give you a tour if you insist on staying."

"How gentlemanly." I made sure to draw out the words in a sarcastic trill. I stepped farther into the cave of the peculiar man.

The statues were taller when you stood next to them, giving each an intimidating stature. I planted myself next to Arkady as he looked up at his work in progress.

"What is it going to be?"

"A woman." He tilted his head to the side. "I'm still blocking it out."

"I see." I must have been looking at him similarly to how he was looking at this block of stone. His clay-covered arms were crossed, and he was tapping one thumb anxiously against the hilt of his chisel.

Off to the side was another work in progress. It looked like two vague forms of clay, presumably two people entangled in a scene. Protruding from certain areas of clay, there looked to be rope, pins, and other material. It wrapped around the figures and surfaced from under the clay to attach to the wrist of one of the raised hands.

"What is the rope for?"

Arkady peeled his gaze from the stone and to me before glancing at the clay sculpture. "To keep the position and form of the supportive material. I cut away and shave down the rope once the ceramics have dried more, in order to build up from the base before firing."

I nodded and looked to the corner, where there was a giant form of bricks, unoriginal to the building. It was like a massive oven, a terra-cotta igloo with a large archway opening and an iron door propped open to expose the ash that was spilling onto the floor.

"What about that?"

"Hm?" Arkady followed my line of sight. "Oh, that's a kiln."

"I've never seen one so big."

"Neither have I. I had to build it myself." His chest puffed out proudly. "The downside is that it is expensive to fire. So it's been a while since I've used it."

"*How* do you use it?" I approached the structure, each click of my heels bouncing off the brick walls just to shoot back at my eardrums. It was intimidating on its own when it was inactive; I couldn't imagine how it would be with a burning fire inside. "How do you keep your sculptures from combusting?"

"Well, my sculptures are mainly organic matter on the inside and ceramic over the top, so they are hollow by the end of the firing process," he explained, shoving his hands in his pockets as he stared up at the brick.

"How clever." I leaned into the arch of the kiln, looking up at the blackened expanse above.

The hair on the back of my neck stood up, a hand by my nape.

I reached up, slapping it away as I turned.

Arkady leaned back, hands up in surrender. "Ah, flighty thing."

"I am not a *thing*." I brushed my hands over my garments, which had collected dust from his arm.

"Oh? Is that so?" He stepped forward.

"Don't be cheeky."

Another step forward for him, another step back for me.

"Cheeky?"

My back hit the brick of the kiln.

Arkady's hands rested on the stones on either side of my body.

My face must have been a wild red, the heat making me wonder how the ceramics must feel when they were fired. Even when I looked away from him, I could still smell his cologne, feel his body temperature, hear—

"You seem agitated." His voice was sonorous, like a freshly rosined bow across a cello. His eyes trailed down to my dress, fixating on the clay dust smudged over my skirt. "I can't help but wonder if that is my doing."

"Clever and receptive," I gritted, staring up at him.

His eyes held a sharp wit that made sure you knew he was watching, a hawk ready to snatch a stray mouse. His skin and hair reminded me of natural clay, not dissimilar to the kind he used. How ironic that someone so alluring was such a sociopath, surely a narcissist at the very least.

"Why did you come?" His face was inches from mine, teasing the air around us with a sort of electric static that shocked me from my thoughts. "And don't say it's because you *missed* me," he teased.

"You didn't come to bed," I breathed.

"I thought it would be rude, considering the circumstances."

"No, you thought I would be easy. You were thrown off."

"You aren't what I expected. I'll admit that."

"I am not of your tastes?"

"I'm trying to be a gentleman." He tilted his head to the side and glanced at my lips. "Unless it is the ungentlemanly types you like?"

His hands grabbed my hips.

"Stop!" I squeaked. My heart fluttered between my ribs like a startled cardinal. "You'll leave prints!"

He raised one hand, gently trailing his finger along my cheek, the other smearing the clay dust up my waist. The heat of his hand lingered, but the hotness was faint compared to my own embarrassment. "I wish I could capture the color of your cheeks when they're flustered, it would make a perfect glaze."

My mouth dropped open to speak, but no words would manifest on my tongue.

"Dare I suggest that it is *I* who is not of your taste?" He retreated completely.

I swallowed hard, not knowing if it was difficult due to dust or apprehension.

He turned his back to me and approached his lonely stool next to the unfinished statue, sitting down to begin his work once more.

"I—I will see you at home." I gathered my resolve once more.

He didn't bother to look my way, though the last thing I saw was a flash of a smirk pulling at his lips, a mischievous glint in his eye showing more interest than he let on. Though, it was possible that analysis was a projection of my own desires.

CHAPTER FIVE

The Artisan

The air was dry like chapped palms over sherpa wool. The day was full of irritants, every event an abrasive particle. The barren air, my unpaid debts—even my wife—were nagging me today.

The embalming room was a cold basement, some cellar windows to let a smidge of light through. Despite the desolate, sterile appearance—there was so much opportunity for enlightenment.

As dreary as the atmosphere was, it was always a great source of inspiration. Bodies held secrets, and if they didn't tell you before their passing, they would tell the mortician. I didn't see a difference between a muse and an artisan.

Lately my creativity had run bare, scraping the bottom of the well. Client work kept me busy, but it wasn't the same as being inspired. It had been months since I'd created for myself, and those were always the pieces that kept me afloat for a year or two.

"Let me see," I demanded.

"Eager for someone who *isn't supposed to be down here*." Kostya clicked his tongue against his teeth as he finished cleaning his instruments.

I sloped my head back and took a deep breath before returning with a more agreeable tone. "May I *please* see now?"

Kostya frowned and pinched the edge of the white sheet covering a newly departed. "That's more like it." He paused and raised a critical brow at me. "You are *not* allowed to bring anything home this time. She has to stay here."

"Christ, Kostya, I may be dead myself by the time you lift the sheet."

My friend finally folded the sheet over, revealing a fair woman, gone before twenty-five. Beautiful, but the beauty stopped abruptly halfway across her face, as it was charred.

"I thought you said this one was in good condition to study." I pulled the notepad from my jacket pocket.

"Well, she's pretty, I never said she was in good shape aside from that. She has good muscle definition. Some freak field-labor accident upstate."

I shook my head and pulled out the pen, beginning to look closely at the skin. I pinched the sheet, pulling it down more to expose her collarbone, her arm, her ribs, then to reveal more charring. Her hand was exceptionally striking, something so dainty covered in a stark singe.

I took a quick sketch of the different parts, but I found myself studying the way the texture changed from smooth to something like bark on the non-surviving parts, only a prominent portion of the bone structure escaping the fire.

She was technically beautiful, but something was missing. A certain vibrance. Perhaps it was because she was dead. I wouldn't know. But, once again, I was going to be leaving the same as I came—uninspired.

"You know, we should take our wives out together sometime, parade the birds around town," Kostya said from the opposite side, leaning on the metal slab.

"Sure, of course." A few more notes jotted, and the loose lines around a few more forms.

"You don't seem thrilled."

"Doing the bear isn't at the forefront of my mind lately." I snapped the book shut.

"Have you spoken to her at all, or have you hidden yourself away in the studio?" His tone was teasing, but he wasn't wrong.

"I *have* spoken to her, matter of fact." I flashed an unamused smile.

"And she thought of you as decent after that conversation?"

I thought about it for a moment too long.

"That's what I thought," he snorted. "You know, having a partner isn't so bad, even if you do not love her."

"She's aware the arrangement is mutually beneficial. I plan on going about business as usual."

"Appearances matter, Arkasha." Kostya sighed. "Especially since her family's money is your lifeline. It couldn't hurt to entertain."

"We get along fine."

"Enough to convince the public that both of you aren't dabbling between other people's legs?"

"Why do you care?"

Kostya combed his fingers through his neatly placed hair. "I know you are a decent man, I believe it, and I know you would rather be alone than surrounded by women—but that's not what the public thinks. Certain occupations come with certain prejudices."

"Why do you care?" I repeated.

Kostya circled the slab and slapped his hand firmly on my shoulder. "Because I want the best for you, brother, and for you to be happy. The public isn't very receptive to the poor, the underprivileged, or immigrants—of which you are all three. Make an effort, and you will find both of you are happier. I didn't watch you claw your way through this life just to see you falter."

I brushed his hand from my shoulder but didn't offer a counter.

He was right, and I knew it deep down, just not enough to validate verbally.

It had only been a few days, so my understanding of my wife's routine was rudimentary at best. She went to bed early and didn't wake up until noon. A single bowl would be abandoned in the sink when I returned by nightfall. It was always covered in a sticky, dried juice—I suspect from her apricots. There were *always* apricots. Her quirks remained cryptic, but I digress.

It couldn't hurt to spend more mornings in my new home while she slept. At least I knew how much time I'd have to myself. Kostya has been sleeping in later and later, even calling in late to work due to his colicky child. It was disappointing to not see him as regularly, but a new, quiet home was just as nice.

The sofa was an improvement from the studio. The decorative pillows were barely used, still plush. There was a kink in the cushions, but it was coincidentally in the right place to support my aching back from the long days of questionable posture.

My roots were settling within my new domain. It was cluttered, but in a charming sense that made you feel like each object was important, of practical or sentimental value. A shrine of some kind. I suppose that would apply to most homes, but especially this one. There was an enchantment to it like some hidden-away place to disappear inside for days. Even the moths were beginning to appear friendly, though I was still working on a way to get rid of them. There was clearly an infestation festering somewhere.

Even with the rough start to my marriage to a complete stranger, it could have been worse. Not as passive as I expected, but that wasn't a problem. I thought she was a pretty thing; it was good to know she was sharper than a rock, duller than a true blade.

I like it here. I do. I promise. This will all work out.

A rasping sound at the front door disturbed my brief moment of contentment.

I sat up from the sofa, stretching my back before reaching for my coffee. By now, it tasted a bit like dust. I would have to clean at some point; it wasn't like she would do it.

More rasping, quicker and louder this time.

They will wake the she-beast at this rate.

I abandoned the comfort of my seat and my less-than-impressive cup of coffee for the door, tucking my shirt properly before answering.

When I opened the door, a strange man stood expectantly, straight as a pin, snobbish as a bird.

"May I help you?" I raised a brow. "If you're a solicitor, you've come to the wrong home."

The middle-aged gentlemen looked almost amused, glancing to the side as if it was a cretinous remark. "*You* seem to be the one in a place you do not belong." He seemed well groomed, but not well mannered to the common man. His dark hair was interrupted by stripes of a duller gray down the sides, but it was plain to see he was attempting to hide them with black salve. His mustache was trimmed short and thin in an attempt to shave some years from his appearance, but it did nothing to hide the stress lines at the corners of his eyes and the way time had weighed on his features.

"I'm sorry, I believe you have the wrong home. This is four hundred forty-four." I smiled politely, tapping the plaque on the door.

"I am aware." He glanced past me, fiddling with a gold signet ring around his pinkie. "Is Miss De Villier home?"

"I don't know about Miss De Villier, but *Mrs. Kameneva* is resting and not receiving visitors."

"Oh, so you're the new fool."

"Possibly but unlikely, as I am not the one standing on the doorstep begging for entry."

"Am I bothering you, good sir? Surely it was not my intention." He smirked, exposing a collection of shifted teeth with tobacco stains at the roots. "I surely don't mean to offend."

"Not at all." I closed the door behind me as I stepped outside.

With one step back, his chest puffed at my gesture. "Tell her I stopped by." He held out his calling card.

Vincent Carlisle
Coroner's Office of New York City

"I am under the impression she isn't going to receive you." I held the card, inspecting the small text.

"She will receive whoever comes." He retrieved a cigarette from his lapel pocket and lit it in front of me.

"Is that so?" I lifted my gaze from the card, pulling out my own cigarette. "Mind me stealing a light?"

"It's the least I could do for any poor fellow who falls between the jaws of Petronille. You're going to need more than tobacco."

I placed the paper in my mouth, and he flicked the wheel of his lighter, cherry-ing the tip.

"I appreciate the concern, Mr. Carlisle, but I am not new to the art of handling women," I assured him with a nod.

"If you can say that so confidently, it is clear you don't know her." He blew a cloud of smoke in my face, stepping closer until we were nearly chest to chest. "You have my calling card now if you ever need her taken off your hands."

I nodded cordially as if his words held any substance for me.

Then I held up his calling card, pressing it flat against my cigarette, and he watched as the ember ring grew until it was a piece of ash in my hand. "And now I've lost it, I suggest *you* find a way to get lost as well."

The man's eye twitched, a bruise to the ego. But what could he do? It was not his house, daylight, in public. His haughty expression faltered and turned to a brief flash of anger. Against his undoubtedly impulsive thoughts, he decided not to act on them at that moment, stepping away and retreating from the front of the townhome.

What kind of trouble have you found yourself in, dear wife?

CHAPTER SIX

The Performer

The next morning was no different from the last. Arkady slept on the sofa, *again*.

I wasn't sure he'd come home at all some days, as he was always at his studio. At least I *assumed* it was his studio. He returned by the time I was asleep and left before I woke. Completely separate schedules.

He didn't speak much if I happened to see him, though it was like he reserved himself until he had something important to say. I admit, this was what I'd wanted, to be left alone. It was no different than before I was married, and he made sure of it.

It was like we were both unsure how to interact with one another, though his stubbornness was juvenile. Hesitation was expected between newlyweds, but was it supposed to be as severe as this?

My morning coffee was getting as cold as my bones. I swore I was never warm no matter how big the fire or however many layers I put on myself. The headache that prodded at my brain surely wasn't helping my appetite.

The soft music on the phonograph beside me was supposed to help ease my tension, but it did the opposite.

"You're up early," Arkady pointed out as he adjusted his jacket, ready to escape the domicile.

I nodded, closing my eyes even if the light still perforated them somehow. A swell of unsteadiness threatened nausea, the piercing phantom pain in my left eye, my sinuses.

There was an awkward rustling of my surroundings, bouncing in and out of my auditory perception.

"Are you studying?" He made an awkward attempt at conversation.

"No, just listening."

"Do you miss it?"

I didn't answer.

"Which symphony is it?" He was closer now. "I'm not familiar."

"Act two finale of *La Sylphide*," I mumbled, leaning my face into my palms at the table.

"Doesn't ring a bell."

"I don't see why it would." My tone would have been more sarcastic if I weren't so focused on not gagging.

"Well, what's happening, then?"

I sighed and lifted my head to the bleary image of him standing by the sofa, collecting things in a satchel for his day. What was the point of asking if he didn't seem to care?

"The protagonist has removed the sylph's wings in an attempt to have her, overcome by his desire. But in doing so, it kills her. One wing drops . . ." I paused, waiting for the sad shrill of the stringed instruments. "Here." I waited for the next beat. "And here."

"Is that the end?"

"Then she is carried off by faeries into the woods, escaping the desire of man at the cost of her life."

"But is she not free?"

"I suppose that is one way to interpret it." I lowered my head back into my palms.

"Are you well?"

I nodded.

Footsteps, louder as they approached.

A hand grasped my jaw and tilted it up. My eyes widened at the man peering down at me. His expression was critical, calculating.

"What?" My voice cracked, not entirely woken up from my slumber.

He used his other hand to pull my bottom eyelid down.

"Stop that!" I swatted his hand.

"You are anemic." He gripped my face to keep me still.

"Yes." I clenched my jaw. "Iron deficiency, I told you."

His eyes seemed sharp, pupils constricting. This may have been the first time I'd seen anything other than indifference, which was both relieving and terrifying at the same time. The pads of his fingers were firm against my jaw. My breath caught, heart pounding so hard I thought it would leap out my throat.

He finally let go, returning to his typical cool demeanor, and he did not comment before the front door slammed on his way out.

What was that?

I swallowed the lump in my throat, rubbing the skin where he'd grabbed. I supposed I could take some comfort in knowing I was right . . . there was something off about him. The more I saw him, the greater the threat seemed.

A watch was ticking, something would happen. My dysfunction was the fact that I was more curious than afraid. *What will he do? What is he made of?* I wished to find out.

"Sœurette!" Cosette squeaked, rising steadily from her seat as she rested a tired hand on her belly, swollen with child.

The housekeeper let me in, and I glanced around the corner into the parlor room.

"Cosette." I beamed. "I heard you were craving the blueberry scones." I held up my basket.

"Yes! *Sois béni!*" She let out an exasperated sigh, pulling me into a hug.

I always wondered if I would have resembled my sisters if I weren't the runt. They were classic beauties: hair like rich hazelnut and an olive depth to their skin even though they were pale, which made their deep blue eyes stand out even more. I shared nothing with them, as I was always sicker, paler, monochromatic—like my mother had forgotten to save that same vibrance for me.

I did not have many friends aside from Félice and Cosette, with the exception of Lorelei, and I liked to hear how their lives were, to live vicariously.

Our parents moved us from the South of France in our teenage years. We joined a ballet in Paris. It was there we gathered our first prospects, connections for our parents to use at their whim. Climbing the industrial ladder until we had enough to move here and begin anew, with rapidly growing appetites and means.

I admitted, I'd been sad to leave the ballet then, and I was sad to leave again now.

My sisters had no trouble making friends. I, on the other hand, never found any ease in the matter. The best I could do was befriend the governess, the milkman, maybe a funny-looking pigeon.

"How have you been?" Félice hugged me next. "I hope everything is well with you and Mr. Kamenev."

"It is fine," I mumbled, "but I don't wish to talk about me today."

We gathered around the tea table. Assorted scones, clotted cream, and margarine paired with our morning tea. My sisters were predictable—black tea, imported. I'd grown to prefer Russian Caravan, since it was gifted to me by a patron years ago.

"You seem pale." Félice reached over to place the back of her hand on my forehead.

"I have been forgetting to eat my fruit." I swatted her hand. "The week has been a bit of a wrench in my routine."

"I see." She sat back in her chair, her hands returning to hold her cup.

"Thank you for the sweets. Charles refuses to give in to my cravings, he calls them unnatural," Cosette complained, eating yet another scone.

She was pregnant with her first, so naturally Félice was here every day to help and support her. One benefit of moving to New York was that we were all a stone's throw away from one another.

Félice almost had a child once. It was stillborn. Her husband expired soon after, though she was in no rush to find another. The assets of her first husband were enough to keep her comfortable for the rest of her life. Our parents always told us that hardship was the only way to find comfort in this life, as women more than anything.

"I was passing the bakery anyway, it was no trouble," I lied. I'd left early with her in mind.

The two were almost comical next to one another. Cosette wore a soft-yellow gown with little bluebell flowers printed on the fabric, while Félice was wearing a nearly black violet one, as she was coming out of her first year of mourning.

Some days I thought Félice was relieved, but I shouldn't have assumed such a thing. I never saw her cry for them, even at their funerals. It was one mourning period right after the other. I don't believe I had *ever* seen her cry; I couldn't imagine it. I supposed after such a sacrifice, you got used to it.

A maid replenished our tea before gathering any loose plates or empty trays.

"How is Mr. Kamenev?" Cosette asked me in French, giving a polite smile to the maid as she departed. All of our private conversations were held in French, as my sister's help strictly spoke English.

"Fine."

"You don't seem very enthusiastic." Félice raised a brow. "Is that why you are sick? He isn't taking proper care of you?"

"He is a distraction." I took another slow sip of my tea.

Félice scoffed, shaking her head. "I don't like him."

"Good thing he isn't your husband." Cosette rolled her eyes at Félice before looking back to me. "So I take it you had a less than eventful night after you left the ceremony?"

"It was eventful, but not in that way. He slept on the sofa."

Both sisters grimaced, their noses wrinkling at the thought of whatever he did to deserve that. I was sure their expressions would be worse if I'd told them it was his choice.

"I know, I know." I sighed. "He is painfully indifferent."

"I suppose that isn't the worst thing he could be," Cosette said, offering her signature optimism. "Though, it is a shame. He *is* pretty."

"Cosette," Félice scolded, whipping her cloth napkin at her.

"No, it's okay." I placed my cup down. "I'm sure he is being *gentlemanly*."

I didn't know if my sisters' expressions were confused or horrified.

"He isn't taking your condition well?" Félice asked cautiously.

"It isn't that. I haven't told him."

"You know he will find out."

"He doesn't need to know everything at once. Men are flighty things, I will tell him eventually."

"He should know soon, you can't hide it for long," Cosette piped in.

"Based on how he reacted to the anemia this morning, I don't know if I want to tell him right now."

"What do you mean?" Cosette's brows knitted together.

"He looked alarmed, almost angry, at my low energy." I shrugged. "I'm not sure what he thinks, he is impossible to read. Maybe he was expecting more of a fight."

"Even with the odd circumstance of your husband, it must be a relief to leave that musty theater." Félice took a relaxed breath.

I didn't comment, taking a closer inspection of my teacup.

"Come now, Petre, the ballet wasn't going to be forever, right?" Félice took on a maternal tone. "We all did our duty, aged out, and gathered our means. This is a *good* thing, Petre."

"I know it's silly"—I shrugged, placing my cup in its coaster—"but I love to dance. Everything else can go except the art itself. It's a shame that the two halves are exclusive."

"I have to agree, I loved the music." Cosette sighed, her shoulders slumping. "Oh! And the costuming! I've never felt so beautiful. I wish we could wear such beautiful things every day."

I laughed and shook my head. "Well, I'm sure Mother would throw a gala just to make that request come true, just for you," I teased.

Félice nodded exaggeratedly, taking a long sip of her brew.

An air of nostalgia wove its way into our conversations, and our morning continued quietly as we finished up our breakfast.

With all of our lives being so different, it was important to me that we all gathered when we could. In my sisters' own odd ways, they were still as supportive as they could be. It was just a blessing to be with them without our parents hovering. Even as adults, we half expected them to be right around the corner, listening in, making sure we were presenting whatever image they wanted us to.

Sometimes it was nice to slouch, to laugh, to be louder, to take up space together in private—away from scrutinizing eyes.

My stomach pinched and growled, whining for something to eat other than cakes and finger sandwiches.

I didn't want to cook anything too labor intensive in case Arkady came home early. So far, he had stayed late at his studio and hadn't shown any signs of changing his habits yet.

The keys at my hip chimed as I stepped up to my front door and fiddled with them to find the correct one for the lock. Not only had the walk exhausted me, but just the front steps had rendered me slightly out of breath. My headache wasn't doing me any favors all the while.

Upon entering my domicile, the familiar smell of my home calmed me, just not enough for me to ignore my other senses.

The earthy colors of the walls reminded me more of a cottage than a city home. The sage-green furnishings were soft on the eyes, even softer now that they had been well loved by my family, then just myself.

The mid-tone wood gave the room a whisper of warmth as if welcoming me with a familiar embrace, like an old friend asking to catch up over fresh tea and old memories.

It was as quiet as ever, a peaceful place where time went to be stolen. A place to lie down on the sofa and rot away in its stillness. Memories are a sort of ghost, and this house was teeming with them. They said ghosts were for keeping people away, but I believed they breathed life into a home.

After shedding my coat, I draped it on a coatrack before letting my shoulders slump, stretching my neck from side to side. The fluttering of a moth greeted me as my coat disturbed it.

My stomach pinched again. A steadfast craving bloomed on my tongue like a lost memory, leaving an acidic taste in my mouth.

The carpet under my shoes seemingly stretched, pulling my eyes in the direction of my basement door. It was like the more I stared, the farther away the door got. Whether it be pinholing or lightheadedness, I wouldn't know. I just knew I was hungry.

With the key pinched firmly between my fingers, I approached the door. The lock was sturdy, a simple brass shape keeping all my secrets safe. The golden glow of the metal was worn down to a muted patina, revealing everywhere it had been touched during the last twenty years.

The steps to the basement floor disappeared halfway down, the only light present from the hallway. Much like the other stairs in the home, these creaked too. The only difference between these stairs and the others was their tune. While the others moaned, these steps screamed. They whimpered and cried upon contact until they were finally relieved of the weight, making the step onto the ceramic floor all the more jarring when everything silenced.

The basement was small, utilitarian. Mechanical forms hid away in the corners, though I wasn't sure what their functions were.

The tiles on the floor were a black-and-white checker. Three of the walls were finished with lath and plaster, the last one bare brick and stained with a buildup of lime. The ceiling was mostly finished except for the places where water damage slowly discolored it. At one point my parents had tried to finish it as a utility room for staff, but then they settled on the idea of building their own custom home farther into Manhattan.

Small boxes were tucked under the stairs in large stacks, a couple of items perched on top for lack of better placement options in the barren room. The pipes groaned a bit louder down here, like witnessing the beating heart of a home in the most clinical sense.

The tenement was a time capsule, burying our history with it. It had been our first home upon arriving to this new city before my parents came into their fortune and outgrew it.

They even left the old icebox, short enough where I could knock my knee if I tripped on it in the dark. The wood was a dull green, pieces splintering and the paint peeling from wear.

Before I could retrieve any perishables from the little box, the bell sounded, followed by the front door's heavy bolt unlocking.

He's home early.

"Hello?" I called out, practically skipping steps to get to the first floor faster. "Leave your shoes at the door, clay is hard to scrub out of rugs!"

When the ground floor was on the horizon, there was no one in the foyer.

"Arkady?" I said, quieter.

I closed the door gently to push it into the frame without much noise. My heart was in my throat, the anxiety a slow squeeze around my chest. I focused on the front door at the end of the hallway, just past the stairs. There were no shoes, not even a new coat on the rack. The moths high on the wall were never disturbed.

I treaded carefully over to the parlor room, taking a deep breath that did little to steady my frantic heart.

My father sat in the corner chair with his signature morose posture.

Despite sitting in the home of his daughter, he always held himself like he was wasting money the longer he was present.

Time is not money, time is worth much more, he would always say. I could practically hear him. His visual was helping with the immersion.

His head cocked to the side, his eyes focused on packing his pipe, not wasting a glance. He sat in his old chair; it remained unused unless he visited.

"You let yourself in," I said.

"It is my house, after all."

"What is the point of giving me the house if you invite yourself in whenever it pleases you?"

"Careful"—his eyes snapped to me—"you have very low leverage in this situation."

I bit the inside of my cheek.

"I was kind to you. I could have used you for a more advantageous marriage." He leaned back in the chair, lighting his pipe.

"But you didn't."

"Because I would need those investors relatively unharmed, for now." He paused, puffing and watching the embers pulse to life with each breath. "I thought you would be more grateful, is all."

"I *am* grateful."

"Have you consummated?" He watched for my reaction carefully.

"Is that not my private business?" I managed a small smile through a clenched jaw.

His laugh was melodic, a lighthearted amusement if it weren't for the topics at hand. "No, my dear, what you do with your body has never been your business." He gathered himself again to take another inhale.

I only noticed I was making fists when my nails began to leave impressions in my palms, stinging as the blood attempted to recirculate.

"I take it that you've scared him off already?" He sighed, standing from his seat and neatly buttoning his jacket.

"We are getting to know one another." My voice shook. "Have you considered he may like me for my mind rather than my flesh?" I didn't know if Arkady could possibly see that in me, but my father didn't know that. The only leverage I had was that we hadn't shared a home in some time.

His head tilted to the side with a smile as if I'd said something foolish. "My dear girl, men are practically born craving the fruit of the flesh."

"I am taking my time."

"How funny, it didn't take much time at all with your past patrons. And your sisters fared well." He moved to pass but paused when he came up next to me. "I thought your experience would have made this go faster, but I am choosing to trust your process while you gather your footing."

There was such venom in his words that an outsider would hardly believe they came from my father. He was collected that way, his perception a mere curation of what he wanted others to see.

Another ring of the doorbell.

"I'll see myself out, it was good to catch up." A pleasant smile graced his features before he squeezed my shoulder.

As I opened the door to let him out, I was nose to nose with my second guest of the day.

"Oh—I didn't realize you had company. I can come back later." Lorelei startled at the sight of my father.

A disingenuous smirk peeled across his lips. "I was on my way out."

He stepped past with a tip of his hat, then flashed me a look before leisurely strolling down the sidewalk.

"How are you?" I mumbled, staring down at my shoes that were toe to toe with hers, only the wooden saddle of the door between us like a line in the sand.

"Could we talk?" Lorelei sighed. She was clutching her little purse, rubbing at the slightly worn handle.

She was never good at apologies, but she *was* good at coming back around.

I stepped aside, welcoming her into the home with a gesture.

Lorelei had already begun rambling about something faster than a racehorse through the gate, immediately making herself comfortable in the living room. I leaned on the archway, her words becoming muffled as my mind wandered, gently being pulled toward the basement door, a loose lock dangling, mocking me as the keyhole stared like some malevolent eye watching over my day.

Finally, I was alone.

My afternoon ritual could begin. A fresh brewing of a new malty black tea Cosette gifted me. She said the hint of chocolate would pair perfectly with the dried apricots. My favorite cups, the cream-colored ones with gold and deep-reddish-orange glaze in the designs around the rim. I only had two, the rest long since chipped, worn, or discarded.

Within the living room, I settled comfortably on the sofa with a novel from the shelf. The only decision I was keen on making tonight was whether I wanted to read a new story or reread an old comfort novel. My own personal library must have been half made up of books I'd read more times than years living, new books I'd bought for how pretty their bindings were, or the small amount that were out-of-taste gifts that I would never touch.

Just as I was settling in, a loud, quite agitating rasping came at the door.

"One moment of peace, I *beg*," I groaned, snapping the book closed again and tossing it on the table, making my teacup clamor in its saucer.

The door practically flew back, smacking me in the forehead, when I simply unlatched it.

"Did you *really* think you could avoid me? How quickly you move on, fickle thing," the coroner scoffed, striding into my home like a debt collector.

I hurriedly caught the door and shut it.

"I wasn't avoiding you, Vincent. Don't be obtuse." I was, indeed, unmistakably, avoiding him.

"You can't just cut me out, you know." He let out a cruel laugh, turning on his heel to snap his head at me, a few stray pieces of hair falling and bringing attention to how manic his eyes were, pupils wide like a feral pest. "Who else will help a depraved little thing like you? Your new husband? No, he would run at the very idea—"

"I didn't cut anyone out," I interrupted, hastily collecting the mail that the door had scattered and placing it on the hallway table. "My hands are tied, it wasn't my decision," I lied.

"You promised yourself to me."

"I don't know what you thought our arrangement was," I started, busying myself slicing through one of the envelopes with the letter opener, "but I did no such thing."

The tall man stalked forward, but I stood firm, propping up my facade of indifference with twigs. If my back weren't turned to him, he may have caught the tremor in my hand.

"You know, just because you are free of the ballet . . ." he began, his stature hanging over me like a guillotine waiting to drop.

In the reflection of the letter opener, his eyes were dark, hungry.

". . . does not mean you will be free of *me*." He placed his hand low on my back, smoothing lower.

"Stop." I crushed the letter in my hand.

"I don't think you mean it." He licked my ear, shoving his hand between my legs and squeezing.

"Stop!" I shouted, reaching down and digging my nails into his hand.

He squeezed tighter, yanking me backward and pressing his hardened bulge against my back.

"I said *stop*!" I screamed, whipping around to slap him with the blunt end of my letter opener.

My aim was miscalculated.

He was too tall.

I couldn't reach.

It wasn't my fault.

A hot sensation kissed my face, clouding my vision with red. The metallic tinge dripped to my lips. I ran my tongue over it, looking down at the bloodied opener and the crimson coating on my hands, spreading to my white tea gown.

A fine line across his neck, going from pink to red immediately. His expression might as well have been mirroring mine, the wound gaping similar to his mouth, spraying blood instead of the profanities I was used to.

He finally let go of me to press that same grip on his neck. He stumbled back but faltered before his back could hit the wall.

"I'm . . . I'm sorry, wait—" I pleaded, kneeling before him, the front of my dress turning pink with every droplet that sputtered from the wound. "I'm sorry, I'm sorry," I wept, trying to press my hands to his neck, which only resulted in more smears and nicking him again with the opener.

I tossed it in horror, blood splattering as it clattered on the floor.

Thank God my carpet was already red. *Did he get any on the wallpaper? Oh, of course, I'm wearing the new tea gown!* It would be too embarrassing to go buy the same one again in such a short time. I wasn't willing to part with it, but I was unaware of what would wash out blood.

His expression—pure and utter shock. It was alien to me, the behavior of a dying man. An awful, terrible, wet gasping coming from his mouth instead of his typical verbal abuses.

Then, the door creaked, the rush of rain showers hissing among the cobblestones.

No, not now!

Mr. Kamenev entered, not noticing the situation at first as his gaze was lowered.

Everything was quiet.

Everything was still.

Everything but my heart.

He shrugged off his coat, popping the collar onto the coatrack. He squinted, brushing some dust from the shoulder. Then, before removing his boots, his eyes followed the spray of blood on the floor until they settled on my patron, then on me.

I finally let go, my situation settling on me.

He slammed the door shut.

Mr. Carlisle reached out, mouthing pleading words.

I sobbed, "I'm sorry—"

Arkady snatched the letter opener from the floor.

I didn't know what to do with the blood that stained my hands, so I held them palms up.

"Call the police—" Mr. Carlisle tried desperately to warn my husband against my transgressions, his mouth moving as fast as it could.

But it slacked when my husband buried the letter opener through the coroner's eye.

Vincent's mouth gaped open and closed like a jittering nutcracker, wide-eyed and all.

With a final shove, he stilled.

"Speechless" was too weak a word to describe what I felt. I wanted to say many things, but I wondered if reminding him of my presence was a good idea after what I'd just witnessed.

There was a long pause. From fear? A lack of an explanation? How would I begin to explain myself?

Why did you do that?

"Clean yourself, you're a sopping mess." Arkady broke the thick veil of silence, dragging his palm and the back of his hand down an unstained part of Vincent's trousers.

"But I—"

"I said," he repeated, looking at me over his shoulder as he rolled up his sleeves, "go get cleaned."

"Arkady—"

"I will take care of it."

All I could do was stare. I couldn't move.

My husband turned to me. All I saw were the eyes of a dog with its lip curled and hackles erect.

Yet, in his face, there was no anger, no confusion, only a look that could cut anyone down to the bone. He tilted his head at me, brushing a piece of hair from my face, smearing the blood across my skin as he tucked it behind my ear.

"Petronille?"

"Y-yes." I clenched my eyes shut, then opened again before clearing my throat. "Yes?"

"Are you *all right*?"

Is he angry with me?

"Yes."

He nodded, taking my face in both of his hands, even leaning down to meet me eye to eye, his instructions slow and precise. "Go run a bath, take time to settle down, and let me handle this. Do not call for anyone, do not leave the house, do not drink." His thumb smoothed over my cheek. "No questions, no qualms. Understood?"

I nodded, trembling in his grip, trapped between the jaws of the hound.

CHAPTER SEVEN

The Performer

After three baths, I was sure the blood was gone.

But what if it isn't?

As I sat there in the basin the next morning, the water ran clear, my skin chapped from the scrubbing and lye. But I could have sworn I saw just one drop, maybe a smudge of blood on my hands, that made me think I was not yet clean.

I sank into the lukewarm water, hoping some of it would soothe my aches, my anxiety.

If I emptied the tub now, I might still have time for my fourth bath since last night.

The smell of rosewater and eucalyptus was so sweet to my senses, it was nearly nauseating. Light from the window pooled into the water, highlighting the faint figure of my legs lurking between clotting bubbles.

I'd awoken in the night many times, paranoid about having blood in my hair, my ears, somewhere I missed. Even after his death, I could not rid myself of Vincent. I'd always known him as some sticky leech; I did not know he would be the mess that became of him.

The morning was so painfully normal, all things considered. You would never have guessed we'd murdered a man the day before. Except for the blood on the floorboards and the wall.

The sun still rose above the skyline, the newsboy didn't lose his voice, the invoices still pushed through the mail slot.

Arkady had disappeared for the night with Mr. Carlisle. Like it was all some inconceivable nightmare, the wool pulled taut over my eyes.

Out of sight, out of my mind.

He'd even abducted my favorite hallway runner; I really loved that rug.

The call came close to dawn, requesting my presence at the botanical gardens. He said to wear something *pretty* before leaving me hanging on the static of the receiver. That boy needed house training; lessons in a proper conversation should be first.

The only remaining itch at the back of my brain wasn't even regarding the murder. What scared me more than my deadly reaction was the way Arkady had seemed completely and utterly unfazed. His expression had been something I would expect if I'd burnt dinner or forgotten to extinguish a candle beside the drapes.

Why would you bind yourself to me, Mr. Kamenev?

There were a million and one ways to handle that situation; finishing the job was, admittedly, not the first to come to my mind. It was an accident. It wasn't my fault. Had he done this before? I had no way of knowing if he would be any good at hiding a body. Could it have been panic? What if he didn't dispose of the body efficiently? I could only hope I didn't have any gumshoes knocking their batons on my door. Of all the things I thought would stress me about my marriage, wondering whether or not my spouse was skilled at body disposal was not one of them.

What if he is turning me in at this very moment?

As a sitting dove, I'd failed to consider that I might very well find out how well he could hide a body, intimately, if I weren't careful.

No, he would have finished me right then, with the same weapon, giving me the same demise as my patron.

I am important, I reminded myself. Not to him, but to his survival.

Surely, I was not in any danger of death, at the very least.

If I simply never left my shelter, I couldn't make any more mistakes. Lord knows how little room I had for them now.

How dare the sun shine on a day like this?

The city conservatory was popular around this time of year, bursting with the excitement of spring beginnings. The glass cathedral of the greenhouse made it feel at least midsummer.

I was sweating. Well, I had been restless sweating before, but now it was just plain sweat.

The dress I chose hadn't been used in quite some time. The color remained a glossy cream, a perfectly soft buttermilk fabric against my skin. The collar came midway up my neck, the skirt skimming completely to the floor. The make was liquid in texture, even more so with the subtle train behind me. The sleeves came down quarter length, white gloves would cover the rest. My hair managed in a twisted plait, the humidity calling out some strays that curled to kiss the dew of my face. The heavy pearls of my earrings made me all too aware of the textures and sensations of the outfit, but one must endure to look perfect.

I didn't like crowds, or people—leaving my home was never preferred either. There were too many different noises, too many conversations, too many smells. Patrons were only tolerable as an audience, forced to be quiet with their attention only on me. The public stage was not as fun.

It may be that I'm a miserable person, after all.

The flowers were in full bloom, planted promptly in the fall to greet us by early spring, maturing by the time pleasant weather joined us in May. Exotics were popular; there was hardly a reason to see native flowers when a garden as grand as this existed. I pitied those who didn't live near such privileges.

A small butterfly crawled along a bloom. I slipped off my gloves to offer it my hand, and it grasped my finger, its proboscis slapping happily along my skin.

At least someone enjoyed clammy hands.

Only when I looked closer did I realize it was not a butterfly but a hawk moth that had snuck in. I had no doubt it had happily eaten its fill of estranged conservatory nightshades. When your lifespan was only a single month, you might as well indulge. Who was I to judge such a thing?

"Those are invasive, you know," a voice said in my ear.

I turned my head. Arkady leaned over my shoulder, looking less than impressed. I lifted the shuddering insect, the clumsy wings flapping and tickling his nose. "You two shall get along nicely, then."

To say he was less than amused was an understatement. As someone pushed past us, he stood straight with a dimpled smile, affixing his public-facing mask. "Put your gloves on, it's indecent."

My eye twitched at his demand, but I reluctantly set the critter free before pinching the white gloves over each hand, not liking how stiff the material felt on my fingers.

Only after did Arkady offer me an arm, and I accepted.

"You look as pleasant as ever with such a virulent expression." He kept a smile, but his tone was cutting. "Shall we walk? Play a bit of pretend?"

"Why did you ask me here?"

"Appearances," he answered.

"What do you care about appearances?"

His shoulders physically tensed like a dog ready to snap at me for getting too close to his bone. "Typically," he muttered in a low voice, barely moving his lips to speak, "the first thing you do to cover up a *murder* is create an alibi. Do you understand?"

I nodded, chewing the inside of my cheek.

A couple passed us, smiling and tipping their heads in greeting as they moved on to inspect the begonias.

He was right. He was right, and it was *irritating* beyond belief.

"All right." I sighed. "You have a point."

His face snapped in my direction, making me physically jump.

I released a short, irritated breath. "What is it now!" I hissed.

His eyes were wide, not unlike a doe's. The simple shock on his face was enough to make me fear what had caused such a reaction.

"Nothing." He blinked a couple times. "Could you say that again?"

"Excuse me?"

"Just that last part."

My brow twitched when I realized he was teasing. "It's bad enough as it is, don't rub it in. Wouldn't it be easier to turn me in?" I regretted the question as soon as it manifested into audible words.

He laughed as if I'd told a pleasant joke, flashing a smile as some people passed. "I would, but then I'd be back to sleeping on the floor of my workspace. You're stuck with me now. *We* are stuck."

"I married you willingly, knowing your financial situation. There is no need for blackmail!"

"Blackmail? No, dear, it's insurance. I'm sure you understand."

"Then make sure we're never caught," I hissed.

He glanced down, gracing me with a smile. "Just do as you're told, and all will be well."

I blew a breath through my nose and looked away.

The gardens were busy today, as it was one of the first pleasant days we had seen all season. The sun burned away the clouds, chasing any gloominess that remained from the sluggish morning.

"About yesterday—"

"No questions, no qualms."

"You said that before. I don't agree."

"Then start to."

"Arkady." I pulled on his arm, stopping under the shade of a small tree.

He stopped but took a deep breath before turning fully to me. "What is it now?"

"Are we not going to talk about it?"

"No."

"I think if we are going to be sharing skeletons in our closet," I started, lifting my chin confidently to face him, "then we have to be transparent."

His expression was utterly unamused; it was as if he were just waiting for me to finish speaking.

"Should we not play as a team?"

"Do you like sweet things?" he finally replied, ignoring my barrage, stepping to my side and leading me forward with a hand resting on my lower back.

He pulled me along, his grip firm as if to reprimand me.

We continued along the path, observing the curation of neatly pruned flowers and shrubs.

His face was as unreadable as his demeanor. If anything, he looked more well rested. I admit, he cleaned up nicer than I'd have thought. The way he dressed was fashionable and young, finely tailored and undoubtedly paid for by my father. Even under the shade of dogwood trees, his tanned skin brought more warmth to him than he deserved. It was foolish to expect the outward expression to reach his core.

Even with his cold treatment of me, a small knot formed at the idea of melting it. It was a foolish thought, but something about him made me feel like I was safe and in harm's way all at once, like a lion grooming a lamb.

Arkady was dangerous, and we were now bound by law, by God, and by blood.

As we came to the corner of the greenhouse, he stopped me by grasping my arm.

I turned to him in confusion. He was suddenly so close, looming like the tree that shaded us in the small paradise.

"Have you ever tasted honeysuckle?"

"Excuse me?" My words could only come as a whisper, as if anyone could hear us under the thin cover of the greenhouse corner.

Arkady reached up. Vines covering the walls and the nearby shrubs presented little white flowers, and he plucked one off. The white flora's petals curled back gracefully, framing the delicate stamens protruding from its core.

I glanced down at it before eyeing him cautiously, a raised brow silently asking him to continue.

He brushed his thumb over my bottom lip. "Open." A smirk graced his dark demeanor when he spoke.

Heat rose to my cheeks. I was reluctant to believe the innocent gesture, but I obeyed. Though, when he spoke to me in that way, it wasn't the honeysuckle I craved to taste.

He pinched the base of the small white flower, pulling a stringlike stamen through—producing one single drop of nectar at the base. He held it to my lips, making me stand up slightly on my toes for it.

It tasted something reminiscent of honey, bitter notes like a perfume dancing on my tongue.

"How does it taste?" he asked, his eyes searching, but it was more distracting than anything.

"I don't know," I breathed, his face hovering.

"Let *me* taste, then." His touch burning into my cheek, face becoming far too near.

I clenched my eyes shut quickly, then his lips were on mine.

My eyes fluttered open again, unable to do anything but stare.

His other hand held my waist to prevent me from pulling away, and he leaned in farther, making me tilt back.

While our first kiss had been sweet, the warmth of a gentle touch, as is appropriate at a wedding, I suppose, this one held something with more initiative. Like it was less of an invitation and more of a statement.

I gasped into the kiss, trying to breathe in between his touches, but I was already getting lost in him.

He deepened the exchange, becoming hungrier as our lips refused to part. The lingering scent of fig and liquor surrounded me, and my arms reached up for him, wrapping around his shoulders. They were lean; I suppose that was necessary when carving through stone for hours a day. Even though it was expected, I didn't realize how solid he was, which reminded me how real everything was becoming.

"What are you doing?" I managed to break the contact.

"Tasting something sweet." His words teased my lips, wanting to taste them again.

"This is inappropriate." I covered his mouth with my gloved hand as if hiding it would keep my head on straight.

He pushed my hand away, making me stumble back as he stepped forward. "I think it excites you."

"I don't understand—" My back hit the honeysuckle-covered brick, his body pinning me there.

"I think you do." His hands settled at my waist, his lips trailing to my ear. "I think you like the idea of getting caught."

"You are just avoiding my questions."

"Is that why you cut his throat?" he whispered, trailing his hand over the front of my neck. "You wanted to get caught?"

"No!" I gasped, turning my face from him and glancing nervously past his shoulder.

Even in the hidden-away corner, I worried about the busy passersby. I suppose they were distracting enough on their own. Wasn't he the one who'd been worried about appearances just moments ago?

"Prove me wrong, be a team player." He cocked his head, leaning down to my ear. "If you make too much of a fuss, someone will hear. Be quiet for me."

I gulped, glancing at the distracted crowds and then back to him.

He took that as an opportunity to continue, gently unbuttoning a few loops of my collar to expose my neck.

"Arkady!" I hissed, balling my fist in his jacket.

He wrapped his lips around the skin, sucking hard on my neck.

My head jolted back and smacked against the brick. A whimper escaped, and I immediately slapped a hand over my mouth.

He trailed his lips to the front of my throat, nipping gently before continuing to the opposite side.

"Please, Arkady—"

This time, he bit me, and I felt ashamed when a muffled moan made it past the cloth of my glove.

It earned a chuckle from him as he stood straight again, hiding me away from any possible eyes. His hands smoothed over my neck before neatly buttoning the collar to the top again, hiding the fresh bruises.

"How well behaved you are," he teased.

"What was that for?" I thought I might cry.

"I'm looking for your boundaries." He grinned. "Would you have let me go further?"

"N-no!"

"I will have to find out another time." He turned on his heel, beginning to walk away.

"Arkady!" I took long strides to catch up and grab his arm.

"It sounds better coming from you."

"I beg your pardon?"

"My name." He leaned over to my ear. "It sounds sweet, even when you are angry."

"You better bite that tongue if you know what's good for you."

He wanted to say something but just flashed a dimpled smile innocently before looping our arms together, placing his hand over mine.

Bastard.

CHAPTER EIGHT

The Performer

"Will you continue to hide away, or will you invite the rest of us to meet your mysterious new husband?" Lorelei nudged me with her hip.

"I am not hiding, nor is my husband." I knocked my shoulder against hers. "He doesn't seem the social type."

"*Pfft!* You are a terrible liar, Petre," Lorelei scoffed, plucking a strawberry from a fruit stand and inspecting it. "Do you plan to leave us behind and become a hermit?"

"You? Never. The rest of the troupe? I could do without."

We met at the market, as I needed to buy groceries eventually. I had been snacking on dried fruits, leftovers from the wedding banquet, or gifted foods from my family's acquaintances.

"So when will you host as a couple?" She poked my arm. "It would be nice to meet the mystery man my best friend ran off with."

I shrugged. "Whenever he is home long enough to receive something other than a cigarette."

"Cheer up, it only means more time to yourself." Lorelei looped her arm in mine as we walked beside the bins of produce.

The weather was cheerier than usual, the sun strong enough to burn through the typical gloomy clouds, uncovering the expanse of blue that hid away all season.

Crowds ebbed and flowed like an ocean tide through the market. Couples strolled arm in arm, gatherings of women looked on at their leisure, and children ran between the passersby.

Our argument from before never resurfaced, but I knew she hadn't heeded my warning. It didn't take an inspector general to see that she had a new hat peaked with exotic feathers, lambskin gloves, and a perfume that stung the nose despite only using a few drops. Such luxuries were impossible to afford, especially for a woman with no career, husband, or family worth noting.

I promised myself today that I would not stress, and that included all matters of Lorelei that were none of my business. Even so, I worried for her. No, it made me *angry* for her. But, again, it was no affair of mine—something I struggled to remember.

The rest of the hour was plain. Useless small talk about the quality of the fruit in season and how the weather forecast might affect next week's goods. Incredibly menial, peaceful. No conversations that may burden the mind, no effort to exhaust the social senses.

Among the bustling people, you could disappear and become just another face. Two women clothed in expensive shades of fabric picked at apples in carts. A man in a rugged smock rearranged large fruit to pass the time. Two men laughed together in front of a stand, leaning up on it as they puffed cigars together.

Then a shock struck me. It was *Arkady*.

I nearly didn't recognize him. Not because he was dressed differently or because he was more cleaned up. No, I didn't recognize him because his smile was genuine and his laugh was melodic, joyful. He wasn't even dressed properly. No jacket, sleeves rolled to his elbows, clay covering his hands, arms, stained on his shirt and tan pants. He had a bit smeared on his cheek as well.

I watched his mouth move and form words from a distance, but I couldn't make out what they were talking about. He seemed warm in the light, details that were lost in the dark now on full display . . . like the freckle beside his eye on his cheekbone, the way you could see veins along the muscles of his forearms, or the green of his eyes alight like spring maple leaves instead of dark like pine.

The sharp dimple of his cheek flashed as he cocked his head, raising an inquisitive brow at his friend as he lowered his mouth to the cigar, puffing it before tilting his head back. As he blew out the smoke, his gaze snapped to the side, catching me in his peripheral vision.

"We should go." I tugged Lorelei in the opposite direction.

"But we still have the rest of the market!"

"Petronille!" Arkady's voice called from behind us.

I froze, my shoulders tensing as I looked over my shoulder.

"What a pleasant surprise." He smiled, acknowledging Lorelei. "I see this is a good time for friendly introductions."

Lorelei couldn't hide her grin and held out her hand. "*Lorelei Hertz.* I've heard so much, yet so little, about my dearest friend's new husband," she said, flashing me a giddy look.

Arkady took her hand, kissing her gloved knuckle before a smile tugged again.

"Konstantin"—he gestured to me—"this is Petronille, my wife, Petronille."

Wife.

I held my hand up. The stocky blond man smiled, his cheeks holding a fullness that made you want to pinch them. The type who probably gave good hugs and was kind to children.

He took my hand. "Ah, the elusive Mrs. *Kameneva.*" He chuckled, kissing my hand. "It is a true pleasure to make your acquaintance."

"Likewise." I pulled a tight smile, glancing at Arkady.

For a moment, his mask was off, his expression cold and distant. But that didn't matter, as no one was looking. When the other two looked toward him, the warmth returned to his demeanor like honey melting through a simmer pot.

"I will take our paths crossing as a sign that it may be time to return home, don't you think?" Arkady looked at me, with a slight twitch of his brow.

"Yes." I winced.

"Well, I'll come by tomorrow anyway." Lorelei smirked, pulling me into a departing hug. "We *definitely* have a lot to talk about."

Lorelei departed as soon as Arkady gave his goodbyes to his friend. Then it was just him and me.

The travel home was quiet despite Arkady's cheerful demeanor only moments before. The walk, the coach ride, even when we entered the town house. Silence.

There was no cheery small talk, no silent expressions exchanged, not even questions about our days.

I retreated to my room the minute we arrived. The putrid feeling inside me was brought on by just the sight of him. I wasn't sure if it was due to his presence or the fact that he was a reminder of what we'd done did. What *I'd* done.

The ornate mirror held a figure, mine, but she felt like a stranger. Staring back at me with such judgmental eyes. There was nothing remarkable about my thoughts as I did so, just that it was clear I needed time alone. Gradually, I worked at undoing the layers of my walking suit.

"Who was that?" His voice spoke from the doorway.

"A childhood friend."

"The ballet?"

I didn't answer, reaching behind my head to fiddle with the top few clasps of my dress.

The creaking of the floors accompanied his moving image in the mirror, his body towering behind me as he reached forward.

I flinched, but his hands brushed against the back of my neck, undoing the buttons with ease. With each button, the fabric became more lax until I could finish it on my own.

"Who was *your* friend?" I asked, but it was only because the silence was uncomfortable.

"Konstantin," he said, the mirror cutting off the reflection of his face so I couldn't gauge his reaction. "We are like brothers." He offered the explanation without asking.

"*Like* brothers?"

"Yes."

I nodded and moved forward, slipping the top of my walking suit off, the thin fabric of my corset cover leaving little to the imagination.

Arkady didn't move, nonchalant in attitude. His hands were in his pockets, perhaps to hide a clenched fist?

I glanced at him over my shoulder, playing with the buttons of my skirt.

"Are you getting shy on me now?" He raised a brow.

I shrugged, popping open one clasp, then the next, letting the skirt begin to fall off my hips, the fabric of the petticoat peeking from under the hem.

Arkady took a step, but I turned around fully, stopping him with a glare.

He furrowed his brow, confused at the gesture.

I dropped the skirt, now only my sheer undergarments on display.

What kind of man was Arkady Kamenev? I still didn't have a satisfying enough answer.

He stood straight, studying my posture, my movements.

I turned around again, pulling the cover over my head, the steel-boned corset on full display. Through the mirror, I could see his eyes, but they weren't on the corset, the dress—no, his eyes caught mine, and instinctually my gaze went to the floor.

This is when he approached again, his hand reaching out to touch my shoulder, the warmth of his fingertips leaving a trail of fine raised hairs.

"Can I ask you something?"

"Just ask," I breathed, glancing as his hand moved over my skin.

"The fruit," he began. "Why are there three crates of apricots in the kitchen?"

"Oh." I turned around. "That's *all* you'd like to ask me right now?"

"Yes, they take up an obnoxious amount of room," he said, though I caught his glance down. "The icebox in the kitchen won't fit them all, it's tiny."

"Really? I hadn't noticed," I mocked, furrowing my brow as if to listen to his concern as I popped open each loop of my corset down the front.

"You have a terrible diet." He glanced at my fingers, raising a brow at me.

"Do I? I think I am faring fine." I loosened the string of my petticoat.

"It can't be healthy."

"Is that so? Maybe you can take a look for yourself," I said, the corset and the skirt slipping off and to the floor. There wasn't much hidden, not much of my shape left to his imagination. Just a set of white combinations standing between his view and my skin.

His throat bobbed, glancing up finally to meet my gaze.

"Well?" I raised a brow. "Tell me, *Doctor*, what kind of shape am I in?"

A small hint of a smirk pulled at his lips, his demeanor settling into something more relaxed at the sight of my attempt at play. He began to circle me, inspecting. Something about being watched so closely, critically . . . it gave me a certain chill.

He traced his fingers down my back, then trailed along my hip as he passed back to the front. When he returned to face me, he cocked his head, a sign of worry. "Maybe eat something more than an apricot a day, and perhaps you may gain some color. You're as white as the sheets on your bed, excluding the marks from your *affinity* for bruising." He glanced down at my legs.

"I quite like my apricots," I hummed. "What would you suggest?"

"Something with more substance."

"I eat plenty. If you were home more often, perhaps you would be lucky enough to witness it." My words were nippier than anticipated.

"Then perhaps I need to start cooking for you. Just to make sure," he teased, then moved closer to my bed.

A twist in the pit of my stomach excited me for a moment, only to see he was reaching for the silk robe draped over the side. He burnished the delicate fabric between his hands, holding it up for me to dress.

The sigh that escaped me came out in a quick huff. I turned my back to him as I shoved my arms in each sleeve, one at a time.

He closed the robe, engulfing me in his arms before tying a near knot in front. His rough, scarred hands contrasted with the sheen of the silk. They lingered for a moment, his lips lowering to my ear. "I could use some company with my wine, if you'll have me?"

My breath hitched. "I may be able to help you with that," I answered, my voice barely louder than the beating of my heart. My disappointment melted into something else, acceptance in defeat.

"In all sincerity," he began, "I'd like to hear about the apricots."

I sighed as I settled back into the couch, looking over at him at my side. We decided to open yet another bottle of wine from our wedding night. It was already half empty before we could blink twice.

"What about them?"

"You can't possibly like them enough to consume so many." He laughed.

I draped my legs over his lap, sinking into the armrest of the couch as I explained, "Iron deficiency, I told you."

"There are plenty of ways to consume a healthy amount."

"I like fruit. The flesh is satisfying to bite through."

"These aren't from the market."

"No." I sighed. "From home."

"Home?" He placed one hand on my ankle, squeezing gently as he sipped his wine.

"We didn't always live here." I laughed. "My parents are new to their fortune. We come from Tournon-sur-Rhône, France. There is no comparison when it comes to stone fruit."

"Is there really that much of a difference?"

"Of course!" I gasped. "How could you say such a thing!"

He held his hand and glass up in surrender. "*Fine!* Fine. What is so special about them?"

I settled back down and took a long sip of the wine. "Well, what makes wine good? It's all wine, is it not? So why is one expired grape worth more than the next?"

"Well, for one, all apricots grow in the same span of time. You don't have to wait a handful of years before you eat it."

"Perhaps." I shrugged. "Maybe it's something as simple as being too sentimental. Extended family sends me dried fruit often. It is better than any candy."

"Is it the sweetness that you like?"

"It is half of it." I finished my glass and reached over to place it on the table. "Do you not have anything that reminds you of home? The one before this one?"

He leaned back against the sofa, a genuine thought stirring. "Certain foods bring back the faintest of memories, but it's as fleeting as the smell of a cigar from a passerby."

"Was it so desolate that you cannot remember a single sweet moment?"

"I am afraid my memories are bland, utilitarian at best," he joked, but I could sense it was only half a ruse.

I sat up, folding my arms over my bent knees as they tented over his legs. "You don't talk about your family."

"There is none to speak of."

"You are being dramatic."

"I am being honest."

"Siblings? Mother? Cousins?"

"Orphaned."

He didn't look at me, but I stared anyway. A deflated, sinking feeling bloomed in my gut, guilty of being too nosy.

It never occurred to me that this could be the case. I half expected a second family or estranged relatives, but not once did I think he was without. His desire for stability might go deeper than fortune, the support of having a family at all enough for him to accept this horrid arrangement.

"Arkady," I slurred, grabbing his jaw and twisting it my way, "I am your family now, and *you* are *mine*."

He chuckled at the gesture, pushing my hand away. "I'm not sad. I can't remember anyone to be sad about." He smoothed his hand over my leg. "Konstantin is the closest I have to what you are asking about. He is like a brother to me, we shared the same foster home."

"Ah, *like a brother*," I repeated, the epiphany only a couple hours late. I leaned forward, sliding myself into his lap as I wrapped my arms around his shoulders.

He raised a brow, setting his glass down on a side table cautiously.

I wanted to kiss him. Now that we were nose to nose, I didn't know if I could do it. Like walking to the cliff, only half expecting to make it to the edge, not knowing you'd have to decide whether or not to jump.

With trembling hands, I touched his shirt. Dust and pieces of clay were rough under my palms, and I was hesitant to touch his skin like it would burn me. His breathing was shallow; his chest rose and fell against my hands.

When I glanced at him, he looked at me strangely. Lord, his eyes were such a thing to get lost in. It almost made me forget that he was some mysterious, unreachable, unknowable creature.

I'd like to pretend he wasn't. That he was something attainable.

I tipped closer, though it may be I was swaying from intoxication, a fruity delirium that maybe my husband would find it in him to hold me, to touch me.

"Kiss me." My lips brushed against his as they formed the words. *"Please."* My voice strained.

He hesitated.

It was like a rope was twisting around my gut.

Then, I kissed him.

His lips were so soft, unlike the skin of his hands. To my surprise, he leaned forward. His tongue was warm and the taste of wine was richer. His hands settled on my shoulder blades before smoothing down low on my back. His tongue danced with mine, his grip on me tight and secure.

He twisted our positions, my back hitting the cushions of the sofa before his body separated from mine.

I sat up to reach for him again, but he placed a hand on my chest, pushing me back down.

He looked down at me with something like pity, or disappointment, or both.

Tears pricked at my eyes, and I took in a shaky breath. "What is wrong with me?"

"What?"

"I must be hideous to you. *God!* You can't even stand to sleep in the same room as me, never mind be near me!" I slapped my hands over my face, trying to hide the inevitable flush. I hoped the cushions would engulf me, eat me up between them, so I might disappear like spare change.

I was so foolish. It had never been this hard to catch someone's attention; he was a *man*, for God's sake! Perhaps something was wrong with me instead of him.

A light chuckle was heard, and I removed my hands from my face. "Why are you laughing at me."

Arkady shook his head, amused at my tantrum. "Is that really what you think?"

"How else am I supposed to take it!" I slapped the decorative pillows when my arms flopped beside me.

"Petronille, we have to work on your confidence." He leaned over so his arm rested on the sofa backing as he hovered. "You're intoxicated. I prefer to have you in better spirits and conscious when I do decide to pursue you. Don't you agree?"

I gulped, staring up at him. "What about our wedding night?"

"You seemed a bit peeved."

"I was."

"And you wanted me to have sex with you then?"

"Yes," I huffed. "It's what you're *supposed* to do!" My voice came out more like a squeak, an irresolute statement.

"I think we are past the point of doing things the *right* way, don't you?"

I shrugged and glanced away.

"We can argue about it tomorrow. Sleep off the wine." He moved some hair away from my face, some sort of glimmer in his eye at the thought.

"Only if you would at least entertain breakfast with me." A hiccup bubbled in my throat, mortification burning into my cheeks. "You have to give me the chance to argue."

"Deal." He stood from the sofa and approached the corner chair to settle himself.

I wanted to call out to him again, but I didn't want to ruin the clever exchange.

As he settled, his pants wrinkled, and I could see now that they were likely self-hemmed. The seated position exposed the small pattern on his socks. He didn't bother taking off his dress shoes. Those shoes were scuffed to all hell, his collar unstarched, suspenders out of date. Yet, he pulled it off. Just the way he held himself was intrinsically fashionable.

He leaned back in the seat and grabbed his pipe. It was as if he had always lived here, making a home out of the parlor room. Perhaps it reminded him of his mess of a studio.

He pulled out a book from a pile on the floor, taking great care in opening it, inspecting the table of contents, the foreword, things not too many would spend such time on. His attention to detail made sense for an artist. I should have suspected it might bleed into the other parts of his life, his mannerisms.

I wanted to be studied. I wanted to know what he would say. If I let him get close enough, truly close, what would he say if I promised I wasn't listening? How did he speak of me when I wasn't by his side? What was it like to be perceived by someone whose entire life was art? Would he see the beauty in my potential, or would he just see raw material?

My vision blurred, my eyelids possessing such heaviness, I couldn't keep him in sight. Carried off to the back of my mind for the night.

CHAPTER NINE

The Performer

It wasn't a dance, more like stumbling around each other in avoidance. Painfully sober, we both were quiet. He kept his promise, he stayed for breakfast, but I was quickly learning he wasn't a morning person.

Good, neither am I.

I was planted firmly by the window table, chewing on a dried apricot as I watched him ready himself for work between cups of coffee.

He pretended to be bothered by my disorganized home, yet his jackets, ties, shoes, and notebooks were playing hide-and-seek with him. I suppose the living room had become his bedroom. If only he knew it didn't have to be that way.

Absently, I chewed on my fruit, watching him as he fluttered about. Now he was looking for his satchel. It was on the floor under the coffee table, but I would let him find it himself for his own mental stimulation.

"Something amusing?"

I looked up, my smile falling once he spoke.

Arkady was staring at me with a cocked brow.

I shook my head, tearing another chewy piece from my snack.

He stalked over, leaning a palm against the table. His body cast a slight shadow as he hovered before me. "You asked me to stay around for breakfast. Will you at least share?" His voice was a little softer, a little cockier.

I picked up a new piece from the bowl, holding it up.

Arkady leaned down, grasping the piece between his teeth before I let go. He tipped his head back, chewing. His brows furrowed together, and he squinted his eyes as if he was deciding whether he liked it or not.

"What do you think?" I finally asked.

He lifted a shoulder before it slouched again. "I guess you won't have to worry about me stealing any from your stash."

"Well, you're not allowed to complain about food anyway." A tinge of defensiveness caught in my throat. "It's not like you are here for any of the meals on any normal day."

"I can be."

I straightened my posture a bit, biting into my last piece. He was looking at me, I could feel it. Expecting some sort of praise perhaps? No, sir, that was the minimum.

"Would you like that?" He picked up a neat curl of my hair, twisting it between his fingers.

"Really?" I looked up at him, his expression soft. No hint of any teasing or insincerity.

"When you say it like that, I'm not sure if it's disbelief or it was a bluff invitation."

I nudged his hand away, but he caught my own in his.

"Noontime," he insisted, forcing his fingers to lace with mine, forcing my attention onto him. "I'll come home at noontime."

"You're not too busy? Will it affect your work?" He was right, maybe it did sound like I was making excuses.

"It can wait." He brought my hand to his lips. "I make my own schedule, after all."

"So are you coming home for company, or are you procrastinating?" I teased.

He shrugged again. "Maybe I just need to sneak a midday visit to save me from my boredom."

"You say that like it's scandalous to see me."

"As long as you don't tell your husband, consider the scandal managed." He winked, finally pulling away to gather his coat. "Wait for me to eat, will you?"

I nodded, sipping my already lukewarm tea.

Even as I watched him leave and say goodbye, it was hard to settle into this new routine. A routine involving just myself took years to manage; it was much more complex with a new addition. Change isn't so much scary, it's laborious. Change takes effort. Effort is exhausting.

I didn't have much energy, even if I summoned it from my core. But this type of morning, where you have someone to defrost with like spring soil, I wouldn't mind getting used to.

Friends are, at the very least, for easing each other's anxieties.

So why was it that every time Lorelei came to me, we both ended up more anxious than before?

"I should pinch you for hiding that tasty thing away!" Lorelei nearly hissed, leaning over her clutched teacup as we gathered around my living room's small window table.

"He's the one who hides," I corrected, taking a long sip of black tea.

"I can see why. He'd be eaten alive by the tabloids if they knew that's what he looked like!" She giggled. "It is a shame you don't use your mother's particular influences—you two are such a pair."

"I don't need any attention, as much as my mother likes to dabble in social affairs."

"Which reminds me, will you host a dinner together? A party? Something I have an excuse to dress nicely for!"

"I'm starting to think you just want to flirt with my husband," I teased. "No parties, I haven't been feeling well lately. I must save my energy for the charity gala. Mother won't let me pass on attending."

"Is it almost time already? I swear the last one was merely a season ago."

"Try an entire year. Though, as time goes on, they do feel closer and closer."

"Are you excited?" Lorelei bit her lip.

I simply gave her a look that said, *What do you think?*

"If I were you, I'd enjoy getting put in the most expensive haute couture in New York for a night." Lorelei pursed her lips, tapping her teacup impatiently.

"Well, then, I will give you a good reference, and perhaps my mother can officially adopt you."

"If she were to do that, at least you wouldn't be able to escape me." She laughed, rubbing her thumb on the rim of her empty teacup.

If she wiped any more, I swore the glaze would wear.

"Petre?" she said softly.

"What is it?"

"Will you be spending less time with me now that you are married?" There was a sadness to her voice, masked as curiosity.

"Is this what has been bothering you?" I set my cup down. "You've been so quick to be angry with me."

"I don't mean it! I swear," she said hastily, gathering herself again before she said anything further. "I can . . . spend time elsewhere. It is all right. I need more hobbies anyway. I could join a club, or make more time for tearooms and such."

"Ma poule." I shook my head. "Even if we may not share a hobby anymore, or there is someone new in our lives, we won't grow apart. You won't leave me that easily," I teased, but I was serious. I didn't have many friends, so I never found it hard to distribute my attention.

She nodded, and her shoulders relaxed a bit at the reassurance as she gave me an embarrassed smile.

No matter what, she would always be my oldest friend. I felt like I owed it to her, a protective urge within to keep her safe from my mistakes, to make sure we both made it out of this life like thieves.

I'd been trying to read the same page for four hours.

The short iron hand of the clock jittered impatiently past the intricate "8" on the side of the face.

Shifting my position in my chair for the third time, I crossed my legs to settle once more, losing my spot on the page for the last time before giving up.

Arkady hadn't come home for lunch, and I didn't know why I expected a different outcome from every other day. The weather tonight was going south faster than my mood. The slow, dark clouds crept across the sky and gave us one less hour of true daylight. They seemed heavy, ready to melt into spring showers.

"Foolish," I muttered to myself, tapping the surface of the kitchen counter as I finished a few small pieces of spiced pears and cream.

I wondered if the night before had been some lucid dream. Perhaps I'd imagined the tenderness, the familiarity. I should have changed before; I looked silly wearing nice undergarments for ghosts. It was past time I retired anyway.

The more I thought about it, the hotter my face got, and the more abuse my lip endured from chewing on it.

I snuffed the candles after I finished my meal. The last candle guided me as my feet dragged along the newly bare hallway. I still wasn't used to the floor being uncovered. There was even a pale spot of virgin wood that had never gotten to see the light until now. Its first exposure christened by an unsightly brown stain.

The front door creaked open, a flash and the chatter of rain smacking the pavement ringing clear.

Arkady dragged himself inside, wiping his shoes on the carpet as he shook the rain off his umbrella, a satchel stretched across him under his coat.

"You're home." I stood straight, placing the candle carefully on the table.

He glanced up at my words as the door closed behind him, a few wet, misplaced strands of hair falling in front of his face, as if I'd interrupted a conversation in his head.

I hadn't meant for my words to be any sort of aggression, but my frustration wasn't unfair.

"I was going to turn in." I crossed my arms, pulling my robe closer. "I can leave the last few candles lit—"

"Stay" is all he said, shedding his coat and tossing it over a hook, water dripping in an unpredictable tempo onto the hardwood.

I squinted at him, unsure if I'd heard him right. "I can leave you to rest, it looks like you had a rough—"

He strutted across the living room, confident in each stride, before he hastily dumped the satchel's contents.

A collection of fruits rolled around the coffee table as they fell from the sack.

"I thought you hated fruit."

"I didn't say that," he said. "I was curious, is all."

"I don't need this."

"Yes, you do." He went to the kitchen, the clinking of silverware sounding as he rustled through the drawers, slapping them shut in triumph when he found his desired tool.

I sat down in one of the armchairs, staring at the pile with my arms crossed, one leg resting over the other.

While I didn't understand his bizarre behavior, it was one step above ignoring me, so I decided to entertain it.

He returned with a knife.

"I thought when you said you'd cook for me, it would be something with more substance."

"Behave, or I'll refrain from bringing you nice things," he warned, gesturing playfully with the knife. "Close your eyes, we are playing a game."

"A game? Are we adolescents?"

"I can't speak for *you*," he teased. "Trust me."

I glanced from the knife to him.

"Do you trust me?"

"Not one bit."

"What happened to being a team?" He smirked.

A sharp breath of air pushed from my nose, and I leaned back in my chair. Reluctantly, I closed my eyes.

In the darkness behind my eyelids, I listened for him.

His footsteps approached, not quite cautious, not quite confident. More like stalking than a playful pursuit. The steps stopped in front of me, and I could hear the crisp skin of a fruit breaking.

I felt wetness on my lips.

"Open," he whispered, gently moving the piece of fruit across my lips, a trace of the juice yet to taste.

I parted my lips, letting him place the piece in my mouth before I chewed. The fruit was sweet, with a slightly sour bite from the skin. The flesh was soft.

I moved the slice in my mouth to chew.

"Ah-ah! Not yet." He grabbed my face, pinching my cheeks inward to stop me. "Patience."

My jaw twitched, wanting to bite down on his finger rather than the fruit now.

"Do you taste it?"

I nodded, holding it in my mouth.

"Did you notice it's sweeter?" His voice stayed close but moved around me. "Or how just letting it sit there, undisturbed on your tongue, agitates the senses?"

I shifted in my seat, holding the fruit on my tongue. The juice dripped down my throat. The temptation to swallow was ever-present, as was my dwindling patience.

"Do you notice the scent is stronger, sweetness only tasted when you salivate enough to swallow, just to wait some more?" he said in my ear.

I nodded again, taking a deep breath.

He grabbed my chin. My eyes need not have been open to know he was *insatiably* close.

"I consider haste a sin. I can appreciate the patience it takes to wait for something. To wait until it's ripened to perfection."

I opened my eyes, and his lips were on mine. His tongue snaked inside my mouth, stealing the fruit from my tongue before pulling away.

"It sounds like you plan to eat me." I exhaled, disappointed that he hadn't allowed me to finish the treat after all that play.

He laughed as he chewed, cocking his head at me. "Maybe. But judging from the look in your eyes, maybe it is I who should be worried about *your* appetite."

He gestured his hands over his eyes, wanting me to close them again.

I did, waiting.

He placed another unknown slice in my mouth, this time allowing me to chew.

"What do you taste?"

"I don't know."

"Think."

"A plum."

"Very good," he said. "Do you want another, or shall I move on to the next?"

"Next," I answered, hearing rustling again. I leaned forward, anticipating the return. He held another piece to my lips, and I let him place it in my mouth. The fruit was stiff like an apple but sweeter. "A pear."

"You have an excellent palate." He chuckled.

"Of course I do." I perked up, posture straightening.

He grabbed another fruit, and I opened my mouth before being prompted.

Another piece, a smooth slice with a bitter sweetness and a peculiar textured skin.

"Easy, apricot."

"No"—he chuckled—"a peach."

My eyes snapped open, looking up at him as he stood in front of me.

"What is the point of this game?"

"You said you like your French apricots because of the taste, because they're special."

"So?"

"I don't believe that to be true," he said, dragging the knife through the fruit again before it was hindered by his thumb, then holding up the knife with the slice on it.

"Why would I lie about a silly thing like that?"

"I don't think you do it on purpose. Or maybe you do, I wouldn't know." He shrugged, holding the knife down to my lips.

I leaned forward, taking the slice from the blade.

"I think it's a sentimental preference."

"How do you mean?"

"You said it yourself, it tastes like home."

"What's wrong with that?" I tilted my head, chewing the fruit.

"I wanted to see how willing you were to leave it, to make a new home from something."

"I have already left my home country," I scoffed.

"So have I," he hummed, "yet you are now married, in the same house, with the same routine, just with fewer friends than ever." His words were like a jab to my gut.

"So?" I crossed my arms and looked away.

"Maybe instead of having the same apricot every day"—his hands rested on the chair arms on either side of me, the knife still in his left—"you should try some new fruit?"

"Nothing is wrong with my routine."

"Petronille."

I glanced at him from the corner of my eye, heat rising in my cheeks. Those pretty hazel eyes were gleaming, a light inside of them full of mystique and certainly bad ideas.

"Did you wear this for me? How nice of you. Ease of access and all . . ." He sank to his knees, his hands moving from the armrests to my legs, then pushing forward to my thighs. He leaned in, close enough that I could feel his breathing through my stockings as the robe lifted. His eyes peered up at me through his lashes. "Will you let me introduce you to something new?"

I gulped, shifting in my seat. "You're not funny."

"Did I tell a joke?"

"How would I know?"

"Why don't you ask?" he suggested, bunching the fabric higher as he lowered his face, kissing above my knee as he kept his eyes on me.

"Arkady—"

"Tell me, what do you like?"

"What do I like?"

His lingering hands froze, looking up at me more directly to meet my expression. "Yes, what do you like?"

I glanced away, shifting again. I wasn't sure if it was the pressure of the position or the question.

"You've never been asked before, have you." It was a question, but his tone was not. "What does sex look like to you?"

I couldn't help a laugh, shaking my head. "Do you think I am a child? I know what sex looks like."

"Not a child, no, but I think we have very different ideas of what it is."

"I'm not comfortable telling you what I think it is."

"Then allow me to tell you what it looks like to me," he said, pushing my knees apart.

"Wait—" I grabbed his hands, but from the way he looked at me, I knew he felt me shaking.

"When I think of sex, I think of art." He used a single hand on my chest to bow me in the chair. "It must be balanced, it must be tangible, and above all else, it must be a conversation: verbal as much as it is silent."

I listened to him, relaxing slightly against his hand. "Then what do you want from me?"

"Tell me how you like to be touched." He played with the lace decorating the top of my stocking. "But that would also mean you have to say what you *dislike*."

I considered it a moment. Whatever benefit he got from this game was unknown to me, as was the reward for asking me these things. Just him kneeling before me with eager eyes and hands made my gut twist, but I didn't know for what. There was nothing particularly salacious happening. He wasn't doing anything taboo or out of the ordinary. So why did all this make me feel so faint? A dizzying spell had captured me from head to toe just waiting here. The worst part was that he had barely done anything at all, just left me swimming with insinuations, with questions. I didn't know what other types of sex there were, for a man, at least, but any attention from him at all was setting me on fire.

"Pick a word."

"Pardon?" I raised a brow at his demand.

"Pick a word," he said, "and it will be our secret word. If you do as little as whisper it, I will stop."

I snorted when I laughed. "What a ridiculous request."

"How about 'apricot'?" he suggested. "Seems to be something you'll remember, since you don't seem to be able to say no to any of my musings."

"Fine." I nodded, moving my hands away from him. "I will play your silly game."

He cupped both of his hands under my hips, pulling me toward the end of the chair.

The back of my head dragged down the backrest from the sudden pull, and I gripped the wooden arms from the jolt.

His hand smoothed down one of my legs to lift it over his shoulder, pushing the rest of my robe away.

He peered up at me with a smirk, raising a brow.

I shifted in place, confused. "Aren't you going to do it?"

"Do what?" he asked innocently.

I bit my lip. *Does he really expect me to say it?* I shook my head.

"Then I won't do anything."

I slouched in protest. This was embarrassing.

If I declined to answer, would he stay like this until I said something? I wasn't going to say what I really thought. He might think I was a degenerate if I said anything as filthy as all the ways I wanted him to have me in my inner fantasies.

Then, I grabbed the half-sliced peach from the table.

If I couldn't say it directly, I would have to get creative.

With the fruit in my palm, I crushed it. The juice dribbled over my pelvic bone, dousing me between the legs.

He raised his brow again, this time in amusement.

"I want you," I began, taking a deep breath through the unbearable heat in my face, "to clean it up. Without using your hands." My face burned as hot as his kiln. "Best not to waste perfectly good fruit."

Stop talking! You are making a fool of yourself!

He lowered his face down between my legs, both him and my pelvis within view. I felt like a voyeur of my own body, removed and attached all at once. I could feel his shallow breathing against the sensitive skin, triggering the urge to flee.

He flattened his tongue between my labia, dragging it up before lingering at my clitoris.

My entire body stiffened. No matter how I justified it in my head, it felt *dirty*.

His hand wrapped around my thigh on his shoulder to keep it still. He lowered again, this time in the surrounding area, cleaning the fresh-squeezed juice from my skin. Licking, sucking, savoring every mouthful.

His warm tongue laved over the sensitive skin, a hotness I thought would melt me faster than ice cream on park pavement.

A shiver shot down my spine, and I could feel the heat rising from my neck and burning my ears in embarrassment.

"How does it feel?" he asked, his lips remaining close, his cheek brushing against my inner thigh. His breath tickled against the skin.

"It feels . . . nice." I was being conservative with my description.

"Tell me more," he said, slipping his tongue between again, probing a little deeper as he ran it through, then sucking gently on my nerves. His tongue circled the spot, teasing me.

"It's warm," I breathed. *"Arkady . . ."*

His free hand moved between my legs, resting on my thigh as he traced around the place he was teasing.

His fingers paired with his tongue somehow made me panic. It seemed both were experienced, though I wasn't sure how to feel about that. His middle and fourth fingers pressed against me, then spread outward, exposing me more, if that was even possible. Then, his tongue dipped in and out, never going farther than what I instructed, only cleaning the peach flavor from my skin.

"Put it in," I blurted.

His eyes shot up, and he smirked as the words registered.

"I want . . . it inside." I winced.

"You're getting good at making demands," he teased. "Be specific."

"Hands"—my face felt like it was beside a furnace—"y-your hands."

He carefully pressed a single finger inside, hot against my skin.

"Not just one."

"Another? Moving a bit fast, aren't we?"

"Forget it, then!" I argued.

"I'm joking." He chuckled. He must have felt my thigh stiffen. He inserted a second finger, his hand palm up now, pushing in and out, testing the metaphorical waters.

I kept my breathing steady, unable to watch.

"Petronille."

I struggled to meet his gaze like I had to pry my eyes from whatever I was focusing on in the distance in order to be present.

He stood up on his knees, putting pressure on his fingers as he whispered against my neck, "Tell me what you want, or trust me to choose for you."

"Choose for me," I said hastily. "I don't want to make any more decisions."

He nodded in understanding, lowering his face back down between my legs. As he moved his fingers inside me, he pushed all the way in to curl them upward, massaging the inside as he sucked on the outside, playing with every sweet, sensitive spot.

I moaned, immediately covering my mouth.

He chuckled as he continued, his warm mouth against my skin.

I could confirm one thing: Lorelei's speculations were correct; he *was* good with his hands.

"Arkady," I breathed, trying to lean up but ultimately deciding to slump farther back, pushing my hips toward him.

He continued to tease me, to play with me like he wanted, like *I* wanted.

I began to move my hips, rolling them in rhythm with his pace, his intensity. I reached for him, only able to grab his hair to pull him closer, to feel him more, to keep going.

The knot in my stomach was tightening, the pressure was building faster, festering. Never had I been able to feel like this with a man, only when I did it on my own. Even then it had felt wrong. And this was worse, in a selfish kind of way. If I just closed my eyes, there was no audience, but there was also the thrill of it not being by my own hands.

He sucked hard, picking up his pace as his fingers moved, smoothing down the inside and pushing on every sensitive place he could find. Every time he heard a new noise from me, he just kept going, chasing the reaction, the validation that came from pleasuring another.

Suddenly and all at once, the tension was released, and I came while his mouth and tongue were dedicated only to me. I wondered if he could feel it, the climax, *le petit mort*.

My thigh tensed before relaxing against his shoulder, then slipped off as I gathered myself. Arkady didn't seem to mind; he licked his bottom lip before wiping with the back of his hand, amusing himself with not only my reaction but how I tasted as well.

I glanced down at him, those hazel eyes looking hungry despite the conquest.

"What is it now?"

He shook his head. "Just watching."

"Are you some sort of voyeur?"

"If I am a voyeur, then you are the exhibitionist." He stood and leaned over me in the chair. "Look at you, it's nice to see the little snail emerge from her shell."

"Stop looking at me." I covered my face.

"You did well." He pulled my wrists from my face. "You have a lot to learn, Mrs. *Kameneva*."

I rolled my eyes, refusing to look at him.

He tipped my face back, cupping it as he kissed me. He tasted like peaches. I leaned up, savoring the kiss before he pulled away.

He grabbed the knife and gathered the half-eaten fruit, taking a bite out of one.

"Arkady?" I spoke up, my voice coming out shakier than intended.

He looked my way, waiting for my request.

"Will you sleep with me tonight?"

"No," he answered, "not yet."

"Why?"

He shook his head as he continued to clean up, like my request was something of the childish sort.

"Arkady," I said again, more stern as I stood from my seat.

"Yes?"

"Come to bed with me. You got your fun, now I wish to sleep accompanied. I am not a toy to use and forget."

A slow grin crawled across his face as he looked back at me. "There it is. She is finally direct with what she wants."

I frowned at him. "Is that all it took?"

"I wasn't going to crawl into bed with a stranger who didn't want me there."

I glanced off to think about it for a moment, and I suppose it made sense to me. I just didn't think it would be as simple as asking—or rather, demanding.

CHAPTER TEN

The Artisan

In all my years, I have never woken up next to a woman.

Surely, I had my experiences, but no one stayed the night, and I never overstayed my welcome.

Even as she lay next to me, it was jarring. Like waking up from a dream and forgetting where you were. That was the risk of a good night's rest, in a proper bed that wasn't your own. Perhaps I was just used to sleeping on anything besides a bed, that was my problem.

Petronille's chest rose and fell as gently as a spring morning's breeze. She was so quiet, not dissimilar to the flutter of an owl's wing.

I brushed my fingers through her silken hair, unable to sleep in the early-morning light. Her perfume reminded me of clementines with a hint of vanilla, sweet and complex. She was pleasant like this, no biting or snapping like the haughty hound she was. Even in this calm state, I missed her quick wit. Someone like me had to be with someone who sharpened the mind, for I was a knife and she was a water stone. Opposite but useful together.

Even as I was sneaking out of my own marriage bed, a new ache was forming. One of those moments you stop and think: *If I fumble all my cards, this can all go away.*

"Damn it," I hissed once my fingers scraped the bottom of the bucket. No more clay, just slick.

Longer rods of steel were needed to prop up the weight. I stood atop the ladder, the last few chunks of clay slapped over the face of my new statue. Luckily, I had a fresh shipment, otherwise it would be quite bare bones for a while. A clumsy first draft, a haphazard form of clay.

A bark echoed from the outside, then another. The sharp yips smacked against the bricks of the yard before they were resounding clearly from the large warehouse entrance.

"Mr. Kamenev!" the man shouted, banging a fist on the doors, making them vibrate.

"Coming!" I shouted, tossing the bucket to the floor before hopping off the ladder. The rampant dog wouldn't let up, barking and snarling before I even reached the door. Simple-brained beast.

I unlatched the bolt and opened the steel shutters, which released a deep moan as they reluctantly opened, rolling along the tracks of the floor.

The landlord stood outside, a stout man holding his insurance on a chain leash.

"I told you I'd be late." I glanced down at the beast, the Doberman staring whale-eyed, his hair standing straight on his hackles.

"I need it today, I've been lenient with you lately." The gruff man shifted his weight. Something told me this had something to do with the nights he'd been spending down at the docks. He'd probably spent his last coin on whores or booze.

"I told you the money from my wife would be coming after due. You said it wouldn't be an issue." I tried to keep eye contact, but the dog was pulling anxiously on his collar, desperate to get into the studio. I held out my leg, blocking the creature.

"Clancy!" he shouted, yanking the animal by the neck.

"Must be the food I left out."

"I told you not to leave food in the warehouse. It attracts the rats."

"I know, I haven't had much time off. I'll clean it. Just give me another day or two for the rent," I explained, searching his expression for any give. "The wife is giving me a hard time."

"Eh, women," the man huffed as if he would know anything about women.

"I'll bring the check to your front door," I offered. "It should just be a little longer, before the next rent payment is due."

He looked away to think about it, absently smoothing down the short hair of his beast. "All right."

"I will see you in a few days. How is two in the afternoon?"

"Yes, but not a minute later," he warned before yanking his dog around. "*Come*, Clancy."

I nodded and smiled, plastering on the expression until the old man waddled off, mumbling to himself under his breath.

The knot in my stomach gave out as I turned the bolt again, locking myself away in my little haven.

One thing I enjoyed about my studio was that it was quiet. I felt like every other place made it hard to think. Here, I could control the layout, the cleanliness, who and what went in and out of my domain. My audience was blocks of clay or stone, crowded around to watch me make another.

Sometimes, they made me feel judged. Other times, I felt less alone.

Beside my recent project was a more feminine statue, still roughly blocked, but it was beginning to resemble a particular person.

Before I knew what I was doing, I gave the statue her eyes, her nose, her delicate hands, her single-portion breasts. Her statue form stood quite proud but soft all at once. Nothing about her was too much or too little. I would expect something of a water nymph, or a woman from some myth chained away from the mortal world, for she was too valuable for the likes of them.

Pulling up my stool, I sat with my elbows on my knees. My forearms were already covered in dust and cracked, dried clay.

"What am I to do with you?" I mumbled to myself.

She didn't reply, of course, but I wished she could. My plans for her might have changed, but that was only because she'd proven to be quite a task herself. I suppose it wasn't the worst thing, as we now shared the same skeleton in our closet. Perhaps she had the potential to be sculpted into something else.

"I swore I did this already." Kostya spoke mainly to himself as he rustled through a drawer.

I studied the embalming-room walls, counting the drawers. Behind each, there would be what was once a person, no doubt. I visited Kostya at work frequently enough that his coworkers treated me like another peer, credulous and familiar. Even if I came alone, they assumed the best of my presence, as if I were just here to fetch something for my friend.

"Would it be childish to blame imps for stealing my tools?" Kostya laughed nervously, and I heard some clanging from behind me.

"Yes, imps don't exist, Kostya," I droned, glancing over my shoulder at my flustered friend. His attitude was light, but I could see the sweat beading on his forehead.

"I *know* that, but I'm starting to believe," he grumbled. "I must be more organized, I can never find the tools I need when I need them."

"Invest in better drawers."

"That's not up to me."

"Then simply be more organized."

"What worm wiggled its way up *your* pants today?" Kostya approached the slab as he tied his smock.

Before I turned, I took a calm, steadying breath. I pivoted on my heel, then approached the slab as well. "Nothing. Irritated."

"Why is that?"

"Landlord" is all I said, and he nodded as if he understood.

Kostya peeled away the sheet covering his new client.

On the slab was a woman. Half of her face was sloping a bit. Kostya said the cause of death was some mystery illness breaking out on farms upstate. It must be prolific if they were sending the bodies all the way to the city for evaluation. What surprised me more was the lack of coverage in the papers.

I stood beside her, tilting my head. Her skin was a warm shade, a few beauty marks scattered across her neck and chest. Her dark hair splayed across the cold table. Even with her warmth, the gas lamps drained her of any color that could have remained in rigor mortis. Lately, none of them came close. She was beautiful, but she wasn't perfect.

It was either a matter of quality decline, or perhaps my standards had changed. Art is nothing without a muse. If I couldn't find another one soon, I might lose my touch. Or worse, I might turn to something else to find what I was looking for.

"Is this one good?" Kostya asked.

"No."

"Really?"

"The left side of her face is too strong compared to the right. Her nose curves slightly to the left, and her lips are asymmetrical." I moved around the table carefully. "She is too lean, and she is also too dead."

"Well, that's what happens when you use *corpses* as still-life subjects, Arkasha. They will look dead."

I looked up so quickly that Kostya physically flinched. I didn't need to say another word.

"You really *are* in a bad mood." He pulled the sheet back over the corpse. "Not even the warmth of your own woman could thaw your stone heart?"

"Do not speak of my wife."

Kostya glared, moving back to his desk. "You know, I'm breaking a lot of rules just by showing you bodies for your little art studies."

I sighed and leaned against the table. "I know."

"You should be nicer to me," he grumbled, "and the corpses."

"They are dead, Kostya."

"It's about respecting the deceased."

"What is more respectful than memorializing them as art?" I raised a brow, pulling a cigarette from my pocket and flicking the wheel of my lighter.

Kostya glared at the sound of the light. "Not all art is respectful."

I shrugged.

"Why not ask Petronille to pose for you?"

I didn't answer, instead pulling a long drag from the cigarette.

"*Hm.* It seems your art is not respectable enough for her, then?"

"That's not true."

"Then why do you do this?"

"Performance anxiety. Old habit." I shrugged, moving toward the door.

"Where are you going?"

"Studio." I stamped my cigarette out on the concrete floor. "I need to finish something."

CHAPTER ELEVEN

The Performer

At the age of twenty-four, I found myself feeling more girl-like than ever before. There I was, standing before the massive doors of the studio with a basket of fruit. I'd thought it was a good idea before I realized how mortifying it would be to present it to him as a gift.

The concrete was dull against the silk of my shoes, dust accumulating against my cream underskirt. I shouldn't have worn something so light. My shoes hurt my feet from insisting on walking most of the way here. Some say sporadicity shows you care, that you'd abandon your routine for something important. So why did it feel so absurd?

I'd imagined my visit would be cheeky, but now I realized it might be completely ridiculous. It was too late, I was here already.

With one brave breath, I pushed the warehouse door aside, soot collecting on my gloves upon contact with the cold metal.

The air was hot and muggy like summer inside, yet outside there was a wet chill of spring. The kiln was red, the light peeking from the seams of the metal door, heating the dim space and filling it with the smell of hot clay.

Arkady stood at the mouth like a knight containing a dragon, ready to slay it should it find itself on the other side of the door.

His arms glistened with a balm of sweat and dust, and clay cracked along his forearms, stopping abruptly where his sleeves had been rolled. Except, there was no shirt. Just a men's undershirt, suspenders hanging at his hips, and his pants filthy as if they hadn't been pressed and cleaned before he left home.

My mouth was agape, and it snapped shut the minute he looked back.

His figure burned into my irises when I looked away at the dim corners, a weak attempt at nonchalance.

"Are you all right?" It could be a hopeful illusion, but I thought his voice held concern.

I shrugged, finally looking back at him. He wiped his hands on a cloth as he approached, slinging it over his shoulder.

"Must something be wrong for me to visit?"

"I assumed there were better things to do." His eyes strayed to my basket, a small, dimpled smirk flashing before his gaze returned to mine. "A gift?"

"No . . ."

He tipped the lid of the basket open before I could snatch it away.

A slow, mocking scowl found its place as he tipped his head. "Ah, I see. A request?"

"I thought you'd be hungry." I turned from him, smacking the basket down onto a small stray table. "Don't be so smug."

Carving tools, lumps of clay, some bricks, and a metal pail of slick were also piled upon the table, surely too dirty to eat on.

"Is that all?" he asked, his voice by my ear, his arms coming into view from behind as he reached around, stealing a kumquat from the basket.

My fingers gripped the edge of the table, face beginning to feel red on its own, unaided by the firing kiln. I affixed a smile to my face before turning around. "I was curious."

He took a bite out of the small fruit, raising his brow.

"If we are to get along," I started, leaning back against the table, "we should get to know one another. It's the natural, sophisticated thing to do."

"Sophisticated?" he mumbled as he chewed. "Is that so?"

"W-well"—my breath caught—"your thing"—I gestured to the kiln—"it's impressive. I wanted to know more about what it is you do."

He glanced over his shoulder at it, shrugging. "It's in need of repair."

"Is that why it's so hot in here?" I tugged at my collar.

"I have to fire it to see where it may need patching. A small flame is enough to find the holes." He glanced back down at me. "Why the sudden interest?"

"I'm making an effort." I glared. "If you don't want it, then fine! I don't have to try any more than you—"

He grabbed my wrist before I could move away. "You give up too easily."

"I don't understand how to talk to you! I haven't had much practice." It was only half a joke.

"How about we skip talking?" His hand on my wrist loosened, his fingers trailing down to meet mine. "I could show you."

"Show me? I see it." I gestured grandly to the statues.

"What good is seeing the product when you don't understand the material?"

"Do you assume I don't understand *clay*?"

"I think you underestimate it." He stole both my hands in his, leading me away from the table and to a different area. Careful to step over the buckets, tools, loose forms littering the ground in his collectorium of rubble.

He stopped in front of this small, rickety wooden thing, pinching the fingertips of my gloves and pulling them off.

"Hey!" I swiped for them, and he tucked them in his back pocket.

"You can't wear gloves for this." He sat me down on the stool.

It was a bit low to the ground. My skirts were already dirty at this point, the heat of the kiln making sweat inevitable, and there was no use fighting off more dirt. I accepted I would be a mess at the cost of his amusement.

Slam!

I flinched as Arkady threw a lump of clay onto a small table . . . a potter's wheel.

"You're going to make me do this?"

"I certainly couldn't force you to do anything, Mrs. Kameneva." He pulled up a stool behind me, his legs on either side of mine, trapping them there.

"Why do you say it like that?" I looked over my shoulder, his face right there, hanging over me.

"What?" His arms further entrapped me as he reached forward, pulling the small wheel closer between our legs. "Kameneva?"

"Yes, that!" My cheeks flushed.

The corner of his lips pulled slightly in amusement. "That is your name."

"I thought *our* name was *Kamenev*."

"It is." He used his foot to pump the wheel, the misshapen lump beginning to blur. "Women, when referred to singularly, have a feminine spelling."

"Oh," I muttered, biting my lip.

Arkady reached over to a bucket, dipping his hand in clean water before letting it dribble onto the clay. Some of it speckled my cheek when the wheel spun, and I wiped it away hastily, checking my palms to make sure it wasn't still smudging.

The flush of my face burned. I might look as if I'd forgotten my parasol in the sun for hours by the time he let me go. I dabbed my forehead with my wrist, moving a stray hair or two out of the way.

"You may want to take that off." He glanced down at my sleeves, leaning closer to the wheel, bending me forward. His hands cupped over the clay, forcing it into a uniform dome.

His arms stretched out, sandwiching me between them.

"Don't worry, the statues won't mind," he teased.

"You are making it difficult on purpose." I flicked the buttons of my top piece, struggling to pull my arms out of the long sleeves, claustrophobic between his arms. I tossed it to the side, leaving myself in only my corset cover. The skirt needed cleaning anyway, so I wouldn't bother. Though, it did feel nice for my arms to be bare.

I looked back at him, his expression pleased with his tomfoolery so far. I wouldn't let him laugh any more, I'd play his stupid game.

"What now, then?" I straightened my back, which pressed against his chest. Just the touch made my shoulders fold to my ears as I slouched forward, all too aware of the limited room for movement.

His hands took mine, wet and sticky from the clay.

"Oh no." I winced. "*God*, what a horrid texture." I nearly gagged.

"You'll forget it in a moment." He guided my hands to the wheel. "Clay is my favorite, because if you don't do well the first time, you can roll it back up into a ball and try again. It's relaxing, if you let loose a little." He took my finger and guided it to the middle of the dome. When he put pressure on my index finger, it dipped straight into the dome and opened wide like a crater.

The form was mesmerizing, the way was so fluid, every small movement of our hands making it dance before us.

He took both my hands along the rim, squeezing them and guiding the clay to a vaselike shape, making the opening smaller now.

"I see," I breathed, leaning back into him. The clay and water were a bit cold, offsetting the mugginess from before.

I watched his arms, every small inflection of the muscles resulting in the soft, precise guidance of his hands.

The wheel slowed to a halt.

He shifted to grab a wire, pulling it along the base to slice the vase from the wheel and hold it up. "See? Do you want to try on your own now?"

"That wasn't hard." I shifted in my seat. "I'll make a cup next."

"It's easy to say when your hands don't have to move on their own." He placed the vase aside and leaned over for more clay, slapping it down on the wheel again.

The lump turned slowly, then blurred as it moved faster. When my hands met the clay, it shook with such force, I had to lean over, squeezing it into a tall form that still wobbled no matter how I molded it. Perhaps I'd spoken too soon; he'd made it look so easy.

"Good, now try to press your hand flat. Into a dome, like last time." He wiped his hands clean with a wet rag.

I pressed my palm down on it, trying my best to force it into the dome like Arkady had. It may have taken me a minute longer, the clay becoming dry by the time it was in shape.

"That's good," he said, "but don't forget to keep it damp."

I scooped my hand in the murky water bucket, watching it trickle steadily onto the material. The matte turned to gloss as it spun, ready to be formed once more. As I cupped it in my hands, pressing my thumbs into the middle, it opened up to me hesitantly.

"Hmm, unsure hands make for shaky work," Arkady said into my ear, his hands resting on my thighs.

"Maybe you make me nervous," I whispered, digging farther into the clay with my fingers, though part of the cup's lip was becoming too thin.

"Do I?" he hummed, his lips pressing behind my ear, hot against my pulse. "Make you nervous, that is?"

My breath shook, reluctant to be released, to be heard escaping.

His hands pressed on my thighs, then found their way to my waist. I held my breath, frozen with my clay-covered hands on the wheel.

"Arkady," I swallowed.

"Hm?" he hummed into my neck. His grip on me tightened as he pressed his body against mine. A soft kiss on my skin, a hand cupping my breast.

"Why must you tease me?" I whimpered.

"Because it is fun." He let out a breathy laugh. "The more you squirm, the less I'm able to resist toying with you."

"You're a dog."

"And you love it all the same," he growled, hand moving up to my throat, only pressing gently to keep me in place.

He let out a groan, his body shifting behind mine. His lips found my neck again, sucking gently on the skin.

I winced and dug my nails into the clay, holding on for dear life.

The fresh bruise on my neck, his breath against my skin, my heart pounding at my rib cage, desperate to be free. Forget the kiln, I could burn up in an instant from his touch alone.

He sucked low on my neck this time, leaning back, my body trapped in his grasp.

"Trapped" was an accurate description, yet it made my insides jump at the thought. To be caught, to be ravished. Just the thought manifested as a weak, needy gasp.

My hips shifted. There was a tension between his legs; I could feel it against my backside.

With his free hand, he reached down, slipping his hand under the waistband of my skirt.

"Wait—"

His other hand went from my throat to my jaw, hooking two fingers in my mouth. I could taste the salt from the clay, an earthy sort of flavor that reminded me of more natural musks.

The fingers below were warm, first just tracing the skin between my legs, making themselves known.

I was breathing hard, trying not to tense up and bite the fingers in my mouth clean off. An instinct I didn't think I would want to fight, but I didn't want this to end.

His fingers under my skirt split, spreading me apart. A wetness was forming; I didn't need to feel it to know. Inside, I was pulsing, begging. The teasing was too much. My hips rolled impatiently.

"So much haste." He tsked. "Such a needy, demanding little thing," he whispered roughly in my ear, which I thought he would bite.

I whimpered, squeezing my eyes shut.

He shallowly inserted a finger, dipping in and out, getting to know my anatomy so intimately, like he was planning to sculpt it himself.

"I can't get to know you if you don't open up." He traced over the entrance again. "I hope to teach you that letting your guard down with me will only lead to good things for you."

My tongue settled against his fingers in my mouth. I glanced down, his hand making a distinct form under my skirt, then I watched it move.

His finger slipped in, just one at first, just like last time.

I clenched around it just to let go, to remember to relax, to breathe.

"Do you know how wet you are right now?" he whispered. "Is this how you touch yourself at night? Imagining it were my hands? Or do you imagine how my cock would feel pressed up in that pretty cunt of yours?" He let out a shallow breath by my ear like his words were letting his own imagination run wild.

With a sharp whine, my hips shifted against his hand as he held his finger inside me.

"More, you say?" He slipped another finger in. "I think you can do better." Then another inside. He spread the three fingers, stretching me.

My legs shook. I realized my toes were pointed and my legs were stiff.

He curled his fingers inside me, pulling them out slightly just to bury themselves deeper. With every repetition, I felt looser, wetter. His palm rested against my clit, that tight bundle of nerves driven crazy from just the contact.

Arkady's hips shifted against my backside, rubbing in tandem with his fingers. The friction was igniting me like live electrical wires touching every time a spark set me alight.

I bucked against his hand, unable to stop from biting his fingers in my mouth. I was so close, it was just out of reach.

His grip was tighter, and he worked faster as if he wasn't going to last long if I didn't finish. It was just what I needed, one last push.

I felt wet again, melting right into his hand.

Suddenly, the vertigo made me slump back against his chest. I could hear his breathing now, harder than I thought, but it didn't match mine. His fingers slipped from my mouth, the others still deep inside me. I wondered if he felt the incessant pulsing, slower and slower, until the orgasm was washed away.

My head fell back, my eyes closing while I recovered, slumped in poor posture against him. The only thing holding me in place was his hand between my legs.

This was better than cocaine.

Before I could open my eyes to face the possible reality or shame of what we'd just done, I felt lips soft as flour and sweet like buttercream against mine. I knew better than to open my eyes, and I kissed back, hoping that it wasn't a dream or some pleasure-stricken mirage.

"You did good," he whispered, his fingers dancing across my temple and brushing my hair into place, "though, I've lost a day's work on you."

I opened my eyes but only to see he was smiling. "If you'd rather work than enjoy simple pleasures, you may be a lost cause, Mr. Kamenev."

"It's all the same, isn't it?"

"Work and pleasure? I wouldn't recommend it, personally."

"Well, you're quite a load of work, so what does that make you?"

"Worth the trouble, I would hope."

He weighed the answer in his mind, then looked before us. "At least you have other talents aside from pottery."

I glanced at our wheel; the form was lopsided, misshapen. I just smiled up at him. "It looks like I may have to visit more often if I am to become better."

"I suppose you will." He rolled his eyes. "Limit your visits to once a week, or I may never get anything done ever again."

"I can work with that."

We'd given up on the day by then. The windows at the top of the warehouse glowed red, the kiln was dying down, and we took our time gathering ourselves before we inevitably would have to leave.

I wasn't sure what spellbound allure the studio held, but it felt infinite. There was so much opportunity for imagination, to let creativity take hold and keep you there. I understood now, I thought, why it kept *him* there so often. This was a home for him, someplace sacred. Just like my family's old tenement, it was an escape, somewhere safe to land.

And now, in turn, I had landed here with him.

CHAPTER TWELVE

The Performer

The bed was cold that morning. It was like no one had ever been there to begin with.

I rolled over, burying my face in the neighboring pillow. The scent of him lingered. His collage of scents teased my nose, the only proof he had been there at all.

It was nearing noontime now, a bit later than my normal sleeping schedule. The rain was steady like a dribble, but the clouds allowed for brief blessings of sunshine, the most beautiful of scenes just outside my window.

Motivation to dress was stronger today. I had nowhere to go, but it couldn't hurt to appreciate some of my less-worn wardrobe. I was tempted to do my hair, to take a full bath with some oils I never used, or maybe to prepare something sweet for later.

Did it matter to him if I made such changes? Or would he laugh?

After dressing, I went along with my routine. Late breakfast was in order. I shuffled down the stairs to the kitchen, digging through some of my nicer bowls and silver, adding extra fruit to my cutting board.

It was only now I realized the coffee grounds were nearly nonexistent. I suppose Arkady had been using them. Should I get more? He'd never asked. It pained me that I could not be plain with him, that it felt like we danced around each other like two desperate birds of different species, misinterpreting every sign along the way.

Today would be for relaxation. I did not have any plans to move unless it was to fill my bowl of fruit or to grab a different book. I would wait for Arkady to come home.

I picked at my fruit, but it wasn't satisfying me in the way that I hoped. The craving was for something savory. I only had scraps, something simple for a stew or even a broth. I hadn't restocked my pantry since *the incident*. It would be enough for my dinner, then I must force myself to the market tomorrow. I was just so tired as of late, even that short trip was a burden on my body.

The rasping at my entryway startled me from famished thoughts.

I hoped the knock would be him, but I knew better.

Upon opening the door, a familiar face greeted me.

"Ms. De Villier," the commissioner acknowledged from my doorstep.

"Mrs. Kameneva, now," I said.

"Ah, yes, Kamenev."

I held my tongue; too many corrections made men unreasonably irate.

James Hunt was a stiff man, no matter how kind he tried to make his face appear. A smile was unnatural on a weathered face such as his. My parents had voted for his office position, as well as donated handsomely to his campaign.

Some people were easy to read. The body was one to tattle on unaware users. He held his conviction in his posture. I already knew this visit was not a friendly one.

"How may I help you, Commissioner?"

"I don't mean to disturb you on such a peaceful day." He removed his uniform cap as his gaze flicked past me, into my home, before returning to me. "May I come in?"

I nodded, pulling the door wider.

His heavy boots stamped mud into my foyer. He didn't bother to shake off his coat, leaving small dribbles on the carpets. To my relief, that meant this visit would be fleeting.

"Did I interrupt dinner preparation?" He pointed his nose to the air like one of his hounds.

"No." I smiled, not bothering to correct his guess. "I was about to eat something light."

"I won't be too long." He smoothed his graying-brown hair back as it dripped from the rain. "I wanted to ask you about a disappearance."

My heart smacked against my ribs, and I could feel the heat rising from my neck, choking me the longer I waited to respond. How did one respond to something like that?

"A disappearance?" My voice was having a hard time relaxing, too squeaky for comfort.

"Yes, have you read the papers?"

"N-no, they're too troubling for me. I prefer things that don't burden the delicate mind." I cleared my throat, brushing the fabric of my skirt as I went back to the living room. "Can I get you something? Tea?"

He waved his hand in a polite declination before glancing around the room. What was he looking for?

"Who is missing?" I tried to keep the conversation going, silence an unbearable sensation.

"A friend of yours." He stepped into the living room, trailing wet boot prints on the carpet.

The sight made me grimace, and I tried to dampen it, but it was too late. He saw.

The commissioner flashed a slight grin. What an unpleasant *thing* he was. "Have you seen Vincent lately, Petronille?"

"No," I said, leaning against the fireplace mantel, making myself small as he invaded on my home, my sanctuary.

"I was under the impression you two were close?" He approached, stopping in front of me. He was close enough that I could see the wiry texture of his mustache. The smell of cigar in his breath was grating, maybe a bit of liquor.

"I haven't seen him." I adjusted a knickknack on my mantel.

"I heard he was looking for you. You don't seem to answer your door often, by the sound of his complaints." He chuckled.

"I informed him that I was married and no longer in the ballet."

"So you *have* seen him."

"No."

The commissioner nodded, glancing down at my dusty, unkempt mantel. "Congratulations, by the way." He glanced back to me. "Where is your husband now?"

"At his studio. He's an artisan."

"Does this studio have an address?"

I looked away. "I don't remember it. It is by the docks, I'm not sure which one. It's all very confusing and congested down there. I haven't been myself. I wouldn't know."

"Of course." His tone of understanding poorly masked his air of annoyance. "How has your family been otherwise? I haven't seen your father in a while."

"He's a busy man." I massaged my thumb against my palm.

There was an awkward pause, then a sigh from my guest. "I have bothered you enough today, I suppose." He placed his cap back on his head, giving a polite smile as he made for the front door.

I followed close behind as he crossed the threshold, my fingers itching to grasp the handle and lock him out. The door sang a pitchy whine, a glimpse of the outside promising the interaction was about to end.

He turned back around, his foot stuck straight in the gap as the door bounced back on his rubber boot.

My knuckles were white, my grip on the brass the only thing keeping my hand from shaking.

"If you think of anything," he started, slipping a card through the narrow opening, "you know who to call, yeah?"

"Right." I hastily plucked the card from him, and he removed his shoe, allowing me to close and latch the door.

As soon as I heard his footsteps descending, my first free breath was nearly a sob. I leaped for the telephone, rustling through the cards before I found the one for Arkady's studio, then I pulled the dial until I heard the call trill to be put through. My leg bounced fast, the tapping of my heel pecking at the floorboards.

Ultimately, the call went unanswered.

My fist ached as it repeatedly pestered the wood of the door.

I heard footsteps from inside, a pause, then the door was unlatched with a squeak.

I was shaking, and it wasn't just from the rain drenching my clothes.

"Petronille?" Félice answered, more alarmed than confused at the state of me.

"I need help, is Father home?" I pushed past her, the wet walking suit heavy on my shoulders as the drips scattered over the glossy hardwood.

The living room was the first thing I saw. Cosette startled when I stormed through, nearly dropping her after-meal tea.

"What is going on?" Her eyes darted to Félice, who shook her head. "Did something happen?"

"I thought the commissioner was still on the books?" I said breathlessly. "Why was he at my home?"

"How should we know?" Félice's brow twitched. "What sort of trouble did you cause if he's at your door?"

The looks on my sisters' faces were both alarmed, annoyed, and all around tired. I felt small again, like I did most of the time. Minuscule, the youngest child, the burden next to the two model daughters.

"Petronille." Félice's tone was sharp. She sounded exactly like Mother, eerily so.

I took a step back, my chest rising and falling, still catching my breath after the haste of walking here.

"Petronille." She grabbed me by the shoulders, giving them a light shake. "What happened?"

"I killed Vincent," I blurted.

"Well, you still have the body, right?"

I shook my head.

Her eyes grew wide, then they darted above my head. The blood from her cheeks drained, but there was a sympathetic look in her gaze when it returned to mine.

"What is this?" The deep, stern voice came from the parlor archway.

I turned to face my father, bracing myself. But nothing in his demeanor showed any haste, not even an iota of concern.

"I need help." The words nearly caught in my throat.

"Oh?" His eyes held more interest than he'd ever shown for me.

The thing about my father was that he loved to be helpful. Help from my father meant striking a deal, and owing him even past paying your debt. My debt was endless, so what was another favor?

My sisters began to gather their things quietly.

"No." Father's voice cut through the room, enough to make them wince. "Stay, I'm sure this will be a lesson learned for everyone." He smiled, taking another puff of his cigar before his eyes slid over to me and he raised his brow for me to continue.

"I . . ." I shifted my weight from one leg to the other, unable to control the blood dropping straight to my feet. "I don't want the commissioner visiting me."

"Why would the commissioner be visiting you?" It was a question, but not because he didn't know the answer.

"I killed Vincent."

A cruel smile broke across his lips. "Ah, my baby girl has finally grown up." His tone was so sweet, undoubtedly laced with poison. "So now you want him gone? Just like that? Your old man fixes all your issues?"

I stared at the floor, waiting for the inevitable drop.

"Is that what you want, child?" He approached me slowly like a snake carefully moving through the tallgrass.

"Yes."

"You know"—he stopped in front of me—"I've paid a lot of money for Vincent's position, almost as much as I've paid for the commissioner's. I was quite attached to him. Good for business."

I glared up at him, but it only made his smile grow.

"Let us do some mathematics, it should be simple for you to understand," he began, holding me at arm's length by my shoulders. "If Vincent is good for business, and Petronille kills him, what does that make Petronille?"

Tears were gathering in my vision. I knew where this was going.

He tapped my nose playfully. "That's right! That means Petronille is *bad* for business."

I swallowed hard, my body aching from holding myself stiffly.

"You don't seem to have a lot of conviction. I've helped your sisters because they do what needs to be done." He sighed. "Now it is time to solve your own problems, instead of being a problem to be solved for once."

The heat was only getting worse, a feverish anger that I hoped one day would be great enough to hurt him. But not today, not yesterday, not any of the times he had brought me to shame and anger.

Not yet, but I promised myself, one day, maybe I would.

I glanced at my sisters; they stood with averted gazes. *Cowards.*

My father looked down at me as if I were still an adolescent. It further solidified my choice to leave, to refuse to take part in this family any longer, to wean myself from their influence. They made me small, and I couldn't afford to be small when my rage was only growing by the day and would inevitably consume everything if not smothered. All they ever did was *feed* it.

I knocked my shoulder against his as I left. Behind me, I could hear him laugh and mumble something snide. It all blended together as I slammed the door, the noises dampened by the sound of rain.

The sensation of the filthy rain was cool, ice over cast iron, cleansing. I could swear I would steam.

Someday, I would be outside this home, and there would be no more snide remarks left.

Not today, not tomorrow either, but *someday*.

CHAPTER THIRTEEN

The Artisan

The docks were as somber as a drunk at dawn. The water sloshed against the ship hulls, just as muggy in color as the ashen sky. The air was the same as it always was but with a more electric edge, like static in a cloud of dust.

I wouldn't call myself a bashful man, but I couldn't stop thinking about my wife's last visit. The way her skin glistened under the glow of the kiln, how her body felt pressed against mine, the amusement of her attempt to *know* me. Perhaps next time I could show her how to carve wood or chisel stone. The only thing she would be genuinely good at would be serving as a model, a muse. It could very well be possible that I enjoyed her company, momentarily.

The looming dread nearly dried up before I noticed my studio door was unlocked, ajar.

"I told you I would bring the check to your office," I called into the studio before I pulled open the massive warehouse door.

There, sitting on my stool in front of my unfinished sculpture of a man, was a crooked thing I hoped I'd never see again.

"Commissioner Hunt, to what do I owe the displeasure?"

He was uninterested, cleaning out his pipe with one of my rags. "I would ask you the same, but this time I come of my own accord."

"Then speak plainly, we are far from strangers, after all." I moved slowly, as if not to disturb a skittish predator. I set my satchel down in front of a statue of a couple embracing, a good distance from the official in my presence.

"It feels like only yesterday I was evicting you as a squatter." Commissioner Hunt glanced up at the grand space, taking in the tall ceilings. He brushed a hand over his bushy mustache, clearing it of any clay dust it might have collected just from sitting there. "Look at you now, pauper."

"State your business, I have been paying my rent regularly enough to avoid you."

"I know you have." He stood from the stool, hands clasped behind his back as he inspected the statue before him. "I keep tabs on those who've caused me the most issues."

"That's quite a declaration considering the state of the city under your watch, no?"

The commissioner's neck snapped in my direction; his mustache could have stood up like a peeved cat with the way he scowled. He was a loathsome bug hiding under a nicely tailored uniform. The most upstanding of them all would always be worse than someone like me, and he knew it. Two magpies replying to the same call.

It pained me to suppress a faint grin, but an expression so full of rage will never cease to amuse me.

"I will have to ask you to leave if this visit is for leisure rather than official." I removed my jacket, and it kicked up a cloud of dust as it flopped onto the used chair.

"There's been a disappearance."

My throat tightened, knotting into a distasteful sourness that rendered me silent.

"I find it quite funny that it's always you at the center of the mischief." The commissioner stalked forward one step at a time, his boots leaving prints on the concrete flooring. "How coincidental that the minute you show up around the De Villiers, something terrible happens."

"You said there was a disappearance." I didn't bother to look at him, instead beginning to pick at a tin bucket of carving tools. "No one said anything about something terrible happening."

"I am willing to bet my week's payroll that you have something to do with it"—he stopped behind me—"or that you know something."

"And what if you're wrong?" I turned to him.

The chuckled rolled like gravel in the commissioner's throat. "I rarely am."

"What if you are?"

He stared for a moment before an eerily calm smile made his cheeks puff. "Then I will make sure to *make it right.*"

"Who is this missing person you are willing to lie for?" I bit the inside of my cheek, not wanting to look more frustrated than I already was. "Though I am sure there are plenty with pockets deep enough to make you do more than lie—"

The thick hand grabbed me by my collar, choking me as the fabric balled in his stout fist.

"Vincent Carlisle was last seen heading to your newly acquired home." His voice was surprisingly calm despite his grip. "Know anything about a thing like that?"

"I don't know a Vincent."

"Your wife knows him. *Quite* well." His lip curled.

"Sorry, I am not my wife. You will have to ask her."

"Have you seen her with anyone?"

"I haven't been home, I wouldn't know."

"He said he was going to see your wife, last I saw him." He raised a brow. "Don't tell me you don't watch what company your wife keeps."

"Ah, I do remember someone visiting, now that you mention it." I gripped the cuffs of his uniform, yanking his hand off my shirt. "He left in a hurry. I suppose he was embarrassed that her choice was clear."

"Any other times?"

I shook my head, brushing the newly formed wrinkles out of my shirt. "I understand he may have thought ill of me, as he left quite angrily upon hearing about Mrs. Kameneva's unavailability. Have you checked the local taverns? A brothel? The ballet, perhaps?"

The commissioner's lip twitched into a sneer before turning from me to inspect the other sculptures. The forms of the inanimate people stood tall over us, watching our every move.

"Well, I guess if she is driving men to run off in their depression, I should keep her locked away. Don't want the hounds to get her!" I joked lightly, though the words felt wrong.

"Is that why you leave her at home unattended?" He glanced over his shoulder. "Not a very foolproof plan."

"Well"—I plastered on my best smile—"the faster we finish this pleasant meeting, the sooner I can tend to the pigeon."

"You know," the commissioner said suddenly, smoothing his hand over the arm of a sculpture, "the De Villier family is very generous, to my campaign as commissioner *and* the coroner's." He rubbed his fingers together, grimacing at the dust collecting on his hand. "I would tread carefully, wouldn't want your meddling to affect Petronille negatively."

"Is that a threat, Mr. Hunt?"

He chuckled, shaking his head as if speaking to a chastised child. "No, just a natural consequence." He sauntered toward the warehouse door, waving his hand lazily over his shoulder. "You have a good night, Mr. Kamenev. I suspect I'll be seeing you soon."

CHAPTER FOURTEEN

The Artisan

"Where did you put the body?"

"Does it matter?"

"Would I ask if it didn't?" Petronille's voice rose from across the dining room table.

I clenched my jaw nearly as hard as my grip on the cutlery, slowly dragging the knife across the rare piece of sirloin. Not only did I not answer her, but I lifted a piece to my mouth and chewed.

"Is this venison?" I asked, the words making their way through my teeth between bites.

"No."

"I must have poor taste, I'm usually good at guessing. Pork?"

"Answer me."

"Thank you for the meal, by the way. I really didn't believe you ate anything savory until now—"

"Arkady!" Her voice was strained.

"Petronille." I gave a taut smile. "Being so loud at the table is unseemly."

Her face grew red, like she would burst at any second.

As I returned my attention back to the supper, I could hear her dainty footsteps light against the carpet as she approached.

Then a knife came down into my steak. The juices crept around the new crack in the fine porcelain.

"A tantrum isn't the way to get my attention. I thought you figured that out *last* time."

"It is the *only* way to get your attention," she hissed.

I took a deep, meditative breath as I placed my cutlery down, folding the napkin from my lap. When I looked up at her, her gaze was as sharp as a tack.

"I need to know where the body is."

"You don't *need* to know anything, dearest."

"The commissioner visited me."

"You get *many* visitors, it seems."

Her palm smacked against the side of my head, and I grabbed her wrist. Even so, she did not flinch. Though the slight tremor in her hand told me everything I needed to know. "I *also* received a visit from our mutual acquaintance."

"What did you tell him? What did he say?"

"Nothing you need to worry about."

"We killed someone."

"*You* killed someone." I squeezed her wrist.

"You disposed of him." She swallowed. "You're complicit."

"I am."

"Yet you don't regard our situation with any sort of haste."

"Mistakes are made swiftly if you're not careful."

She only continued her glare, twisting her wrist in vain.

"What were you thinking?" I stood from my seat.

"What do you mean?"

"You stuck a letter opener in a man's throat. What were you thinking?" I lowered my voice, closing the distance between us. "If you were thinking at all, that is."

She didn't answer me, which was an answer in itself.

"Petronille." I backed her against the table. "What would you do if I told you?"

"For my safety, I want to know all the information."

"I think you like it."

"Excuse me?"

"You heard me." I smirked, placing my hands on her waist, letting one drift down over her hip. "Does it excite you, thinking about what I did? What *we* did?"

"No."

I could practically feel the heat coming from her blush. Those supple cheeks were so expressive, so telling.

"Do you ever wonder," I began, gently bunching her skirts, "if I'm capable of doing something to you, *Petre*?"

The sound of a less formal name made her straighten her posture, leaning back on the table slightly.

I lowered my face beside her ear. "Would it get you hot knowing what I would do for a sweet thing like you? To know someone is hidden away, deep in the ground, because you cut the fox's tail and sent your hound to *chase*?"

"No, it doesn't!" she hissed, but her darting eyes couldn't give me any confirmation that her words were true.

Under her skirts, her silk stocking caught slightly on the scars of my worn hands; such a lovely fabric was nearly as soft as she was. Her thighs were trembling. They were also incredibly warm to the touch.

I felt between her legs. *Wet.*

I chuckled in her ear. "What did we say about denial?"

"Get off me!" She shoved my chest hard.

I threw her back, pinning her to the table, the plates and cutlery chiming together as the tablecloth dragged.

"You know very well which *word* I respond to." I towered over her, leaving a gentle kiss on her collarbone. "I'm well trained."

"The *hell* you are," she bit out.

"Already bored of your pet?" I began to undo the gown. The garment alone must have cost two weeks'—no, three weeks'—wages. Though, no matter how expensive the pelt, I was more interested in the meat. "You wound me, Petre. Here I thought I was becoming one of your favorite playthings."

As the buttons popped open, her flushed skin was exposed to me.

I expected to count the beauty marks on her skin, feel every dip and rise of her form, but it revealed something better.

Yanking her gown down her torso revealed these *strange* markings. A littering of birthmarks resembling brushstrokes that spiraled in different ways across her stomach, straight through her sternum.

Blaschko lines, a rare pigmentation of the skin.

"You hide so much from me. Every time I open you up, I discover something new," I taunted, but admittedly, I was distracted by the patterns. My fingertips brushed against the trail mindlessly. It reminded me of a mosaic, or patterns on fancy pet birds. I leaned down so my lips could replace my fingers, tracing the unique finish on the expensive porcelain of her skin.

Her breasts rose and fell with her harsh breathing, but she only watched me.

Say the word.

The buttons ran out, and I pulled the gown away from the form I so desperately wanted to see. I must have been jaded before to not look closely, but she really was a specimen of symmetry, of good composition.

Say it before I lose myself in you.

Her breasts fit perfectly in my palms, but that seemed to be a theme all around. The anatomy of her muscles and tendons let her physique shine. They framed her body perfectly; I could see every movement under the skin, a lean animal in prime shape.

She somewhat reminded me of the skittish little things they let run at the derby. All muscle, little to spare.

I can't stop . . .

My disillusioned state shattered as I looked lower—and I could see bruising, more and more as I followed the length of her legs.

I nearly forgot she was a dancer. I never expected such elegant creatures to be marked so brutally by the sport.

A jolt of something disgusting flipped in my stomach, souring at the back of my throat as it threatened to manifest. Could it be jealousy? The feeling dissipated as I thought of replacing those bruises with marks of my own.

"You're just cruel." Her words were angry, her eyes something more like mortified.

Why would you look at me like that?

I glanced up at her, but she'd already gathered her dress, slipping out from under me, and her rushed steps sounded along the whiny stairs.

"Petre!" I shouted before the inevitable slam of a door.

Perhaps staring was not the most mannerly.

Now whenever I closed my eyes, the map of her body spread before me. Every freckle, every curve, every inflection of a muscle, that exact deep pattern across her torso.

The perfect muse. The one you can't forget. The one I didn't want to ruin.

CHAPTER FIFTEEN

THE PERFORMER

If there was to be a show, it would be at The Brass Globe or not at all.

"Prestigious" was not quite the word, but "infamous" might be. A prime example of grit, talent, and the constant comings and goings of star protégées. It was the place to be if you knew what kind of night you were looking for.

The thing about The Globe is that it was shiny. A shimmer that could entrance anyone at first glance. Everything from the tall chandelier to the performers was flashy—but that's all it was. A bright light to attract the moths. If a hair lighter than the illusion required, you could see every scratch in the wood, every creak of the building, every flaw down to the bedbugs wedged between the seats and the men who lurked behind the curtains.

Much like the activities within, the theater had its own part to play in the performance.

The gaslights were sore on the eyes at full brightness, and the smell was too much some days, which is why they were always on a low dim by the time the guests arrived. We would have to open the skylight behind the stage to air it out, sometimes as early as the morning before the first matinee.

Seeing a theater during rehearsal was like seeing a woman with her hair down. Unrecognizable, yet her true image became clear the more time you looked. No bells, no whistles, just being.

A body or two darted through the doorframe, nearly crashing into me on my way in. In the grand ascending aisles, a costume rack and two seamstresses. In the seats, members of the company waiting to be fitted. A small group in an ocean of upholstered seats.

On the floors, the thumping of ballet shoes as dancers ruined them until completion. Crushing, snapping, testing their handiwork as they broke the shoes on the hardwood. Some with needles tucked between their lips, ready to sew in their ribbons. A few had to alter the color, dyeing them to their skin tone or costume.

The wings of the stage were crowded with either sprites in tulle or creatures in suits. The two parties shifted in the shadows; some exchanged friendly words, some became *too* friendly and disappeared in twos. If you were lucky in this business, in escorting, you might find yourself as a mistress, kept or otherwise. The goal, after all, was to leave. Not all were so rewarded in their efforts by the time they aged out, and opportunities were fleeting.

On the stage were dancers, some standing and some sitting while completing their stretches and warm-ups. Barres were placed along the back, where one familiar brunette would be.

Lorelei, with her leg up and foot pointed to the ceiling, using a well-dressed fellow's shoulder to rest her shoe. They were speaking, although breathless. When she looked away, he touched her leg, though it wasn't to help her stretch, I suspected.

Her face was stern, mature. She almost held herself like an adult when no one was looking and she was determined to get something. Then her eyes drifted and found me at the edge of the stage.

"Petre, darling!" she squeaked, her leg whipping off the man's shoulder so fast, the breeze misplaced his hair. She fluttered across the hardwood, falling to her knees between two lamps lining the very edge of the stage. "You're early, I thought you'd be here half an hour later than you are!"

"I thought it would be nice to decompress somewhere familiar before we go." I smiled. "You'll have to reserve me a seat for the premiere if you end up with the principal role."

"You'll have a seat with your name on it, I promise." She winked. "Give me a few, I'll be ready to leave once I redress." She practically skipped backstage.

I watched her retreat, but I wasn't the only one.

The man, cigarette in hand, eyes trained like a hound, was watching her move off the stage as if tempted to lunge. His hair was slicked back, no facial hair, perhaps an attempt to look more youthful. Though the aging of his skin placed him a little over mid-age. His attempt at a fresh-faced mask had failed, but it was hard to ignore the quality of his suit and shoes. Not one piece of lint, not one scuff on his shoes. This man could afford to groom, and to be groomed.

His eyes only settled when he realized I was watching, and he took a long drag of his cigarette before slinking off the other side of the stage, the snake slipping through the grass. If she and I weren't spending lunch together, I couldn't imagine what they'd be up to instead.

What Lorelei didn't know about this business was what lurked under all the success stories and glamour. There were things, men, that she wasn't ready to handle—and her current prospect looked exactly the type.

I only prayed that she fully understood the transactional nature of the work, and not to confuse it for something like *love*.

CHAPTER SIXTEEN

The Artisan

Rare steak with delicate fat marbling the flesh plated upon fine china, a matching silver set meticulously arranged in a specific order. Only one of three wineglasses was full, one of the three forks used; I was unsure of when I would need the others or why they were present. I didn't expect so much cutlery to eat one damned steak.

Using fine porcelain under a meal that required a sharp knife was like some sort of cruel game. You either eat stress-free or leave a hundred-dollar mistake slashed across the smooth surface.

The juices of the meat dripped as it was sliced, mingling with the almond-roasted greens and buttery potatoes, endless steam teasing my nose as I leaned close, not letting a scrap go to waste. It was hard to eat slowly, my stomach empty from the long day, insatiable in my current state. It was like I could only focus on eating, all energy dedicated to such.

"Is the food to your liking, Mr. Kamenev?" Petronille's mother asked.

She put up a quick smile by the time my glance made it to the end of the table.

A kick at my knee.

I swallowed hard, glancing across the candlelit table, my wife's scowl cutting through. She raised a brow, cutting her steak slowly into a mouselike portion before pulling it from her fork between her teeth. Her brow twitched pointedly with a glare before she continued to peck at her food.

I straightened my posture, her father concealing a small gesture of amusement.

"My apologies." I tried to seem gracious, whatever that would be. "It's truly delicious. Compliments to the cooks."

"Don't be so hard on him, he's a young man in need of real food. He is welcome to eat as much as the cook can throw." Her father chuckled, offering a bit of a teasing look at her mother, who squinted at him, clearly unamused.

"Well, if Petre fed him, it would prevent the near choking he's about to cause from such mouthfuls," she muttered into her wineglass. "What do you feed him at home?" She turned her head to Petre.

She mumbled something.

"What was that?" her mother chirped.

"I haven't had time to go to the market." She didn't bother to raise her voice, pulling a piece of meat off her fork sharply before chewing.

"Is your butcher out of town?" The tone seemed . . . mocking.

Petre refused to answer, becoming fixated on her greens and sawing away at the fillet.

"Or can you not afford such a delicacy anymore?"

Petre's plate cracked; her mother flinched.

Petronille threw her cutlery down and kicked the chair out, emitting a horrid screeching sound as the legs dragged against the flooring, spending not a second more looking at us before she tossed her cloth napkin to the floor.

Then she left me with them.

Why must she make every gathering so painfully awkward? Now I'm stuck with . . .

"I suppose her temper hasn't dampened." Her father sighed, throwing his napkin beside his plate. Even with the attempt to salvage the awkward encounter, there was amusement in his tone, and it even brought a slight smile to her mother's face as she finished off her glass.

Something about the way they pushed her made me lose all appetite, like watching a cat play with something half dead already.

Hopefully these visits would become less frequent, for the sanity of both of us.

Instead of a ballerina, Petre should have been a magician. She was good at disappearing, or just hiding. Or it could be the gratuitously large house with all too many rooms.

The staff was cleaning up the dining room, which meant our visit was coming to an end. I made my best effort to find her. It was bad enough being alone with her parents; the least she could do was help me entertain them for a little before we took our leave to avoid being accused of being uncouth.

Each door opened into a completely different scene, a new theme and display, lush with furniture that I suspected hadn't been used yet. I had worked on this house since they'd begun building it. They had wide plans for entertainment, and were prepared for hosting and other things I didn't have a clue about. I still couldn't wrap my head around having so many rooms and places to be. I would get tired just trying to find the water closet at night.

I propped the last door open to find her mother tenderly clutching a glass of harder liquor. She tipped her head over and grinned at me.

"Arkady." She sounded almost relieved, patting the sofa next to her. "Come. Do you enjoy bourbon?"

I glanced over my shoulder before entering the parlor. This room had a theme of deep greens and creams among a medium-stain wood. I sat in a chair rather than next to her. I was afraid she'd sink her claws in and take a bite.

"Have you seen Petronille?" I cleared my throat as a glass was shoved into my hand.

She patted my hands to make sure I wouldn't drop the crystal, nodding as she leaned back on the arm of the sofa. "She's around, I'm sure."

The burning scent of the bourbon pinched my nose as I lifted the glass.

"You would think she would have outgrown these fits once she was ready to be a wife." She sighed, taking a long sip of her drink. "I guess it falls on me for not house-training her."

The way she spoke about her daughter was jarring. It was as grating as chalk across slate, a kettle screeching in my ear. Family wasn't something I was comfortable speaking about due to lack of experience, but I couldn't imagine what would possess someone to say something so demeaning, like she were some house pet.

From what I knew about my bride, she wasn't one to listen to or obey anything she didn't want to be a part of. She was stubborn, tightly wound—but even I wouldn't describe her this way. So why in God's name did she stay around them?

No matter, we would make it a point to ween her off whatever she still needed from this particular familial connection. They weren't good for her.

"You know, this is your fault too."

My eyes snapped to Mrs. De Villier, but she was already sneering. "Excuse me?"

"I told her to pick a strong man, one with a firm hand," she scoffed. "Oh, I had great suitors lined up for her. Several, actually. A duke, a statesman, those of the entrepreneurial spirit. I even considered the coroner, since I never knew how many Petre would chase away."

My grip on my glass was the only thing keeping me from lunging at the hag.

"I shouldn't have been so hasty. I just wanted her to be a wife, to come into her own, my sweet Petre. So when she said, *I want the grimy simpleton who crafted the mantelpiece*, who was I to deny her?"

My jaw nearly cracked from how hard I was biting my tongue.

"I would have thought someone who owns a mallet would know how to correct—"

"Perhaps the best correction is knowing when to sculpt rather than chisel," I interrupted with a tense smile. "Why labor and hit dry plaster when you could guide the material while it's still malleable?"

Her mother's mouth fell agape, opening and closing like a beached fish.

"It is good to practice foresight, Mrs. De Villier. Or else we all may exert ourselves from ill preparation of due process."

"My wife has had enough to drink, it seems," Mr. De Villier spoke from the doorway, an edge to his tone that made Mrs. De Villier sit straight, like he'd yanked a string on a marionette. "It's time you retire, dear."

She blinked a couple times, eyes glassy from intoxication or embarrassment as she wiped a bit of liquor from the corner of her lips, suddenly overly concerned about appearances. Fear is, indeed, sobering.

"Arkady," he beckoned, "come with me."

The study was exactly as you would imagine. Dark and intimidating, all too clean for everyday use. The only part of the room used was the top of the desk; even the guest chairs didn't look like they were as popular compared to the office seat.

The mantel was antique, possibly fourteenth century, yet the hearth was barely stained, not much evidence of experience to match the age of its facade.

"I apologize on behalf of my wife." Petronille's father grunted, unbuttoning his suit jacket as he sat on the edge of his desk. "She is better at public relations than private ones."

"That's a peculiar type of vice, especially in one so used to catering words."

"The difference is that the words from her mouth are rarely copywritten," he joked, beginning to pack his pipe.

"Sounds dangerous."

Mr. De Villier lit his pipe, puffing to get the ember glowing. He never seemed in a rush to do anything, relaxation afforded to few. Yet, you would think it would reflect badly on how little he valued other people's time. Mine was a dime on his dollar, and he didn't shy away from the insinuations.

If I weren't already a bit agitated from his wife's words, his general demeanor may not have bothered me so.

His lips moved, leisurely puffing tobacco while not even bothering to look at me as he spoke. I could grab him by the whiskers and pull as hard as I could, show him what a working man's hands actually felt like as I buried them in his face, or plunge that exorbitantly gilded pen into his eye the next time he glanced sideways at me as if to check if I was lifting anything from his trinket collection.

"Did you hear me, boy?" He muffled a cough as he exhaled.

My eyes snapped to his, and for a moment I thought he could read my thoughts. His expression wasn't one of fear, no, it was similar to the look you gave a child who you knew was about to scream in public.

"No, I was preoccupied with the craftsmanship of your study." I smiled. "I can appreciate good taste. It's rare that it is all in one place."

"That's because you're one of the good ones." He chuckled. "One is either wealthy in money or in skill, rarely both."

I wanted to roll my eyes, but they stayed fixated on the ornate desk he sat upon. I approached the front, touching the carvings of the edge, the quality of the wood. The grain was fine, old. "Redwood?"

Mr. De Villier nodded, getting up to gather some of the papers to show me more of the surface.

"Expensive for something used so often, no?"

"On the contrary, a man's desk is a sign of his status, his life's work. It is the modern equivalent of a throne. A desk isn't just about utility. It represents all you have built."

I offered a mumble coupled with a nod as I listened, debating on whether my next question was something I truly wanted to know. "How does one manage to garner such success in such a short amount of time?"

The question came off more aggressively than intended, garnering a sharp look from Mr. De Villier.

"Your company is relatively new. It must be some biblical type of luck to become so large so quickly," I clarified, pinching myself mentally for not being concise the first time. "Now I am just curious about where it started."

He sank into his office chair, leaning back to take in the question, or perhaps to be strategic about how he answered. His eye caught on a small frame propped on the desk; you could have assumed it was a photograph of his wife or his children, based on the wistful smile. He pinched it between his fingers and twisted it to face me.

A photograph of him in front of his first factory, here in New York City. The iconic *LAGO* signage painted on the doors.

"We began as just a manufacturer of pharmaceuticals," he said, twisting the photo back so he could admire it again. "We moved into development shortly after."

"That's quite a path."

"We used nearly the last of our money to buy the warehouse. It was the purchase that would let us be the company we are today." He sighed.

"What did you do before?"

Mr. De Villier's expression faltered in amusement, only briefly. "We owned an orchard."

"Do you miss it?" I leaned closer. "I saw that you've expanded into buying farms, setting up clinics and housing. It seems like a great deal of charity for something so different than pharmaceuticals. Is nostalgia a reason?"

"Because I miss it? No, never," he scoffed. "But I remember what it was like, how desperate conditions become if the crop isn't thriving. The conditions that are standard. It seemed like a logical opportunity."

Before I could chip at him any longer, shouting from another part of the house made both of us question what we were hearing.

Both of us stood quickly once we realized it was Petronille.

We were barely outside the study door when we heard the quick footsteps and another shout of crude insults.

As we approached the main room, Petre hurried down the grand stairs with a red face, her mother nipping at her heels. Though, Mrs. De Villier seemed to recollect herself when she spotted us on the ground floor.

"You're being dramatic," her mother hissed.

"You *choked* me!"

"See?" She laughed, throwing her hands up in gesture to her daughter as she looked to her husband.

It only made it worse, every word out of her mother's mouth fueling the dainty blond. She stopped in her tracks, her mother nearly bumping into her as they reached the bottom floor.

"You are an ugly, *awful* monster!" Petre shoved her finger into her mom's chest on every emphasis, gaining some ground in the process.

Mrs. De Villier was now almost as flustered as Petre, a quirk in her brow and tight-lipped as if to keep the illusion of levelheadedness. She didn't say a thing in return.

Petre sneered, a smile of victory, but at what cost? More an expression of righteousness and knowing that, for now, she had a firm stance.

For a brief moment she looked at me, and so did her mother. Then I realized her father was also staring.

Everyone was waiting for a word from me; in defense or reprimand?

"Coward." Petre audibly scoffed, turning on her heel for the door without her coat, her things.

"Fetid moppet." Her mother's venomous words before she retreated back up the stairs, fussing with her necklace as if she'd just experienced something putrid.

"I suppose this is good night, then. Good luck reeling her in." Her father patted heavily on my shoulder, somberly following his wife.

At first I walked, then jogged lightly, toward the door. I gathered our coats in my arms, the rain smacking my face in thick droplets as I walked outside. Looking left, then right, I saw Petre, a small, wet silhouette halfway down the block already.

"Petre!" I shouted, my shoes splashing as they smacked the puddles, my socks already becoming cushioned with the water logging down the insoles of my shoes. I extended her coat to her. "It's raining—"

"What is the point of having you as a husband if you can't stand up for me!" She whipped around, slapping the coat from my hand, where it sulked onto the sidewalk, overtaken by a puddle.

"You were doing fine on your own."

"I wasn't! And you were utterly useless!"

I didn't answer right away, not with words. The streetlamp made the water glisten on her face, casting a dark shadow over her eyes. Her chest heaved, jaw tense like a bull-baiting dog unwilling to let go. Stubborn.

She spun on her heel, her shoes clicking as I got a full view of her hunched shoulders.

"Petre, stop!"

"Why?" Violence in her tone. Her sogging tendrils of hair slapped against her face as she turned, the white dress translucent in its dampened state. "So you can laugh at me? So you can wallow in misery at my very presence? To feed me to the dogs the moment I need something as little as one singular loyal word from you?"

"Loyalty?" The word fell from my mouth, but the next ones were more violent. "You want to speak of *loyalty*?"

She stumbled back like the words were physically thrown at her.

"What about you, *dear wife*? What have you done to show even the slightest bit of appreciation for my service to you? I can name some of your gratuities. For one—the way you stormed from the dining room table with lead feet, child's play at the tender age of twenty-four!" I laughed into the air, wiping my wet hair from my face as I stared up at the sky as if to beg God not to let my mouth run on too long. "How about putting me in as many awkward situations as you can afford? Have you thought about how your actions affect *me*?"

"I didn't—"

"No! No, you haven't, of course. Because no one exists outside of your influence. You can't hold yourself socially, you scream at your hosts, I bet you'd cry if I made you finish the greens on your plate."

"That's unfair. You're being cruel!"

"You *petulant* child. How dare you accuse me of no loyalty when you've done *nothing* to earn mine."

My throat burned, my breathing suddenly quick and heavy, like I'd endured some great labor—emotionally at least.

"I *killed* for you." I swallowed. "I promised to keep you safe. Is that not enough?"

Petre was so still, I wondered if she'd heard a word I said.

In the world of a greedy, spoiled child, nothing would ever be enough.

I put on my sopping coat as I brushed past her.

"Where are you going?"

"Home."

"Without me?"

"You have free will."

I almost made it to the corner of the block before feeling a sharp blunt hit to the back of my head, then a clatter.

I raised my hand, rubbing my scalp as I looked behind me on the ground.

A single dainty ivory shoe.

When my eyes lifted to her, I expected her to be livid, given that she was now missing a shoe in an attempt to assault me. I expected a tense brow and a beet-red face, at least a few more insults.

Her breaths were stuttering, lip trembling. Though I'd seen this expression before. Red eyes and a shaky white-knuckled fist. This was the image of a child who was never listened to, and was still ignored into adulthood. While she was older than I was, I felt nostalgia seeing her this way. Unfortunately, I saw my angry, bitter younger self.

This didn't absolve her of her transgressions in my mind, but my understanding of her cleared ever so slightly in that moment.

"I . . ." She swallowed, laughing to herself before raising her hands just for them to fall by her sides in defeat. "I *hate* you. I hate the way you make me feel, I hate the way you don't want me, and I hate that everyone loves you. *Everyone* does. No one questions you, misunderstands you. They accept you with more ease, with no leverage, and I *hate* it."

"The problem with everyone loving you . . ." I picked up her shoe, watching her shake as I approached for the last time. Her eyes were red, searching, possibly puffy from tears. She shivered under my stare, more so when I let my sentence linger. Did she really think my life was so easy? I pitied her. "Is that you sacrifice what you really want to say, how you really want to act, at all times. You are a portrait of what you wish to portray, unable to speak and only there to be observed. As a woman, I would have thought you'd understand this most of all."

"I'm tired. I'm tired of it all. I feel as though the only way to be true to myself is to be exceptionally loud."

"I may have agreed with you at one point." I knelt down, holding the shoe out before she reluctantly lifted her foot, stepping back into it. "But you can't be on the offensive constantly. Some ropes will strain on their own; let them snap and avoid the friction burn."

"The only reason to act that way is to be accepted by those creatures," she said, her words laced with spite. "Appeasing them won't make you one of them, even through me. They're vultures ready to pick the bone clean, to use every part of you for their gain. It's foolish to please them while they eat you alive."

"Maybe. But knowing that is power"—I looked up at her—"and when you play the classes, being aware is the best defense you have. Keeping a level head allows you to shape the narrative rather than force it."

She was silent, the adrenaline finally wearing off.

"You may not think I am familiar with the games of your parents," I said, softer, my hands still on her ankle, "but you get a lot of practice when you come from the bottom. I would say *you* may be more blind to them than me."

Then she knelt before me, on both knees, eye to eye with me.

"I don't hate you," she recanted, her voice sounding like a guilty child's admission. Her hands balled into fists in her soaked skirt.

"I know," I said softly. She had a hard time meeting my eyes now.

I touched her face, cupping her cold cheek. The streetlamp cast a dull light over her face when she looked up at me again. The rain mixed with her tears, her eyes tired from whatever war was going on inside her mind. She made herself so small, as if in anticipation. Belittled all her life.

"You're not my enemy, Petre." Our lips were so close. "You are my wife."

An instinctual lunge, her arms thrown around my neck, and our lips crashed together. I enveloped her in my arms. I balled my fists in her wet blouse, squeezing her against me like it would be possible to just absorb her there, two pieces of wet clay kneaded together.

I held her in my arms as we caught our breath, and I pulled her head into my shoulder in our embrace.

"You'll fall ill if we stay out here," I breathed, holding her frame like it was merely a doll, light and delicate.

"What's the point, I'm already sick." If I didn't know better, I'd think I caught a breathy laugh.

The night may have been a failure, but it seemed like maybe it wasn't a waste, after all.

CHAPTER SEVENTEEN

The Performer

"What's wrong with it anyway?" I didn't even bother watching as I kneaded a small ball of tawny clay.

"It needs to be patched. The pressure isn't holding, and heat is escaping somewhere," Arkady said, slathering parts of the bricks with wet cement. "It's yearly maintenance. A kiln this big needs it. I can't fire any of my new statues until it's finished."

"Right." I nodded as if perfectly acquainted with the standards of the trade. "Is that what keeps you here so late?"

He gave a tired laugh, taking a break to sit on his ladder. He wiped his rough hands with a dirty cloth hung over his shoulder. It could be my ladylike hormonal nature—but why was he more attractive when he was covered in dirt and dewy from a light sweat?

"Petre."

"Hm?" I blinked.

"Are you just going to play with that ball of silt all day?"

"What, do you expect me to help patch your kiln? You're the one who repeats *Don't touch anything* all the time." I tried to mimic his stern tone.

He shook his head and sighed, turning back to his work as he realized I was probably right.

Arkady was the same in his studio as he was outside: focused, stern, task-oriented. It wasn't a complaint, just an observation as to why he was the way that he was.

The studio wasn't disorganized, it just looked that way because you could see lots of clay and dust. It was dirty, not messy. Wooden crates categorized by scrap material, types of tools, even broken pots to be thrown back into the slick pile. Tins of glaze, brushes, smaller sculpting tools organized in the drawers of a secondhand filing cabinet.

"Are you worried?" I began, pressing my thumb deep into the clay after rolling it into a near sphere in my palm. "About the commissioner digging? There isn't much to find on me, not anything that he wouldn't already know from his proximity to my father."

"No more worried than I've been before." He didn't look at me as he scraped his pointing trowel against the brick. "At some point, the constant and steadfast threats become meaningless."

"How does he know you?" I blurted the question quicker than I thought.

"I wasn't the best behaved in my youth."

"And you somehow *are* now?"

He threw a sarcastic smile over his shoulder. "You are full of jokes today. Does something have you in good spirits?"

"More like nothing has agitated me yet. Keep speaking to me and it will all be back to normal." I tossed my clay mush back into the slick bucket.

He watched me for a moment like he was debating what he was about to say.

"I was violent, angry. I don't entirely blame him for past reprimands," Arkady admitted, "but I was getting old, too old to be a ward of the state, at least. I was just a kid who felt the world was failing him with every passing month. It isn't easy, you learn a lot of hard lessons about life and its consequences on your own."

"So he has a grudge? Against adolescent actions?"

He shrugged. "You could say that. Prejudice, I am sure, played its part."

I walked up beside his ladder, staring at his handiwork before my eyes wandered, finding some comfort now in the greeting gazes of his statues. Some covered in cloth, some under construction, a few finished.

"How do you get your ideas?" I touched the hand of one of the female forms. "Do you hire models?"

He hesitated to answer.

A piercing in my stomach, a jealous bile working up to burn my heart. *He is a professional,* I reminded myself.

"Sometimes, yes." He stepped down from his high place on the ladder. "Though I mostly settle on sketches. It's more efficient and financially responsible."

A refreshing breath of relief cleansed my lungs.

"I could model for you." I stared down at his shoes beside me, then trailed up to meet his eyes. "I won't even charge you, since I am *so* kind."

A quick smirk tugged at his lips. "Is that right? What has afforded me such charity?"

I shrugged. "Anything to help a starving artist."

"You could just feed me."

"You are hard to flirt with." I clicked my tongue at him.

"Model for me now," he said.

My heart fluttered, my head whipping toward him. "Now?"

"Why not?" He lifted his shoulders, retreating to the back of the studio to the stairs leading up to the overseer's office.

The hairs on my arms and neck stood, my senses alight as the insinuations settled. I had to remind myself we were *married*, this was *not* scandalous . . . and I might be a prude, despite all my hard work as a retired escort.

I followed him, having to jog to catch up, as he was already halfway up the flight.

The overseer's office from the building's previous occupants looked to have been converted into a bedroom.

The loft area was high above the ground floor of the warehouse, viewable through foggy, stained windows. The lighting was better than expected; it almost made up for the dust.

This must be where he lived before.

The walls were brick, too poorly insulated to be tolerable. There was a mattress on the floor in front of an impossibly large circular window, the crescent nearly floor to ceiling. In the corner was a chewed-up chair that may very well have been considered *nice* once upon a time, if it hadn't fallen into such sloppy hands. A mess of shapes crowded the wooden shelves and scattered over one lonely, plain desk. Hands, heads, incomplete busts, an animal or two—all in different earthy hues of gault and stone.

It would be cozy if not for the missing fourth wall. Just a foggy grid of windows with a propped-out pivotal pane for whatever airflow it could manage, even though it might as well be trading dust from one space to the other.

I imagined he would live in some measly dark hole. Well . . . it had rather exceptional lighting. But it was a hole nonetheless.

"On the bed," he said, gathering a stool with a sketchbook and a compact charcoal stick.

"The bed?"

"Well, standing completely still for long periods of time is harder than it looks." He picked up his pad and dusted off his seat. "It's more comfortable."

"Should I . . ." I stared at the bed, then pinched my skirts. "Do I undress?"

"Do you want to undress?" He smirked.

A frustrated blush burned at my ears. "No."

"Then don't." He settled in his seat, one leg crossed over the other as the back of his sketchbook stared at me.

I sat on the corner of the bed, brushing down the sheets. "What should I do?"

"It doesn't matter as long as you're still," he answered, an amused spark in his voice. "Look away, it'll be less awkward."

I huffed, turning to the side for a profile. It allowed me to get a better look at the view outside. The perfect scenery for a therapeutic watch—still, not entirely as to make it less alive in picture.

The scratching of the paper was calming, but the anticipation was what made it hard to sit still. The temptation to ask, *Are you done yet?* I wouldn't. This was a rare opportunity. He had allowed me into his space, his haven. This was another step into his mind, this person, knowing him deeper than the skin. I'd ruined many opportunities with my mouth lately. I would practice keeping it shut for now.

"You're doing well," he commented, his voice tickling my ear, as he was out of sight.

"Because I'm speaking less?"

"I was going to say that you are a natural," he corrected. "I suppose I shouldn't have expected less from a ballerina."

My shoulders pulled back, my posture alert. "Really?"

"In the short time you've known me, have I ever falsely flattered?"

"I wouldn't mind seeing a jackal grovel"—I caught him from the corner of my eye—"especially if it is me you get down on your knees to."

"Haven't I already?" I couldn't fully see his face, but I heard the slyness in his tone. I simply smiled and looked back at the harbor.

He stopped scratching at the paper.

"Can I see it?" My posture unfroze.

"You can see it when I sculpt it."

"That's not fair."

"I'll name it after you; you won't miss it."

"Please don't." I covered my face.

"Don't worry, it will be flattering." He laughed.

"I don't trust you." I tossed his deflated pillow at him.

To my surprise, his smile seemed genuine. Enough so that his dimple cratered in his cheek, and I could see that his natural smile was at a slight slant, a little higher to his left. The beauty mark on his cheekbone shifted when he squinted, his face contorting with authentic, unmasked emotion.

I could get used to seeing his face soft like this instead of placid like the stone he carved. It was like the entire world opened up at the slightest, simplest interaction.

I was starved of him, and it was, in part, my fault for creating the distance.

Just one taste could sustain me until he allowed me another.

CHAPTER EIGHTEEN

The Performer

Drowsiness stung my eyes and made it hard to hold attention. The cup vibrated in my hand, spilling the faintest drop of Assam tea onto the cotton napkin on my lap. Every ripple of the sheer surface sent a wave of lightheadedness through me, making breathing more manual than ever. The voices around me materialized as mumbles, then words, then my name.

"Petronille." Lorelei placed a hand on my arm.

My friend, as well as friends by extension, were staring at me from all points of the tearoom table.

I stared at Lorelei, nudging her foot under the table to clue me in.

A fine dark brow shot up at me. "You must be tired. I trust we can assign blame to Mr. Kamenev." She winked.

The girls surrounding us erupted into a quiet chorus of mousy tittering. I had to remind myself that *I* was the old one, these were just girls.

"Yes, not much rest to be had." I set my unsteady china on the table before any more tea became a stain.

The blue details of the cup matched the rest of the Blue Moon tearoom, named for its famed wisteria blossoms covering the facade as well as the walls of the inside. The droopy violet blooms hung above us as if listening in on all of the chatter. You could see the vines through the stately windows, flowers swaying in the breeze.

The guests of the room were just as flowery, wearing whites and rich accents of color. Their perfumes mixed with one another and the blossoms; it would be overwhelming if the tearoom were any smaller.

"Does that mean you won't return to the company?" Helen asked. Her expression was haughty, young and bright like a well-fed fire. I had seen her many times at auditions and rehearsals. The first time I saw her, she was maybe fifteen years of age. Time is a thief, but it was generous with her.

"No, I've retired," I answered, turning my attention to a small snack on the table, my shaky hand pinching it between my fingers.

The girl's impish grin flicked up when she saw me reach. "Clearly."

Despite the chatter around us from our companions, her words interrupted me mid-bite, making me abandon the snack altogether. I looked at Lorelei, only to find her intensely focused on her tea, though I knew she'd overheard. I nudged her with my shoe again, but she ignored me.

Perhaps I've truly outgrown this group in more ways than one.

"Petre retiring is the only way you have a shot as *The Sylph*." Lorelei's tone was playful, but she meant it. "I would be thanking her for the opportunity. Or else you may forever be stuck in the background as a tree, not even a faerie."

"You say that like you aren't gunning for the same role. Keep up that *manly* footwork and you may find yourself in the role of Gurn."

"Pardon me." I cleared my throat, excusing myself from the table and making directly for the powder room.

The light from tall windows in the establishment trailed as I passed like a malfunctioning silver screen. Faces looked at me, or were they looking away? I kept my breathing deep and steady, reminding myself that not everyone was watching me like I thought they were. I was being paranoid in a fit of uneasiness.

"Surely there must be something wrong," I insisted, "for such a sudden change."

"Many things change instantly." She shrugged. "Your symptoms don't worry me yet. It sounds like you have just gotten older."

"Your answer is that I'm *old*?" The word was spat like it was unsweetened clover candy.

The botanist shook her head, but when she turned, she was most definitely laughing.

"Not old, just *older*," she clarified. "You will never be like you were when you were a young lady. Nobody is. Aging is part of it, you're simply maturing." She raised a brow. "Physically at least."

I laughed and shook my head. "Now you are calling me childish?"

"Never." She furrowed her brow in mocking reassurance. She took my hand and placed a bottle firmly into my palm. "Take this nightly, see how you feel. If you feel your disposition is getting worse, come visit me again."

I tore my eyes from hers and looked to the unlabeled bottle in my hands. It seemed to be some sort of chalky liquid, I didn't imagine it would taste any good.

As if she could read my mind, she said, "Take it with a cocktail, it will taste better."

I couldn't say I was excited about this mystery remedy, but it wasn't like I had anything better to do.

The park was supposed to be calming, serene. I couldn't find the ease within me, not now.

The day was nice, the park was beautiful, all signs for a good day, yet I was suffering from a seed embedded deep in my gut that something was amiss.

Within the park was a tall fountain, the dribbling water rippling the surface, hiding the shimmer of pennies gilding the bottom. I saw a mother pushing a stroller along the pebbled walkway, a couple promenading, then lastly, a lonely elder woman sitting on a bench.

She looked wise all on her own, lost in thought. Perhaps burdened by old memories, age, or maybe just her breakfast. It was hard to read strangers. Oh, to be able to be idle, unbothered.

My thoughts disappeared into the movement of milky liquid in the bottle, a brief loss of place—before a gruff hand snagged my arm.

"Petronille." The strained voice of the commissioner manifesting my name made my stomach drop back into place from before my moment of bliss.

"Commissioner." The word came out cracked like dry clay.

"I just had a few more questions, I couldn't catch you at your home earlier—"

"I don't have much time, I'm already a bit behind schedule."

"Oh, this won't take long!" he insisted, forcing my arm to loop with his as we walked along the pavement. "I was wondering if you gave some thought to where Mr. Carlisle may have gone."

"I am not his keeper. He was hardly a friend." I spoke as quickly as my steps, since it took two of my strides to keep up with one of his.

"Really? After all the years he's paid patronage to you through the ballet? Or the midday visits to his office? Or perhaps the visits to your home—"

"I don't see how it is your business. He is in my past."

"Where were you two weeks ago, Tuesday specifically?"

"I was at my sister's place," I answered.

"And what about your husband?"

"Commissioner!" I planted my feet into the crack of the pavement, halting our stroll abruptly.

The commissioner's expression twisted like a hound who'd spotted the fox on a run. He clasped his hands behind his back, attempting a calmer expression this time.

"Listen here, dove"—he took his time checking his timepiece—"there is much respect here for your family. They are generous when they need something done." He glanced up sharply from the face of his ticking watch. "Don't think their greed won't be used against *you* to clean their slate, if you're keeping something from the law."

"Is that a threat?"

"A promise"—he chuckled—"from your *father*, not I."

My hands went numb, and I couldn't feel the bottle anymore. My limbs ran cold, all the blood rushing to the back of my head, engulfing me in heat like a fire had been lit under me. I would love to say I laughed it off with grace and poise, but it came off as a choke as I averted my face, hoping to negate any more insinuations of guilt.

"It doesn't have to be like this, Petronille." He stood by my side, pretending to watch across the street. People passed us, some coming from the bakery, some from the park in their nicest fashions, some children running their way among the skirts and legs of the pedestrian herd. "If you prefer it this way, I may be inclined to extend a line to the papers about your extracurricular visits."

"Father will have your head."

"No"—he snorted—"he will have *yours*. It was his suggestion. I suppose to avoid certain . . . liabilities."

I clenched my teeth, rubbing them back and forth to stave off the immense impulse to bite.

"Pick your next words wisely," he suggested as he turned to leave, "and choose them soon."

CHAPTER NINETEEN

The Artisan

My hands were cramping, constantly moving and sculpting the form. The body was rough but recognizable. The face was the most formed thing about it.

The sculpture sat upright, hands by her sides, her face tipped up at me. I worked on the face, scraping and smoothing the clay until it finally resembled someone familiar. I held my breath when I looked into the eyes before trailing down to the breasts, then the abdomen.

The small tool scraped across her chest, swirling it before letting it continue across one breast. I couldn't remember the exact pattern. It seemed there was much to learn about her before I could properly bring her to life.

This bout of inspiration was different. It was draining, yet it tortured me with mania until I saw it through, until I was satisfied. It was like I saw her flesh, and my imagination started reeling. Itching to get back to work. Then once I got to my studio, anything I did paled in comparison to what I wanted to create in my mind's eye.

Inspiration is fleeting. It's clumsy and uncertain. There was no knowing when it would come or go, but it plagued my mind like the worst kinds of sicknesses. It would suffocate you in a fever if you didn't know what to do with it.

I brushed my finger across the cheek, the slick on my hands and arms already dry and cracking, pulling at my skin.

The earthy scent of my creation teased my nose. Dragging my finger over her lip, I wished it were warmer, softer.

I leaned in, half expecting my inanimate sculpture to move. One hand on her waist, one on the side of her head. The clay was wet and damp but still malleable under my grasp. It was in some way ironic how, every time I was around her in person, I wanted to squeeze her—out of anger, frustration, or possessiveness, I hadn't a clue.

I lowered my mouth to the salty clay, soft enough to not disturb the form. I wished the lips were in the flesh, but much like the sculpture, I didn't believe I could express anything, not without hurting her, punishing her for the feelings harbored deep inside.

My lip twitched as I smoothed my hands down her waist, mindlessly carving out the divots on each side of her hips, distracted by the memory of her and the form before me. I grabbed a handful of slick from the bucket to cover the area, gently working the clay into the form I remembered, the body I *strived* to know.

How frustrating it was to have a desire to capture her in clay when I had only seen parts of her, never fully observed, never fully mine.

The slick dripped over the legs, and my hands glided between them.

Perhaps I could carve from memory, no matter how brief it was. The slick felt no different than the juice that covered her when I got just a small taste.

Slowly, I pressed my fingers into the clay, between the formed legs. It felt dirty, inappropriate, despite the sculpture's inanimate state.

The wet clay felt similar, but it wasn't the same. I curled my fingers upward, scooping out the material. How lewd.

My other hand shook as I pulled the waistband of my trousers down.

I held my cock in my hand, the divot between her legs in the other, and I closed my eyes.

I imagined her on the table again, bathed in warm candlelight, her skin pink and flushed as I stared at her while she was at my disposal.

What would have happened if I'd kept going? If she hadn't left? Would she have let me take her then? It was hard to entice her when she got stuck in her own insecurity. What would she do if she didn't hold back? What would *we* do?

I spread my fingers inside her; she flinched. I swiped my cock along the entrance, teasing her with her own slick. I'm sure she would bite her lip, or her cheek, depending on if she was titillated or refusing to show me how much she liked it.

I pressed in . . . it was cold, a bit uncomfortable. As I pressed deeper, it made room for me, squeezing tight. I placed a hand on the table beside her, beginning to move.

Ah . . . Arkady, she would say. Would she grab me? Touch me?

I thrust in, the suction created by the slick making me shiver. Her hands grabbing my shirt or the tablecloth, maybe wrapping around my throat.

Would she ask for more? Yell at me to stop?

The thought made me throb harder, move a bit quicker. My body was producing enough heat to make the cool sensation melt away. It was so soft. I dug my fingers into the divots of her hips, burying them in her sides, the wetness making it easier to move, to squeeze. I imagined pulling, clawing at her skin, crushing her in my grasp, breaking her open and savoring her for dinner.

I reached upward, my nails tearing through her abdomen, hooking up under her ribs until I felt it, the throbbing, withering heart. I crushed it in my fist.

I finished.

I opened my eyes, the clay a misshapen form on the table, my cock pulsing. The former sculpture ruined beneath me.

I caressed the side of the face, squeezing it between my fingers until it escaped through the gaps. I suppose I would have started from scratch regardless, no matter what I did.

"Sweet Petronille"—a heavy sigh—"how do I entice you without ruining you?"

CHAPTER TWENTY

The Performer

My ears rang like a gunshot had gone off beside my head, and my hands were clammy enough to suggest that may have actually happened as well. I could barely hear the door slam behind me as I was swimming through my own consciousness, dropping my purse and neglecting to take my boots off at the door, the chatelaine on my hip chiming.

I almost didn't notice my husband reading quietly in the corner of the living room.

"Oh," he mumbled, "I thought you were in your room." He didn't take his eyes off his book as he delicately flipped the page, thin spectacles rested on the bridge of his nose.

"You would know if you bothered to *check*," I shouted, my ears ringing as I hurled my purse at his head. "You self-absorbed *narcissist*!"

His reaction wasn't fast enough, as it smacked the side of his head. He stood abruptly, but I was already halfway up the stairs. His footsteps boomed behind me, and I realized too late I wasn't running fast enough.

When I reached my room, the door slammed against the wall behind me and my arm was grabbed, yanking me into a livid Arkady. His nostrils flared, and I swore I could picture steam coming from them like a bull. His face was slightly flustered, but I wasn't sure if it was from the temper or the slap.

"Oh? Now I am visible to you? You've finally figured out I am no specter that you can just walk through? Do I have to cause a scene to make you less passive?"

"This anger is not for me," he said steadily, but his eyes told me I'd reached the end of his patience.

"Who else would it be for?"

"Well, that's what I was hoping you'd tell me," he said through a clenched jaw, loosening his grip on my wrist.

Tears pricked at my eyes, my throat sore enough to croak.

"I wish to bite someone. Enough to draw blood! Splatter it everywhere and paint the walls! Only then will I be taken seriously." I yanked my arm from him and paced toward the large chest at the end of the bed, angrily plucking at the buttons and clasps entrapping me.

"They will take you as seriously *ill* if you do that."

"Better than not at all!"

"Petre, what troubles you?"

"It would be easier to tell you what *hasn't* troubled me."

"Then start there."

"Pastries. They don't disappoint."

A hand slipped past my waist to the front, pulling me away from my rummaging. Then another arm looped around and held my back to a strong chest.

His cologne overwhelmed me; it seemed stronger now that I was overstimulated. A tickle of breath fanned across my neck, his lips hovering. I watched his thumb brush over the fabric of my blouse, and suddenly wet spots began to appear. One by one, tears fell before I realized they were mine. My tears. Just as the slightest touch, cracking like ice after a clean pour of liquor.

"Tell me about it," he whispered, his hands smoothing over the front of my torso.

I swallowed my words with an audible gulp, not that they would have been coherent if they'd manifested.

"Biting your tongue isn't good for you," he said as he dragged his lips over my ear and down toward my jaw, over my shoulder. I stole a glance at him, and his eyes met mine. He was one of those men who looked like they were always up to no good, no matter how charming they acted.

"The commissioner caught me in the street," I breathed, not trusting my words to be solid if I spoke any louder.

His eyes narrowed, and I saw his pupils get small enough where they could fit maybe a pin. "And what about it?"

"He's going to blackmail us."

"With what? He has nothing"—he lowered his lips to my shoulder, kissing the fabric gently—"or else he would have us in custody by now."

"But he said—"

"You need to stop taking every man's word as gospel," he snapped.

I gulped and looked away, but his hand left my waist and grabbed my jaw, making me look at him through the mirror in the corner.

"As long as you keep quiet, we will be fine." His tone was assuring, but his grip was a warning.

"What if we aren't fine?" I blurted. "Will you kill him for me?"

That brought a smile to Arkady's face, but his eyes didn't change. "My dear, after all I have done for you thus far, you *still* question my loyalty?"

"I mean it."

"So do I." His smile dropped, and so did his hand, releasing me from his grip. "Your mother rang for you. It is best you go out and make an appearance." He backed toward the door. "I fear you may be too fussy to keep cooped up here."

I turned to him. "Will you come with me?"

"No." A finality in his words. "I have full confidence that you can handle them."

"So you're abandoning me?"

"I am not abandoning you, this is an exercise," he emphasized. "Play the game, play nice, so they give you the things you need—knowledge or material."

I must have given him a pleading look, because he laughed after I looked his way.

"Go on, I know you're smart. Apologize for raising your voice but not for what you said or believe to be true. I have full faith in you."

He was right, I knew that. But it was an idea I hadn't had much time to swallow. Would they see right through the act? At this point, they might become suspicious if I began to act civilly. The only way to know for certain was to test my skills in the field.

"How are you and Arkady?"

I looked up from my dinner at Félice's question. My expression must have given her the answer she sought.

The women of my family were gathered in Cosette's home tonight. The charity gala would be soon, which meant my mother was about to become *insufferable*. It was a miracle if you could escape the gala season with anything less than five fittings. I was grateful my presence was only required for those, as Cosette helped mother with the rest of the planning. I was under the impression that she liked it, it gave her something to do. She took after our mother when it came to an excitement for design. I couldn't help but wonder if it was a distraction from the sudden changes.

I suppose that is why we met at her place more often now, to help her nest and settle into what would be her new life, with a new family, new ambitions. Sometimes I wondered if that was what Cosette wanted . . . or if it was what *Mother* told her she wanted.

No matter, today was for happy thoughts. Cosette was like a thoroughbred, high-strung and easy to perturb, so none of those concerns would manifest today.

"Petre," my mother's voice piped up from the end of the table, "could you come help me place something in the nursery?"

I glanced at Félice and Cosette, both whispering among each other as if to pretend not to hear. I nodded and placed my napkin on the table to rise.

My mother and I left the dining room and went up the stairs, the sounds of chatter floating away as we removed ourselves from our company.

The nursery was the first room that greeted you upon arriving on the second floor. It was a ghastly mint color. It reminded me of an infection I got when I was an adolescent. I cut myself on the jagged wood of a ladder at the theater.

"How is your little issue?" My mother's voice cut through the room. She smoothed her fine fingers over a blanket in the nursery chair before sitting down.

"There is no issue."

"If there weren't an issue, you wouldn't have gone to your father."

"It is handled."

"Is your husband aware?"

"Extremely."

She nodded in calm understanding as she picked at the woven fabric of the blanket, her gaze floating to the crib next to where I stood. It was like she couldn't bear to look me in the eye, as if I'd greatly offended her personally, despite it having nothing to do with her.

"Why isn't he handling it?" Her eyes finally met mine, but they were absent of any sign of lenience. "Surely that's why you came to us."

"He is handling as much as he can."

"You should have listened to us. We suggested Mr. Carlisle for a reason."

"I didn't want that—"

"Want, want, *want*," she mocked, shooting up from her seat to approach me, shoving an accusatory finger at me, her neck craning like a mantis. "You selfish brat! Everything we do is for our family; you owe everything to the sacrifices your father made—"

"You mean, *I* made." It was hard to hold back a sneer. "*Félice* made. *Cosette* made."

My mother's lip twitched, as did her eye when I stared long enough. I held her gaze, waiting for a hit. Her lip curled slightly. "Everyone must make sacrifices, my dear."

"Your own daughters?" My voice was stern, but I didn't dare go above her tone. "I suppose that *is* a sacrifice. Veal for the wolves."

"And here you are, unable to please the husband you chose for yourself. Must be poor-quality veal," she taunted, her posture returning more upright, tucking away the monster she hid within. "Perhaps we should allow you back to the ballet, maybe you're out of practice."

I bit back what I wanted to say; it wasn't going to change her mind or how she felt. "If rumors start in the papers about my connection to Vincent, the ballet, it'll be to your detriment."

Her laugh was melodic and filled with poison. She shook her head and smiled. "I disagree. I think you should sensationalize it more."

"You want me to admit to escorting?"

"No, that's not what I said." She turned her attention to the dresser, opening the drawers and fussing with the neatly folded blankets and clothing. "I *said* sensationalize it. Lean into the image, the iconography. You could have a whole career and not do any real work."

"How so?"

"Well, if you're worried about being seen as a whore, you already have half the reputation from the ballet. Become a sex symbol instead. Accept it. You and Arkady are a painfully stunning pair. Use those pretty faces properly and you'll find it most profitable."

"You want me to sell my integrity instead of my body."

"It is all the same, my sweet pet." She sighed. "You should know this." She then turned to me, a newspaper clipping in hand.

She slapped it across my palm. This silly slip of paper. A simple piece of pulp and ink. It should have been as insignificant as a billowy piece of ash breaking away from a bonfire.

So how come I could feel only *disdain*?

The clipping heading:

> FORMER MISS DE VILLIER WON BY NEW YORK'S NEW UP-AND-COMING ARTISAN. SECRET WEDDING DETAILS LEAKED EXCLUSIVELY.

The title was just the beginning. Below was an article, my portrait illustrated—but so were the individual undergarments I wore on the day of my wedding.

The article detailed their fabric, the cut, the bones of my corset. All done without even a lick of my knowledge.

All I could do was look at my mother, mouth agape. At a true loss for words, and the manifestation of too many intrusive thoughts I wished upon her in that moment.

"Did you think I would let you marry so inconveniently without *some* benefit?" She laughed, her eyes raking me up and down. "You should be happy. The whole city will know your name."

"Because of one article?"

"No, my dear hermit"—she went to pass me, squeezing my shoulder—"but if the tabloid says you're infamous, the public believes it, intrigued by this new name. Because why would they put a nobody in the paper? They won't—unless it's paid for. And as your name is seen more and more, they will remember you. This week, you're a headline. The next, you're an icon. It takes time to build infamy. Do you not keep up with the tabloids anymore? Now is a great time to start."

The paper crumpled in my clenched fist, rolling her hand off my shoulder. There was nothing left I could say to her. Nothing that wouldn't accompany my hands around her throat.

CHAPTER TWENTY-ONE

The Artisan

All I could say about the day was that it was productive. It was no secret that I lost time in the studio more often than anywhere else, but I hadn't realized how late it was.

The town house looked rather strange compared to its neighbors on the outside. Most of these homes were warily lit with hints of curtains or bustling company concealed within—but Petronille's home was dark. Only one homely light on the ground floor, the rest of the building seeming utterly void, leaving an ominous absence of human life.

A soft hum of the gramophone welcomed me after I cracked the front door. A classical piece, a Russian composer. Around the corner in the living room, she sat with her knees pulled to her chest as she wrote in a journal. For once, she looked truly delicate, vulnerable, less like the combative creature that clawed its way out of her.

She did not demand anything of me upon coming home. Which was a relief, but equally a concern.

"Petronille?"

Her eyes shifted subtly from her paper before returning to it, not even bothering to move her head.

"Don't be like that." I caught my tongue clicking against my teeth as my bag and coat slipped from my shoulder and to the spare chair in the corner. "Something is wrong."

"When has it been right?"

"Pessimistic." I shoved my hands in my trouser pockets, standing before the curled-up woman.

She continued to write, though it was in French, so not very helpful in deciphering her current state of mind.

"Is there something I can do?" I offered.

"No."

"You want something, or else you wouldn't be pouting."

"I want many things."

"Name one."

Her diary snapped shut. "I want to not be repulsive."

"Repulsive? Are you referring to your attitude as of late?" I teased, but I caught a sharp twitch of her lip, then I noticed the light dappling her waterline—tears.

"Why else would my husband avoid me until he is forced to talk to me?"

"Is that right?"

"You tease me. Constantly. Leading me on. Pretending to be interested, only to leave me sitting with my palms open and not a crumb given."

"What do you mean?"

She raised her voice. "You know exactly what I mean!"

"I promise you, I don't."

"The fruit, the touching, the attention—" She gulped. "You can't even go all the way!"

"I see my efforts are *most* appreciated."

"You are a horrid rake, and you know it!" She stood from her seat, but I snatched her wrists.

"A rake?"

"Let me go."

"Where is this coming from?"

"Nowhere. It comes from *you*! You insufferable tease!"

"Petre." I searched her face for some indication of drunkenness, but there were no cups or wine in sight. She was drunk on insecurity fermented by her own delusions. "Tell me"—I spoke steadily—"why do you think you disgust me?"

"Because you won't . . ."

"Won't what? Tell me when."

"Our wedding night, you—"

"You were drunk."

"And when we were right there on the couch—"

"Barely conscious."

"But then the fruit—"

"Petre!" I shouted, jolting her slightly in my grip. "You couldn't even ask me for what you wanted. How was I supposed to assume you wanted anything more?"

I saw the knot bob in her throat, her lip twitching again. Like the words she was choking on, the words she was going to say before biting them back.

"When I greet you, it is like I cast some sort of shadow over your mood. How am I to guess what you want from me when I'm not even welcome in your dwelling?"

"I just . . ." Her words trailed off.

"I don't know what you're used to, and you are under no obligation to tell me, but do not mistake me for whatever sad, limp pieces of flesh who have had you before."

All she did was stare at the spot on the couch.

I grabbed her jaw, forcing her to look me in the eye. "Stop doing that to yourself. While I don't think you're ready, I also think letting you believe you are something disgusting would be a disservice to you."

The way she looked at me then was something I would never forget. I'd never seen her look so *hungry*. Eating every word I spoke until she craved more when they stopped.

She was silent for a moment, but that was how I knew she was sober. I took in everything, from the feeling of her skin warming under my palm to the way her pupils grew large, in danger of sucking me into the deep-brown abyss that were her eyes.

"Do you believe me to be awake now?" She drew nearer. "Conscious enough?" She stood on her toes to close the distance. Slow enough that it felt like she may have been scared I'd run off. "Sober to your liking?"

Her lips just barely touched mine, inviting me without making the move herself. They were soft and pink like fresh marmalade, possibly tasting like it too. I had to know.

I kissed her gently, closing my eyes to fully feel it. My hand at her jaw smoothed over her cheek and to her head, letting my fingers weave through the fine silk.

Her gasp was so gentle, it made my heart hurt.

Her nightgown was silk, thin enough that I could feel the heat of her body on my palm, only making me hold tighter as if she would melt through my fingers.

I found myself picturing her body again, the way it was splayed out on the table. I couldn't remember exactly where her beauty marks were, but I remembered they were favorably placed. The pattern of her birthmark was tawny, or was it more of an earthy soil? It only made me want to see her like that again. To take another look. To *remember*. Just one more peek to hold me over.

She removed her lips from mine to trail them across my neck, gently sucking on my skin.

I closed my eyes and tilted my head, allowing it for now.

I needed her under me, on me, clinging to me. I wanted her nails to dig into my skin and pull out every organ. Her breasts pressing against my chest made me want to squeeze them, to grab her and crush her bones in my grasp.

"Stop," I gasped, not sure if I was willing to create distance.

She kept kissing, nipping gently, and I didn't let her go.

"Stop . . ."

She bit my shoulder with her teeth this time.

"Petre!" I grabbed her hair and tugged her head back, tears in her eyes and a smirk on the corner of her lips. Then her soft lips curled into a cruel smile.

"Why is it so hard for you to accept me?" she asked with playful humor in her tone, but behind it was a sharp simmering of rejection.

"I'm afraid." I took a deep breath to control myself. "Of hurting you."

"Why?" She raised a brow. "Do you think about hurting me often, Arkady?"

I let out a shaky breath, though it may have been a slight tremor from my body and the dopamine that question prompted.

Against her lips, I whispered, "All the *godforsaken* time."

"I don't believe you," she said, a daring sharpness to her words. "Be rough with me. I am not a porcelain plate, I won't break."

"You're not ready."

"Try me." She was breathless, desperate to prove herself. "Pleasing a man is an art, but it isn't hard. Let me have my hand."

"I don't think you want me to be the one to tame that attitude of yours, I promise," I hissed, my grip tightening on her hair.

"By God, I'm *begging*!" Her tone was exasperated with a bratty edge as her knees nearly buckled from the thought.

Fine, if this is what she wants.

Like steering the reins of a horse, I yanked her by her hair, forcing her to her knees.

She yelped when I let go, looking up at me from the ground. Those big brown eyes, which I thought would hold malice, were filled with a hungry determination that I could only imagine was fueled by my stubbornness.

"Let us use this as a lesson." I stood straight. "Do what you wish—but you must tell me what you're doing as you do it."

She frowned, her brow twitching. "Must everything be a lesson?"

"How else do you tame a brat like you? Structure is important," I teased.

She balled her fists on her thighs, her eyes falling lower. Forcing her to restrain herself unless she could commit to an action was the only way I thought she might think before she acted on her impulses. An alienist had taught me this at one point, though it was for intrusive impulsions rather than hypersexuality. I was sure it worked all the same. Saying a thought out loud could put it into perspective.

She touched my pant leg, squeezing my thigh, her lips moving but no sound audible.

"What was that, dear?"

She glared at me, eyes squinting as if to figure out if this were a ruse or genuine—it was undoubtedly both.

"I'm touching you."

"Where?"

"Do you have eyes?"

"Where?" I repeated.

"Your thigh." She glanced back at her hand, then her other joined it on my other leg. "Both of my hands are touching your thighs."

I nodded at her to continue, reaching into my pocket for my pipe.

She watched me relight the old tobacco, taking small puffs to foster the embers.

Leisurely, I took in a breath, blowing the smoke down at her.

She coughed, her nose wrinkled like she was about to sneeze.

"If you're done, we stop here." I tilted her wrist up, checking her dainty timepiece before dropping it, her hand landing in her lap. "It's been ten minutes already."

"I'm . . ." Jaw tensed, she crawled closer on her knees. She placed her hands to the front of my hips, one of her fingers hooking into my waistband. She stared up at me through those featherlight lashes, placing her cheek on my thigh. "I'm touching your belt, my head is in your lap." She took a deep breath, her hand smoothing over the front of my pants, cupping my cock through the fabric. "I'm holding you."

"Say it."

"Your *cock* is in my hand, and you're getting stiff." She smirked as if she'd achieved some grand victory.

I took another inhale of smoke. "I am a man, after all. What will you do about it?" I tilted my head at her and moved my foot forward, the leather shoe slipping under her gown. Then I tipped my foot up on its heel.

She flinched, and so did her grip on my cock. Just that reaction made me twitch; I was sure she felt it.

Her ivory cheeks steadily became red, the color spreading as she let the actions ferment.

"Please"—she was glowing, glassy-eyed, and squirming on my shoe—"let me use my mouth."

"What for?"

"I . . ." She twitched as I slid my shoe between her legs more. "I want to feel your cock pulsing at the back of my throat, hot and eager." Her voice dropped, rich like an imported cigar. She cupped her hand between my legs and placed her lips on the prominent bulge.

God, the mouth on this woman makes me think I should attend a confessional just for hearing her.

Her hips rolled against my ankle, her abdomen flush with my shin.

"You know, they say positive reinforcement works just as well as conditioning," she started, her eyes fluttering up. "Do I get a reward for this lesson?"

"Do you deserve one?"

She swallowed whatever clever words she'd reserved for her next response.

"I would think the simple friction against my shoe would be enough for you," I taunted, keeping a careful eye on her expression. "It's quite a sight to see the pampered pet groveling, quivering with even the most meager contact. Why don't you finish? Is that reward enough for you?"

The corner of her lip twitched, her hands balling in my pants. With the most wicked smile, she said, "No, I want more."

"What you want and what you are allowed are two different things, princess." I laughed. "Do you need a moment to correct your attitude and try again?"

"Or what?" She smirked. "Will you punish me?"

"I may." I shrugged, though my veil of nonchalance was being whipped away with every retort. "Do as you are told."

"No." The single word was breathless, like the resistance was just as arousing as the friction between her legs.

"Very well, then." I reached down, yanking her up by her nightgown.

I stepped back, sitting at the far end of the sofa. With one tug, she was over my lap, her torso over the arm of the couch.

The silk was soft in my hand as I ran my palm flat against the backs of her thighs, her hips in my lap. The silk lifted, her bare skin exposed. I paused, just in case, but there wasn't even an utterance from her. Though her legs were shaking in anticipation.

She was finally getting her reward.

I brought my hand down across her backside. She yelped, clutching the edge of the sofa. A red impression of my hand formed.

"See what you do? Princess treatment only comes when you're good." My hand came down again, and the sound that came from her was like a mewl. "Brats get a special type of handling."

"Is that what I am?" She smirked over her shoulder, the absolute bliss on her face making her appear nearly drunk, glassy eyes and all. "Your hand is soft, you're going far too easy."

My hand raised, coming down on her backside again with a sharp slap, the sound cracking through the air.

Her legs tensed, then relaxed again. "Light as a feather," she moaned. "It tickles."

Slap!

Her nails dug into the sofa, her faced burying into the pillow to muffle her yell. "Again, my God, I can *almost* feel it! When will the discipline begin—"

My fingers in her hair, pulling her head slightly back. Far enough where it was difficult for her to talk, not too far where she couldn't breathe.

I leaned toward her face. "Maybe next time I should find something to put in that *mouth* of yours."

Her lips slowly formed the daring impression of the word *please*.

"Take it without talking," I whispered.

Slap!

She flinched, biting her lip.

"What a good girl," I praised.

Slap!

Her eyes clenched shut, a tear sprinting down her cheek.

I raised my hand and paused.

"Look at me, dear," I instructed sweetly.

She opened her eyes; they were red but not distressed.

"You're doing so well. Can you take one more?" While this was entertaining, and putting me at my own limit, I needed to know if she wanted it.

She swallowed thickly, a silent nod with eagerness.

The last slap cracked through the air, my hand maintaining contact with her skin before slipping between her legs.

I glanced over her backside, completely red; it would certainly be bruised tomorrow. As my fingers slipped between her legs, I smirked.

"Ah, it seems like you claimed your reward before we finished." My fingers played with the wetness between her legs.

I let go of her hair, brushing my fingers through to undo any knots I may have created, rolling her over in my lap.

She slumped with her head on the decorative pillow, her face and chest as red as her behind. Even her breathing was deep and therapeutic, like she was recovering from some great undertaking.

"Did I tire you enough to retire to bed early?" I pulled her gown over her legs, shifting beneath her into a more comfortable position.

She simply nodded, unable to open her eyes any longer. Even as I held her, she trembled slightly, charged from the shock of orgasming on her own. She seemed comfortable enough here, so I didn't move. I reached to the side, grabbing a sketchbook from the small pile on the floor, then dug between the cushions for my pencil.

If I would be stuck serving as her sleep cushion, I may as well take the time to relax too.

CHAPTER TWENTY-TWO

The Performer

Attendance for any of my mother's events was mandatory. No negotiation.

Her gatherings were the place to be, and if you weren't there, it was a laughable offense. Anyone who thought they were anyone important would be there. In her defense, this cruel sense of entertainment and social engagement wasn't for naught. The couture we wore would be auctioned, along with the other art pieces on display for the evening. The proceeds from the gala today were going to the orphans of Saint Lucia's in Hudson Valley.

In the receiving room, people would arrive and be greeted before entering the ballroom. The entertainment room was cleared of any furnishings to make room for a full band, the piano, and small banquet tables for a champagne tower and a display of sweets. An auctioneer placed a podium at the base of the grand staircase. On the plateau joining the twin staircases leading down to the first floor were various items laid out for buyers to prepare their wallets: five sculptures, twenty paintings, and a few miscellaneous showpieces.

The gathering was more formal than her last few, with full catering that had had the staff holed up in the serving kitchen since morning. Many of her friends attended—from editorialists to the press to socialites to Mother's tearoom birds—as well as Father's business partners. They all came, no matter what. Though, by the way people dressed, I would have assumed this was a gala for some sort of royalty, which we were not, despite my mother's ambitions.

My dress for the evening was a rich cream silk with layered sleeves that hung just off the shoulder, collarbones only serving to complement the accessories around my neck, choking me. The earrings dangled, tickling my skin as they swung. A pattern of dusty-pink flowers was embroidered into the dress, real blossoms pinned in front of my bodice. A matching fan in my hand and white lambskin opera gloves covered me up to mid-forearm. At least if I felt silly wearing something so extravagant, I remembered that my sisters would be wearing dresses similar in extravagance and color somewhere within the gathering.

It was so much, too stuffy, though that could just be the flowers. At least if I cried from overstimulation, I could blame it on the pollen.

"Ah, how fitting for a blooming flower!" a voice sounded from behind me. I tore my attention from my mother beside me to an older gentleman confidently approaching. He cupped my hand and kissed the knuckle of my glove. "It feels like ages since I've seen you," he said, his smile making him appear red in the face as he greeted my mother next, touching cheeks.

"Blooming just in time for spring," my mother piped up, shooting me a look as if to remind me of my manners.

"How generous a compliment." I could feel the tension in my jaw.

"And now I hear you are a wife!" he exclaimed, then turned again to my mother. "Congratulations."

Something about the way my mother received congratulatory remarks instead of myself always sat a bit sour in my stomach. Though it suited her, and she accepted them like a gluttonous hen picking at someone else's dough.

Like flies to sweet cream on a summer's day, the initial greeting invited more to our midst. People nudged their shoulders so they could physically participate in conversation with my mother. Offering sweet words of gratification and awe for whatever they could notice, to fluff her ego like a staff to her pillow.

Soon there was a shoulder in my way, then a torso, until, in their infatuation, I was physically removed from the conversation entirely. As telling as it was about my place in my own family's home, it was an excuse to leave the swarming flies who salivated for a bite of my mother's change purse.

I didn't know many here, only a few familiar faces. Business partners, a banker, possibly an old neighbor. The younger women in attendance were tethered to their mothers like foals to a broodmare's teat, waiting to be weaned off and handed to the next eligible man.

The ballroom was newly constructed, not even five years old. The wood floors had barely a scratch or a scuff, a fresh coat of white paint freshened the walls, and a new set of paintings garnished the room.

The house was always under some sort of work, additions upon additions. I supposed there wasn't much else to do when you had an overactive wife who was instructed to stay at home with an entire reserve at her disposal. My mother didn't spend money because she needed to. When you'd hoarded the amount of wealth my parents had, you didn't spend out of necessity. You became something of a peacock, flaunting it for fun or assuming status. People tended to take you seriously when you could sign checks without looking at the price.

"I'm impressed you're still sober."

I glared over my shoulder at none other than Arkady. He was dressed decently, but clearly it was something new. I'd never imagined him in a suit this expensive, not without some paint stains or clay dust. He raised a brow as he lifted his champagne flute to his lips, then extended an extra one to me.

"Are you trying to tempt me?" I teased, plucking the glass from his hand and turning away to spectate the crowd.

"Not that it takes much convincing," he said from beside me, joining me in my voyeurism.

"I wouldn't mind temptation. Even from someone as stale as you."

"It seems like I do well enough, based on your advances."

"It means nothing." I sipped. "I am just bored."

He leaned down to my ear, his lips impossibly close. "Denial is an adorable color on you. Wear it more often for me, will you?"

"Insufferable."

"Yes, you must be tortured." He rolled his eyes. "Who are you hoping wins you tonight?"

"Excuse me?" I snapped.

"I overheard your mother talking about the auction for your attire." He cocked his head with a smirk. "What did you think I meant?"

I smiled through a clenched jaw. "Yes, very funny for a man who can't afford to bid."

"Who said I can't afford it?" He loomed closer. "Or are you assuming I don't think you're worth bidding on?"

I blew a frustrated breath from my nose, snapping my neck toward the crowd.

Arkady leaned down, brushing the hair away from my shoulder. "If I were you, I'd start hoping I win," he hummed in my ear, "because if I'm going to spend that much money, I'm expecting more than just the dress."

His words made me dizzy. I couldn't tell if this was just another one of his teases. When I turned to look at him, he was gone, disappearing into the crowd.

"Casanova," I mumbled into my cup, suddenly losing the need to drink any spirits when his words alone sent me into a head high.

As more people arrived, music played in tandem. Staff with trays of bites to eat fluttered around to the congregating groups like bees in a garden, prompting the guests to indulge. The tower of champagne glasses was poured, and the golden liquid glistened as it cascaded down the crystal.

No matter how many people I conversed with, I couldn't stop thinking about Arkady. What was he doing? Was he talking politely with a stranger? Telling a group a wild story about his figure studies? Talking to a woman about one of the sculptures being auctioned tonight?

Just the thought put my stomach in an upset, my mouth a bit too dry to partake in any drinking with much joy.

I scanned the crowd, looking for the brunet. It might have been a bout of sudden loneliness, but I wanted to speak with him.

Among the chattering faces, I spotted him. He looked charming and light, unlike how he really was—indifferent to such pleasantries. If only he would put on such an act for me. Perhaps it was an honor to know what he was really like. I wished he would lie to me, pretend for *me*.

Maybe that was why I wanted it. Because I wanted him to know I was not as unpleasant as our interactions suggested, that I *did* want it to work.

Just as I feared, as I drew closer, I realized he was talking to another woman. She was a dazzling thing, in a dress of fine making and colors that suited her perfectly. Her smile was especially delightful, her laugh melodic. And then there was Arkady . . . He was laughing with her, perfectly at ease.

It made me sick to my stomach.

I glanced down at my trembling glass, my reflection bubbling in the untouched champagne. I abandoned it on a passing serving tray.

Why is it so difficult for you to be pleasant? My mother's voice rang in my subconscious, making me wince at the shrill tone.

It might be clichéd to say I forgot to breathe, but in all honesty, the rush of air in my lungs made me nauseous, and breathing felt all too manual of a process.

Breathe in, hold, exhale.

A gravity weighed on my ankles, my wrists, my heart. Everything was just so *heavy*. An inescapable sinking.

"Petre."

I heard Arkady's voice, but my legs carried me elsewhere, anywhere but there. I no longer had the energy to keep up a facade, a smile, an exterior. I wanted to go home, to curl up in the corner of my living room with my journal. A moth or two to keep me company.

Before I could exit the room, I was grabbed by the waist and swept onto the dance floor. A waltz of many couples twisted around each other like a well-oiled clock, with a cog such as myself being accidentally shuffled in during the exchanging of partners.

Every face on the floor was a blur, as all I could do was remember how he'd looked with someone other than me. I kept my face down, the murmuring of voices and music fading in and out as the room glimmered around me, the peripheral fading, helpless but to focus on the cravat of a stranger.

I was handed off again like a marionette changing hands as one puppeteer swaps with another. It was nice, as all I had to manage were the movements. It was less awkward than wallowing in my own misery by the liquor.

Another change of partners; this one gripped me tighter.

"You won't make it up the stairs tonight if you keep up such a dance." Arkady's voice in my ear, his hand gentle at my waist, but his grip on my hand rather tight as if he was unwilling to hand me away during the next exchange.

"I'm sure I won't be the only woman who complains of such a thing."

"Are you jealous?" If he was offended, he didn't let me know.

"Of course not! We are going our own way, living our own lives." I stuck my chin in the air, finally looking upon his face. "I understand the arrangement."

He was so handsome, even when he was angry with me. "You're drumming up a promiscuous character tonight. Leave the poor champagne to rest. The other guests may have a fighting chance in the race to complete inebriation."

"Is that what you think of me?" I tipped my head at him and laughed. "It seems to be what everyone else thinks too!"

His brow furrowed, pinching as he looked at me. He glanced around us as if he thought people could hear. "What are you talking about?"

"Oh? It seems you're the last in Manhattan to know." I traced my gloved finger up his chest and along his neck, making him flinch at the sudden touches. "Everyone knows what I wore the day you rejected me, on our first night home. The irony is, old men and young women get off on the idea of what I was wearing when I was fucked by the handsome artisan, only for the reality to be much more depressing." I sighed, tracing my finger over the place I'd bitten him the night before. "You poor thing, stuck with a salacious creature like me."

Arkady yanked me as we took a sharp turn, then the tune of the dance changed. We stood there still, only briefly. Close enough to hear each other's breaths, such an intimate moment for a busy occasion. The band tuned up and the new pace was set.

He looked down at me, his thumb smoothing across my knuckles as he held my hand. "Sometimes we have to play a part to get what we want."

"I don't want to pretend—"

"You're a performer, Petronille." He squeezed my hand, leading me to the floor again. "People will see you exactly how *they* want to, might as well enjoy it in the meantime."

His words made me straighten my back a bit, allowing him to lead me.

The trill of the band changed, a new dance. Each step matched a note, Arkady circling me, with his hand smoothing around my waist as he did so.

I followed him with my eyes only. I didn't wish to seem wanting.

Even when I managed to find his gaze snagged on mine, it was different than before. No smugness but a hint of a challenge in his look. From there, we didn't part.

Our hands touched; I wished my gloves weren't a barrier. It wasn't the touch I craved, it was the connection. Since meeting, there'd been nothing but walls, those built by the two of us against each other. It was time for a change.

We neared, and he held me close, properly. I rested my hand in his, relaxing my posture—a relinquishment of any momentary mistrust.

My chest pressed against his. So improper, uncultivated, but it didn't matter.

Our hearts pounded enough to feel, banging as if they wanted to escape and run off together right there. Every touch, despite being sparse, was electric.

People were looking; the thin hairs on my neck and arms told me so. Ironically, it had the same thrill of a stage.

Arkady's touches brought me back, and there it was. A smile. Pure and absent of malice.

"Is something funny?" I whispered.

He shook his head. "You're radiant."

A bell chimed, dampening the music of the instruments and inviting a chorus of excitable chatter.

Even when I tried to pull away, Arkady's grip on me tightened. My breath caught in my throat. The crowd began to move to the adjacent room, yet he held me there still. His eyes looked sincere, like there was something else he wanted to say.

I waited for it, but it never came. Like it caught in his throat and dissolved the instant my attention was drawn.

"I have to go." I twisted my wrist in his grip.

He snatched it, but the touch was gentler as he raised my hand to his lips. He kissed the back. "Then I suppose I shall let you go"—he studied me for a moment—"for now."

He released me, but I was already overheating. Though I think it had to do with being ripped from such a moment of bliss and thrust back into the reality that exists outside of ourselves.

The crowd gathered at the bottom of the stairs, a sea of leering strangers. The auctioneer poised at his podium with a gavel and papers. The first items were to be auctioned in order of starting bids, lowest to highest. I positioned myself beside the banister with my sisters and my mother, ready for our turns when they would come.

Félice forced her hand in mine, squeezing. I looked at her, and she only raised a single brow. I furrowed mine at her to ask why she was looking at me. She swiped a finger across her undereye in a gesture.

I blinked and touched my face. It was hot and wet; a tear had slipped through. I wiped my cheek and sighed. Félice squeezed my hand again, this time in silent reassurance rather than to seek my attention.

The auction items went fast, and not just because of the quick speech and shuffling of the crowd. There was a painting from my parents' private collection. Miscellaneous accessories, jewelry, antiques, and more fine art than the most esteemed museums. Lastly, a statue of a couple dancing collected from Arkady. Did it hurt him, seeing his work resold, or was it a badge of pride?

Was he watching?

Cosette was first to the stage after the sculptures. Her figure was immaculate. She was a slight bit taller than I was, her pregnant belly carrying low, which complemented the sweeping fabric of her gown that went straight to the floor with little bunching or draping. Her train connected high in the back like a cape. A soft dusty pink that matched her cheeks and a few of the flowers in her hair. If anyone was having a good time, it was her. She smiled and walked in a circle, displaying the dress before the auctioneer announced the starting bid.

This was when the *real* auction started. It was funny seeing grown men fight over a dress, throwing out life-changing amounts of money for something they had no use for, perhaps an outfit their mistress might wear for them once and never again.

I shouldn't have judged; this was for charity, after all. Maybe some of these men were honest and would gift it to their wives, maybe daughters. But I couldn't be blamed for my pessimism, as they'd all been spotted not less than five times at the ballet. Some seats even had their names on them.

Félice let go of my hand. She was next.

The farther she got from me, the more my ears began to ring. The crowd got taller, the room larger—or maybe it only appeared that way from feeling all too small. I tried not to look at the faces, my environment. It would be my turn soon. One more performance and I could go home. I could discard the dress, the jewelry, the tight hairstyle, this life.

I wouldn't do another year of this. No, I was not in the business of pleasing people any longer.

The auctioneer's voice cut through, announcing my own cue to enter. I took a hard swallow to ease the dry despair, then climbed up the long steps until I reached the plateau, letting my gown settle at its intended length. I stepped in a small circle, making sure the short train would gather gracefully behind me on the floor.

It took a moment to build up the courage for my eyes to leave the pattern on the carpet, slowly focusing on the crowd ahead. A sea of people, glittering with wealth and inflated self-importance.

"Opening the bidding at three hundred," the auctioneer called.

Immediately, little white numbered paddles popped up all through the mass of people. They began bobbing up and down. If I squinted, it could look something like prairie dogs peeking from their burrows.

The squabbling fast-talk of the auctioneer registered so foreign, it might as well have been a separate language, aside from the "sprouts of numbers," as he called them.

Four hundred, six hundred, one thousand.

All I needed to do was stand, smile, and be quiet.

I scanned the crowd. Did Arkady see me from wherever he was? Was he off getting a drink? Talking with someone else while he waited? It was no surprise that he hated gatherings; I suspected he may have been as claustrophobic as myself.

The numbers began to slow, five thousand so far.

Finally, it's almost over.

To my surprise, a paddle went up.

Attached to the little numbered sign was Arkady.

My brows nearly creased together before I realized people were still watching.

Is he dragging this out on purpose?

More paddles went up, the auctioneer picking up excitement as the numbers rose. Each time they slowed, Arkady's paddle would rise again. Another round of signs and chatter of excitement as the numbers rose. Again and again he would repeat, eyeing some of the bidders. I noticed the remaining bidders were only men.

It was then I understood.

They were bidding against Arkady for the fun of it.

If only they realized that Arkady didn't care, not one bit, and he was playing *them* like fiddles. These men were brittle, fragile. Getting off on some odd display of dominance, of wealth, of reputation. Throwing money around for a quick ruse.

"Twelve thousand," the auctioneer rang.

Once, twice, over.

It was over.

CHAPTER TWENTY-THREE

The Performer

It was like the minute my heel hit the bottom of the stairs, I was snatched in an instant.

"Have you gained weight?" my mother hissed, pinching the side of the dress, then my arm, to test her hypothesis.

No response at all was better for mean-spirited interrogations.

The crowd dispersed around us. The staff tagged, moved, and prepared the art pieces for their intended destinations after the event. Félice and Cosette had already had their costumes changed so they could gather the dresses for the proud new owners.

"Come." My mother dragged me toward the hallway, a spare dress draped over her arm. "We should get this off of you before you ruin it."

"Petre." Arkady grabbed my opposite arm.

My mother's brow twitched, scrutinizing the interruption.

"Allow me, Mrs. De Villier," he offered, a kind smile to pair with it. "You have been working so hard on such a stellar event, perhaps you should take time to enjoy it as much as everyone else."

Her face contorted. First it was tense, then it relaxed into something more accepting. Her grip loosened on my arm, my skin red where her manicured claws laid into me. She let out a bashful huff, smoothing imaginary stray hairs.

"I suppose you're right." She sighed happily, the beast pleased with his flattery. "But please use extra care when handling the dress."

"I will handle her with great care." Arkady smiled pleasantly, pulling me along before she could make any more requests.

"What are you doing?" I hissed at him.

"Undressing you. You really don't listen to your surroundings, do you?"

We ducked into my father's library study, the large door chittering as the new wood settled back into its place.

The room was exhausting to look at. Too claustrophobic, even when organized. Despite its craftsmanship, it still had the infant scent of linseed oil on the carpentry. The books were all new. Not one cracked spine, not one dog-eared page, not even the smell of well-aged paper.

A wealth of money was easy to fake, but a wealth of knowledge was much harder.

"I thought you'd burst into tears out there." Arkady helped himself to some scotch from the bar cart in the corner.

"As I'm sure you would have taken great joy in the spectacle," I snapped.

"I guess we will never know, will we?" He turned, sipping the liquor. Though he suddenly became distracted with the taste, second-guessing his drink.

"We have our whole lives to try." I crossed my arms, remaining beside the door.

"Time is on our side, luckily." He placed the glass on the corner of my father's desk, tilting it with a single finger to watch the light from the gas lamp dance through the crystal. "An eternity to get under each other's skin."

"Did you not hesitate the last time you saw *my* skin?" The words came so quick, it was like I hadn't even said them.

He smiled at that, but it was not a pleasant one. Irked, he abandoned his drink for a quick approach.

I grabbed the door handle.

He slammed it back shut, already towering over me, holding it closed no matter how hard I yanked.

"Self-deprecation is second nature. It lives under your skin, makes a home in your heart until it rots in comfort." His voice vibrated in my ear, his face so close. His chest was pressed firmly against my back, with my white-knuckled hand gripping the handle of the door still. "That is, only if you allow it."

"Will you, then?"

He didn't speak.

"Will you allow it to make a home in me, Arkady? Or will you offer another creature habit to replace it? To fill the void before it can burrow?"

Silence.

It was impossible to keep still, to sit in the vacant air, the awkwardness. I wanted to speak again; it was harder to keep quiet. *He* didn't need to speak. He wanted to hear what my heart would say if squeezed hard enough.

Movement at my neck, his free hand startling me as he pulled my hair aside. His fingertips brushed between my shoulders, then over the hem of the dress backing.

I bit my lip, not daring to speak, waiting for him to do something. *Anything.*

I pushed against the door, but he leaned closer, trapping me.

"Where do you think you're going?" His hand smoothed down the back of the dress. "Can't have you running off with something so expensive."

"You make it seem like you want to steal it."

"I have no use for dresses."

"Thieves don't steal for utility, they steal for value."

He leaned down, his face by my ear. "There is something here worth the trouble of stealing, and it isn't the dress."

He grabbed the back of my neck gently, pinning me against the door like a scruffed animal.

"Arkady!" I squeaked.

"Hush," he scolded, putting pressure on my neck before sliding his hand down. "You wouldn't want them to hear you, would you?"

My words hitched in my throat.

The guests on the other side of the door were talking, champagne glasses chiming nearly as loudly as the laughter. My mother would be hovering close by like a buzzard, no doubt. My father would be lost somewhere, anywhere but beside his wife.

Arkady pinched the seam together, releasing the small clasps down my back, his knuckles brushing over my skin before slowing to a stop.

Warmth on the nape of my neck, his lips. A shaky breath audible, unsure if it was mine or his.

The rough skin of his hand pressed flush against me, smoothing over the bare skin. Slight pressure on the tips of his fingers as if to mentally note every dip and curve. Was this what it was like to be one of his sculptures? Oh, to be art. To be the object of his infatuation.

"Isn't this what you want, Petre?" His words were soft, sincere. "The luxury of being desired?"

"Not just to be desired," I breathed, glancing over my shoulder at him.

His eyes caught mine, and he leaned in. "Will you let me?"

I neglected to answer, we were too close. Claustrophobic. If I spoke, our lips would touch with no room for words.

And I was right.

Our lips met, skittish at first, then with more confidence, more reassurance, with every breath we could steal. He began pulling my dress up the front, digging desperately until he could finally touch my skin, cupping his palm between my legs, the warmth nearly melting me in more ways than one.

I gasped, my hand grabbing his arm, but not willing to pull it away. He pressed into my backside, his arm securing me in place. His fingers slipped between, gently pressing on the nerves before reveling in the wetness, the arousal.

His lips twitched into a smirk against mine, shifting the gathering of fabric to the back.

I expected the warmth of his fingers, to be touched and teased.

No, something else.

The chiming of his belt. Pressed firmly between my legs was a hot, smooth sensation. It wasn't his palm. I didn't dare look under the bunching of fabric.

I rolled my hips forward, along the shaft of his cock. I only felt length without an end. The lack of visuals making the mystery more unbearable.

I leaned back against his chest for stability, going up on my toes.

His hand guided the tip, swiping it between my legs, teasing the entrance.

He gasped, slow in his movements as if to savor, gathering the slick of the arousal.

Is he stalling? Hesitating?

I crossed my legs, his cock firm between them. I reached down, and he thrust forward, the wet tip hitting my palm.

So hot. So hard.

I was getting dizzy. I couldn't believe the size, the thickness. I was fully prepared to be let down, with the way he avoided sex, but now it was clear it wasn't out of embarrassment.

His arm wrapped to the front, his palm pressing on my chest to keep me close. He ground up against me, his chin resting on my shoulder with his eyes closed, tense with focus.

"Arkady," I whispered, rolling my palm over the tip of his cock poking out from between my thighs.

He exhaled shakily, kissing my shoulder as he pulled out, using his leg to push mine apart.

The moisture dripped down my thigh. I was so hot, so ready. I was worked up like a cat in heat, mind and body eager. Even if it was only an inch, whatever he would give.

He touched me first, making sure I was ready. He began with two fingers, aware of my willingness. He curled them inside, knuckle deep, as my muscles twitched in anticipation for much more.

"How malleable you are," he whispered.

"Careful, even lithe things *break*." My chest rose and fell against his palm, my insides pulsing against his other.

His hand slid up my chest and to my jaw, caressing my neck as he kissed me. He removed his fingers, my body wanting to collapse from the disappointment of being empty. My adrenaline was the only thing that kept me upright.

Then was when I felt it, the hot tip of his cock prodding timidly, carefully, as if afraid I'd have teeth down there.

I pushed my back against him, eager for entrance.

He leaned down, kissing my neck. The scent of figs and cedar, of bourbon. The softness of his lips contrasting with the roughness of his palm on my neck.

Then, he sucked down hard on my skin.

I flinched, a whimper escaping.

He pushed inside. My insides filled gradually, all too willing to accommodate the intrusion. It was beginning to feel sore, and before it could hurt too much, he retreated, taking careful inventory of each breath, each sound I made.

Yet, I was doing the same. Listening to how he let himself exhale with a shaky breath, the tension in his arms as he held me, the pulsing of blood in his cock against my skin. Locking away each memory, each touch.

Was this what it was like to be obsessed?

His other hand placed low on my abdomen, holding me against him as he went in again.

He groaned into my shoulder, keeping his head down as he pushed inside once more.

I scratched at the door, his arm. I moved my hips, gasping and whimpering.

"I want you," I said quietly.

"I need you," he replied raggedly, keeping me tight against the door.

The pressure of his body against mine was grounding, letting me savor every inch he allowed, slowly, until there was no more to give.

Then, he thrust.

My hips knocked against the door, but he kept his hand above my pelvic bone to avoid too much impact, preparing me for what was to come.

I swore the heat coming from my face would steam, my insides would melt, my words would disintegrate the minute they tried to manifest past my throat.

"Arkady," I whimpered, making him grip tighter, thrust harder, bottoming out inside me.

"Tell me to stop." His voice was strained.

"*Stop* holding back," I begged. "I want all of you, every last *unsavory* piece of you."

He grunted and left love bites down my shoulder, the back of my neck.

"I'll ruin you." His voice low.

"Spoil me," I gasped. *"Like I'm worth the trouble."* I went up on my toes as he plunged into me, the arousal only making it easier to submit to his size and vigor.

He was angled in such a way that was meant to undo me, to form and unravel the knot wound tight inside me. The knot that has been building since the day we met, the nights we shared, the secrets we traded. All threads of fate meant to be tied.

"Petre." He bit down on my shoulder.

I covered my mouth before I could yelp, my hips slamming into the door with every rough jolt of my body.

An involuntary sound came from me; I didn't recognize it.

My body shook, the coursing shock so violent, so vicious, I had tremors—inside and out. Wetness dripped down my leg, soiling the dress. My head was light from holding my breath, from releasing the tension in my legs.

Arkady was still, his body pressed to mine, his cock held inside. He felt the wetness too, because it wasn't him.

"What a mess you are." He let out a breathless tease.

"I didn't . . . I didn't mean—"

He rolled his hips slowly as his cock pulsed steadily inside. "I thought you were worried about ruining the dress?"

I shook my head, swallowing, the twist in the pit of my stomach settling.

But God, it was worth it.

He pulled out slowly as he kissed the bruises along my shoulder. My body wanted to collapse, refusing to accept the emptiness he left behind.

Then, he wiped between my legs with the skirt of the dress before using it to dry his cock.

"Arkady!" I scolded.

"It will raise the value, if anything." He slipped the dress off my shoulders and discarded the petticoat. "Turn. Let me help you dress."

I covered my chest, turning to him so I could step out. I straightened my shoulders, letting him take the clothing.

He undid the front clasps of my corset, leaving me in my combinations.

It was intimate, more now than what we did before. The way he was careful, detail oriented. Making sure to undress me carefully, like he was taking stock of what was underneath. He gathered the dress and placed it over my father's chair. The soiled fabric would probably dry before they suspected it was ruined.

My mother will kill me.

He reapproached with the plain cream tea gown my mother had handed him. With the dress draped over his arm, he stopped in front of me. Only when I recovered from my internal mumblings did I notice he was staring.

I didn't know if my expression was projecting my anxiety, but I knew my lip was trembling. Something about the scrutiny of his gaze, being nearly naked in front of a fully clothed man. Though disheveled, he was still more dressed than I.

"Well?" I snapped my fingers before holding my palm out for the dress. The burning in my cheeks went from arousal to embarrassment. I thought I'd evaporate if he let me steam any longer.

"What kind of man do you think I am?" He laughed, undoing the back of the dress.

He knelt down, opening the garment.

I sighed, placing a hand on his shoulder as my shaky legs stepped into the dress. He pulled it up over my waist, then moved my hands into the sleeves. It was light, clean, and freshly softened.

He circled me, clasping up the back all the way to my neck; conveniently, the collar was high enough to hide the fresh markings.

I spun around, slapping his lingering hand away. "You're being too nice."

"A gentleman doesn't allow his lady to dress herself." He cupped my face. "Here I thought you *liked* attention."

I huffed, too tired to argue any further. "I want to go home."

"I'm glad I've worn you out enough to make a retreat."

"More like I'm tired of *you*," I hissed.

He chuckled, leaning down to kiss my head and wrapping his arms around me. The pressure easing some tension in my shoulders.

I felt the prickle of tears in my eyes.

He rested his chin on my head. "Do you want me to cut you some peaches when we get home?"

I nodded, balling my fists in his shirt.

There were other things to say, other insults I wanted to unwrap from my tongue. I don't know why, I didn't understand my anger. Perhaps it was just too many emotions at once.

I'd gotten what I wanted, but it only made me realize I had something to lose. Giving him my heart meant it was possible to break it. To make oneself vulnerable was to give them the blade with the tip to your chest.

But for now, he was a guilty comfort.

For the first time, a truce.

CHAPTER TWENTY-FOUR

The Performer

Why was it that getting dressed for a promenade in the park was the equivalent of dressing for war?

I tight-laced for the occasion, a walk with my sister.

It was of the utmost importance that I didn't wear anything plain or embarrassing, as she would nag me. Before her mourning period, her marriage, everything, our trio of sisterhood would put on our best, better than our Sunday skirts. One thing we all had in common was our fascination with fashion. I suppose our mother rubbed off on us in a single positive manner, and it was style. Some days I forget she was a master seamstress; she barely used those skills for anything other than weaving stories, rumors, whatever would feed her greed for infamy.

"Is this new?" Félice gestured to my dress.

I looked down, pinching the material as I walked. It was the color of buttermilk with a pattern of white roses with green leaves dotting the fabric. Lace lined the trim and the collar around my neck, the fabric over my upper chest lighter and more sheer.

"Not new, but never worn," I answered.

"Well, you look simply radiant." Félice smiled. "How is the household? Have you gotten sick of one another yet?"

"Tolerable." I had to bite my cheek, punishment for a lie.

"Tell me, Petre," she began, looping her arm in mine as if keeping me under her parasol would shield us from whoever could be listening. "Be honest. How does he treat you?"

"Like a colleague."

Her face twitched, a confused brow rising nearly to her hairline.

"He is indifferent, but he is fair," I lied. "There isn't much to it."

"If that is true, why do you keep him?"

My neck snapped from how quickly I looked at her. "Is this a conversation you want to have *in public*?"

"You act like I asked how you plan to do it." She laughed. "I know you went against our parents' matches, I just wasn't sure if that changed his indispensability."

"If I already went against the plan once, what makes you think I would suddenly fall in line with the usual?"

"Come now, Petre, don't throw one of your fits," she scoffed. "It is the natural progression. We all do it for the family, for our own well-being. Keeping him is costing you an opportunity. You are still young."

"Just because that is how you decided to get ahead doesn't mean it will be my choice."

"Who said I wanted to get ahead?" She squeezed my arm. "It is the only thing a woman can do to be comfortable in this life, is it not?"

"Our ideas of comfort are very different, Félice," I warned her.

Her eyes were sharp. The blue of them always scared me, like staring down a wolf with its hackles up. That same sharpness never left, even as her eyes snapped somewhere else, accompanied by a smile. "Lorelei, what a surprise."

My head whipped over my shoulder.

There was my dear friend, bright like a summer flower with a crow propped on her shoulder, waiting to pick her clean of spring seeds.

"Who is this gentleman?" Félice teased, surely saving this detail for later gossip.

It was the man Lorelei was with at the theater.

"This is William, he is the new ballet master." Lorelei's chest puffed, her arm looped in his proudly, even without a ring.

William could be considered handsome, just not quite enough to attract Lorelei without added benefits unseen to the naked eye. Slick hair, shaved face, and, unfortunately, fashionable.

"Does William have a surname? Or are you afraid little sprites will steal him if you tell us?" I raised a brow.

Lorelei's eyes flicked my way before returning to Félice, ignoring me. "I will be working closely with him on the new production of *La Sylphide*."

"I didn't know auditions had already ended." My jaw tensed.

"I suppose talent doesn't have to audition if you know they're perfect. Sometimes it's just meant to be," William replied, undoubtedly pleased with himself. "The minute I saw her perform, I knew she would be perfect for *La Sylph*."

"Oh, is that what *talent* gets you?" I smiled, though I suspect it was more of a grimace.

Lorelei glared, begging me to be quiet.

I thought I had appealed to her better senses last time I warned her, but I suppose it fell on deaf ears.

Lorelei had never even owned a dress nice enough for a promenade, and suddenly she was wearing something worth more than any salary she'd ever made. When I looked closer, my heart dropped. A diamond and garnet brooch in the shape of a sparrow was pinned upon her coat. It was one of a kind . . .

Or at least, that was what my mother used to say when *she* wore it. I wouldn't forget a piece like that.

This poor girl, being groomed into a position that would wear her down to the bone by the time there was a "two" in front of her age.

I couldn't say that I wasn't once in her shoes, but I thought I could break the cycle for her.

Even now, my cycle wasn't over yet. Vincent continued to haunt me, lingering like a spirit clinging to the spine, shivers warning against the upper hand he still had. Much like a specter myself, I had unfinished business with him.

Like receiving some omniscience from beyond, my body wouldn't quit its sheepish tremor. My hands were unable to still except when they were holding my skirts.

The coroner's office was a bleak thing. The offices were entrapped in a cold brick building, a leaky, miserable place to spend most of your time. I would say it was at least sterile, but I had my doubts about that too.

A cold corridor led to the stairs, which spiraled down to the basement. It was ill lit; every complexion would be washed in the ailing light. I was familiar with the office space enough to know where to go but not enough to remember precisely where Vincent's office was.

The hallway smelled of the sickly sweet putrescine cadavers. I couldn't cook any dried offal because of the same off-putting musk. It stuck in your nose for days, and it would take serious scrubbing to make it leave the senses.

One by one, the doors passed. A storage closet, autopsy room, laboratory, then the offices. I peeked into the next room, the embalming room. It was brighter than the hallway, and the smell all the more apparent. The only difference was a tinge of sulfur and bleach.

The next door was an orange wood, the frosted glass dark, and I could almost feel the same dread as when he was alive.

The door creaked as it opened, the cheap wood on new hinges alerting whatever ghosts remained within. It was as musty as any office, maybe just as much dust despite the abandoned nature. Everything was exactly where he'd left it.

The only light came from the hallway, spilling across the dull gray stains on the carpet, the utilitarian furniture, all the way to the worn walls, likely from the sweating brick foundation.

It was painfully ordinary. His desk to the corner, no windows, papers scattered on every surface. The piles of folders never seemed to make their way back to the cabinets, always in vertical stacks. A skyline of evidence, justice to be neglected.

I approached the back of the desk and sat in the dry leather chair.

If I were a forbidden memory, where would I hide?

I picked at the peeling leather arm, scanning over the photographs. To anyone, this was a normal working man's desk. This could be how he left it; men were allowed to be messy. They were allowed to abandon responsibilities, especially if they were elected. The only hint that he may have intended to come back was the half-full coffee mug, a film of fuzzy mold flourishing on the sour drink.

I brushed through the papers, my posture slouched and focused. Employee checks, crematorium records, police reports.

Within one stack of folders, cases from upstate that had made their way down here. Mysterious ailments of farmers, all escalated and never reviewed, yet their bodies had already been marked as *cremated.* The log stopped where expected, as there was no one to continue it after him.

I pulled open the first few drawers. Only paper clips, notepads, a crumpled bill or an invoice here and there. Then the last drawer, all the way at the bottom.

Stuck.

Another yank, only to brush my thumb over a keyhole below the knob.

My heart dropped directly to the pit of my stomach, a tingling at the back of my neck prompting a dry swallow.

It's in there. I know it.

Arkady may have been correct about my ignorance of Vincent's whereabouts affording me some protections. But now, I absolutely needed to know.

Asking for Vincent's keys and belongings would only make Arkady ask more questions. I doubt he would extend the same trust to me. *No questions, no qualms.*

I would find it myself. I had my suspicions about his studio, as I would hope he didn't hide Vincent's things in our own home.

No, he was smarter than that.

CHAPTER TWENTY-FIVE

The Artisan

Most days, the stale, unmoving air of the house took on the smell of wood and dust. Tonight, it smelled like a steadfast simmer of rosemary, the slow-cooked soul of broth, and the tenderness of meat that slipped from the bones.

Petronille allowed me to witness her cooking, which was a different pace than usual.

I learned exactly how much she loved to cook. Specialty knives and an expert navigation of the flank. It wasn't anything particularly fancy, a bit lean, but it smelled so good, I suspended my belief in her cooking skills.

She was different when she was occupied. She still had her home work clothes on with a clean apron, her sleeves rolled up to her elbows, and hair secured in a braid.

A silver chatelaine chimed by her hip; that was how you knew she was a woman who ran her own home. Each chain held another teeny item. A set of small sheers, a bobbin, a perfume vial, and a couple of brass keys.

She laid out another cut of meat, her knife pulling through the thick of it, carving through fat and cartilage and discarding a couple scraps that she didn't look too impressed with. The cut was prepped and laid carefully in a large pot, then set aside to cook.

I should have guessed earlier that she was serious about this hobby. Her house was outdated, in style and structure, yet she had this year's Richmond stove to cook on. The kitchen and its utilities were the most updated part of the house.

"I don't think I can wait four hours for dinner," I complained, leaning against the kitchen table as she tidied up.

"I have confidence that you will endure." She shook her head with her back facing me. I was sure her eyes were rolling.

"You know your way around a piece of meat."

"I've had practice."

"With whom?" I joked.

"My grandfather was a butcher, his father was a butcher, his father—"

"Was a butcher?" I cut her off.

"No, a cobbler."

"Oh," I mumbled to myself.

She wiped her hands on her apron, turning around and leaning back against the counter to face me. She took one of her knives, carefully wiping it of any remaining pieces of the meat.

"I wouldn't have guessed someone like you would enjoy cooking." I watched her closely. "I suppose you *are* self-sufficient."

"Only out of spite," she admitted, tilting the blade after cleaning it. "I would like to think nothing would change in my likelihood of survival if my parents and their fortune suddenly disappeared."

"You say that as if you weren't raised with a silver spoon and an inheritance."

"Things in this life change quickly." Her eyes shot up to me. "Some people lean on their upbringing so much that they stop learning about what keeps the regular folk alive."

"So you cook?" I scoffed at such melodrama.

Her eyes stayed on me, unamused. "I learn. You die when you don't adapt. What you don't respect in life will kill you."

"I suppose that's fair." I pushed myself away from the table to approach. "I wouldn't be opposed to a lesson or two from a thing like you."

"What makes you think I want to teach you anything?" She lifted a brow, then the knife tipped in my direction, the blade hovering in front of me.

"I think I've taught you a few things in our short time together. A lesson for a lesson?" I offered, lifting my hand to hers and pointing the blade upward, anywhere but at my chest.

"Who said your lessons are worth it?"

"You keep coming back for more, don't you?" I tipped my head at her, unable to hide a grin. "Or do you just want to see me beg?"

My hand on her wrist slipped up to her palm, stealing the knife from her hand.

She didn't fight, didn't protest. Perhaps this was a test, the hunger of curiosity getting the better of her. The flare in her eyes told me everything I needed to know.

"How often do you sharpen these?"

"Often enough."

"Oh, really?" I lowered it to the strap of her apron, flicking it outward. She flinched, and the strap slipped away, the front corner of the apron folding down. "I suppose you weren't lying."

"Why would I lie?"

"I don't know, Petronille, I wouldn't imagine that you had any reason to lie to me, correct?" I hovered the knife over the other strap, cutting that one loose too.

"Of course not," she whispered, her hands gripping the edge of the counter she leaned on, making me aware of my imposing position.

I reached past her, our faces getting close as I grabbed an apricot, holding it between our lips.

"You swear it?" I whispered.

I could hear her breathing. I could imagine her heart thumping wildly like a rabbit's foot against frozen ground.

Her frightened eyes darkened, and she pushed the fruit away. "You have my word, I *promise*."

"Shall we make an oath, then?" I suggested, pointing the knife to her left breast, the sharp tip hovering over her blouse.

She leaned forward, pressing it to the fabric; a tiny blotch of red blossomed.

I dragged it once, then again.

"If you turn on me, the knife won't be in your back, it will be here." I tapped the middle of the X. "No matter how wrong I am done, I will be honorable."

She took my hand in hers, redirecting the knife to my peck, dragging it in a neat single hatch. "There will be no confusion as to where you may find my blade or a bullet buried."

The knife returned upward between us, a hint of red glistening.

"We have a deal, then."

"This has always been the understanding." She smirked, leaning up. I thought she would kiss me. No—she was hungry for something else. Her tongue dragged up the flat side of the blade, the red of our blood staining her tongue, her lips.

It was easy to become taken with something like her. She should be angelic and pure from looks alone, only to find she was much more elusive, so many pieces left unknown, an enigma to be solved. The only thing she would not be is tame, and that was very good or very bad for my own demons to cavort with.

I dropped the blade, our lips crashing together before we could even hear the metal blare against the tile. I lifted her onto the counter, and her legs found a place around my waist. The taste of blood was off-putting, strange, primal. I felt some sort of release, some satiation as my fingers dug at her side, her nails against my back.

She grabbed at my shirt, tearing it open to expose the fresh cuts. She flattened her tongue on it, and the sting subsided after she moved to bite me.

I grabbed her hair, yanking her head to the side to bite back. She smelled like a sweet, like a pastry tempting a passerby in the bakery window, an expensive delicacy. Her skin was smooth like cream; I just wanted to sink my teeth in.

It would be so easy.

No.

So easy to pull her apart. If I bit her as hard as I could now, I think I'd break right through.

Stop it.

Her nails dragged along my skin. Her moans in my ear coming from those soft lips, her legs tightening around me in a way that could trap me here. She was toxic, all-consuming.

I stopped. Against my will, I stopped. Steadied myself. Urging myself to cease before I couldn't any longer.

"Arkady?" Her voice was wavering, or was I dizzy?

I pulled my head from her neck to look at her, my grip on her shaky.

"I . . ." I shook my head, unable to know what to say. Would she hear me? Or would she use it against me if I told her?

She lifted her hand to my cheek, her fine nails brushing over my skin. "Are you well?"

"No."

She nodded, dragging her nails over my scalp, allowing me to regain my bearings with no explanation needed.

"Hungry?" she offered, her fingers dancing in my hair.

I lowered my head back down to her shoulder, closing my eyes. I could feel the tension melting like the fat on the meat she was cooking. For once, the fever of destruction was tamed without even the least bit of interference.

"That must be it," I whispered, but I didn't let go. My arms engulfed her waist, and I let my eyes rest for a few precious moments.

I needed to remember this sense of control. She might not be the ruin I thought she'd be. It gave me a brief vision of hope that maybe I was good for her, and that was all I needed to sustain me.

"Something is wrong with me."

"Which part? You have to be more specific than that."

She glared, flicking water from the tub.

"I mean"—I cleared my throat—"*whatever do you mean, my most perfect, sweetest wife*?"

At least that made her laugh.

Petronille sank farther into the water, the bubbles crowding as she gathered them with her arms. I settled on the stool next to her, just watching as I leaned against the tub.

"I just . . ." She tried to brush it off, but her eyes were glassy.

I took one of her hands, extending it in front of me as I used the washcloth, smoothing up and down her arm, massaging her palm gently as if to ease out her words.

Her lip trembled.

"Petre," I said. It only made her tremble more. "What is wrong?"

"I liked it." She swallowed. "I liked it *a lot*."

"I would be worried about re-instilling our special word if you didn't," I teased, but I recognized this conversation.

"Am I so depraved that I need violence to feel that level of excitement?" She rested her head on the side of the basin.

I reached over, wiping the cloth on her shoulder and cleaning the mark on her chest from before. "It is not the violence you like, it is the control."

"How?"

"You were in control the entire time. With a single word, it would all stop. You aren't odd for liking it. A lot of people enjoy control, especially during sex."

"I never thought of it that way," she mumbled, playing with a wet tendril of hair.

"You're just coming down from the excitement. It's normal to feel a certain way after something so intense. That is why we do this . . ." I gestured to the tub.

"Bathe?"

"More like doing something *nice* afterward. To give you a safe place to break down, to ground you and remind you that it isn't real."

"Do you not feel anything, then?" Her eyes grew sad. "Since it isn't real?"

"Of course I do. I was just as excited as you." I laughed, tracing my hand over her knee, the bubbles sliding down her skin. "But it's my job to remind you that if it were to escalate, in the end, you were always safe. You will *always* be safe with me, Petre."

She stared for a moment, not saying a word. She stilled, some sort of sadness still burdening those brown eyes of hers.

Did I say something wrong?

She shifted in the tub, wrapping her wet arms around my shoulders and squeezing tight.

I returned the hug, soaking my clothes as I wrapped my arms around her waist. She huffed a muffled sob into my shoulder. I rubbed her back, tipping my head against hers, and just let her melt into my grasp.

"Let me get your nightwear," I muttered. She freed me from our embrace first in acceptance of the offer.

She sank back into the bath, more relaxed than before, as I retreated.

Gathering her day clothes, they chimed. I hesitated before wrapping the chatelaine in her petticoat to stifle it. I glanced back to see she paid no mind to the noise.

CHAPTER TWENTY-SIX

The Performer

For the first time, I couldn't find Arkady at his studio.

My foot tapped involuntarily, accompanying an awkward slouch as I sat on his mattress. My fingers brushed over the fabric; dust collected and puffed into the atmosphere, shimmering in the morning light.

I reserved my judgment for his previous living conditions, try as I might. It helped to romanticize it a little. Arkady could make even the worst environments enticing.

I might be exaggerating—this was far from the worst.

The studio was becoming a familiar comfort. I could imagine myself reading a book up in the loft while the chimes of a chisel sang from below. Or the smell of clay and cold coffee on days when we stayed up until morning.

The window was irregular and large, quite old as it was. It was facing east, so the light would be this soft every morning. Oh, to be a muse, bare-skinned and bathed in the light. Nowhere to be contractually, smelling of earth and cologne, arms to pull you back into the warm nest of blankets among the chill from the poorly insulated hideaway.

I can't say I snuck in to surprise him, but I found myself almost looking forward to seeing him. Before I knew it, I wore a smile as involuntary as a jacket in the cold, kept warm by the thought of him.

Yet, he was nowhere to be found.

Stupid, getting your hopes up. Don't be a girl.

An empty paint can clattered along the floor as I stood, then I kicked it farther on my way out.

Even as I descended the stairs, the mass of sculptures made up a daunting crowd. I didn't like to look them in the eye. They would tell him I was here.

Though, they became less intimidating with each visit. Soon I knew their poses, their expressions, even some names that had been inscribed on their pedestals.

One in particular was new.

It was a woman, lying on a slab in bliss. Her arms through her hair, moths coming from her chest and all over her hair and body.

They were coming out of her skin in a familiar pattern across the torso.

I would never compare myself to art, never in the slightest, but it was hard to convince myself that this wasn't a sculpture of . . . parts of me.

All the humility in the world couldn't compete with the idealistic vision of a lover. To him, I was art. But only to him, and I believed that was enough.

And just like that, as if to remind me of my true belonging, a memento mori beside her.

A table . . . full of knickknacks, tools, cloth. And Vincent's silver cigarette holder.

I picked it up, rolling it in my palm. My fingerprints smudged over the patina of past hands, reflection distorted from dents and other proof of love. Only the most prized treasures were used so reverently. The dust collected in the identifying *V.M.C.* etched on the flat of it.

I almost felt warm until I looked closer at the pile. The familiar item wasn't enough to distract me from the rest of the strange collection.

Each item seemed odder than the last. Belts and buckles, various sizes of cigarette cases, rosaries, artisan hooks from walking canes.

Though, none of these gave me any heartache . . . not until I saw the chatelaine.

At first I thought it was my own. No, of course it wasn't. Mine was on my hip, I was touching it right then. This belonged to someone else.

The back of my scalp became hot, right where the spine connected to my head, threatening to let it roll off.

No, this means nothing. These are knickknacks. He collects.

Still . . . this chatelaine wasn't like mine. It was nicer. Too expensive to be discarded, too polished to accept it was forgotten. A souvenir from another woman?

Like there was a last-minute pull, I dug through the pile again. Knacks clattered to the floor, tangled together, screaming for me to stop looking.

There they were.

Vincent's keys.

I grabbed the small loop full of tiny assorted keys on a large round ring. I recognized them from every time his long fingers gripped them, fiddled with them when he was trying to fake a confident stride—which was often. I suppose it reminded him of the world he held in his palm. And now it was in mine.

"You smell like earth." Lorelei's lip curled into a sneer.

"My husband touches me with the same hands he sculpts with." The muscle in my jaw twitched. I couldn't help a small smile. "I suppose that is why you smell of cheap booze?"

"You know what cheap booze smells like?" She gasped. "Maybe your pauper is rubbing off on you."

"I'm sure you wish yours would rub you off."

"Not for free, he won't."

"Is this really how you're going to act?" I hissed, my arm tightening on hers.

"I'm not acting any different than you," she replied innocently, twirling her parasol above us. On her arm, a new purse. The handle most notably unscathed. "Perhaps we both bring our men out. Long walks are encouraged when keeping dogs in shape."

"Arkady isn't a dog."

"Yes, *Petre*, I know he isn't a *real* dog," she scoffed. "Can I not tell jokes now? Have you become that soft?"

"Perhaps I've outgrown your humor." I shrugged. "Or it could just be that your joke is in bad taste."

"Like you would know *good* taste."

I dug my heels into the pebbled walkway, tugging her arm back. "Why do we keep doing this? Why are we going in circles?"

"It's a promenade, we walk one big circle."

"Don't get smart with me, child," I snapped.

Lorelei's eyes widened, some sort of delight. She clicked her tongue against her teeth, a smile gracing her painted lips. "I almost heard your mother right then. You might be growing into your maternal figure sooner than you thought."

"I know you must be feeling smug. Between your patron—"

"He is my intended."

"—and whatever associating with my mother is getting you, it isn't worth it," I finished.

"Who said I was talking to your mother?"

"Come now, Lorelei"—I laughed—"you were wearing her brooch, her gown pattern from two years ago, and you had her old purse last I saw you. Did she let you raid her past-season closet? What did she ask you to do in return?"

"Unlike some people"—she paused, a twitch in her brow—"she has asked nothing of me in return, just my company."

"Company? Or has she offered to mentor you?"

Lorelei lifted a shoulder, twirling the parasol as she turned away. "Keep up, or I'm leaving you behind," she chimed.

If I let my blood boil any longer, it might come out my eyes, my ears, spewing from my mouth in the form of profanities.

I walked beside her, too disgusted to talk. Though, she didn't seem to have a problem resuming her gossip as usual. Her expression was so bright, so positive and energetic.

Lorelei did well because she kept her composure. I supposed she couldn't afford to fall out of line. I understood some of my privileges in that sense. I could throw fits and get upset without losing any stability in my life. But there were better ways than this, and I didn't know what would come first: our friendship ending or her inevitable demise. It made the whole thing quite bleak. I felt like I could see the future, like watching a silver screen.

We arrived at my town house, but I was barely there. Lorelei didn't notice; she was too busy talking. Even as we crossed the threshold and settled like birds into the living room, she was *still talking.*

She peeled off her gloves and set her parasol aside, her lips moving feverishly, but I couldn't hear a sound.

"Eugh." Lorelei swatted in the air, a moth fluttering by her hair. "You should really do something about these things. I don't know how you live like this."

"I don't remember your living situation being much better."

She ignored me, leafing through some photographs on the table, smiling brightly at one before pinching it between her fingers. "We should all have a night at the opera! Oh, how fun it would be! Don't be miserable, let us do it!" she squeaked.

I stared at the photo, all the blood leaching from my body, as if by some type of vampyre.

"You can't wear your usual—it needs to be nice. William likes to show off. I'm sure Arkady wouldn't mind if he could show you off as well."

She turned the photograph toward me. "Memory lane!"

It was a photograph of us. Me and Lorelei. Me, Lorelei, the rest of them. The whole troupe, when we were all whole.

"Petre?"

Her words fading, my focus waning.

Skinny, awkward legs, all at different paces of growth. Lorelei's bangs curled in the front, awkwardly grown in. I remembered that day. My mother had scolded me that very morning for outgrowing my uniform for the third time that year.

All of us sat on a knee each, as if we were posing for a family photograph. Vincent, James, among other men's faces I would learn to block out whenever possible.

"You know, it's really a drag to talk to myself—"

"I suggest you get comfortable with the idea of being alone."

Lorelei stared, mouth agape. "I'm not—"

"You are." I slammed my hand on the table, photographs scattering. "You are alone, and you don't even know it. You are a lamb whose cord was cut too fast by wolves with greedy palates."

"What has gotten *into* you lately!" she shouted. "I'm just trying to include you—"

"The sooner you accept that you're not one of them, the better off you will be." I spoke low, rising from my chair and leaning over the table. "Even in my *state*, as you enjoy pointing out, I will always be born in a different class than you. They would rather accept me at my most tarnished than you at your finest. Because you will never be one of them. *That* is the game my mother plays. There is no prize. You will always be the second choice."

"You only say this because your mother chose *me* over you." Lorelei swallowed, her eyes shifting the closer I got.

"You don't know anything in the slightest." I looked down at her, and for once, she almost looked pitiful. Such blind optimism. "You wouldn't know a phantom from a cheap illusion, even if the mirrors were in full view."

"You are being cruel!"

"I am the *only* one being honest with you."

"It seems unlikely that all but one are secretly my enemy. I knew you were pessimistic, but now I truly do think this is a bout of envy."

"A child's school of thought."

"Says the one throwing a tantrum!"

"That's the problem with you." I laughed, pointing a finger at her. "You are young. You don't have to do any of this to get far—"

"I'm farther than you ever got! You are just mad you quit early!"

"No"—I shook my head—"you joined late. You weren't there for the worst of it. Yet here you are, jumping headfirst before the ink dries on the new catalog." I slammed my fist on the table again. "You could have made it out! You almost were!"

"Maybe I don't want to get out!" she screamed back at me, standing from her chair. "What if I don't want to leave? Not everyone has to feel shame, to feel like this is a burden. I'm a woman in my own right and can choose for myself!"

Even though we had only been exchanging words, our breathing, our posture, my fatigue on the subject made it into a long and weary battle.

This was it. This was the end of us, our friendship. It was clear she would never understand, and she wasn't going anywhere useful. Maybe it was best that it ended now before I got to see them ruin her.

Leaning against the table, a sharp sting. I flinched away, my blood on the tip of the letter opener resting among a pile of opened letters, the crimson pooling on my finger in a singular drop.

"You know, I thought you would understand." Her voice was uncertain, like she was struggling to sort her thoughts before she spoke. "Now I realize you've hated me this whole time. A by-product of jealousy or otherwise, I do not know."

The tension in my jaw made each pulse of blood through my temples throb, an ache so strong I thought it would burst through my forehead and sprout horns of a raging bull.

"Poor Petre, so *hard* to love! Not your mother, not your friends, quite possibly not even your husband! You are lucky he is poor, or I fear he may have run for the hills the minute your personality came *shining* though. Yet you still think it is the fault of all those around you? Years of complaining about the same hardships in relationships, and you still never wondered if it was no coincidence that the common denominator was *you*."

"Stop it," I demanded. "Stop it now."

"And the one man who was obsessed with you has suddenly disappeared. Not a trace! By God, I thought once upon a time that Mr. Carlisle was *so* obsessed, so taken with you, that you would have to kill this man if you ever wanted to be rid of him!" She paused, biting her cheek as she laughed with teary eyes, fiddling with the sparrow brooch on her collar.

My fingers curled around the letter opener, crumpling an old love letter under it within an iron grasp.

One last look to keep her in mind like a picture, unbruised by experience, unsoiled by the desires of man.

I would be free of her.

Then she would be free of *them*.

CHAPTER TWENTY-SEVEN

The Artisan

The house was so cluttered that it could probably compete with my studio.

Rugs, drapes, silverware, every home accessory you could think of. A barely used candelabra that was entirely too fancy for Petre's current decor, drape ties, used cookware, and miscellaneous china with incomplete sets.

"I like the rug." I smoothed a wrinkle out of the hallway runner with the heel of my shoe.

"I'm happy to hear." She lifted a pile of linens to the table. "You can help me decide where the other five will go."

"Where did this come from?" I shoved my hands in his pockets, inspecting the mess.

"Cosette."

"Why?"

She shrugged, holding up some tasseled curtain cords. "Do you think this would be too much for the living room?"

I stepped forward, touching the velvet and smoothing it between my palm and thumb. "A little."

"You don't seem amused."

"Have you been sorting through this all day?"

"Most of it."

I poked through a bin, pulling out some metal contraption between bottles of arsenic pesticide. It looked like some sort of pump with a sharp spike at the end, then a needle and tube coming out the side. "Do you even know what this thing is?"

"For gardening. Aerating, I suppose."

"We don't have a garden. Or a yard."

"Well, what if we do get one?"

"Unless you mean flower boxes in the windowsills, I'm not sure how that's possible."

She snagged the items from me.

"We don't have room to keep it all." I followed her aimlessly.

"I know, but I like nice things." She crossed her arms. "It can't hurt to sort through."

"Would your friend take it?"

Petronille's eyes widened, a flash of disgust settling before she waved her hand as if dismissing a thought. "No. She wouldn't."

"Did I strike a nerve?"

"We aren't friends any longer."

"Oh," I mumbled. "Did something happen?"

Petronille pushed past me as if I hadn't asked her a question.

"You seem a bit wound up." I stepped behind her, placing my hands on her shoulders, pressing down gently. Her body leaned back when I did so, resting against my chest as her head sloped tiredly to the side. "Are you sure there isn't anything I can do to help?" I peered down at her.

"It would be like grounding a lightning bolt. I feel like I'm made of lead. If you threw me into the Hudson, I would sink." She sighed.

"I think most things would sink if you threw them into the Hudson," I teased, but she shot me a brief glare over her shoulder. "What are you stressing over now?"

She leaned back into my chest, and I could feel her breath hitch. Her shoulders slumped. "There are too many messes to clean."

"Maybe if I tied you up and forced you to be still for once, you wouldn't be so stressed."

"At least I would have an excuse as to why I cannot fix everything."

"Allow me, then." I pulled away from her suddenly.

She nearly tipped backward, turning to watch me leave. "Allow you?"

I picked up the long drape cords and gardening shears. I turned to her, holding them up. "Trust me on this."

She looked from the cords, a critical stare, to me once she realized I was sincere.

I raised a brow. "Let us call it therapy. You remember your word, correct?"

She nodded, the idea settling in. She crossed her arms again, tucking her hands under. She lost herself, retreating into her head as she focused entirely too hard on the new hallway runner.

Oh, don't get shy on me now.

I stepped forward, tilting my head as I tipped her chin up.

Her lips parted, either to speak or out of surprise. I lowered my lips to hers, kissing her ever so gently, just a taste, an *ask*. In order for this to work, she had to get comfortable letting someone else take the reins, to trust me to help her.

She leaned in, a bit more hesitantly than expected, but did it nevertheless. I rewarded her with more contact, holding her face in my palm. I closed my eyes, enjoying the sweet scent of orange blossoms in her perfume.

I grasped both her hands in mine, lifting them to my lips to kiss along her knuckles, then I looped the rope around her wrist in a knotted cuff, the navy blue stark against her skin.

"*Shibari* has a very long history, you know." I tied loops down her forearms. "It was originally used to contain criminals."

Her eyes flicked to me, a critical look, but she didn't give me any indication to stop.

I turned her around slowly, wrapping the rope around to the back and beginning to bind the torso. "The knots used to symbolize the crime, a type of public shame when leading them through the streets," I explained, my hands lingering by the back of her neck, whispering close to her ear. "Some said the knots and colors of the rope were used to trap demons inside the so-called sinners." My knee went into the back of her leg, making her kneel on the couch with her elbows propped on the camelback of the sofa.

In one hand, I held the rope, pulling slightly, allowing the strands around her to tighten. She made a small noise, more like a breath of relief. My free hand touched her leg, smoothing up to lift her skirt.

"Your ropes are blue," I said, leaning forward to reach the front of her hips. She flinched, her face hidden in her arms. Her legs trembled as I touched her, cupping between her legs roughly. "Reserved for the most impactful crimes, taboo to the community, something unforgettable and heinous." I pressed my hips into her, pulling the ropes a little tighter. I rubbed her slowly, gently, with purpose.

She gasped, her breath hitching. I could feel every breath through her back pressed against my chest.

"Breath control is important." I took her earlobe between my teeth, nipping her gently as I smoothed my fingers between her labia, wet with anticipation.

Just the visual of the ropes rubbing on her skin, turning it pink in its grasp . . . I had to take my own advice and *breathe*. This exercise wasn't for me.

"Does it feel good to wear your shame?"

"I don't . . . know what you mean," she answered.

"Clearly you did something to find yourself bound like this," I said against her neck. "What sort of sin did you commit to deserve this?"

"I don't know—"

"Do the knots match the crimes?"

"No!" she sobbed.

I stopped, the tone of her voice concerning.

"Apricot! Stop!" she cried.

At the drop of the word, I pulled the last knot for a quick release, picking her up to gather her in my lap as I undid the ropes.

Her face was stained with tears, her eyes and nose pink from distress.

"I'm sorry," I whispered, tossing the ropes to the ground.

She wrapped her arms around my neck, nearly choking me in her grip. She wouldn't stop shaking. My heart beat hard, fast. I hesitantly wrapped my arms around her. I rubbed her back, holding her for as long as she needed.

"I'm sorry," I repeated, kissing the side of her head as I rubbed her hair. "You did so good. I'm so proud of you," I whispered, tilting her chin up. "Look at me."

She blinked away her tears, her breathing calming down, though the anxiety was still left over. "I'll be ready next time. I can do it next time."

"You don't have to be if you don't like it. We don't have to do anything," I assured her, wiping away some of the remaining wetness from her cheeks.

She shook her head quickly. "No, I did like it. I just . . . I just panicked. I'm sorry."

"Don't apologize. There is always next time, and even if you stop it again, I would assure you all the same."

"I want to . . . try again. Not now, maybe another time?" she suggested.

"If that is what you want."

I kissed her forehead before pulling her to my chest, enveloping her in my arms with my chin resting comfortably on her head, my fingers playing with the hem of her skirt and tracing delicately over her ankles.

"I *am* proud of you, you know."

"For what?" She laughed, a small snort.

"You're learning to set boundaries."

"I said 'apricot,'" she mumbled. "You are making it more than it is."

"Whether you say the word 'apricot' or dictate a contract's worth of things you will and will not do, it is something you've never done before. And for that, I am proud."

She let out a small laugh, possibly too tired to argue. As long as she knew that I saw her, that was all that mattered.

CHAPTER TWENTY-EIGHT

The Performer

The walls were moving, spinning, on my descent to the first floor, weighed down by my heart. Last night was a warning, the universe telling me I was a drunk walking too close to the water's edge.

The living room was empty except for the dust and abandoned organization. It was like I cleaned one section, then another would become more cluttered than the last. My own Sisyphean task.

I grasped at my hip.

No chatelaine.

Battling against my vertigo, I stumbled back up the stairs, catching myself with my palm on the step as I scrambled.

I pulled open the drawer to my nightstand, trinkets clattering against the inside before my hands could rummage through. Another minute of frantic clawing, knowing it wasn't there. The keys weren't there.

"Shit. *Shit!*" I cursed, my throat clenching in distress as I already found myself skipping steps on the way back downstairs.

I yanked the miscellaneously shaped pillows and cushions off the sofa. Nothing but spare change and crumbs were revealed before I was flat on the floor, squinting under the couch at silhouettes of dust and a long-dead insect or two.

I sat up on my knees, raking my nails through my hair.

Slowly, I balanced on my wobbly legs, sore from the sudden burst of panic, undoubtedly expending whatever energy my poor body would have saved for the day.

"Please," I exhaled up at the ceiling, praying to the cracks in the plaster. "Please let it not be so."

With steady steps, I stood in the hallway, eyeing the door at the end. As I approached, some details inspired hope. The carpet was unmoved, the floorboard underneath creaked the same way it did before, unfixed.

The padlock on the door was firmly in place, no signs of damage, and still locked.

Arkady's coat and bag were hanging on the banister, things I wouldn't imagine he would stray too far from. He would be returning.

If these things were true, I attempted to reassure myself that nothing was amiss.

With raw fingers pushing on the back of my aching neck, I went to the kitchen for my routine. Nothing was unusual, nothing aside from my own imagination.

Then, on the counter, I saw it.

My chatelaine, keys intact.

I sighed with deep relief, my elbows hitting the cold counter as my fingers tangled in the fine chains, holding it firmly to remind me they were here and all was well.

With the chatelaine secured to my skirt, it was time once again to dig through the mountain of hand-me-downs my sister had so graciously given me. I couldn't imagine how I would ever get the house clean. Perhaps today I would work on the boxes of smaller items.

I sat at the table, pulling a box forward. It wasn't terribly heavy, and it seemed to be a file box, something with papers. I swore that if this were expired tax reports or other rubbish, I would be having a word with her about getting their own waste disposal instead of handing it off to me.

I slid the lid off the box, a bit of dust puffing from it when it finally released. The good news was that it may not have been garbage, after all.

I pulled out a stack from the top, photographs of our old home in France. *Tournon-sur-Rhône, '87* scrawled on the back corner. New York was a sight to behold but nothing compared to the south of France.

Stone houses lined the street, tall, rocky hills overgrown with grass just beyond the steeple of the square. It looked to be spring or summer; it was hard to tell from buildings and lighting alone.

Another of an orchard, taken from the top of a hill. A river could be seen just past the trees. This would be late June, as there was someone picking apricots.

Then another—people, this time.

There was a woman and a man who resembled softer versions of my parents. My father, absent of a stiff-starched collar and wrinkles in his eyes. My mother in lighter clothes and shoulders, her hair dared to be tucked out of place, effortless. Then there were my sisters, standing side by side.

I should have been there, but I wasn't. The only other person was another grown woman, a bit younger than my mother. She looked to be the help, as she stood on the side of Mother, a hand on Félice's shoulder as if to keep her still for the photograph.

I checked the back, only to see: *The De Villier Household, '79.*

I should have been in this picture, I thought. *I would have been two.*

I tucked the photograph in my pocket, containing the rest in the box and closing it. Something about this mysterious box made me feel like Pandora. There were secrets in there that I wasn't sure if I wanted or cared to know.

I needed more than just an afternoon to dig, and I had other investigations planned for the day.

I returned to the coroner's office, a bottle of wine in hand. A man at the front desk spotted me, nodding as I passed. No one questions you when you walk with purpose and have something expensive in hand. I knew where to go this time, I remembered the way.

The edges of the stairs were clear, the concrete of the walls more detailed upon second passing. The office was where it was supposed to be, unlocked due to the absence of its owner. Down the stairs, third—no, fourth—door on the left, tucked just around the corner of the hallway where it split.

I took great care to look both ways, then again to make absolutely sure no one would bear witness. I turned the knob quietly, carefully. Not one creak from the door as I slipped inside, closing it delicately so as not to make any loud clicks as it settled back into the doorframe.

Now, I could get to work.

I fell to my knees in front of the drawer, digging around in my pocket. I produced the dull keys caked in remaining flakes of plaster. It was dark, the desk lamp wasn't very bright, so it was a struggle to find the keyhole. I scraped it along the brass lock until it finally clanked into place.

It wouldn't turn.

I flicked to the next one, shaking as the key clattered clumsily against the hole; this one was too large.

"Come now," I cried quietly, squinting at the ring of keys as I moved to the next one, then the next.

The smallest key worked, sliding in easily, and took very little effort to turn.

The drawer was heavy, papers shifting and falling out from fullness. I gathered the small pieces of paper, catching a couple more as the drawer opened farther, until I could see some of the mess inside. There were folders, many. Varying in thickness, some photographs loose from the piles and haphazardly thrown in.

It was like they wanted to be found, practically leaped into my hands.

The first one was a woman, a robust figure, curved in every way, her neck and arms soft in feature with no detectable sharp angles.

The next was a group of women in nightgowns, a candid of sorts. Not completely staged but not completely genuine.

Then the last one shifted between my fingers, reminding me of why I was here.

A ballerina, awkward in stature, soft in nature, and a smile not yet grown into.

A tremor overtook my body, my limbs becoming cold. The adrenaline was wearing off, fully actualizing my predicament. I dug through the folders.

Madeline. Dolores. Adelaide. Mary. Margret. Anne. Mary-Anne Margret.

Then—*Petronille.*

The pads of my fingers left small smears on the folder as I held it, my name written across the stiff pulp. It would almost make me feel better if this were a folder detailing my death, rather than my life.

The folder was spilling, the papers within thick and numerous. A few photos had slipped out when I disturbed it. I dug into the drawer. Not one must escape.

Then, echoes of fine shoes in the hallway, each slap of a sole traveling off the concrete walls like gunshots—and I was the rabbit in the way.

I shoved the drawer closed, gathering the file to my chest and tucking myself under the desk, pressing against the wood.

"Seems the janitorial staff left it open. I'll have to speak with them about closing the doors." A familiar accent.

"Is the coroner's office always this indisposed?" Mr. Hunt's gruff voice accompanied the scuffling of shoes.

"I couldn't say, I haven't seen him much at all, never mind in his office."

Shoes dragged along the cold floor, a pair coming into view next to the office chair.

I pressed my hand over my mouth and nose, taking careful inventory of each breath going in and out, slow and silent.

"He only really comes by every week, less so now, since I assume he has more important things to do for the upcoming reelection," Konstantin said, then laughed. "I suppose there isn't too much competition for his spot. Those who've stepped up in the past dropped out pretty early on."

"It's a hard job that not many men are cut out for," Hunt grumbled, leaning over the desk, the sliding of papers hissing against the wood. "I appreciate you letting me take a look. Did he have any logs? Visitation and employees?"

"I do, but you will have to get a warrant. It's policy, apologies." Nervous laughter from the young mortician. "The living as well as the dead are accounted for in a place like this." A crude attempt at a joke.

There was a contemplative silence from the commissioner, then shifting weight on his feet. I could see his shoes, smell the leather, they were so close.

"Well, is there anything missing lately? Any odd behavior you'd want the police to know about?" Mr. Hunt asked.

"Missing? No, nothing is missing. Not anything out of the ordinary, of course. Well, what I mean is that sometimes the *bodies* have missing things—but they come that way." The mortician stumbled on his words, a nervous chatter not unlike a bickering bird.

"Well, you know who to call if you do think of something," Mr. Hunt said, stepping away from the desk.

I let out a breath all the way. I was safe, I just had to wait a bit for them to leave.

Then, he stopped.

I didn't need my hand to muffle my breathing; I held it.

His hand reached down, I could see it by the drawer. The key was still in it.

No!

He hooked his finger under the handle, sliding it open. There was a pause, then a breathy laugh. He lifted his hand, rustling in his coat before his hand reappeared with a handkerchief, reaching for something in the desk.

"Ah!"

I nearly hit my head on the desk the way I jumped at the mortician's sudden exclamation.

"His secretary—*she* may know more about the coroner's travels and schedule, if you are concerned about his whereabouts and safety. Here, let me write you her address."

Mr. Hunt reluctantly stepped away from the desk, not even closing the drawer as he walked away. "That would be especially helpful, I appreciate your willingness. Not everyone nowadays is dedicated to keeping our city safe." His voice got quieter, more distant, before it echoed into the hallway, words disintegrating into mumbling patterns.

That was close. Too close for comfort. I could feel the absence of blood making my head light, my neck cold.

I clutched the folder with sweaty palms, tipping my head back just for it to knock against the wood of the desk.

It was over, I could rest. I could lay my worries to die.

CHAPTER TWENTY-NINE

The Performer

Central Park was for stealing moments with nature between all the brick and concrete. You could almost forget you were in the city if it weren't for the tall buildings watching over the green space.

The season was maturing, the sun luring out every body in Manhattan. You started to truly believe that three million people somehow lived here on days like these.

The fresh air mingled with the passing smells of perfume, horses, or a pipe. The trees shimmered, the cherry trees and the magnolias dancing above. Sunlight filtered through the greener trees, painting splotches of light along the dirt footpath. You could see every cloud of dust kicked up by hoof or shoe, beating the path we walked along.

It was the perfect day to be an ice-cream man, handing out cool glass cones and fresh vanilla cream. The cafés were busy, leeching customers from the crowd that gathered to listen to the music coming from the gazebo—there would be several concerts, luckily not all so close in vicinity. The sheep were out today, grazing and gathering under trees in the meadow as their shepherd stood by. The menagerie would be open by now, and sometimes you could hear the song of a loose peacock roaming about. No matter how they tried, the pigeons and peacocks were impossible to contain.

"How about here?" Arkady's voice broke the surface of my thoughts.

I squeezed his arm, readjusting my parasol to follow his pointing. There was a free space in the grass just along the perimeter of a pond, shaded by a looming tree.

We settled down, laying out a blanket and opening our picnic basket.

"What a hassle, we are lucky to get a free space with this crowd." I sat down on the blanket, folding my parasol beside me.

"Focus on the positives. It's a beautiful day, the activity is good for you, and the sun will give you some extra energy." He began to take out some strawberries we'd bought at the market, as well as some cheeses, crackers, and a small jar of marmalade.

I watched the field, picking absently at the cubed cheese. Blankets dotted the green space like clover buds in late summer. Even with the park's natural beauty, the most interesting thing about it would always be the company. Couples sharing lunch, not unlike us. Groups of girls gathered, parasols planted in the grass to shade them from the sun. Kids running around a leisurely mother. Some of the loiterers were familiar.

"Look." I nudged Arkady, taking a bite from a strawberry before tilting my head. "Do you see the couple? Five blankets away, blue pinstripes?"

He leaned back on his hand to look past me, legs crossing as they were outstretched. "The couple? Middle-aged?"

I nodded, scooting closer to him while glancing in their direction. "They're patrons—*were* patrons of mine."

"The two of them?" His brow creased.

"Yes"—I smirked—"except neither of them knew."

His brow raised high, and he offered a small smirk of his own. "And how is that?"

"They would never come at the same time; neither of them knew the other was visiting the ballet. It was phenomenal. I wondered when the day would come that they both arrived on the same night and discovered they were hiding the same secret."

"It sounds a bit messy"—he took a bite out of a cracker—"and unnecessary."

"Many things, especially in my circle, are unnecessary." I laughed, picking at some of the other berries. "Some days it feels like strange and unusual punishments. The customs, the socializing, the rules."

"The rules?"

"Just the act of remembering them all. The goalpost moves by the day, it's hard to keep up with."

"Is that why you insisted we didn't go so early?"

"A habit." I shrugged. "First meal shouldn't come until ten or after."

"Is that really a rule?"

"Well, my mother said only the working class eat so early."

"Afraid of mingling with the working class?" His tone was serious.

"It isn't like that—"

"Would you be ashamed of being seen with me in work clothes, then?" He looked stern, his shoulders tense.

I took a second too long to reply, so he shook his head and looked away.

"I don't . . . care about those things. I wouldn't have married you if that were the case," I explained, though my hesitation was hard to brush off.

"Why do you care about these rules, anyway?" He tilted his head at me. "If you struggle to keep up with them, why bother at all? You don't even like being in public."

My fingers picked at the pilling blanket as I took my time with his words.

"If you want to be free of your parents, their expectations, whatever they may be, you have to allow yourself to be uncomfortable. I think you find safety in the privileges of your parents, even if it is to your detriment."

"It isn't easy, you don't know them," I snapped.

"Oh? Did I hit a nerve?" He smirked.

"No I . . ." I pushed a sharp breath from my nose, gathering my next words. "I want to be free of many things. But I don't think it would be possible unless I disappeared into obscurity. It's hard to wean yourself from a life you've known for so long. It takes time to weed by the root."

He nodded, seemingly entertained by the idea as he looked out in the distance.

"Run away with me, then," he said finally.

I laughed. Perhaps I shouldn't have.

"Is it so foolish an idea?" He nudged me.

"Someday"—I placed my hand over his, squeezing—"may it be."

"It could be today."

I shook my head, then leaned to rest it on his shoulder. "Ask me at another time, maybe the answer will be more in your favor."

"Arkasha?" a voice said behind us.

Arkady twisted his head, looking behind us before his face brightened. "Kostya! What luck we have running into you." He laughed, reaching his arm up as his friend hoisted him to his feet.

I rose to greet him. Much like ourselves, Kostya was paired up. A blond woman with a pram, I assumed his wife, stood idly beside him, smiling and giving a tired nod to myself and Arkady. She rocked the covered baby trolley back and forth on its wheels.

"May I?" I whispered to her as our husbands finished their hardy greetings.

"Yes, of course, she is sleeping off the meal," the woman answered, lifting the hood of the trolley.

A small baby, plump with red cheeks, sleeping soundly in white cotton.

"What a darling." I beamed at the tiny swaddle. No matter how normal children were, it was always hard to believe they were so small. Frail, pudgy things that somehow learned to eat and talk on their own. "Oh, where are my manners? Petronille Kameneva." I pulled a card for her.

"Emily Bezkorovainyi." She traded her card with mine. "I've heard much about you. Konstantin keeps me up to date with his dear friend's endeavors. I think he talks about him more than his work."

"I don't blame him, I wouldn't imagine cadavers are cheery to hear about after a long day."

"You have a point." She laughed, sighing as she wiped her temples with a handkerchief. "Would you like to join us? We were just heading to the menagerie."

"Yes, of course." I glanced at Arkady, who was occupied talking to Kostya, though even within earshot, I couldn't understand. It sounded vaguely Slavic, I wasn't sure which kind. Whatever it was, the conversation was lively, excited.

The zoological gardens were so small, it was hard to imagine fitting so many animals inside. Though once we entered, it became clear how they managed.

Along the paths were either cages or bars, depending on what animal lurked inside. The camels stuck their heads between the metal, allowing the visitors to feed them small carrots and oats. Peacocks fluttered about freely, as much as they could with those heavy tails behind them. Their calls were odd, so exotic. If I closed my eyes, I could imagine myself somewhere tropical, especially in this heat.

The lions lay on the concrete floors of their cages, napping soundly in the shade. Birds and monkeys took their turns squawking, sitting on high stoops in their enclosures. A buffalo used the bars of the gate to scratch its side, its massive form making the metal shake. I'd always wondered what kept the beasts from running free through Manhattan. I suppose it could be pure luck that one hadn't decided to make an effort to escape.

"It's very nice to see you keeping out of trouble," Kostya said, slapping Arkady's shoulder with such force he nearly stumbled.

"You say that like it's a common occurrence." Arkady rubbed his shoulder after the hit.

"No! No, I know. You've been a straight arrow for so long. It just feels like yesterday we were young and causing havoc. Ah, are we truly getting so old?" He laughed. "The way you used to run from that lumpy fella, you'd never have guessed he would become a commissioner. It certainly wasn't from chasing down criminals, not that he could catch anything that way."

Try as I might, I still found my shoulders tensing at the comment. I supposed we couldn't escape our stress, not even on a day out.

"The only way he can close a case is if he pins it on others," Arkady replied bitterly.

"Yet not you, not yet—I won't manifest it." Kostya knocked on the wooden fence.

I looped my arm with Arkady's, falling behind Emily and Konstantin.

"Has he really been on you for that long?" I asked.

"He used to respond to the calls during any disturbances at the homes," Arkady explained. "He's been on my tail ever since, convinced that I couldn't have possibly changed in ten years. I suppose it's easier to pin the blame on vulnerable people than actually solving crime."

"Do you think he will find a way to pin Vincent on you? Without evidence?"

"Can't call someone a murderer before you find a corpse." He shrugged. "Which he won't. I promise," he assured me.

"I'm not getting into that thing."

"Come now, Petre." Arkady held out his hand. "If you fall in, I promise you won't melt."

"I know you're not above pushing me!" I crossed my arms, chewing my lip.

The line for the rowboats was long, people waiting at the boathouse for their turn. I wished I could have the excuse to stay on land with Emily, but she and Kostya left because of the baby fussing. The glimmering of the water around the dock made me dizzy. Everything was too bright, I just wanted to leave.

Then, hands at my waist.

"In you go." Arkady grunted as he lowered me right down into the boat.

"Stop it!" I demanded, clutching the sides of the vessel.

He tossed the folded parasol and our basket at my feet, stepping in.

"Let me out." I tried to stand; it only made the boat wobble more. "Pull it to shore."

"We're doing it. Look at you!" he said as if encouraging someone far too young to be me, his tone patronizing at best.

"Pull this boat around now." Tears pricked my eyes. "Turn it around!"

Arkady whistled a happy tune, gracefully rowing us through the water. The lapping sounds against the wood encouraged the nausea, the movement not making it easier.

I shakily reached down, opening the parasol to shield the midday sun from my eyes. I could feel my scalp beginning to redden; the same would be true for my cheeks and nose.

"See? It isn't so bad." Arkady stilled the paddles, looking at the other boats around us.

"I'm going to be sick," I muttered, taking deep inhales through my nose.

"Here, a prize." He reached inside his coat pocket. I thought he was going to offer at least a cigarette, only to see him pull out a silver flask.

"Arkady!" I shoved his hand down, out of view of anyone else. "Do you want people to assume we are some pot-shotten derelicts?"

"Your dress costs half a year of the average working wage. Trust me, no one thinks that." He looked unimpressed with my word choice, then held it up again. "Take a sip, relax."

I straightened myself, holding the parasol low over my face. With a swipe of the hand, I held it close, gingerly flicking open the cap. The liquid was cold yet stung my throat with a floral sweetness.

"Gin?" I glanced up at him.

"Isn't it fitting?"

"I suppose it's . . . immersive. Why walk in the gardens when you could drink them instead?"

"That's the spirit." He took the flask back, taking a sip himself. "I may need educating when it comes to your world, but *you* need lessons in *loosening up*."

"I *am* loose."

He rocked the boat slightly.

I gripped the edge quickly, nearly dropping my parasol.

"Right." He laughed.

"Please, Arkady," I begged, my stomach beginning to sour, "I've entertained your outing. I've done all you ask. Please, can we go home?"

He sighed, leaning forward with his elbows on his knees. "I don't know, do you deserve it?"

I lowered the parasol to the side, hiding our faces from shore. The shade from the fabric made his eyes so bright between his dark lashes, his tanned skin. As I leaned forward, we were almost nose to nose. "Can I earn it with a kiss?"

"Depends on the kiss."

"I was hoping for one as sweet as the marmalade in our basket."

"Perhaps. I'll need a reference." He reached down, digging the small jar from the basket at our feet.

He popped the lid open with a snap, his eyes never leaving mine as he did so, locking me in a trance. He dipped his finger in, then brushed it across my lip. The aromatic jam made for a sweet balm.

"Will you taste just as sweet," he whispered, "or will you be bitter?"

"I suppose you will have to tell me," I breathed, closing my eyes.

His lips were always so soft, though when I felt his tongue dancing in the marmalade, my stomach fluttered, heart pumping loud in my ears.

He cupped my face in his rough hand, our kiss mingling with the fruity taste, made all the richer by each other's taste. His cologne of figs and cedar heightened the palate, making me hungry for more.

As soon as the sweetness faded, he broke the kiss but not the contact.

I opened my eyes hesitantly.

He smirked, his thumb running over my cheek. "You make it very hard to be in public when you look at me like that."

"I'm not—"

"We better get you home before our appetites get us in trouble," he joked, pulling away.

I rolled the parasol in my palms, fighting it upright again above my head. "I don't know what you mean." I licked my lips, brushing a finger at the corners to check for leftover jam.

CHAPTER THIRTY

The Artisan

The impression of the key was clear in the slab of soap. The morning was spent filing scrap metal to match the impression until I could slip the key seamlessly into the original shape. It was more time-consuming than melting down and filling a mold, but soap was the best thing I could use for the impression in a pinch.

As I approached our block, a figure in black—obvious mourning attire—hurriedly came down the steps of the town house. As I neared our home, I could see that it wasn't a visitor who wished to stay.

A plain box was placed in front of our door. I looked down the street in the direction the woman went; she was already gone. Turned a corner, swept away by a crowd, however of the many ways to get lost in Manhattan.

"I suppose you're a special delivery, then," I muttered to myself as I gathered the box.

The house was empty when I opened the door. Glancing at my timepiece on my wrist, it read ten o'clock. Petronille usually didn't wake until about this time. But today, I found she wasn't even in the house.

I placed the box on the dining room table, tossing my keys next to it and my coat over the back of a chair. The box was dusty, much like the things she had collected from her sister's donations. The cardboard had small stains in the top corners, and not much on the outside indicating the contents.

I slipped the top off, glancing inside. Photographs bent out of shape, receipts, papers with dog-eared corners and wrinkles.

How boring.

I picked up one of the photos; it seemed to be of the family, taken someplace warm. When I shifted the papers, a white blur startled me. Several moths puttered out of the dense memorabilia, crawling quickly as the wings slapped, tumbling across the surface. I swore there were more and more of them every time I blinked. I would have to place more traps.

When I lifted another photograph, it seemed to be just the siblings. A candid. Two brunettes crouched on the ground, looking at something in the dirt. A small blond girl was next to them, yet even standing, she wasn't taller than the others. She was dressed differently, I suppose in a hand-me-down. Clothes aside, there seemed to be an invisible wall, a disconnect, between the brunettes and the pale-haired child. It was hard to see all the finer details from the photograph.

There was another; this time I knew Petre instantly. The faded blond with two beauty marks next to her lip. She was with five others, all posed nicely in their tulle skirts and silk shoes. It was adorable how stern they all looked, like professionals, despite being lanky and small.

The last photo was one I couldn't part with. It was a portrait, cropped to a simple bust, professionally done. I suppose this would be her eighteenth birthday, according to the date. Her dress was simple and handmade. Her hair was curled and styled with moonflowers. Her gaze, even her smile, was lighter. I didn't believe I'd seen her like that before. So at peace, so hopeful.

I tucked the photo in my pocket, hesitant to hide away the image like a secret, like it was something I wasn't supposed to see. A sacred illusion that I didn't want to forget.

Under the photographs were folders, all varying in fullness.

I plucked one from the box, letting the cover flap open.

Coronary Report.

On the lines following were rather mundane, technical details. A name, date of birth, place of death. Occupation, farmer. Something about the notes poked at my subconscious, screaming at me to look. Nothing good would come from recognizing anything within a dead man's file.

Cause of death: Unknown.

Observation: Enlarged kidneys.

Within some of the folders were photographs. The first one, a few white-coated individuals standing in front of some shack, vast fields in the horizon. They were shaking hands with farmers, tanned and dusty from working out in the open.

The next one was just a woman, sitting. She looked familiar, but I couldn't quite place her. She was pretty, so perhaps I was associating her with some celebrity.

Flipping to the next photograph, it was darker, indoors. There were people in white coats and bandannas, white cloth masks over their faces and rubber gloves up to their elbows, all hunched over a table. There wasn't much to see, as the grain obscured most details from poor lighting.

Then, the woman again. But now I recognized her.

The last photograph, she had half her head shaved, metal pieces holding a long scar together, one eye concave and stitched shut.

I placed my hand over the butchered half of her face. But the next paper confirmed my suspicions.

I'd seen her before.

The last photograph, a small one clipped to the report: her cadaver scorched in all the places they'd disfigured her while she was still alive . . . almost half of her entire body, from what I could see. An experiment gone wrong, and they didn't have enough of a soul to admit it.

Used, then discarded. Like an animal.

I squinted down at some small text. A few words were repeating, familiar as of late.

I held the file in one hand, moving quickly near the door to gather an old, crumpled newspaper.

LAGO PHARMACEUTICALS PROPOSES ON-SITE MEDICAL CARE FOR UPSTATE AGRICULTURAL FARMS.

I skimmed the article for the one line of tiny text I was looking for. Halfway down, I saw it—Ghent, New York.

I held the file next to the paper.

Place of Death: Ghent, New York.

The distinct taste of bile nipped at the back of my throat, then became stronger the more the insinuation fermented. My fingers shook, the paper almost slipping from my hand.

I threw the file on the table, tipping the box over and spreading the others out across the dining room table. I opened each one, the newspaper in hand as I read through them.

Ghent, New York.

Ghent, New York.

Ghent, New York.

They all came from the same town, had the same occupation . . . on the same farm, I assumed. Yet, their deaths were spread across months. The oldest being a year ago, the newest being last week.

Why was this left for us? Was this a threat or whistleblowing? Did Petronille know the extent of her father's business? I couldn't even hold it against her if she knew, because what *was* there to do? The more I learned about her family, the more I realized her behavior toward them wasn't unwarranted but had been earned in full with capital. Which made it clear that I needed to hide the evidence in case this was some sort of ploy.

CHAPTER THIRTY-ONE

The Performer

When the sun fell, the city woke. Friday night, mild weather, and the twinkling of occupied windows as plentiful as the stars. There were no stars in the sky because they were all down here, shimmering in the streets after dusk.

Surrey and barouche carriages would be making their debuts with horses just as flashy as the mobiles themselves. Though now you could hear just as much sputtering of engines as the clopping of hooves.

With all the luxury of transportation, one forgot the art of meandering. Arkady and I took to the street, arm in arm. There was no rush to be at the show early, and the theater wasn't far. To be fair, no establishment was that far here.

The balletomanes crowded in their place of worship, their regular tithing, the stage their church, the performers their prophets. I did not know if I believed in God, but I believed there were things in this world that could move the soul, art being among the most powerful next to death.

A swarm had already gathered. The slow trickle of people disappeared one by one through the doors as their tickets were checked.

I stopped in my tracks, the block alight from the electric bulbs of the marquee sign, *The Brass Globe*, proudly atop the fixture.

La Sylphide

The letters black and bold, like seeing the face of someone who's since passed.

We were here to see the premiere. Most importantly, it was supposed to be Lorelei's debut.

Just remembering made me want to walk a couple more blocks, to postpone the showing. There were many feelings I couldn't quite come to terms with. Could it be jealousy? Guilt? Going at all felt too much like a confrontation; I didn't even know if I could stay for its entirety.

Skipping would be a waste, as I'd gone through the effort of looking nice. A silk gown, cream with white datura embroidered down the front. The sleeves were a short white lace that tickled my arms. The opera gloves fashioned from the same cut of silk. Pearls were light in my ears, much more comfortable than any rock. Glimmering on my fourth finger was my engagement ring, a deep red like blood orange.

"You're hesitating," Arkady said, standing in front of me to pull me from my fixation.

"We aren't in a rush." I thumbed my engagement ring, twisting it absently.

He placed his hands on my shoulders, pressing down slightly.

I sighed at the pressure, my head loping back. "Would you be upset if we didn't go?"

His fingers cupped either side of my face, letting my head relax into his touch.

"I don't know why you bothered with all the finery if you didn't want to go," he hummed, glancing at the theater, the crowd almost finished filing in. When he looked back at me, he had some wicked glint in his eyes; a terrible idea had graced his mind, I was sure. "Do you trust me?"

"Yes," I muttered.

He patted my cheeks before grasping my hand. "We don't have to go, but I won't let the night go to waste." He was already pulling me in the opposite way that we'd come from.

"Where are we going? Wait!" The theater got smaller and smaller in my vision.

He walked faster, the gas lamps lining the streets burned, people becoming fewer and fewer as he led me to the heart of Manhattan.

"Stop!" My voice was strained. I twisted my hand away from his. "Just let me . . . catch my breath."

The tall gates of the park hung over us. The iron bars and sharp hooks, to keep all intrusion out, were intimidating. But it seemed as though the scarier the fortification, the grander the reward. Even as we stood before the gates, you could hear the dribbling of running water within. The frogs were chirping, the one place they could perform their song that felt like home, before us mere people moved in. Each breeze carried the scent of cherry blossoms, tulips, and other botanicals yet to be discovered. It was a temptation, and we were not supposed to indulge.

"Come." Arkady stood under the gates, his hand extended.

"Come where?" I crossed my arms, glancing around us.

"It is a public park, you act as though we are stealing," he joked, taking a step closer, grabbing the air between us to beckon me.

"It feels wrong."

"The park is open for another two hours, we have time," he assured me. "I promise."

I looked down the sidewalk, then to my other side. Not a person in sight.

"Petronille," he called to me adoringly.

I finally looked at him again, his hand still there for me.

"It's time to practice letting go a little," he said.

I raised my hand, hovering it over his palm. It wasn't like I was not going to take it. No, I was weak to his charms. Arkady was the type who could talk the most sensible people into leaping straight off a wildwood cliff. He had that air to him, the kind that made you feel as if you could fly. An aura that promised adventure, even in small pieces. That was the most exciting of all, the small adventures woven within the mundane, entirely accessible and never ending.

It was then I took his hand, and our adventure had just begun.

Flowering trees canopied over the walkway, the slightest breeze sending the wilting petals down on us. The path opened to tall hedges, blooming shrubbery, like witch hazel and aster.

It wasn't much of a maze, but it did lead to a pond with a fountain.

The chittering of the frogs was louder now, their calls intermingling with a lone musician somewhere in the streets beyond the park.

My heels sank into the grass. I kicked off my shoes, the soft manicured lawn tickling against the soles.

Arkady laid his jacket neatly on the edge of the fountain, swiping off his suspenders, and he tugged his freshly pressed shirt over his head.

"What are you doing?" I whispered.

"Going for a swim," he said as if it were obvious. His arms slipped around me, holding me close. "And so are you."

Before I could object, he picked me up, submerging us with one quick dip in the pond.

I gasped at the chill, blinking the water from my eyes and shoving his chest. "Bastard!" I hissed.

"Apologies, did I get Her Majesty's hair wet?" He pulled me farther into the water.

"C-cold! Dear Lord, it's cold," I chattered, hugging myself as we waded.

The ripples of the water cascaded through the water lilies, the frogs silent from the sudden commotion. For one small moment, the city seemed quiet.

I caught my breath, wiping my hair back as it fell from its updo and hung in damp waves that stuck to my neck and face.

The dress was becoming heavy. I felt I was weighed by lead.

"Arkady, help me with something," I beckoned him, reaching to the back of my neck, looking over my shoulder to see if he understood. His hands steadied on my shoulders before moving my mop of hair away from the dress clasps. The touch was warm against my skin, even the gentlest graze.

When the fabric loosened on my shoulders, I waded away, lowering my body fully under the surface to slip it off. The water made my underthings sheer, floating like ghosts under the murky water.

The moon rippled in the reflection, obscured as Arkady swam through it.

His hand touched my waist, then my hand. The newly bloomed water lilies bobbed in our wake, and as the water stilled, the night came alive again.

The frogs whistled and crickets chirped. The water was warmer now, or at least I was used to it. I was so entranced with my surroundings that I nearly forgot he was here, watching me this whole time.

He pulled me in close, a slow dance like swans circling.

Even in the dark, the green of his eyes looked as if they were grown right here within the garden. Nothing could compare to the softness they held now. I knew, in this moment, that the intimacy was no illusion of mine.

"We'll get caught," I whispered, but it wasn't the first thing I wanted to say.

"Just let me steal a few more moments." His forehead rested against mine.

"Thief," I teased as we sank a little lower in the water to keep the breeze from chilling us. "At least steal something less fleeting."

He let go of my waist and hand, cupping my face between his palms. His brow taut, his voice stern. "There is nothing of greater worth when the world is in my hands."

My lip trembled. I could blame it on them turning blue from the cold night air.

I wrapped my arms around his neck, leaning into his kiss.

His hands on my cheeks squeezed as he leaned back in the water. The grip was desperate, a grounding reminder that it was real. He backed us into the shore of the pond, turning and setting me down between the towering cardinal flowers.

The sharp breeze sent a tremor through my body, limbs bitten by cool air. My clothing stuck to me, dripping wet.

Arkady crawled over me, kissing my lips several times like he couldn't resist stealing another before moving down to my neck, my chest, between my breasts, fingers pulling the wet fabric.

I glanced up to the tall stalks of the cardinal blossoms swaying against the dark sky. A shiver overtook me as I glanced around.

"Don't worry," he whispered, "no one will find us here." His breath hot against my skin, his hands smoothing up my calf, then over my knees, as he pushed up the soaked petticoat.

I didn't tell him to stop, just watched, crossing my arms over my chest.

"No, that won't do," he said, pulling me up and reversing our positions.

"I'm cold, please." My hands pressed against his chest, my shivering thighs straddling his hips.

"Let's warm you up, then." He leaned up, hooking his arms under my legs and yanking me up to sit right on his chest.

"Wait a minute!" I squeaked, my fists balled in my undergarments now, but even with my pleas, he maintained a smirk. I didn't know how he expected me to act with his face nearly between my legs.

He nudged me forward again.

"What are you doing? You'll suffocate!"

He ignored me, yanking my hips forward. His hot tongue flattened between my legs, and I nearly keeled over in shock.

"Wait!" I whined, followed by a moan when he sucked hard, holding my hips down on his face.

My breath shook as I exhaled, the warmth melting me as his tongue danced across every sensitive place he could find until he ventured farther within. A wet slurping sound made the heat rise from my thighs all the way to my cheeks. My hand slapped over my mouth to contain my moan, fearing we'd be discovered—especially in *this* position.

Soon enough, my thighs were tired from tensing, and I hesitated to relax, wary of my entire weight being on his face.

It didn't seem to bother him, it made his fingers dig into my thighs and his movements more pointed, voracious. He dug his tongue inside, sucking hard as he did so.

My head tipped back to the sky, eyes watery from the stimulus alone. It was easier if I didn't look, if I closed my eyes. The tall stalks of the pond flowers brushed against my shoulders, my cheeks, as they swayed. My hips moved, slowly, at first, against his face, beginning to ease into every sensation he offered me. At this point, I wasn't sure if the warm wetness was from the pond or myself.

My legs tensed again, feeling a rhythm snap into place, rocking steadily against his mouth. I reached down, entangling my fingers in his wet hair. He hummed in response, making his tongue still as I moved against it.

"It's hot . . ." I moaned. "*God*, it's hot."

My hips flinched, thighs trembling when I couldn't move them any longer. An orgasm pulsed until my hips slowed to a halt, no longer able to hold myself up as the sensation worked its way through me, from my core to the tips of my toes. I could practically hear the electricity buzzing in my ears . . . or was I just hearing my own blood flow?

Finally, I opened my eyes, taking deep breaths as I tipped back, raising my skirt.

"My turn." He licked his lips, sitting up and sliding me back to his lap.

"I don't think I can lift myself any longer," I said breathlessly.

"You don't have to." He kissed me as he used one hand to undo his belt. I could taste myself on him, mixed with the earthiness of fresh water.

His cock was hot under my skirt, pressed flush against my pelvic bone. He lifted my hips as I placed steadying hands on his shoulders.

We didn't break our kiss, we just continued to melt in each other's arms. His cock pressed between my legs, a couple failed prods before I reached for it, hot in my hand as I guided it, relaxing down.

I gasped against his mouth, and he captured my breath between our lips again, holding me tight as he rocked my hips back and forth, comforting, like he was easing me into an embrace.

"Do you think," I whispered, eyes fluttering open, "this could be how Eve felt in the garden?"

He smiled like it was a silly question. "If the snake were half as lucky as I am now, I would consider the temptation worthwhile."

He lifted my hips again, then settled them back down.

The feeling of being full, accepting his length. It stretched inside me, overwhelmed my senses. Though, it was only half the sensibility. He spoke to me in soft kisses and fleeting glances, the art of entwining one's self with another. The language of the body, the soul.

I gasped against his lips, kissing deeply as if to distract from the fact that we were baring ourselves publicly. I lifted myself in tandem with his support, his grip tightening as his hands wrapped around my waist. It was like every sound, every unspoken word, made him clutch tighter, yet he was forcing himself to savor when all he wanted to do was devour. It was the type of hunger where you crave for a person, for the flavor of their lips against yours. To hold each other's hearts, hoping neither one of you will squeeze harder than the other.

The more he allowed me to see and feel, the more he invaded the very core of my chest cavity, filling up my heart and replacing my blood until the only desire within me was *him*. Just him. A deep, primal instinct to eat him whole.

"Arkady!" An overwhelmed cry.

"You have me," he breathed against my neck.

"Please . . ."

"I'm yours, completely and utterly yours." His words were so light, I almost assumed he was saying them to himself.

I dug my nails into his shoulders, resting my head against his, my hips rolling desperately as his hands guided me. The quickness of the pace and the warmth of our bodies teased even the most stubborn of senses. Complete relinquishment of any goal other than to be pleasured, to be desired.

"There you go. Again," he whispered the demand in my ear, "give in for me."

One of his hands slipped under my skirt, and he distracted my lips once more as he did so. The sudden stimulation was too much, overwhelming when paired with the rest of the attention on my body, on his. I swore my gasp came out as a cry, a shock up my spine that made me sit up straight, but he held me tighter.

I sat fully down on his lap, with only enough energy to rock slightly. Though I assumed he'd finished long ago, as not *all* of the wetness could be my own. I supposed we were both distracted.

"Mine," I breathed, resting my head against his. "By God, if I desire anything on this Earth, it is you."

"And if the devil doesn't strike me down, may you have it." He caught his breath, a bright smile on his face as he lay back, holding me close to his chest.

And like the critters of the pond, we spent the last of the early-morning hours staring up at the sky between the mudflowers. The wind between their stalks whispering to us of the secrets we shared, of the moments we stole, and the night our hearts dug their roots into each other and made a home.

CHAPTER THIRTY-TWO

The Artisan

Seeing your art up close after a long period of time absent from it feels like seeing an old friend.

Mantelpieces, carvings in stone banisters, even statement pieces were all familiar, yet it felt like a surprise to run into them. They were what made the home luxurious, a simple statement of wealth and taste, all of which could be considered narcissistic to say since they were all mine.

Yet I couldn't help but feel like their ownership was my first sellout, not just creatively, but that I'd given pieces of me away.

Even so, now it felt like I'd traded them for a wife.

"Arkady!" Mrs. De Villier appeared at the top of the grand staircase, shimmering as she fluttered down the steps to meet me like she had so little time but much to do. "My husband is in his study; go straight down the hallway and in the first door on the left."

I knew *very well* where the study was.

Even on arrival, it was a lot different in the full light of day.

Adrien De Villier was tilted back in his leather chair leafing through papers. The light from the outside shifted over the desk and rug. The birds fluttered around the bushes crowding the window, shadows flickering from behind the figure.

"Mr. Kamenev! My good man, how are you?" Mr. De Villier glanced up from his papers, gesturing to the seat in front of him. "Come, sit."

"Faring fine." I slid into the curve of the wooden seat. "You summoned me here, it sounded urgent."

"You sound tired. My daughter hasn't worn you down, has she?"

"Of course not, nothing outside of my abilities to manage."

Mr. De Villier snorted, shaking his head as he tossed his papers on his desk with a slap. "I am glad you are a good sport about it. Everything is less fun when people aren't team players."

"I am no stranger to wild women," I joked, forcing a genial smile.

"Me and you both." He reached over for a decanter and two glass cups with a single hand, pouring a drink for each of us. "Speaking of, I have a favor to ask of you."

I reached for the glass, inspecting the liquor that stung my nose when the scent finally reached me.

"Unless it has to do with artwork, I'm not sure how I can help."

A small smile pulled at Mr. De Villier's face. Not a pleasant one, an expression of slight annoyance. "That is where you are wrong, my good fellow."

I placed the cup down on the arm of the chair, turning the glass and watching the light break on its way through the crystal.

"Get Petronille under control."

"Pardon?" I looked up at her father, his expression blank and cold, losing the previous hospitality.

"It's easier than you think, I promise." He sipped his drink, looking absently at his bookshelves. "I'm beginning to think you are a neglectful husband."

"I assure you—"

He raised his hand and sighed, shaking his head at me. "I mean this as no insult. She is difficult, of this I am *painfully* aware; for the past twenty years, I have become accustomed to her tantrums and outbursts."

I didn't care to comment. I barely cared to be here. I had no desire to do him any favors after the way he spoke of her. While Petre was strong-willed, being married to her never felt like a chore. In the beginning, it felt like cohabiting with a stranger, which was what our union was.

My father-in-law opened his desk drawer, producing two pieces of paper. He held them up pointedly, looking me in the eye before sliding them across the desk. "Take her out. Show her off. Keep her away from those she shouldn't fraternize with. Building a good rapport with the public will always be a smart investment, especially as two young people with the means to do so. So far, they love you. But be warned, they can turn on a dime."

I picked up the pieces of paper. I didn't have to read the bold typeface before seeing the illustration of a horse and jockey. Derby tickets.

"People ask me all the time, who is my artisan? They know your name but not the face!" He laughed, slapping the desk with his fingers before wagging one playfully. "It's about time you showed it off. What better way than at the derby? She can dress well, and so can you."

"It is generous of you to support our endeavors, sir." I tried to seem grateful as I clutched the flimsy paper in my hands.

"Of course! You are doing us such a favor. The poor thing, she isn't well."

"What do you mean when you say things like that?" I tapped my foot impatiently.

All he did was smirk at me with an air of pity. "Oh, it's nothing. I am sure she will explain her affliction to you."

I nodded, carefully choosing my words. "Yes, she has told me of her anemia, it was a feat convincing her to eat something other than candied apricots."

Her father burst into a snark of laughter. "Oh, did you now?" He shook his head and finished his drink, standing as he adjusted the buttons of his vest. “Good for you. I don’t mean to laugh—truly, good for you! She is so very lucky to have you.”

I stood, knowing my company was no longer needed.

He chuckled, slapping my shoulder when he came around the desk to lead me out. “Just make sure you two get some air, it’ll be good for the both of you.”

CHAPTER THIRTY-THREE

The Performer

This may have been the first time Arkady had asked me to attend anything formal with him, officially. Something of his own idea, his own will, not due to any hidden bodies or social formalities. Which was either evidence of our bond—of which I did more speculating on than anything—or it was cause for suspicion. I would like to believe the former.

Morris Park was a sight to behold on days like this. The Belmont Stakes was equal parts pageantry and gambling. The stands packed people in like tinned fish, accompanied by questionable scents intermingling with perfume and sweat from the adrenaline or the anxiety of lost wages. On the other side, those who did not partake in the stands had parked their carriages and set up picnics in preparation to watch the ever-so-fleeting event.

Such excitement and intrigue, attending at my husband's insistence, might be the only thing that would bring me into Westchester.

The dress I chose was cream in color with rustic orange ribbons as details, matching the florals on my fascinator. My parasol was made of the same fabric as the dress, ribbons and all. I would have felt quite pretty if it weren't for the distracting smell of horse manure.

Arkady wore something nice, his accessories matching mine.

It was too perfect, even considering the occasion.

The clubhouse building kept a careful eye over the park, welcoming its visitors for the brief spectacle. Women in their finest, a sea bobbing in fascinators and hats, ribbons and flowers, parasols and fans clutched in their modestly gloved fingers. Men were nice in appearance and tailoring, but never in demeanor. The only gentlemen at the racetrack were the stallions.

We were headed toward one of the viewing areas before I was led beyond the stairway.

I squinted at Arkady. "We passed the stairs."

"I know." He had some sort of mysterious smirk.

He held my arm a bit tighter as he led me down to the working area. We passed through to the backstretch of the track.

From far away, these horses were unremarkable. They had four legs, were usually brown. There wasn't much to them. But up close, I could see the appeal.

Even as one passed, side by side with their lead ponies, the thud of the hooves against the ground was assertive, proud. They were larger than life, or at least the stature of the jockeys made it seem so. The thoroughbreds' muscles rippled under hides, vibrating engines ready to be released onto the track.

"High-strung," I commented, "that one is already sweating."

"Just like you," Arkady teased, "though I would pay to see you in sport."

"Not a chance." I glared at him, fussing with the pins of my fascinator.

"Which one will you put your money on?" He leaned low to speak in my ear.

I bit my lip, looking from horse to horse. They all looked the same to me, not much to go on in terms of the sport itself.

"I like the polka dots," I said, pointing.

"Which one?"

"White and blue."

"Are you choosing based on the silks or the horse?"

I shrugged, squinting up at him. "It is all based on luck anyway. Why does it matter?"

He smiled and shook his head. "Fine, how much?"

"Perhaps we bet on something less monetary." I smirked, twirling my parasol between my fingers.

He nodded, thinking about the proposition a moment before speaking. "If your horse wins, I will be indebted to you for a favor. And you will be indebted to me if it loses."

"And what will a favor be good for?"

"Anything."

"If I win, I can ask for anything?"

"You're beginning to worry me now."

"I'm just making sure I hear the wager with clear ears." I held my hand out. "Deal."

He shook my hand firmly. "May your luck be plentiful."

As the horses finished their warm-ups and the trainers had their last words with the jockeys, the trill of trumpets demanded they begin fitting themselves in the gates. Below the doors were pacing hooves, one thousand pounds wound into these tightly coiled marvels of nature, and pacing shoes from anxious money holes, a gambler's dance.

Everyone was quiet as the last horse was ebbed into its gate. I leaned on the railing to look, but so was everyone else who stood trackside.

Then, the shriek of a brass bell, and sudden thunder rumbled the entire ground as beasts whipped past us so fast that if I blinked, I'd miss them. I lowered my parasol quickly, dirt kicked up as they passed, smacking against the fabric instead of my face.

Whistling and shouts of encouragement erupted, as if it would feed their horse of choice and bless the wind under its feet. I swore if the rapture came, the crowd would mistake it for a nearby derby and reach for their wallets.

By the second lap, the jockeys were already covered in as much mud as the bottom of my dress. The horses glistened as they whipped by, covered in mud and sweat, frothing at the bits as they lived the most freedom they'd had in their three years of life by far.

The last lap was due. I readied my parasol again, and before I knew it, my fascinator was blown off by the last pass of the herd.

Men on all sides were either exclaiming or throwing their hats. I supposed there would always be more losers than winners, but it was hard to tell from the crowd.

"Shoot, I missed it. Who won?" I mumbled.

Arkady rolled his eyes; he didn't answer.

"Does this mean my polka-dot pony won?" I twisted the parasol playfully between my fingers, turning my chin up to Arkady. "Sore loser about your debt, now?"

"No," he mumbled. "Remind me to bet money next time you pick a horse."

I looped my arm in his, tapping my head on his arm. "Next time, after I cash in that favor."

He nudged me, but I caught a sly smile.

"What will your favor be, then?" He sighed in defeat.

It was one thing to have a favor, it was another to pick only one.

"France." I looked up at him. "One day, with all your riches from being the most famous sculptor the world has ever seen, I would like you to bring me back to France. Far away from people, just us."

"You're trading a favor for a hypothetical?" He smirked. "I'll accept it, but I thought you'd ask for something more instantaneous."

"I could have, but it gives me something to daydream about, don't you agree?"

"I'll agree with whatever you like, it's your favor." He shook his head, amused by my conjecture.

I closed my eyes among the noise. I thought I didn't like events, or socializing, or *people*, for that matter. It could be that I just had never gotten to experience anything with people who were fun. Arkady made everything new, he made adventure fun again, even if I wouldn't admit it to him.

Something warm inside me blossomed at the idea. He and I against the world. What a blissful thought.

CHAPTER THIRTY-FOUR

The Performer

The scent of moth repellent burned the inside of my nose. My fingers flipped indecisively between catalog paper, the edges slightly warped from how many fingers had handled the pages. Even with less modern wares, my seamstress was the best. The shop was a nondescript hole on Fifth, but no better work came from elsewhere. I first came here to fit my ballet costumes; later, I came for everything else.

I couldn't decide between different sets of combinations. New colors were in fashion, yet I wasn't sure how it mattered, since nobody but your maids and husbands would see.

The thought made me pause, some new clarity dawning on me.

Did Arkady have preferences? Not that he really spoke of them. I suppose it was a good sign that he hadn't voiced anything that would make me think I had to change. Did he like one color more than the other? Did certain fabrics irritate him to the touch? Were there details he didn't care for? Or perhaps it was all the same to him, and I was thinking myself into a paralyzing hole.

The shop door slapping its bell made me startle, my heart leaping out and yanking me from the back of my mind.

"Petronille?"

I glanced over my shoulder. "Helen." I nodded politely.

"You know, you've always been so pretty." A sly smirk across the haughty features. "It must be nice to have attention even when not in the spotlight." She turned to one of her flock. "Don't you agree? Isn't she darling?"

"I'm not sure I'd like to know where the sudden compliments are coming from." I kept my expression steady, careful of any and all reactions. Everyone knew that jealous compliments were bad fortune, even worse for those who reacted incorrectly.

"Nowhere in particular." She giggled, turning to the other girls. "Should have known we would find you here."

Their fleeting gazes flicked to and from us as they shielded their laughter with gloves or fans.

At the beginning of the season, this may have bothered me some. But now, I felt that not only could I not understand the catty jokes, I didn't care to either.

"Have you spoken with Lorelei lately?"

I looked at her again; this time, she seemed less of an antagonist. "No."

"I doubt that. I'm sure you finally succeeded at talking her out of the ballet."

"I'm not her mother, her actions and whereabouts are her own and none of my business."

"Could have fooled us." She smirked, a couple of flighty laughs from either side of her. "I should be thanking you if you did, as her understudy. William was furious when she didn't show for her debut."

"You are awfully optimistic." I clenched my jaw, now feeling the soreness tense in my neck and head.

"I can't help but shine at a bright future." She pointed her chin in the air, a smirk of victory. "Well, as the old passes, so come the new. I sincerely hope you are enjoying your retirement."

I stopped looking at her, keeping both hands on the catalog to prevent them from seeking out the supple flesh of her face. Another hard chime of the door slapping the bell to mark the other customer's departure, the high-pitched irritants muffling with distance.

I slowly let out a long sigh, like holding it would keep unsavory words from forming after the interaction. The small optimist in my head told me to ignore it and continue on with my day, but the overwhelming pessimist that was cemented in my personality told me to go home and hit something in private.

As I was in no mood to take any functional highway, I did as my lower sensibilities craved. There was no need to be outside today anyway.

The arrival back home was as regular and ordinary as the walk there. I walked up each of the seven steps to my townhome, was at eye level with the window flower boxes, and to the left corner of the door was the daily paper.

I knelt down to grab it, the curled wad of paper dry, as a familiar face jumped at me.

I flipped the paper tube over to move up the headline.

What is this?

I scrambled to open the paper, unfolding and nearly tearing it with the force I pried at it.

This can't be real . . . no, it must be a sick dream. I am ill, I am asleep, it must be the fever.

I crumpled it, tossing it aside. Pressing my palms into my eyes as if to will the news away; it was a prank and not something printed across every paper in the city.

"Petronille Kamenev?" The gruff voice spoke behind me as if to clear his voice.

"Yes?" I frowned, turning to see not only Mr. Hunt but two uniformed men from his office. "What is this about?"

"Your presence is requested at the station."

"Am I under arrest?" I couldn't hold my voice, which wavered at the very words. My throat closed up, threatening to choke me, not caring if it was suicide.

"I can certainly do that, if you'd like," he said as if in a somber joke. "I'd rather not give the press any photos of you in cuffs. What do you say? I just have a few questions down at the station."

The commissioner was a poor actor. Despite his words, he was giddy about it all. His hand fiddled impatiently with the cuffs at his side as he pretended to be a patient and merciful man. In reality, he loved this. Like one who hunts for sport, not for sustenance.

I smoothed my skirt, stepping down from the front of my townhome and back onto the street.

Even with ill intentions, he was correct. I couldn't afford the bad press.

"Coffee? Water?"

"Tea?"

"No can do." Mr. Hunt shook his head. "Water, then?"

I blew a frustrated breath from my nose, crossing my arms as I leaned back in the chair.

Mr. Hunt stalked over to his desk, sitting comfortably as he interlaced his fingers and propped up his elbows. "Thank you for coming down here without a fuss."

"Right, because you gave me *so many* alternatives."

"Mrs. Kamenev"—the name was awkward in his mouth, as he was chewing enough that I barely recognized who he was addressing—"where were you the day of Vincent Carlisle's disappearance?"

"I already answered this!" I huffed. "I was home."

"I understand, we are just doing our due diligence," he said sincerely, but I could feel something coming on. He glanced down at his notepad, his woolen brows clenched together. "You said you were at home?" He glanced up without moving his face back to mine.

I stared back. My breath held hostage as I thought, as if all oxygen must be used to remember. *Damn it, remember.*

"Yes," I said slowly.

He pursed his lips, nodding as he pulled the notepad closer. "When I first visited you, you said you were at your sister's."

"Y-yes, that's where I was that morning. You didn't specify a time," I replied carefully.

"Was that Félice's home or Cosette's?"

"Cosette, we were having tea. She asked for biscuits, she has been craving them throughout her pregnancy," I lied, hoping that if asked, Cosette would just assume it was correct that the event was a couple days earlier.

"So when were you home?"

"I came home after."

"Did you leave your home later in the day?"

"No."

He nodded, pausing to reach over for his rounded spectacles. They sat crooked on his face as he produced a pen from his pocket and wrote something down on the pad. "Can anyone confirm you went home?"

"Lorelei . . ." I paused, gulping, picking at my fingers. "My friend used to stop by often. She may have come by, I don't remember."

"I spoke with her." He began writing quicker but didn't elaborate.

"You did?" I nearly laughed. "And what did she say?"

"She had some interesting things to say about your whereabouts."

"How long did you harass her before she agreed to play along in this petty investigation?" I watched his hand carefully; he stopped writing.

He placed his pen down, leaning back in his chair. "She volunteered this morning, actually."

Caught you, liar.

I eased into my own seat, uncrossing my arms and leaning back, elbows on the arms of the visitors' chair. "We don't speak much anymore. Her testimony would be as good as snake oil."

"I will need someone other than your husband to corroborate."

"My sister, then. Félice and Cosette saw me leave."

"But they didn't see you in your home."

"I don't see why I would lie about going home."

"Your husband seems to lie about going to his studio, so why not his wife lying about being home alone?"

I balled my hands in my skirt, a physical representation of my grip on my temper. I lifted my chin, raising my brow at him. I knew this game; it wouldn't work.

"I appreciate your concern for my marriage and well-being, Mr. Hunt," I said with the sweetest of smiles, "but I trust my husband wholeheartedly. He has odd hours, odd schedules. He is an artist."

He chuckled as he folded his spectacles, tucking them into his vest breast pocket. "Are you aware that your husband comes from a troubled home? Several, in fact."

"I don't see how someone's childhood is of any concern to their current life."

He smiled at me. "That's interesting that you say that, Petronille."

He reached down to his drawer, which squeaked as it opened, and produced a file. He placed it on the table before him like he was about to unwrap a Christmas goose and eat it in front of me. He opened it and leafed through a page, then another, in no rush to share his insight.

"Violent outbursts. Evidence of antisocial personality. Unnecessary cruelty toward his peers and staff. Disordered sleep schedule. Threatening his foster family with a splintered yardstick. Threatening a nun in service at Saint Lucia's." He stopped, holding the papers up but out of reach. "It was severe enough to be evaluated by an alienist."

I shifted in my seat, unsure how to defend the behavior. There had to have been a reason. There *must* be. It didn't sound like him at all.

"I will ask this once, and I need you to find it within yourself to answer honestly." He tucked the folder back into his desk before settling. "Where was your husband the day of Vincent's disappearance?"

"At his studio. Maybe until eight in the evening?" was all I could say with confidence. "His hours are unpredictable."

"That's all right, you are an honest woman, I appreciate any answers at all," he assured me. "Do you know where he was on your wedding day?"

"At the wedding."

"No"—he pulled up his notepad—"the papers detailed that your wedding was held privately in the afternoon." He leaned in slightly. "Do you know where he was earlier that day?"

No, we met at our wedding, I wanted to say.

"I don't know. It is bad luck to see the bride in her dress before the wedding." The answer was almost a sneer. "Why does it matter?"

"There was a disappearance of a couple." He slid over a photograph. Two people in a portrait, of good wealth but not of good breeding. They seemed lovely, young.

"I'm sorry, I don't see how this has anything to do with me."

"You will understand," he said cryptically. "You can ask him yourself. I will move on."

"Please," I insisted.

I knew the commissioner thought of me as dim, as well as most women, but I didn't appreciate his attempts to drive a wedge between myself and my husband.

"Are you aware that your husband visits the morgue nearly three times a week?"

I squinted at him, waiting for the other shoe.

"Interestingly enough, they're missing some files," he mentioned. "You wouldn't know a thing about that, would you?" Mr. Hunt slid over a piece of paper—a visitors' log.

On the list, there was Mr. Kamenev.

But there was also another stack beside it, the cremation logs.

It was like gravity was about to grab me by my ears and slam me down.

He knows. He knows about the deliveries.

I looked up at Mr. Hunt, his expression some mix of victory and satisfaction, a stare that pierced me to my core, seeing straight through me.

He knew this would not just distress me but violate me.

CHAPTER THIRTY-FIVE

The Artisan

"So everything is better?" Kostya bumped his shoulder into mine.

My whiskey sloshed against the glass. "It is fine," I mumbled.

Quiet mumbles of the morning mixed with the haze of sluggish cigarettes and dark roasts. Walnut from floor to ceiling with the exception of the mirror behind the bottles of the bar and the haze of the windows between the smoke and café curtains. The gilded painted lettering on the window read backward from inside, clear against the light greeting those with hangovers. Kostya and I nested ourselves in the pub corner, my friend's morning beer in hand with espresso on the side.

"Now that you're getting along with your wife, Emily has been asking for a double outing." He grinned. "We could try something fun, a show and dinner, perhaps?"

"Now why would you assume that?" I laughed.

"Oh sorry. I just thought . . ." He sipped his tall glass awkwardly, like he'd gotten too far ahead of himself.

I shook my head and took another sip of whiskey, then frowned. "Wait." I whipped my head back to him. "What are you talking about?"

"I thought you took my advice regarding reputation." He shrugged, frowning back at me, equally confused by my reaction.

"Why would you bring it up?"

"Have you not seen the papers?"

"What does that have to do with anything?"

Kostya looked over one shoulder, then the other, before standing and heading toward the door of the pub, checking behind a chair before digging out the paper from the morning in the garbage tin. He brushed it off, unfolding it as he sat next to me again.

The bold typeface of the headline read:

> NEW YORK'S RISING SWELLS TURNING HEADS—NEW YORK'S ILLUSTRIOUS SWEETHEARTS OFF TO THE RACES.

The main image was a photograph of the two of us promenading about the event. It was a nice photograph, though I hardly recognized myself next to her, dressed for her tax bracket. They caught something rare in the photo, not just my new tailoring but a small, fleeting smile on Petronille while she was with me. It was so brief, I didn't even remember it.

It would have been a great photo . . . if it weren't for the image below, accompanying the article.

It was another photo of Petronille, one I couldn't recognize. It was old; she looked just barely eighteen. She was only wearing combinations, a helpful illustration beside it detailing the exact design and where to get it.

While I would expect the design to be outdated, it seemed Petre's allure was enough to bring it straight back into fashion.

Interestingly—there were even quotes.

> The secret to alluring a man is your sense of fashion. Every detail, a tell-all. Invest in yourself, and a quality man will follow. That is why I recommend L'Atelier de Rhode for the finest catalogs, custom in cut and dye, the finest feel for the most exceptional value.

There isn't a single chance on earth that those words came from Petronille's mouth. A branded impersonation of my wife, at best.

This would surely affect her, though the article wasn't scathing. Which was odd, as the free press didn't hold back often.

I knew I hadn't been invited to Mr. De Villier's office the other day out of charity. No, he'd planned for this—paid in full. A trade-off was expected; he didn't seem the type to do anything without a motive. I just couldn't have guessed he would do *this*.

The slam of the door made a sharp cracking sound, a few officers rising from their desk from the commotion.

"Where is he?" I grabbed one who approached. Another man attempted to pull me back. "Where is he!" I shouted.

"Just the man I wanted to see." Mr. Hunt stood in the doorway of his office, laughing smugly as he waved me inside. "It's all right, he's harmless. Let him go."

Cautious stares as they hesitated to release me, their eyes telling me all I needed to know. Young, jumpy men all too willing to beat someone at the slightest inconvenience. They turned their noses up at those in the streets, as if they were somehow above the working man. Blue collars who believed they were white. Little did they know they were closer to being us than they were to being the lobbyists they protected with their badges.

They said you couldn't be an intelligent cop, or else you'd be promoted to politician—only the stupid believed the law served the people, and the men who served made fools of us all.

"Come have a seat, Arkady," Hunt said, stepping aside to hold the office door open.

I shoved the paper at the commissioner's chest. "I want to press charges."

"Is that so?" A new voice as the door closed. "What for?"

Adrien De Villier sat behind the commissioner's desk, reading this morning's paper.

"You used my wife's image and disgusting insinuations to sell overpriced scraps of clothing."

"Insinuations?" He seemed disinterested. "I believe you have me confused with the lingerie company. They paid for their placement in the papers."

I shoved the paper down from his face. "You gave them the photo."

Mr. De Villier glanced at it, a smirk rising on his face. "The photo looks better than expected when it's printed so large."

My arm snapped out at his tie, yanking it forward. "You did this."

"There is no foul play here, Arkady," he said, calmly placing the paper down on the desk. "We have permission from the photographer."

"We?" I pulled tighter. "This is defamation."

"It's just good business."

"What is your game, old man?"

Mr. Hunt approached us at the desk and reached for his pocket, slowly producing a photograph.

It was of Petre, her pale silhouette stark against the background. An older photograph than the one in the papers . . . but completely nude. I slapped my palm over it quickly as if it would protect the image's dignity.

"Rumor has it that this will be in the papers in two days," Mr. Hunt informed me. "It'll get pulled very quickly for being obscene, but it only takes one spark to set the tabloids ablaze with opinion pieces."

"You can't do that."

"Who will you call to complain? *My* precinct?" Mr. Hunt laughed.

"There is no point to this but to be cruel or entertained. I should hope not the latter, considering it is your own daughter. What do you gain from this?" I demanded from her father.

"An opportunity."

"What do you want? What will make you stop this aimless crusade?"

"I fear there is nothing to be done." Adrien shrugged, glancing at Mr. Hunt. "Though, there could be something . . ." He trailed off, leaning over the side of his chair.

With one hoist, a bag thumped in front of me on the desk. And with one quick zip, a flash of green. More money than I'd ever seen up close. My stomach lurched.

"I have one last favor to ask of you, for Petronille."

"No." I didn't need to hear his request. I already knew it wasn't something I could do. I wouldn't betray her, especially knowing this man would ruin her if nobody stood in his way.

"I thought you'd say that. You drive a hard bargain. Good man!" He laughed, leaning back down and dropping another bag on the table with a grunt.

Before I could open my mouth to repeat myself, he put his hand up in pause.

He reached down on the other side of the office chair and stood, throwing the third bag at my chest.

The impact almost toppled me as I caught it, the weight nearly forcing the air from my lungs.

"You're a smart boy. I know you'll choose well. It's simple. You killed Vincent. Well, Petre said *she* killed him, but, of course, I know my little girl well. The poor thing is squeamish, that's why Vincent always did everything for her. I expected it was probably you. Even if it wasn't, I'll make sure the law *thinks* you did. Do you understand me so far, boy?" He took his seat again in the commissioner's office chair, Mr. Hunt standing by his side.

I eyed him carefully, my grip on the bag tightening.

"You deserve an easy life, Arkady. Mr. Hunt has told me quite a bit about your history," he said. "Isn't that why you married her? To save her reputation? Come now, boy. Do her this one kindness and free her of you."

"You want me to abandon her and volunteer a confession to fill your quota?" I sneered.

"No, my dear son, you are being paid to disappear. We will announce your confession after you are long gone. It will be the story of the decade. She will be free to remarry above her class, her love story will skyrocket her to infamy, you will have more money than you could ever spend in your lifetime, and no one will see the inside of a prison."

"No one?" I laughed. "Not even you?"

The charming geniality in his face faltered, daring to show the wicked monster that lay within, before the facade hardened. "If you'd like to propose a threat, be plain with it."

"The farms." I was firm in my accusation but couldn't let him know how much I truly knew. "Is that why you wanted us on the front pages? Embarrassing your daughter for a headline to bury the ones about your farms? I'm sure a plague would be an even bigger story than a woman who married an alleged murderer with no evidence, not even a body to be found." My jaw tensed as I forced myself to chew and swallow the words I *really* wanted to say.

"That's quite a story. Would you be willing to gamble with it falling flat?" Mr. De Villier asked, tapping the hollow desk. "You are young, I admire your optimism in our press. The truth is, they're *just* farmers. Even if you warned of some catastrophic act of God that would kill millions, the press would ignore it until there is a Caucasian casualty, upper-middle class at the very least. These people come from far and wide to work the fields, with no family, no connections to the land or the community, just there for a paycheck."

"They're people," I said sharply, looking to Mr. Hunt. "You harp on probity so often, I almost believed you had some sense of decency, in your own snobbish way. You are a harping fraud! How do you go on, knowing you'd rather harass people for petty crimes while you're covering for such a molestation of justice?"

"There are necessary evils in this world that are inevitable," Mr. Hunt said. "You will understand, as you mature, that this is how the world works. There is give and take."

"You are a coward," I snapped at her father. "Throwing Petre to the wolves won't help you. Isn't it *bad for business* that your daughter's in the press?"

"My boy, the public didn't even know I *had* a third daughter. Their first impression of her was with your last name attached to her face, along with a gossip piece about the exclusive private wedding of a retired ballerina. Her brand is her own." They both laughed. "You and Petre could have been a decent distraction, and yet you've made my job harder by killing the man disposing of our bodies. If you'd just held out a bit longer, you could have faded back into irrelevance if you wished."

"This is a good deal, for all parties," Mr. Hunt said. "You don't want to see her hurt, do you?"

"It isn't me who is hurting her," I said.

"You can choose what you like." Adrien sighed, leaning back in the chair. "You can deny the money, save your confession, and stay. But will you be able to live with yourself when she suffers, and you knew you could have prevented it?"

I clutched the bag in my hand. I could feel the distinct bound stacks of paper poking through the edges and giving it a lumpy shape.

Mr. Hunt, her father . . . nobody was there to protect her. She wasn't a person to them, just a pawn like their working-class slaves or lab rats. They wouldn't stop, not until they got their way.

With all that in mind, I left the precinct that day with three bags.

CHAPTER THIRTY-SIX

The Performer

The docks were different at night. During the day, they were crowded with gruff men, the shrieks of squabbling gulls, and the sloshing of water lapping at the posts. But at nighttime, it all went away.

The moon glittered through the water, the black expanse dazzled in the middle like some celestial spotlight. The only sound was the faint harmony of water whispering sweet nothings to the hulls of the harbor boats.

Even Arkady's studio looked different. A simple old warehouse. The tall metal doors were dark and looming yet cracked open enough to emit a dim warm light.

The statues were gathered at the edges of the studio like a thistle-lined field, a thick tree line before an expanse, the mighty overseers of something peaceful, a haven.

It was a silly thought, but I was in need of something whimsical and unserious after the day I'd had. Escapism might not always be the answer, but it remained the only place where I controlled the narrative—to express without being perceived, to desire without shame. Control was the ultimate phantasm.

I stepped out from the crowd of statues, my foot nudging something small. At the feet of the statues were candles of various widths and burns like the lining of a makeshift stage. The flickering shifted, casting shadows from the marble and clay creations—an audience.

In the middle of the studio was a form, a small speck on the stage.

I knelt down beside it to unfurl the discovery.

My old ballet shoes, with a sheer, gauzy fabric resembling gossamer wrapped around them.

The hazy sound of a phonograph, scratching to life before the music paced itself with ease.

With the fabric in hand, I looked up at the fogged window of the overseer's office. There was a shadow of a man, the small cherry of a lit pipe.

A balletomane?

As I listened to the ebbs and swells of the recorder, I knew I recognized it. It was transitioning to the prelude to *La Sylphide*.

My heart throbbed; I could only close my eyes to take it in. I took off my shoes, my skirt, and my top. I hiked up my petticoat to put on my ballet shoes, flexing them after I tied off the ribbon. The bare corset allowed my arms to be free yet my posture to remain intact. The phonograph stopped. I stood in the middle, waiting.

The prelude began again, and I closed my eyes to feel it, to imagine how it was before. The stage was a place to breathe, to stretch the mind and the legs. I saw a dark expanse, only the small lanterns separating the stage and the unknown critics, the impression of chairs that disappeared into the auditorium, then the chandelier hanging above. The stage, *my* stage. Despite the crowds that swell to see your performance, in the moment, you were alone in all ways that mattered.

With the gossamer draped over my shoulders and arms, I embarked into the unknown.

I moved to the center, standing up on the box of my shoe and lifting my arms, letting go of my tension to replace it with the music.

I kicked my leg back and fluttered to one side of my stage, moving my arms slowly as if they would lift me into the air, to imagine I was feather light. Turning, I went to the opposite edge, extending my arms, lowering and raising, stretching out as if to reach someone in the dark.

There was no feeling like a performance. To somehow translate music into dance, a language that most could understand with no prerequisite.

As I turned and stretched, the movements felt like I hadn't even left the ballet. They were as familiar as a childhood meal, the scent of a parent's cologne, the eyes of a loved one after too long apart.

I spun on just the tip of my shoe, holding the pose before I expected to come down—except I didn't. Two hands at my waist, supporting me to make the moment last a little longer, to delay the conclusion.

I didn't open my eyes.

His hands smoothed up to my rib cage, then along the undersides of my arms, and Arkady collected the draped fabric in his hands before pulling it over my eyes and tying it in back.

He smelled of cocoa, cedar, and smoke, and it wafted around me like a ghost, something to entice the soul and tempt me to follow. The blindfold allowed me very little visibility, especially in such a dim setting, yet made the space seem larger, grand with possibility.

He spun me gently, my hand in his as my body relaxed.

His hand touched my hair, then traced over the fabric of the blindfold.

In a swift motion, he lifted me in his arms, my hands steadying on his shoulders before he placed me down, seated upon a hard, smooth surface. Marble. Shaped like a chair, I thought . . . then realized it felt like a body, a male figure seated in a reclined, leisurely position, except there was a stone jutting out in front of my pelvic bone like the horn of a saddle.

My partner shifted, backing away from me. I couldn't see much through the fabric over my eyes, just a vague figure leaning against the sheet of a covered statue, the small amber of his pipe lighting and dimming. I could smell it, he was so close yet unreachable.

"Arkady?"

"I don't know that name," he said, the sound of smoke blowing through lips. "I am simply an admirer."

I swallowed, shifting on the marble. I felt the stone, smoothing my hands over the form to discern it. Legs, an arm, a chest and torso behind me. Which meant . . .

It was phallic—the *horn*.

"Don't let an audience stop you from such a lovely performance," he said. "Continue."

"What do you want from me?"

"The better question is"—he approached, his voice getting much clearer, like the smoky scent—"what do you wish for?"

I held the cock of the statue, warming the marble between my palms.

He leaned in, my mysterious admirer. His bottom lip brushed against my earlobe, then my jaw. His hand placed my hair gently over my shoulder. "You're not allowed off until the *finale*."

The stone was smooth but thick. My hands squeezed around it, gathering what warmth I could muster to prepare. Though, it was the anticipation, the churning in my stomach, like the flutters you get before your cue behind the stage.

My hands steadied on Arkady's chest as he lifted my leg and hip.

"A performance can be ruined by a stiff partner," I joked, overcoming the heat that inevitably lit my face afire.

"It sounds like you need a new partner," he replied, his hands holding me above the inanimate member.

The cold tip brushed against me, my hips moving forward to test how I felt between my legs, to see how relaxed I really was. I let it go in, just slightly. The cool material encouraged a tremor.

"That's it." Arkady's hand gripped my thigh. "But I fear you're being too modest."

Then, he lowered me onto the cock, and my hand left his shoulders to cover my mouth.

He stilled, not moving a single muscle. I leaned my head against his chest, a shaky whimper escaping before I relaxed, a moment of recovery as my hands held on to his shirt. I could feel his bulge against my stomach, pulsing when I tilted my head up.

He brushed my cheek with his fingers. "How do you feel?" Though his voice sounded more like himself, as if he wanted to ask, *Are you okay?*

"I would feel better if it were you," I breathed. My feet didn't touch the ground from the lap of the statue. I had to spread my legs, thighs gripping the statue to lift myself up, then lower back down. "But I suppose I can pretend . . . for you."

I held on to Arkady's shoulder, steadying my movements.

"Is that what you want, sir?" I palmed his pants, feeling the pulse. I leaned up. "Do you take more pleasure in the thought of me or the visual I've created just for you?"

I heard him swallow, and I lowered myself back down on the stone. I let him go, leaning back on the lap of the stone man. As I moved, I put my hands to better use. Teasingly, I used both hands to lift my skirt, exposing only my knees.

Arkady touched my leg.

"No," I said, "wait."

I lifted it higher as I moved, exposing my mid-thigh. As I lowered myself again, I released a small moan, a mewl like some feline in heat.

"I suppose it is quite an experience to watch two masterpieces at once," he hummed.

Even if I couldn't see him clearly, I knew his eyes would be positively fixated on me. "So you prefer to watch?"

"There is no greater pleasure than that of a woman's, even if only seen and never disturbed."

"Truly? No greater pleasure?" I teased. "Not one thing?"

One hand on my thigh, the other cupped the back of my neck, pulling me slightly forward. He pressed me down, slow and hard on the marble piece.

"Do you still wish it were me?" His voice was low in my ear as the cock bottomed out. "Are you that desperate?"

I shook my head, his fingers laced in my hair.

"When I ask you something, you *answer*."

"Yes," I whimpered, my legs shaking from the repetitive motion.

"I'm not convinced." He pressed his hand to the front, rubbing between my legs; it only made me buck against it.

"Yes! God, yes!" I cried, my hands balling in his shirt as I felt it coming, my focus bleeding into a blurry bliss. "Please!"

He yanked my face forward by the grip on my hair, kissing me so deeply, my tears of pleasure stained the silk of my dress. My tension tight, then blooming as relief washed over me, a pulsing inside as I settled onto the stone, my legs too sore to lift any longer.

Arkady let go of my hair, gently rubbing the back of my scalp and smoothing my hair down. I slumped against his chest, needing to catch up on my breathing, my body twitching from every subsequent touch.

"You did good," he whispered to me, leaving a kiss on the top of my head. "You were perfect."

I dug my toes under the quilt, leaning back against the window that took up most of the wall behind his mattress. Pillows stacked behind me, stowed away to make room for the spread.

Arkady had assembled some wooden trays, covering them in cloth to appear either fancy or just to hide the paint and clay stains. One of the boards was covered in all types of charcuterie: figs, cheeses, aged meat. The other had more sweets, soft stone fruit, and fresh heavy cream. A safe distance from the bed were more candles on the floor, each in its own reused piece of pottery. On the low stool beside the bed was wine, the last of our wedding gifts, shared between us like an intimate secret.

Arkady was up, draping my day dress over a chair and rummaging for clean glasses and an extra blanket, as it got cold at night by the shore.

I glanced over my shoulder, the wind whistling to me like some message lost far away at sea, tapping against the old glass. The water looked not as expressive from up here, but the wider picture was so beautiful. A distance away, you could see the flash of a lighthouse, a bridge connecting one of many little islands we called a city. If you looked far enough west, the glow of dreams, of mammoths built to the sky out of iron and brick, the man-made towers we built to greet God at his door.

"I promise, they're clean." Arkady sat beside me on our picnic mattress.

In his hands, two mismatched jars, one for jam and one for pickles, filled appropriately with wine that cost more than his rent.

"This is nostalgic." I graciously accepted my jar.

"Oh yes, from a time where you had only one house instead of two?" he joked.

I let out a small laugh. "More like comfort meals."

He looked at me oddly with a quirked brow. "Your family fed you like a mouse? With all of that money?"

I nodded. "They seem giving . . . kind, even. But they are crueler than you know." I shrugged. "Though I suppose I am to blame. For a long time, I was angry at everything except them, it seems."

"Was it because of your sport of choice?"

"No, though it was part of it," I mumbled, eating one of the sliced pieces of aged meat. "They cut corners. They call it 'good business,' but it's negligence. As a child, I didn't understand. And then I suddenly became an investment. It felt like a savior when offered as an alternative. *Be useful or starve,* my mother would say. A witch, she is. I suppose that is why I was reluctant to leave dancing behind."

"What is there to eat in the French countryside?"

"Cheap meat, good fruit," I said.

"I would hate to imagine what circumstances would make such frugality necessary."

"You have too big of a heart," I said softly. "I wish to share that with you, but my heart no longer believes it to be true. I *thought* my heart was just large, but instead, I grew into it, and realized that some people only have their own interests in mind."

"Is that what has caused your affliction?" He leaned back on his palm, tipping his head at me as he ate a peach slice.

"Yes."

There was a short silence, though it wasn't bad. It was more contemplative for the both of us.

"Did you ever think you'd be in his situation?" I turned to him. "I'm sure if you expected to marry rich, she would have been a lot more interesting."

"No," he answered immediately, "but I couldn't imagine it any different now."

"Oh, really." I smirked. "Am I the best you've ever had, Mr. Artisan?"

"You are the *only* one I've ever had."

I blinked, registering his words in my mind. "Don't lie to me. I am no fool."

"You are anything *but* a fool." He laughed, lifting a piece of fruit to my lips after dipping it in the wine.

"You're too experienced. You know too much," I said as I chewed. "Not that it is bad, I clearly benefit from it."

Even looking at him now, I couldn't find a single joke in his expression.

"You're telling the truth?" I gasped.

"I have a habit of putting people before me," he tried to be playful, "including other people's needs before mine."

"How is that? Why? You've never once thought to do it?"

"It makes me feel good. Like I *am* good." He swallowed, glancing away. "Petre, is this a good time to be honest with you?"

My gut clutched at his words. "Of course."

"I have my own affliction, intrusive thoughts," he admitted, not willing to look at me, "of hurting people."

I didn't speak. I was afraid of interrupting, of making him feel cut off all over again.

"During moments of higher emotions, like anger or passion, I worry I will act on those impulses. I avoided most meaningful relationships and penetrative sex altogether," he explained, his words shaky. "I am fine using my hands, my mouth, my words—but there is something about opening up to someone in that way, the intimacy, that makes the thoughts stronger. It's violating. So I remained a virgin in the *traditional* sense."

"So you weren't joking when you said you think about hurt—"

"I would never," he cut me off, finally able to look at me. His free hand squeezing mine. "I'm . . . glad it was you."

I squeezed his hand as I watched the candles dance in the reflection of his eyes like little sprites celebrating the union. A small fracture from my voice as I pulled my hand from his, cupping my jar of wine and observing my *own* reflection. Then the surface rippled, and the light blurred in my vision.

"Petre." Arkady's hand held my face, guiding it toward him so our foreheads touched. "Is something wrong?" His voice shook, as did his touch.

I shook my head, rubbing my cheek into his hand and undoubtedly getting it wet with tears. "I'm overwhelmed."

"How do I help?"

I shook my head, closing my eyes to banish the tears before staring back.

He released a calming breath, banishing whatever brief anxiety I had caused him. He lifted his cup between us, and so did I. We twisted our arms together as we lifted our cups to our lips.

A shy glance was exchanged, met by closeness and intimate messages through our breathing alone. Then we drank together. The action was silly, meaningless to anyone except us.

Arkady reached over the side of the bed, putting the needle on the phonograph to play *La Sylphide* from the beginning. There, we watched the stars wink over our candlelit dreams.

CHAPTER THIRTY-SEVEN

The Performer

A heavy bell rang sluggishly as I opened my eyes. I rolled onto my back, the birds riding gentle winds against the rich reds and purples of dawn framed by the large window. The harbor was just beginning to wake around the time my dreams slipped from me.

I reached to my side to grasp an empty bed. The office loft was dusty, the light exposing every speck in the air. I suppressed a sneeze before sitting up, pulling the sheets close to me. On the stool beside the bed was a note.

Gone to get breakfast, will be back soon.
A

I pulled on my corset cover and my underskirt, just something to protect against a stray breeze. I took my time redressing in yesterday's clothes, the smell of clay dust tickling my nose as I smoothed my skirts before I reached the ground floor.

The daylight washed away all apparitions from the night before. Without mingling shadows, the statues were as such: statues. The candles were cratered, dried to the floor with limp wicks.

On the small working table was an abandoned cup of water with some small sculpting tools soaking next to the morning papers. The circular window cast an oval eye over the bare floor. Scuffs in the dust across the floor replayed my dance from the night before.

I dragged my fingers over the table, flicking a few metal tools that chimed together before swiping the paper. It was a little wet from this morning, some of the ink bleeding at the edges.

> SEVERED ARM HUNG OUTSIDE LAGO FACTORY: WHISTLEBLOWER ACTS OUT AGAINST POSSIBLE HUMAN RIGHTS VIOLATIONS.

It took several moments of an empty stare for the headline to register. I read on:

> Early this morning, our chief editor received a tip leading to the discovery of remains belonging to the now former New York City coroner Vincent Carlisle, outside the Kings County LAGO factory. The severed arm was nailed to the doors, bent at ninety degrees, and pointing to a large stack of papers also pinned to the wood. Sources haven't confirmed the identity aside from an initialed signet ring on the deceased's finger.
>
> These papers allege human experimentation carried out by LAGO Pharmaceuticals, complete with photographs, names, and laboratory reports. The whistleblower remains unnamed. We confirmed with sources at all NYPD offices that an investigation is underway.
>
> Chief Commissioner James Hunt leads the ongoing investigation of both the factory and the murder, assures the matter is being handled with upmost care.

There was no illustration of the scene, only a portrait of a decade-younger version of Mr. Carlisle smiling peacefully, knowing his body was found and that I would soon be caught.

My stomach dropped.

Below the table were bags, one open. Neatly folded clothing, a comb, a straight blade.

I fell to my knees.

Is he planning a trip?

Under the clothes, something else. My hand dove in, elbow deep before I felt it. A papery material. As if obscured purposefully by the clothes . . . piles of money hidden beneath his belongings.

No . . . he is going to leave.

I tossed the clothes to the floor, revealing more. It was like the bag never ended. I opened another bag, then the third. The same.

He was either stealing or taking bribes; I begged this wasn't goodbye, either way.

Scrambling to stand, it was like I'd lost my land legs, shaking and wobbling as if my first time with feet. I bumped into one of the statues, nearly tipping it before I caught it by the arms—or rather, arm. Broken off.

I stared at it, the clay becoming heavy from the weight of where my mind went. Then it slipped from my hands, and it shattered, clay pieces skating across the floor before all was still.

Frozen. Everything. My train of thought, my body, the pieces on the floor. Enough to think, to conclude my initial gut feeling.

My dear Vincent, why must you haunt me so?

The smell of horsehair and fire starter, a dusting of ash.

Black grime beneath the fractured ceramic, like I'd simply dropped a flowerpot. A dark, brittle material. It broke apart like charred meat within, molded around a support. If I told my mind often enough, it *could* be. This was all just dirt to hold flowers, the clay an elaborate containment of earth and life.

The bones were just stones, a drainage layer.

There were no bones, there was no Vincent, if only I closed my eyes and walked away.

Turning to the porcelain crowd, I feared my heart would not handle looking them in the eye, afraid to make the insinuation. To accuse them of harboring secrets much like my own.

Suddenly they felt more lifelike than ever before, always watching, always judging. They would look down on me for as long as I knew that they were not unlike me. The small difference of animate and inanimate.

The door slid open, then closed. A soft whistling as footsteps echoed across the warehouse.

"You lied to me." I looked over my shoulder.

"About?" Arkady said distractedly as he stepped out from the statues with a small bag in hand. He looked at me in confusion and with caution, shrugging off his coat and placing it on the arm of a statue, placing the bag on its lap.

Then he saw, his secret spilled onto the floor, the clothes, the bags. His expression fell, but in dread.

"You . . ." My legs were moving, but it felt like I was falling. "*You* did this!" I shouted, slamming the crumpled newspaper into his chest.

He let the papers fall to the floor, looking to me with a stern expression, not needing to see to know of my discovery.

"It was necessary." His hands reached cautiously for mine.

"You said you would protect me!" I threw his hands away from me. "You were going to leave me, is that it? Teach me to love, possess my body and soul, just to leave me more shattered than when you came?"

"I had to," he said carefully, but then seemed to bite his tongue on any more explanations.

"All you had to do was keep him hidden! Get *rid* of him! Why did you keep him?" My throat caught, and I couldn't stop shaking my head. "At my father's factory too? You then led a trail of blood right back to us."

"This is for your own good." He was more reserved, cutting himself off from me. "You will understand soon." He reached for my hand.

"You are sick! And selfish!" I seethed as he grasped my shoulders.

He held me at arm's length, bending to meet me at eye level. "Calm yourself, I need you to listen."

"No! You take your money and you run, you coward!" I cried, covering my face. "He will kill us, Arkady. *He will!*"

Arkady pulled me back into an embrace. "He won't touch you—"

"And neither will you!" I screamed, shoving him so hard, I stumbled back.

"Petre."

I felt a hand on my shoulder before slapping it away. "Don't touch me!" My voice shook as much as my hand, my head light, stomach too empty to feel the spell of nausea.

"It was for the better—"

"The statue you donated," I breathed. "The one of the couple, for the charity auction."

He shut his mouth, swallowing thickly.

"Was it . . ." I knew in my heart what the answer would be.

"Please." He reached out to grab me, and I jolted back.

"Were they people?" My lip trembled uncontrollably. "Have you been doing this all along?" I whispered, so softly it was likely no sound came.

He left me with no answer.

"I need to be away from you—"

"Let me explain—"

"*Far* away," I said sharply, already making for the door.

"Wait—" He grabbed my arm.

"What part of *don't touch me* do you not understand?" I yanked my wrist from his hand like it burned the very skin it touched. "Leave me! Leave me like you planned and spare me any more heartache!"

I didn't wait for another moment, another opportunity to falter. His charms were no longer effective, not while I was seeing clearly.

The disgust in my gut, the rot in my heart, was reserved just for him. A small part of me wondered if my reaction was somehow a reflection of how I felt about myself, but I wasn't in a proper headspace to dissect that inclination.

I needed to be away . . . not to hurt him, not to abandon anyone, but to think. To process. To finally escape this hell.

CHAPTER THIRTY-EIGHT

The Artisan

Cards from the index box were piling up on top of my shoes. All the numbers were looking the same, the wheel of the telephone making me dizzy in my repetitive insanity. I phoned the theater, the tearoom, her parents' home, as well as Lorelei's. All those who answered couldn't place her; all those who didn't answer were suspect.

She had been missing all day. I had no way of knowing if she'd gone to the police to turn me in, or to her father to beg him to spare her, or if she'd run away altogether in light of the minimally satisfying options at home.

Why couldn't she just trust me? I had it handled.

Smoothing down my hair for the half-dozenth time, my jaw turning to stone from how long it had been clenching, I kicked away the pile of calling cards scattered across the floor. Pacing incessantly as if to warm up my blood for more efficient flow to the brain, to magically clear my head and give me all the answers.

"Fuck!" I shouted, kicking the cards again, a few of them fluttering in the air, accompanied by several larger moths.

Crunch.

I stopped, tilting my shoe to reveal a fatally pressed moth against the sole. It winced, shaking as its own fluids stuck it to the floor. Another crawled past, sticking itself in its partner's mess. Doomed by the spillage of one another, no flailing would save them now. Then another crawled out from the paper.

"Where are you coming from?" I muttered, brushing the cards from the floor in search of more clumsy trespassers.

The vibrations of my footsteps sent a few scuttering from under the brand-new rug.

Moths coming from under something was never a good sign.

I pinched the tasseled edge of the hallway runner carefully, lifting the corner.

The underside was moving, shifting.

At first it was a dizzying illusion, then I saw in between the fine threads were even finer strings of translucent larvae, falling away in their gluttonous state as the carpet lifted. They pittered onto the floor like boiled rice, thinking themselves stealthy as they rolled between the uneven hardwood.

I tucked my nail into a gap, the wood remarkably ill fitted and loose.

Tossing the carpet away, I inspected the surrounding flooring. One notoriously jutted panel of the hall stuck out awkwardly, several bent nails holding it in place. I assumed it was just poorly fitted wood, but it seemed to be a haphazard mend.

I hurried to the kitchen, digging between chemicals and cookware under the sink for something useful. Neglected in the back of the cabinet were a few small tools, nothing worth using.

I went to clear the clutter from the living room tables, the chair. I checked inside boxes, to no improvement in my luck.

Then, the fireplace. A small stand with a poker and sweep collected dust beside the hearth. "That's it." I grabbed the cast-iron poker.

With swiftness, I drove the pick between the floorboards, bending to try to lift them. The poker jolted, releasing the plank from the hold of the nails. Upon freeing it—the most egregious smell permeated the air.

In the long, narrow view between the neighboring boards, a pale, stiff hand.

"My God . . ."

I broke the plank, then was able to wedge up another, then another.

Just the breaking of planks and movement of the musty air was enough to encourage the reek. A scent so natural and primal, it was smothering, the earthiness of a dying flower, completely uncultivated *faex*.

Her arms were bent rigidly across her chest, no more color to her skin than the powdery wings, dehydrated and void of life, pale in the eyes from what I could see between the moths.

The insects were as still as she was. Which might have been an unremarkable observation if she were not covered by hundreds, if not thousands, of them in various stages of life.

Her gaze was lowered, as if in disappointment at the state of her being, doomed to watch her body follow the soul. Her face youthful yet sunken, with the exception of the hole in her cheek and nose. The moths had almost gotten her eye, but they'd expired just before they could dig in. Luckily, I couldn't see, as their wings shielded that wound from view, like a painting, still and delicate.

At this point, I had no choice but to cover my mouth and nose with my own handkerchief. Deep breaths of composure, telling myself it would be all right if I just breathed.

She was nude, petrified moths breaking off at their feet and crumpling as they fell back between the baseboards at the slightest disturbance.

Brittle blood crystallized around a hole in her chest. Black stains trailing like a starburst from the wound. Her skin was so pale, yet the cavity seemed full. It was such an unnatural gray-and-purple hue against the dry, tangled hair.

Something glimmered from beside her, hidden in the darkness of the narrow grave.

I used my hand to touch her stomach, and she leaked a diluted rusty liquid from her puncture. The contents of my own stomach nearly joined in.

Then again when I saw the bottles of arsenic pesticide tucked around the body. All the evidence discarded in one place.

My back hit the wall as I scrambled away, pressing as if I could run from the sight before me. With every breath, the smell was stronger, richer, now that I knew what was causing it.

With my arms crossed, I tucked my knees to my chest. It wasn't something I wanted to believe; I wished there were any other option to offer as reality. It was like witnessing a quiet creature finally snap. Sure, anyone could be capable of anything. Great joys, explosive anger, you could probably even imagine someone you know killing someone, perhaps even the way they'd do it, deducing from their individual personality.

I'd witnessed people harm children, terrible accidents in factories. I'd seen the fire in a woman's eyes when she discovered her husband had cheated. I'd seen the wrath of men who struck women who questioned them, police beatings for daring to look at them sideways.

I'd killed. I'd seen Petronille's attempt at self-preservation. I'd seen my dear friend Kostya exhume a body for autopsy.

What I couldn't imagine was my wife attempting an embalming at home.

A blanket of red-eyed moths covered the body, stuck to the skin and sheets like they served as some final barrier of divine modesty. They were like sprites looking to carry her to the next realm, bite by bite, until they'd consumed the body, and none was left for the world to defile, if the arsenic didn't get to them first.

This would forever be known as Lorelei's finale.

Petronille . . . what have you done?

CHAPTER THIRTY-NINE

The Performer

My fist was becoming numb from banging on the front door. My hair stuck to my face, and so did my clothes. It wasn't raining in any considerable volume, but I was kept waiting so long, it had completely soaked me without the protection of a coat. There was a light somewhere from deep within the heart of the home, so *someone* was present. Though, the service staff wouldn't keep only one light on, so they may have retired already.

I looked down at the intricate handle of the door. My aching hand wrapped around it, squeezing before a slow push.

It opened.

What had once been a richly lit abode of gold and marble was now a dark and tumultuous landscape of dull brass and plain rock. Without an audience, there was no need to posture, not even for the house.

Past the grand entry, a light flickered from beyond an archway.

The ballroom was larger than life or, at least, larger than any single family needed. It seemed bigger when empty. The tall windows allowed you to see almost as many stars as if you were standing outside. The night cover painted everything in an illusion of blue and purple shades.

One single source of light, the fireplace at the other end, and a silhouette feeding it little by little, pausing in between paper tossings.

The tapping of the raindrops on the grand windows nearly blended in harmony with the snapping and crackling of paper in the fire. Two opposites that seemed to have an understanding.

"Bold of you to come." My mother's voice was grave.

I approached slowly, each click of my heels more awkward and unsure than the last. My skirt was soaked, releasing moisture drop by drop to mark my trail.

My mother held up a photograph. The light of the flames flickered across her face, highlighting every crease at the corners of her eyes, the hollows beneath her cheekbones, and the tired skin of her neck.

She smiled briefly, like a glimmer of a memory presented itself to her through the photograph, before tossing it directly into the fire.

Beside her was a box full of papers and photographs. The one from my home.

"I heard you were going to disappear," she said. "I thought I would give you a head start."

"I'm not disappearing."

"Then you would be unwise." She tossed another paper into the fire, sparks puffing up into the chimney.

"You can't erase me."

"I should have. A long time ago." She sighed. "This is what I get. No good deed goes unpunished, dearest Petre."

"I don't understand."

"Of course you don't." She laughed, looking over at me in disbelief. "You know, I thought I did you a favor putting you in the spotlight. All you ever wanted was *attention*."

"You didn't have to put that in the papers." My lip trembled. "I don't even remember those photographs—"

"You loved to pose for them," she interrupted. "The publicity is more than you deserve. Pity. I told your father it was a waste of resources."

"What do you mean?" I closed the space between us.

She plucked another photo, her eyes flicking over it before turning it toward me. "Pretty thing, wasn't she?"

I took the photo, my hand shaking.

The photo was of a blond maid, her face smudged, smock dirty, yet the linens she was hanging were clean.

"She really was a dear," my mother said wistfully, plucking the photo back and tossed it into the fire, along with a couple more crumpled papers. "She was a good maid, almost as talented at pretending to be a friend. She was even better at opening her legs."

I winced at her words. They felt personal, like I'd walked in at a bad time.

"I tried to keep you as my own, I really did, but there was just too much of her fire left over."

"Is *that* why you neglected me?" I hissed, grabbing her wrist before she could toss another photo into the fire. "You *tortured* me. And now you tell me about a mother I've never known? I don't know how else I should react to the fact you stole my childhood, my *real* family, my middle years, and you planned to take advantage of the rest too, didn't you?"

"I went *above* and *beyond* for you, you sickly harlot!" she shouted, spit flying as she snapped her wrist from my grip.

"You've cursed me with such an affliction, an unholy appetite I can't control." I took a deep, steady breath. "You made me sleep outside with the dogs!"

"You were constantly sick. I couldn't let you sleep next to my children," she scoffed. "One day, you will understand. You can't let the cuckoo lay her brood with another. I would have thrown you out sooner if she hadn't survived as long as she did."

I shook my head, the tears in my eyes mixed with the rainwater dripping down my face. "I ate with the dogs too."

"How spoiled. You're lucky I fed you at all. It was good meat—"

"Was it?" I whispered. "Because I have a sneaking suspicion that I would not suffer from my affliction if you'd just helped me—"

"We did. We *did* help you. And how do you repay us? You should have listened and gone with Vincent. I suppose it is ironic to say he would have taken your secret to the grave." She laughed.

"What a cruel thing to do to a child," I scoffed, "all because you couldn't bear that Father would stick it into anything but you?"

"You're an ungrateful *bastard* child!"

"Is that what I did to deserve this curse? Punished for the sins of my father?"

"You deserve *worse*!" she said. "The curse of the flesh is to be consumed. Your mother was a slave to it, so it was only fitting you suffer the same."

I stared at her for a while, configuring the odd words in my mind. "What did you do to her?"

She smiled, her hands resting in her lap. A pitiful expression. "Darling, I know Vincent has been dead for a moment, but not *that* long. Did you already forget why he was on our books?"

"The donations to his reelection?"

"Yes, the campaign." She spoke pointedly, like she was leading a lecture. "Do you remember what his job was?"

"Coroner. He doesn't file the paperwork," I said slowly. "Then passes the evidence to me."

My mother nodded, raising her brows knowingly.

"You said no meat is worth the waste," I whispered, eyes burning with tears.

"I don't mean to avoid your question, dear." She sighed, standing from the chair and brushing off her skirts. Just before she passed, she leaned over, her hand on my shoulder. "Your mother wasn't a waste of flesh, after all."

CHAPTER FORTY

The Artisan

If I weren't already recognizable to the front staff, they may have written me off as insane. Though, I was running too fast to see if they thought as such, despite the familiarity.

My footsteps pounded down the stairs to the lower level before I began skipping steps altogether.

"Kostya!" My voice echoed almost as loudly as the slapping of my soles on concrete, and I picked up a faster pace as I rounded the corner and went straight into the embalming room.

Kostya stood by the table, leaning on it with his hands gripping the edge. I hardly recognized my mirthful friend, as his face was stone and his posture rigid. I knew the news had gotten to him, in the form of Mr. Carlisle's arm on his slab.

"Kostya." A breathless plea. "I need your help."

His eyes lifted from the severed limb to me, his eyes dark and sleepless. "Why?" was all he could manage. Then, louder: *"Why?"*

I approached the table slowly, understanding the sensitivity of the situation.

He scoffed in disbelief, shaking his head. "Hunt said this was *your* doing. Is it true?"

"It doesn't matter, he will say it is me whether he has evidence or not," I explained carefully. "My father-in-law wants me to disappear, and he's going to make sure I do. But before I do, I have a favor to ask."

"I want to believe in my heart you are a good man. My friend, my *brother*. My brother would not do this."

"I don't have much time." I swallowed.

"I imagine so." He checked his timepiece. "Reception would have phoned the police when they recognized you."

"I need your help."

"I don't know if I can give more than I already have. I'll already be accosted for letting you down here. I may lose my job."

"I didn't want you to get caught up in this."

"Well, now I have! By God, Arkady, you murdered my employer!"

"He deserved it." I dug around inside my bag.

"You aren't the one who gets to decide these things!"

I tossed Kostya my evidence, and he caught it, posture freezing.

In his hands, my justification was wrapped neatly in butcher paper. Though, the smell was more apparent now that it had left my satchel. The paper was deteriorating already from the moisture, dripping onto the table as Kostya cupped it as if I'd just tossed him a duckling or something to be handled with great care. I'd argue that was what she deserved—to be handled with care, to have her truth be told.

"Arkady . . ." His tone was steady. It always was when he was stern.

"Open it, Konstantin." I knew he would recognize the smell, at the very least. "I just need confirmation."

He peeled back the soggy paper, undoing it carefully so as not to disturb the contents. He peeled back the last piece of paper, then placed it before him on the table, right next to Vincent's arm.

A hand, severed at the wrist with a surgical bone saw. It was easy to see there was an experienced technique at work here, though it was half burnt and improperly refrigerated for far too long.

"Where did you get this?"

"I found it in my wife's icebox." I neglected to mention the other samples I'd found. The body had been separated into sections. I'd have brought it in and reunited the limbs, but some were missing.

My throat had been dry since I'd found them, a manifestation of my inner dealings of the matter. Hard to swallow.

Embarrassingly, I assumed Vincent had paid money for her past *services*. Now, I realized they were bartering with something much more illicit.

Kostya looked alarmed, in that way you would expect ringing in the ears amid genuine shock. I couldn't tell him the whole truth. Would he judge her? Would he judge *me*?

I knew he would.

"I think Vincent was making her dispose of evidence." In all fairness, this wasn't a lie. "I need you to confirm it's her," I finished, sliding him my pocket sketchbook cautiously.

He opened the sketchbook to the charcoal etching of the hand from the last body I'd observed in his laboratory. I knew it was the same, I'm a man of detail—it was an exact match. I needed *him* to see it. To trust that I was no monster.

His eyes flicked back and forth between the hand and the sketch, his mind making the connection, already beginning to justify my actions. With a long, dizzy sigh, he nodded.

Kostya was silent for a moment, staring down at the larger appendage before us, hyper-fixated on the glimmering signet ring against the sterile flesh. "So you *did* do it?"

"Yes."

He looked me straight in the eye. "Answer me this once, as a kindness. *Why* did you do it?"

"I did it for her."

He nodded, weighing my answer against a feather in his mind. "Did you have anything to do with the disappearance of our fosters?"

I was careful about my words. "Would you believe they deserved different if I did?"

Kostya was known as a sensitive man, but this was the first time I'd seen him moved to tears.

"I'm sorry," I whispered.

"They'll be here soon."

"Please, Kostya, help me," I begged, taking his hand and folding his fingers over a paper. "Call these numbers, at the specified times. Tell them where I'll be. If you do this for me, there will be no one to punish you. You can testify against me if this doesn't work, tell them I threatened your wife and child."

"I would leave." He cleared his throat, tucking the paper in his smock pocket, turning his back to me as he leaned against the table.

I nodded, stepping back to the door, but one thing kept me.

"When Hunt comes," I began, Kostya glancing over his shoulder at me, "tell him I will be at the ballet."

He looked confused, squinting as if I'd told a joke at a funeral.

"He'll know what I mean"—I released a deep, assured exhale—"trust me."

CHAPTER FORTY-ONE

The Performer

I would say the feeling of belonging to nowhere was a new sentiment, but that would be a lie. Now it was more of a feeling of comfort, of being right all along. To be unattached was a gift; I just didn't realize why until now.

After visiting my mother, I had no place to go. I attempted to return home, only to be met with a letter addressed to me at my doorstep, reminding me that I mustn't remain there either. The night was lovely after the rain, so I preferred to be alone someplace new, a third place not for belonging or unbelonging.

I flipped the cream paper envelope in my hand, tracing over the jagged ripped seal. I didn't move from the park bench until dawn awoke the bees and the birds for their morning routines. I felt silly. My tan walking suit was wrinkled, awkward water stains getting worse as it neared the bottom. My hair was nearly completely undone, half of it fallen from its pinnings.

It didn't matter. Silly things mattered naught when you would soon be on the run from either your family or your husband.

Whether this show would be a comedy or tragedy, I couldn't tell. He'd left me a rather cryptic message.

Dearest Petronille,

Wherever you have gone, I do not care. You may run far away from me, and I will not argue with you. I will not plead with you, even if it is what I ache to do. I would like to begin with—I found Lorelei. I do not hold it against you, as I am sure you had your reasons.

I am aware your affliction was more than you were letting on, but I didn't realize it was so dire until I saw the contents of your icebox. I assumed it would be money you traded when escorting Vincent; I realize now that I was gravely misled to the nature of your arrangement. I know you received the bodies from Ghent. I suppose it was a nearly foolproof solution to hiding evidence.

As for your appetites, they will be hard to cater to, but I am a man of craft. I will find a way.

Before you disappear far from me, please entertain me one last time.

He was just as arrogant in his writing as he was in person. I could practically hear him in my mind, speaking to me with such directness.

Allow me one more chance to show you my heart. If you have seen it and still despise me, I will accept it, albeit wretchedly. You have an appointment at Blue Moon tearoom this afternoon.

Whether you come or not, there will be one last show.

With all my heart,

Arkady

The tearoom was at its busiest hour, and I looked less than presentable for the reservation. The amusing thing was that I no longer cared; perhaps the lack of vanity was personal growth.

The staff stared at me, unsure, before looking back down at the reservation note as if there would be some magical portrait appearing to confirm my identity, trading glances before asking, "Are you Mrs. Kameneva?"

"Yes," I answered, raising a brow.

They surveyed me from head to toe.

"This way," they finally obliged.

He'd reserved the table by the window. A fresh centerpiece of datura and fresh-bloomed orange blossoms. It was a table for two, yet on the other half, dozens of bound journals of sorts were stacked in neat piles on the table, and one on the guest chair.

Before, I would have been embarrassed by the unusual request he seemed to have included with his reservation, but the proposition interested me.

When I sat, I didn't have to pick my beverage, since he'd ordered ahead, choosing the orange white tea.

I picked up a journal placed atop the large pile directly in front of me. Its pocket size stuck out to me.

Inside were sketches: small graphite drawings, some instructional sketches, a grocery list included occasionally, and a number of long-lost whispers of problems through the years.

The next book I picked up was clothbound, the paper thicker. Inside were what I assumed to be studies. Anatomy with and without skin. There were hands with poses ranging from simple to peculiar. Every couple of pages, the body part would change, then some rough studies of bodies and poses, plans for larger sculptures and compositions. In the corners, sometimes there was a palette smear, small details to pull the vision together.

I veered from the main pile to a lesser one, lifting a somewhat new notebook of thick bound paper. Along the edge, the paper wavered, presumably from fingers grasping the pages.

It started with full anatomy, dried rings of coffee stains here and there, the charcoal still loose enough to be wiped away by my curious finger. The forms were stiff, clinical.

As I turned the pages, they got looser in form, and something familiar grasped at the back of my mind. I started to see my face, my posture, my clothing invaded on this closed door of expression, my likeness bleeding through, possibly subconsciously.

Then, it was no longer a question of the representation being accidental.

An entire page dedicated to my reading positions. At the table, curled up on the chair, lying in bed. Some of them made me all too aware of my posture, even now.

Facial studies on the opposite page; my favorite was the one with some sort of angry expression, nearly a pout.

Do my eyebrows crease that much when I'm angry?

Upon flipping the page, there was a nude spread that crossed two pages.

I held it to my chest, my face becoming hot as the staff brought the food items, small and stacked delicately on a three-tiered stand.

I nodded in thanks, waiting for them to walk away before peeling the book from my chest, getting a glimpse at the sketch. There was no uncertainty about her identity, my markings were proudly smudged across the chest. Yet, I didn't recognize myself, not in this way. Nothing was particularly fantastical. My proportions were accurate and favorably depicted.

Most men, when they imagine a woman, wish for changes. The length of her legs, the mass of her bosom, even the shape of her teeth or the color of her hair. When men wish for fantasy, they wish for something different.

my last performance. A knot in my gut forming, adrenaline building, until I decided whether I wanted to run or leap.

My body had other plans as it pulled me into the light, the glare blinding me as I stepped out cautiously, the dark, empty expanse serving as my audience. I could see a faint shimmer of the chandelier, larger than life for such a lavish establishment. The looming empty levels of seats along the sides, and a dark shadow to block the floor and orchestra pit.

It was empty . . . or so I assumed.

"You came." A voice from the crowd, such relief in those two words, I hardly recognized Arkady as the source.

"I saw your message." My own voice betrayed me, but it seemed he was hungry for my answer as well as my attendance.

I couldn't see him in the dark, but I knew he was lingering about. The creaking of a seat, then the echo of one person walking through such a vast and empty place. His form only became known when he appeared by the steps at the front of the stage. Even then, he seemed reserved.

"I want to explain." I swallowed.

"We can talk about it later." He approached slowly, ascending the stairs.

"I had to—Lorelei. It isn't as you think."

"Like Vincent?"

"No—but, well, yes."

"What about the others? In the icebox."

My breath caught, twisted in my lungs.

"A better question would be, who did you feed to me?"

"I don't know—"

"Be honest."

"I asked him to not tell me their names." My answer was cowardly, but it was true.

He stood still at the top of the stairs, his face hidden from me as the spotlight glared from behind. His expressions were a mystery to me; I had no clue as to whether he was angry or disappointed.

I took a deep breath, opting to wait for him to speak.

"Why didn't you tell me?"

"I did—"

"The truth."

"You got the truth. It was just in pieces, or skimmed from just above the surface. I always gave an answer," I said sternly.

"What did you neglect to tell me, then?" His voice became cool, his shoulders still tense from what I could see. "You know my secrets. It is only decent to share your own."

"I would have told you, in time."

"You ate them, Petre."

The words rang in my ears, bouncing off my canals like a deep-rooted tinnitus.

The silence was taken as an answer, and he laughed. As if it were some tired joke.

I considered the answer carefully. "Some on my own, some fed to me."

His form rummaged for something, stepping closer as he pulled out a photograph. He held it straight in front, stepping forward enough for me to see it.

A little blond girl, kneeling beside two massive white guardian dogs, an empty metal bowl shared by all three.

"When did you start?"

My eyes shifted from the photo to his hand, blood on his fingers and smudged on the corner of the paper.

I stepped back, and he stepped forward quickly, his other hand extended in a halting motion.

"Wait." He was visible now, smudges of dark red stuck to his face, his eyes dark from either the poor lighting or some other force entirely. "I want to know how long he was helping you."

I shook my head, covering my face as if it would hold back the sob swelling in my throat.

My hands were pried from my eyes. Arkady holding them far enough away where I couldn't hide, I couldn't resist. His eyes were so sharp, I couldn't read them as they cut me down to something small, something to be dissected.

"You lied to me," I cried. "You told me you'd never given in to your urges! You promised me I would be safe!"

"And you are," he said with such certainty, I could have believed it.

"That's why you didn't tell me where you kept Vincent," I accused. "Is that why you called me here? To finish the job? To bury your secret?"

His lips curled into a grin, dimples forming as he shook his head.

"No, my love"—he tipped his head toward the audience—"we are finishing it together."

I stared in silence for a moment, following his eyes slowly to the audience. I squinted, blinking to let my sight adjust to the darkness.

Somewhere in the void, movement.

My head snapped back to him. "Arkady, what have you done?"

He let me go, reaching into the back of his pants for a folder. He then emptied it onto the floor in front of me.

All of the photographs were of me, older, newer . . . all of them. Even the one from the papers.

Arkady stepped to the edge of the stage, settling in a comfortable stance and shoving his hands in his pockets. "I'm missing a few patrons of yours, but that is because I used them as muses."

"What do you mean?" I looked at him, his backlit silhouette somber in such a desolate scene.

He sighed. "I wanted to be respectful and let you do the honors."

"I don't understand." My lip trembled as I stepped to his side.

"My muses were used to fill the sculptures," he whispered, "and I still regret giving such divine opportunities to the likes of them."

I stood stagnant.

Arkady looked to me, his steady hand engulfing mine. "The first sculpture of mine contained Kostya's foster father," he began.

I watched him, and now that he had my attention, he turned to me to collect both my hands in his. "The second one was *my* foster parents, after I became a ward of the state. The third was Sister Margeret from when we were moved to Saint Lucia's. She liked to burn us with cigarettes. The latest? My last foster parents. They rented us out to the factories. We were lucky if we just lost fingers, as some never came home."

"So you *have* hurt people before?" I whispered.

He nodded. "I didn't lie to you entirely, just as you did with me. I never acted on an innocent, I only acted *for* innocents. I am not angry. I wanted to show you that I understand." He lifted my knuckles to his lips and kissed them, releasing a shaky breath as he closed his eyes. "I rid the world of my demons, allowing me to finally be free. I just want the same for you."

I looked out into the still dark. Now that we were at the edge, I saw them.

All of them.

Forms to the front, slouched from apparent concussions and tied to the theater seats with rope. Several shifting heads and flighty glances. Some of them unconscious, some just coming to their senses.

Among them, a group of patrons at various stages of consciousness, most bound and gagged. Officers, including the commissioner. Next to Mr. Hunt was Vincent, armless and decaying. His body was almost all bones, dried clay keeping the bugs from speeding the process. One more seat over, my mother . . . and finally, my father. The only ones not gagged were my parents, I suppose to plead their case, as they were the reason for everyone's attendance at the heart of it all.

My hand tore from his to cover my mouth, gripping tight as I felt the tears finally escape.

"Some of your patrons overlapped with my muses. I suppose abusers rarely commit once," he said, chest puffed out proudly. "Further proof we were fated to meet."

"We can't do this." I shook my head. "It isn't right."

"Yes, you can." He stepped behind me, his hands smoothing down my arms with his head tipped beside mine. "This is the time to let the truth be free. To heal is to first be believed, to testify. Allow me to be your witness."

I stared out into the crowd. My mother began to sob, the commissioner was barely conscious, and my father held my gaze with such eerie steadiness, I believed he knew this was his restitution for whatever deal he'd made at the crossroads with whatever devil he held dearest.

"They developed an appetite for killing . . . and I, the taste for flesh against my will."

"What did they do?" he prompted.

"They fed me alongside the dogs."

"Who did they put in the food?"

"Anyone they wanted to disappear," I said. "Félice married a politician—the one running against Mr. Hunt for position of commissioner."

"He was the first?"

"No. I'd lost count."

Arkady's fingers brushed over my wrists before intertwining our fingers. "Who was the first?"

I stared at my father, and he never broke, his wife inconsolable beside him as if she weren't equally to blame. "My mother. They fed my mother to me."

I couldn't stop shaking, my limbs becoming cold from the heaving of emotion.

"They knew I was sick. A sour kind of luck where one thing led to another . . . I couldn't help it." I swallowed. "The coroner would give me meat belonging to the evidence of their experiments. After a while, it became too frequent. I couldn't do it anymore. Couldn't keep up, there were too many bodies. I was becoming too *aware* of my meals, and I just . . . *couldn't*. I thought it was the most ethical way to satiate my cravings, but they abused it. They abused *me*. My condition that *they* gave me."

"That's good, Petre," Arkady praised. He leaned down to my ear to whisper, "You asked me once what type of man I was."

I nodded slowly, looking at him from the corner of my eye, his hand still in mine.

"You have a choice. If you wish to be free of this, of me, you may leave. You can walk out of here and go far away, these people and myself gone forever. You don't need to know what happened to them. You won't ever see me again."

I squeezed his hand, hot tears spilling faster as I turned to him.

He held my face between his hands with something like reverence.

"I was always going to be on your side, no matter what," he said at my lips, hesitating only slightly as they nearly touched.

My mouth hung open to say something, anything, but his lips were gone.

As he began to pull away, my hands cupped over his, holding them before they left my face . . .

"Wait." My voice rang clear. "I have something to say."

His eyes flicked between mine, stepping back, allowing me the spotlight.

I turned directly to the crowd, gazing at each set of sad eyes looking at me. For a moment, they seemed hopeful. Likely praying over and over in their heads that I would do something. That I would tell Arkady to stop and this could all be over. That they could return to their homes, their families. Eat a warm meal and tuck themselves into clean sheets for the night. That tomorrow, they would wake up lighter knowing they'd survived their sins one more day.

It would not be so.

"My house is full of moths," I announced, my small audience looking at me. I knew they would hang on to every word by the glassiness of their eyes in the dim light. "Infested. There's hundreds of them. The pesky type that stowed away in between apricots, tucked into the corners of the crates."

Arkady watched me as I looked over at him. I managed a small smile and a deep breath, turning back to the crowd.

"My parents used to send my sisters and me to catch them. Whoever caught the most would get a bowl of wine-soaked peaches. Though, I suspect we got that anyway, since it would make the three of us little ones sleep very soundly by seven in the afternoon."

That earned a few nervous shifts, and the stillness of my mother, apparently giving up on her damsel charade.

"My mother explained that these were pests of the nastiest kind. They ate *everything*. Not just my mother's fine silk or the foliage after harvest. No, they would eat the fruit, fresh or rotten. They would eat the insulation of the house, the grains in the pantry, even the meat hanging for preservation," I explained.

I stepped to the very edge of the stage, my shoes between two lanterns, my skirt nearly touching.

"You've always been shortsighted," my father said. My mother tensed beside him, but she didn't take her eyes off me. So stubborn, standing by his actions until the end.

"I accepted the way this family works for longer than I should have." I was firm with my words. "If your actions are just and good, why not tell the public?"

"There is a reason there are very few people who change the world." He leaned back in his chair, wincing against the rope restraints. "Not everyone understands when evils are necessary, they only recognize the rewards after."

"Everyone is collateral to you." It felt so good to say, to scold him.

"Yet the papers would rather know the inches around your waist than report on the expendables dying somewhere in the middle of nowhere. Don't be foolish. You know it too. One lowly farmer dies, three more show up to take his job. They died serving a greater purpose—medical advancement. Who knows, if someone else is doing what *we* were doing, we may have a cure for your monstrous disease."

"Expendable," I repeated, breathless. "You are all the same, you know." I laughed, rubbing my face tiredly. "You chew away at everything, down to the bone, until the carcass is no longer fruitful."

I turned to Arkady, noticing a sternness to his brow as he listened.

"I don't want to disappear, to let it eat me alive," I said softly. "I am spent, I've given all I can. I don't want to give any more."

He approached. Before he could take my hands, I stepped away, back to the edge of the stage.

"Let's see. Father, are you replaceable? Expendable? You think of yourself as God, you play His game. Tell me—does God burn?"

I lifted my skirt, using my foot to tip over one lantern.

It shattered on the floor of the orchestra pit, oil spilling, as well as the flame.

The audience lurched in the opposite direction, muffled shouts in reaction to the bright light.

Then the next lamp, the oil spilling farther, closing in on the spectators.

One after the other, they spilled and caused such a brilliant light that the chandelier seemed to glitter.

"Petre!" Arkady shouted.

I turned to him, and he embraced me. The firelight danced in his eyes as he looked at me, his hands caressing my neck, my face. Then, he kissed me. So deeply that I thought I may float, the heat of the moment or the blaze sending me afire in more ways than one.

He broke the kiss with a faint laugh. A gleaming smile met with a warm caress. "A beautiful farewell to a stunning career, your artistry will be deeply missed."

"May our next chapter be brighter than the last," I breathed.

"You fools! You're *dead*!" my father screamed, thrashing in his seat as the fire crept closer. My mother sobbing, wailing beside him, slumping in her seat and kicking at the flames, her skirt catching.

I couldn't pull away, entranced by the sight. My father's slicked-back hair now disordered and ashy from the toil between the blackened smoke. His breathing rough, spit misting like an angry bull with bared teeth. In the reflection of his eyes, the fire blossomed.

In every woman's life, she must either overcome her parents or join them. The apple falls beside the tree, or a bird carries your seeds somewhere unknown, uncertain you will ever grow.

This was my moment, my time to plant new seeds.

It would almost be worth it to die here, just so I could watch my parents burn.

Arkady grabbed my hand, pulling me offstage past the curtains. I got only a single glimpse of my handiwork before I no longer felt the heat on my face or the smoke in my nose. It was like the lights aglow after the final act.

Revenge was an unconventional choice of gift, notably in the form of hellfire.

EPILOGUE

The Performer

The mountains guided coastal winds through the river valley.

This time of year was lighter in all ways, more vivid in all ways, than can be interpreted by the senses. The mountains greened as they met the river, its waters a seamless match with the cerulean sky. The town a beating heart in the distance, a humble steeple keeping steadfast watch for centuries, and it would continue to do so for many more.

The sky concentrated from blues to soft pinks and reds. My cheeks tingled, burnt as proof of my daily devotion to the sun. A testimonial to freedom. Basking in it every day.

A wreath of apricot blossoms adorned our villa's front door, the sweet smell of them greeting us every time it opened and closed.

My window was shaded by the surrounding trees, the orchard blossoms beginning to wilt and flutter through the sky, littering the ground in preparation for the next growth.

Waterfowl picked at the overgrown clover, sheep and goats bleated behind the wooden fencing. Two *Pastous* panted in the shade, attentive to their flock.

Arkady sat across from me, packing his pipe beside the open window. The curtain fluttered behind him like a gentle ghost. His skin was deep and sun-kissed, his eyes richer and without stress. He lit the pipe, taking a deep breath before he looked over to me.

I smoothed my hands over my dress, the linen soft under my palms. My ring all the brighter against the stark white. It had been reset for a more comfortable fit, fashioned with two new pearls, one on each side. Made with my own tastes in mind. The sunset sky competed with the ruby, to no avail. It sparkled as I placed my teacup on its saucer.

I touched Arkady's hand, and he grasped it gently from across the table.

"They should be fruiting soon," he hummed, focused on the orchard outside.

"Not too soon, but it looks like they'll be plentiful, based on the buds." I turned his hand in my palms, clay under his nails. My eyes flicked up to him. "Spring serves those who are inspired, doesn't it?"

His smile softer, his fingers left my hand to brush over my forehead, tucking hair behind my ear. At one point, the less-than-immediate answer would have worried me, angered me. Now I knew all good things came with time, even if it was just finding the perfect string of words to make a moment priceless. Sometimes that meant no words at all.

When he pulled his hand back, a moth pitched from my shoulder. It landed in my tea, quivering, leaving a dusting of chitin powdering the cup. The tea stained the chalky-white wings as red as its eyespot pattern. The sprite drowned.

Arkady's brow rose, followed by relaxed shoulders. A leisurely shrug followed by our silent admission.

I held the cup, turning it between my fingers, before lifting it to my lips and taking a sip.

We both sat in leisure, watching as the last sliver of sun dampened over the horizon. One of many fluttering moments that would sculpt the rest of our days, nights, years.

No matter how long, nothing changed. We grew together like the orchard—slow, steady, trusting that spring would come, the sun would rise, and nature embraced.

Acknowledgments

Fruit of the Flesh is my dream debut. Born of my obsession with the ways we are consumed by things we cannot control, the desire for justice, and those who transgress us. This book is wholly about many frustrations, shared personally, but also everything I wanted to hear when I felt the most lonely, used up with nowhere to go. This was a story that ate away at me, gnawed down to the bone, until it forced my hands to the paper. Once upon a time, I would have been looking in a mirror with Petronille, a loud young woman who was tired of not being heard, so I began shouting, hitting, and biting. This is a love letter to my more vulnerable self, and I hope that others will see that you're allowed to take up room, to light a fire when injustice rears its head. Survive yourself because no one else will.

To my agent, Angie: I was an independent artist just toddling along before you grabbed me by the neck and said, "You're coming with me." Every day I'm grateful that you chased me down and showed me that my stories have a place, and that they deserve to be here. We have so much mischief ahead of us.

To my editors, Megan and Kelli: You make editing fun, I mean it. I can only thank you endlessly for your excitement and enthusiasm throughout this whole process (and for dealing with calls where I ramble about Victorian embalming practices). Kelli, I hope you can forgive me for all the moths, considering your mottephobia. It only means it was truly, ironically, meant to be.

To my partner, Ryan: Thank you for letting me tell you about the plot of this book for two hours before you proposed to me. I can't believe the story was so good that it made you say, "Yes, I want verbal essays on all her stories for the rest of my life." In all seriousness, I love you, and thank you for entertaining my madness.

To my parents: Why are you in here? I told you not to read this! But also, thank you for being so wonderfully supportive of my author journey and your endless curiosity about publishing! I look forward to sending you many more copies for your collection.

To my beta readers, Grace and Jake: You are real ones for suffering through my first drafts. Your positivity and willingness to entertain my ideas will always earn you a special place in my heart.

Lastly, to my readers: I am so incredibly privileged and lucky that I found you. I am able to do what I love full-time because of your endless passion for my work. You are the reason I keep writing, and I look forward to feeding you more.

About the Author

Photo © 2025 Isabel Malia

I.V. Ophelia is the author of *The Poisoner* and *The Arachnid* in the gothic vampire series The Poisoner. Born in small-town New England, she now haunts the streets of New York City, writing the most unhinged tales she can conjure. When not crafting gothic romance, she works as a full-time artist, hoards nineteenth-century gowns and antique furniture, dotes on her menagerie of pets, and plots her next literary transgression. Discover more of her deliciously dark world at www.ivophelia.com.